ONE BIG ITCH

SARA WILLIAMS

Printed in the United States of America

ISBN 979-8-89114-002-8 (sc)
ISBN 979-8-89114-003-5 (hc)
ISBN 979-8-89114-004-2 (e)

Library of Congress Control Number: 2023912205

2023.10.11

MainSpring Books
5901 W. Century Blvd
Suite 750
Los Angeles, CA, US, 90045

www.mainspringbooks.com

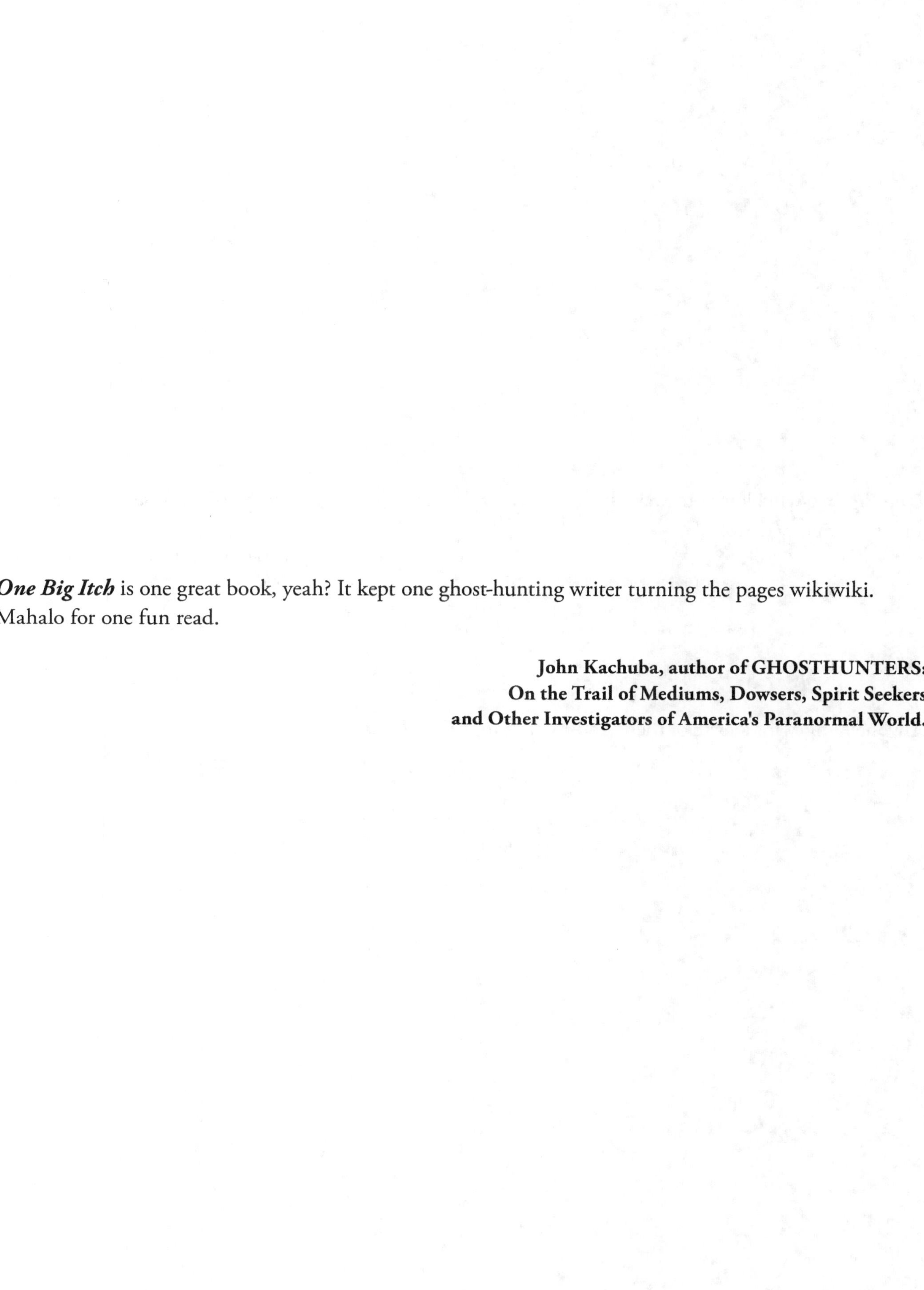

One Big Itch is one great book, yeah? It kept one ghost-hunting writer turning the pages wikiwiki. Mahalo for one fun read.

John Kachuba, author of GHOSTHUNTERS:
On the Trail of Mediums, Dowsers, Spirit Seekers
and Other Investigators of America's Paranormal World.

One Big Itch will blow you away like the wind off the Pali. Here's one novel with a real sense of place and a most intriguing hero.

-- Bob Morris, author of A DEADLY SILVER SEA

Anyone hungry for a taste of the Islands will devour *One Big Itch*

Elizabeth Becka/Lisa Black
Forensic Mystery Novelist

CONTENTS

PART ONE Friday, June 12

PART TWO Saturday, Sept. 10

DEDICATION

For my beloved sons of Maui, Colin and Winston

ACKNOWLEDGMENTS

For legal and procedural issues I am indebted above all to Steve Whiting, Honolulu P.D. detective (ret.), and former Seattle Police Chief Norm Stamper, author of **Breaking Ranks**: A Top Cop's Expose of American Policing, both of whom patiently answered my many questions; any flaws in legal or judicial procedure are, of course, entirely my own.

Jennifer and Dennis Short, Alan Haire and Robert Doktor, Ph.D., of Honolulu helped me find the right settings and sort out the language; mainland core readers Anne Remington, Bill Koch, and Phil and Julie Coyle, Marilyn Erly, Rusty Brown, Bill Tanner, Maureen Bashaw, Carole Rachlin and my friends at the Tuesday Book all read early drafts and let me know when I'd lost them. My friend K. Misti Wilcox patiently combed through several final edits, offering the insight of an avid mystery reader.

The Poet's Truth sake cocktail was first poured for me one night by Adam Farish of the Outlook Inn, Eastsound, WA.

One Big Itch is an erotic poi-pourri of Hawaiian intrigue brimming with deceitful hula-gans. From beginning to end, One Big Itch twists and turns dizzyingly and will have you reeling.

William Tomicki, Editor and Publisher
ENTRÉE Travel Newsletter.

The city and environs of Honolulu are brought to life in ***One Big Itch.*** The reader can almost feel the warm trade winds and see the mountains rising above the city through the descriptive phrases. ..Mystery lovers will embrace the twists and turns of the well-plotted story line and be sorry to leave behind the many-faceted characters when the book ends.

Susan Campbell, *Author*
STAINED GLASS WINDOWS, *co-author/editor*
POTAWATOMI TRAIL OF DEATH

One Big Itch...is full of twists, turns and bumps in the road. Just when you think you know where you are going, there's a "Y" in the road that takes you another direction. When you think that John Spyer has given the mystery away, the story is not over yet... Put some nice hula music on your IPOD, lay back and let Sara Williams escort you to this sunny Hawaiian Island for a fast and exciting adventure.

Connie Walle, *Poet and Director*
DISTINGUISHED AUTHOR SERIES

Enduring the last, dragging days of a lingering northern Michigan Winter as I was, Sara Williams' ***One Big Itch*** came as a welcome diversion. A great story with a strong plot, shared with Williams' unique voice, allowing this Missaukee County boy to escape Spring doldrums and visit the sweet, warm islands of Hawaii. *Mahalo nui loa*, Sara... and people are wondering why I'm calling everyone 'Brah'.

Lynn Elliott *Editor*, **MISSAUKEE SENTINEL**

One Big Itch takes readers on a trip to the tropics laced with liberal splashes of murder, mayhem and steamy romance. Author Sara Williams knows Hawaii and it shows. Rich Hawaiian language incorporated into clever dialogue and vivid cultural descriptions (along with a helpful glossary) add authenticity and interest.

Lynne R. Christen, *Freelance Travel Journalist,*
Author of **TRAVEL WISDOM**

Sara Williams takes her readers on a joyride with a bunch of crazy, wonderful, lovable characters in ***One Big Itch***.

Maureen Bashaw
Freelance Arts Entertainment writer

Sara Williams' fast paced novel brings the reader a taste of South Pacific culture in her murder mystery, ***One Big Itch.*** Set on the Hawaiian Island of Oahu, the clever use of Hawaiian island slang terms and words allows the reader the perspective of a local. Escape to the Islands, blend yourself a Mai-Tai and enjoy this romp in paradise.

Mike Hollywood, *travel writer/author,* **PALAU**
ISLANDS & COOK ISLANDS HANDBOOKS

I love a good mystery that keeps me on the edge and ***One Big Itch*** fits the bill. Just when I thought we couldn't have another twist, Private Investigator John Spyer comes up against one more. The added benefit is all the Hawaiian culture woven throughout and makes me yearn to return to Hawaii.

Barrie-Louise Switzen
THE WOMAN'S CONNECTION

Obsessive love...murder...mystery...an exotic setting. And throw in quite a bit of Hawaiian culture. How can you miss? ***One Big Itch*** starring Hawaiian P.I. John Spyer is a welcome addition to the genre.

David Wilkening, *freelance author of books,*
magazine articles and newspaper stories

One Big Itch is a high-energy mystery cocktail laced with more than a little Hawaiian punch. Sara Williams' novel is a glorious blend of the Island of Oahu with all of its fragrances, tastes and textures, all the voices and patois, and all the good sense and superstition of its varied population. Hawaiian P.I. John Spyer is a man of intelligence, loyalty, sensitivity, humour, and heart — whose exploits readers can only hope will be continued.

Phil Jason,
FORT MYERS MAGAZINE

One Big Itch is a page turner of a murder mystery….Spyer is an intriguing, fully-fleshed character. The well-crafted plot races toward a suspense-filled climax. The setting is the still beautiful Hawaii of haves and have nots that tourists seldom, if ever, see. A splendid read!

Prudy Taylor Board
BOCA RATON NEWS

One Big Itch is one wild ride! With her quirky characters and roller coaster plot, Sara Williams weaves a slyly entertaining tale that combines the lush Hawaiian landscape of travelogues with the gritty reality of its urban streets. Alive with authentic native voices, this fast-paced/mystery will leave you wanting to hop the next plane for a tropical adventure of your own.

Diane A.S. Stukhart
Author of ***PORTRAIT OF A LADY,*** 2nd in the Leonardo da Vinci mystery series

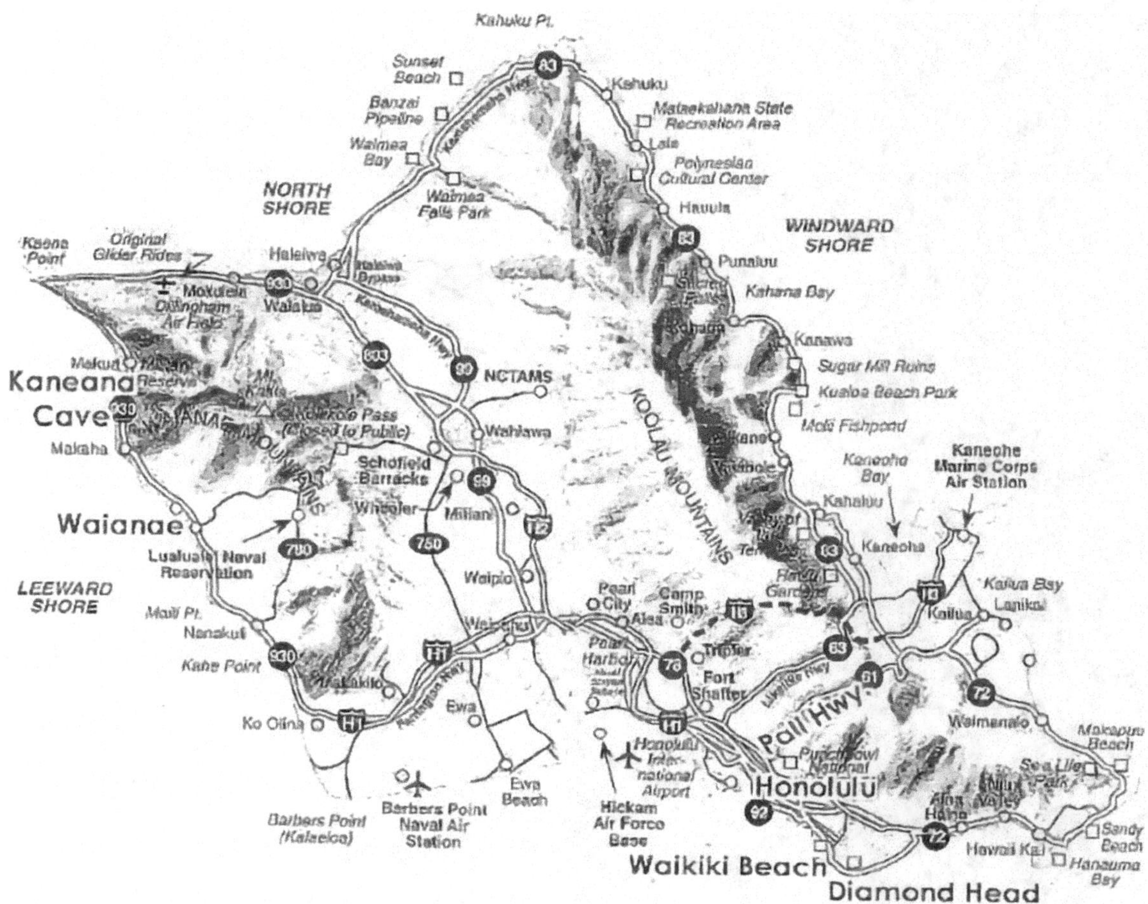

As if a page-turner of a murder mystery isn't enough, **One Big Itch** also offers up an explosion of glorious Hawaiian colour: expanses of a mountain and sea, legends of a native royalty, lots of local patois, and pizzas loaded down with pineapple, ham, and edible flowers. Not to mention a private investigator with a taste for Drambuie and vintage sports cars. Riding the New York subway, I almost felt I was in Diamond Head.

Matthew Goodman
Author of The SUN AND THE MOON:
The Remarkable True Account of Hoaxers, Showmen, Dueling Journalist, and
Lunar Man-Bats in Nineteenth-Century New York

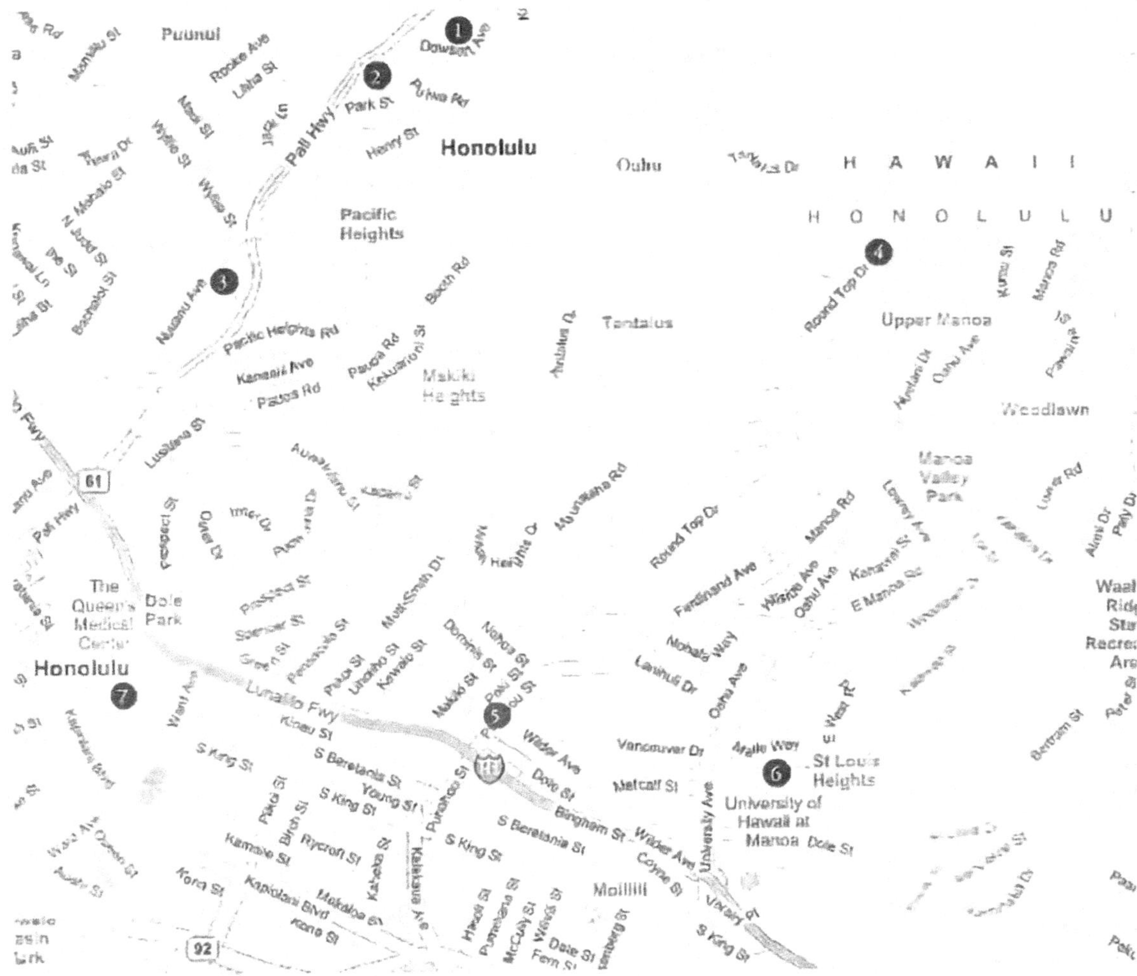

1. Haverhill Estate
2. Queen Emma's Summer Palace
3. Royal Mausoleum
4. Eva's Hale
5. Punahou Downtown School
6. University of Hawaii
7. Honolulu Police Department

If you want a novel you just can't put down, pick up Sara Williams' ***One Big Itch***. The fast paced story and the colourful Hawaiian scenery and dialect will keep you enchanted all the way to the end. And what an end it is!

Lorie Thompson, Heber Springs AR SUN-TIMES

One Big Itch is a gritty tale of murder and intrigue set against a lush tropical backdrop. The mysterious Hawaiian Islands are the perfect foil for the conflicted John Spyer. ***One Big Itch*** is a swirling trip through traditional native culture, modern mores and viscous human emotions. Read it and enjoy it.

Rick Klein, Executive Producer
MISSISSIPPI PUBLIC BROADCASTING

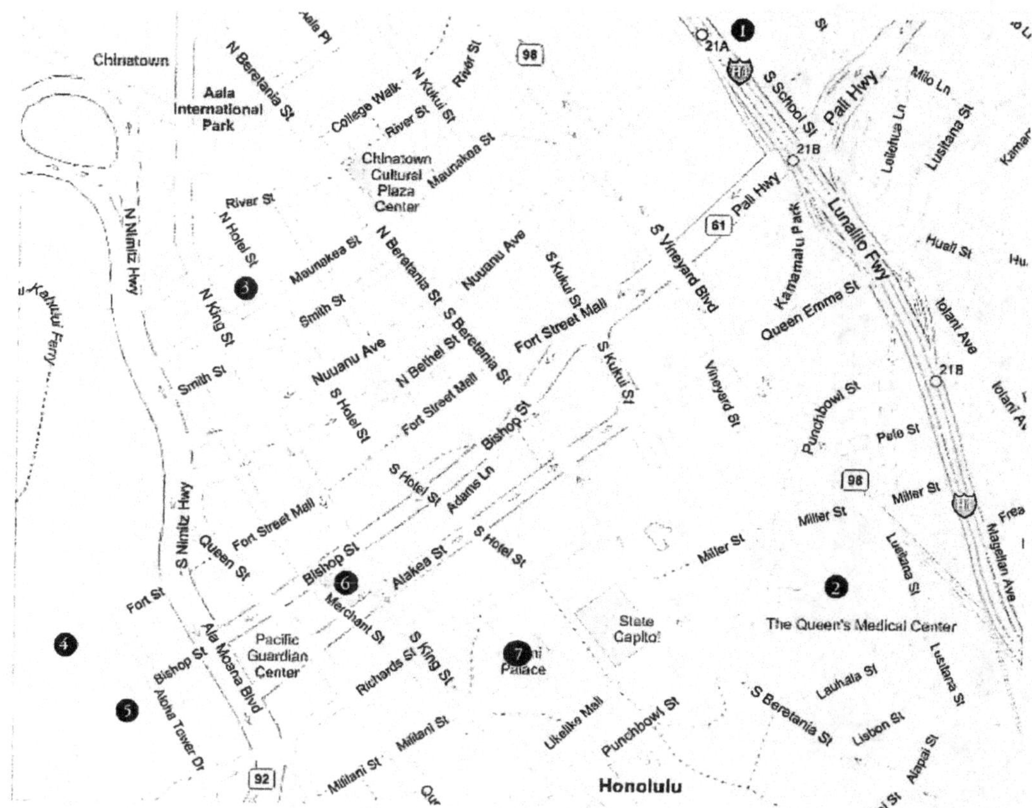

1. Twice-a-Slice-a
2. Queen's Medical Center
3. Monica Fat's Bail Bonds
4. Aloha Tower
5. Falls of Clyde
6. Bishop Square
7. 'Iolani Palace

One Big Itch is the real deal---a fascinating murder mystery with more shake-ups than a Hawaiian volcano. Sara's latest novel is a start-to-finish riveting read with a carefully planned plot. Say Aloha to this Florida resident writer extraordinaire.

Doug Cifers, Publisher
FLORIDA MONTHLY MAGAZINE

Spyer is an appealing mixture of John D. MacDonald's Travis Magee and Mickey Spillane's Mike Hammer, with an exotic locale thrown in for spice. Williams has caught the rhythm and feel of Hawaiian life and lifestyle. Her characters are real, three-dimensional, interesting people, whose actions grow naturally out of their characters, not some arcane plot demands. And the plot of **One Big Itch** is a gem, with layer upon layer unfolding as Spyer investigates the murder of a childhood friend.

Rodger Nichols, Editor
THE DALLES CHRONICLE

1. Diamond Head
2. Outrigger Canoe Club
3. Kapiolani Park
4. Honolulu Zoo
5. Leahi Avenue
6. Flower Gardens
7. Cousin Duke's Hale
8. Wizard Stones
9. Police Substation
10. Surfrider Hotel

I love a good mystery that keeps me on the edge and One Big Itch fits the bill. Just when I thought we couldn't have another twist, Private Investigator John Spyer comes up against one more. The added benefit is all the Hawaiian culture woven throughout and makes me yearn to return to Hawaii.

Barrie-Louise Switzen
THE WOMAN'S CONNECTION

Absorbing the Hawaiian spirit in every line of One Big Itch is the next best thing to an island getaway and it provides a perfect contrast to the head-spinning mystery that confronts John Spyer. The plot twists continuously amazed me.

Brian Bandell, Reporter
SOUTH FLORIDA JOURNAL

One Big Itch is a compelling story I didn't want to put down. I could smell the Hawaiian countryside, described to a "T"... And the plot? Down to the wire in good readin'!

Edna Wheless, editor/owner/publisher, DESOTO PARISH TODAY

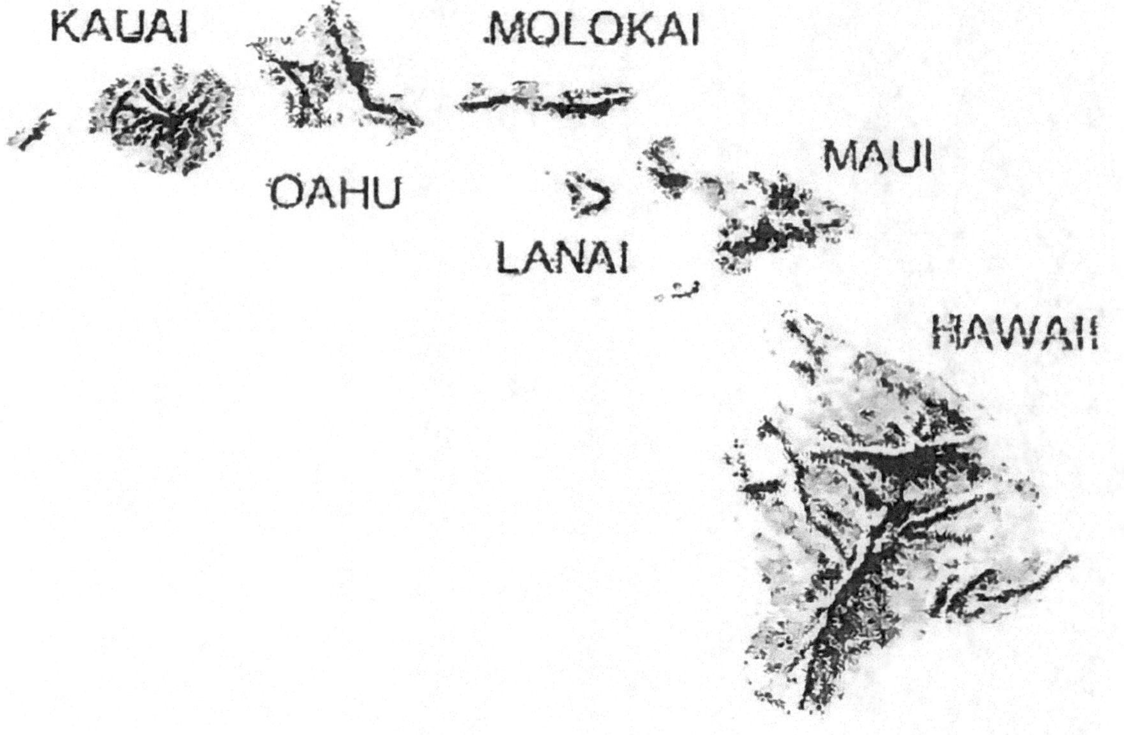

PROLOGUE

I came to with a start. A pain shot through my jawbone, sending trails of sweat coursing down my forehead. I blinked, trying to clear the sweat from my eyes. I saw nothing at all against the blackened and dripping cavern walls, neither a shadow nor a shiv. I flung my head around, trying to shake away the pain clamping at my jaw. Fully awake by this time, I realised I'd been fighting a phantom attacker in some half conscious state, a daze, a stupor. The real problem was bad enough. My cheek was resting on the jagged end of a rock.

I shifted my face to another location but found my nose in a puddle of dust, went into bouts of sneezing and my eyes ran. My temples throbbed. My sinuses swelled shut. I had to keep my mouth open to breathe. I tasted sulphur in the dirt as bits of grime slid down my gullet, and slaked my thirst on my own blood as it trickled down my torn cheek.

I snaked my body, trying for a more comfortable position. My hands and feet were numb—trussed behind my back. My shoulders throbbed. My lower back screamed, very much on the outs with me. The constant dripping in the cave was hell on the nerves. Then came the moaning I had heard off and on the whole night through, but I have to admit I could no longer distinguish night from day and had no clear idea how long the moaning had been going on and how long I had been out of it.

How did I get here?

It all began with that ominous incident at Randy Haverhill's book signing and his odd denial that anything was terribly wrong after it happened. I lay face down eating grit, asking myself once again just how it was that I had failed to see disaster in the making...

PART ONE

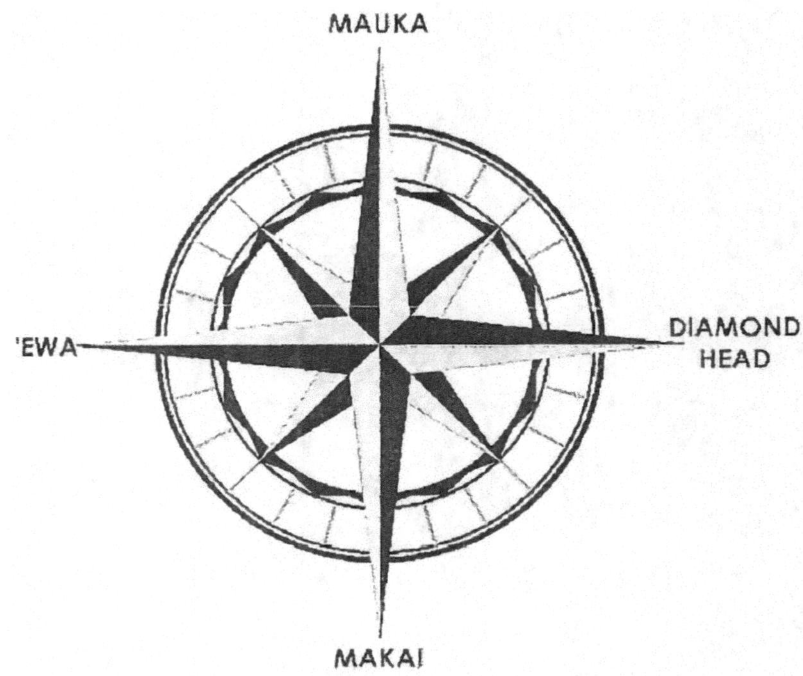

ONE

FRIDAY, JUNE 12TH

A tropical city is all about play, and when I arrived in Honolulu, once again I found myself laughing out loud. I was seeing things: Jefferson Hall, one enormous fungus rising out of damp earth? I blinked my eyes and shook my head, but there it was, Jefferson Imam Conference Hall, hub of the East-West Center, the University of Hawaii's claim to international fame, an outsized flat roof balanced on a squat stem.

One great architect, I. M. Pei, had modelled this renowned building on a mushroom sprung from the ground? I had to laugh. No kava vision this was; I hadn't had a bowl of the brew in months. I sucked in one of my scratchy honks and let go, and I must admit it felt good to be laughing in Honolulu once again.

Honolulu might be playful, but the city is also haunted, as any Hawaiian will tell you. Some ghosts we live with, some we leave behind. This was the painful message I took away from what has become known as the Haverhill case. Of course I had no way of knowing any of this on the night when it all began. Now I see that my skewed view of Jefferson Hall may well have been Madam Pele's opening gambit in the Haverhill matter. The other strange happenings of that very night suggest as much.

I'm John Spyer, by the way, with one of those four-banger, Hawaiian-style handles, starting off with a proper first name. After the missionaries arrived and Hawaiians converted to the new religion, public law decreed that we must each and every one have a Western style first name, and so officially I am John 'Oluhana Maalaea Spyer, but please call me John. Such a name pegs me instantly to any other Hawaiian. I'm hapa haole, half white. Where Honolulu and her ghosts are concerned, I'm only half inclined to believe in them, but as we talk story about Randy Haverhill, it's quite possible that you yourself may become one hapa believer. Yeah?

It was mid-June, finals week on the Manoa campus. I was running late to a book signing in Jefferson Hall. Doctor Randolph Kealoha Bishop Haverhill had just published his latest bestseller. Engraved invites, heavy pupu this thing was, and Doctor Randy was one of my childhood buddies. Truth be told, I was not up for this. I was more eager to sip some kava and hear some fine Hawaiian music than I was to hear my old friend Randy Haverhill hold forth about the economic ailments of the Pacific Rim. I'd missed a couple of other Haverhill invitations as well. I'd been invited to the New Year's luau celebrating Randy's elopement with Hillary, his new bride, but Randy—of all people—would understand my absence. He knew I had every good reason to stay out of Honolulu.

Randy Haverhill and I grew up together in the Nuuanu Valley, but it wasn't as if we still hung out together. Here was Dr. Randolph Haverhill, this celebrity economist, bent on saving governments from themselves, while I'm engaged in the far more modest business of salvaging people, one client at a time. The trouble started with a note tucked inside the engraved invite. John please come. You must. We need your help. It was signed H.H. for Hillary Haverhill, Randy's new wife. One client? Hillary? The new Mrs. Haverhill? Let me tell you, I was not eager to get involved, but Hawaiian protocol demands that I go to her, hear her out.

TWO

I caught a ride from the airport with my usual taxi driver, Soon Amorin of Taxi Service Soon. He drives one of the English taxis that add class to the Honolulu fleet. Not only is my friend Soon one expert on Hawaiian music, but also his black taxi is equipped with the finest sound system in the fleet.

And Soon, he drives a taxi the way his musician buddies play, pihi wiki, hot on the keys. Soon had dipped and dodged through the heavy traffic on the H-1 freeway. He squeezed us onto the Manoa campus through the back gate; we sat idling in a traffic snarl on East West Boulevard listening to a falsetto singer soaring into the musical stratosphere.

As Soon's taxi crept mauka, toward the mountains, one of our efficient tropical sunsets sluiced a coppery sheen over Jefferson Hall. The late afternoon light, maybe? The steepness of the road? Whatever. There it was, Jefferson Hall, one fungus. At the sound of my sucked-in honk, a wounded look crossed Soon's face: "You don't like the music, brah?"

"Your boy is fine, Soon. Put your money on him." This falsetto dude was trying out for the Aloha Festival, our tropical version of an ancient harvest rite, come September. My lady friend from the mainland, Maya Menecal, had assured me she was coming for it. "Jefferson Hall, brah. I've seen it hundreds of times and I never noticed until now. It's one big fungus among us."

Soon grinned, showing his tobacco-stained teeth. We listened to the singer's final soaring notes, and as the line of cars crept forward another few feet, Soon switched off the demo tape. Soon is either Filipino/Irish or Irish/Filipino, I can't remember which, but he's a pointy-head of a guy with a shock of red hair and the long face of one of those Filipino monkeys down at the Honolulu Zoo.

The wide flat roof of Jefferson Hall forms a deeply sheltering plaza. When we finally arrived in front of it, the plaza was jammed with exotic-looking party goers, pulsing in the day-glow swirls of tropical colours, the women in flowing muu muus, caftans, saris, pareau wraps and such; the men in aloha shirts or lacy white barangs, Filipino dress shirts. Some guys were turned out in the finest of Hong Kong tailoring and exotic ties. A few arrived in their lei-draped, tanned, and well-oiled pecs and lava lava skirts. No doubt there were also a couple of māhū guys who turned out as women, an accepted Hawaiian tradition.

The entry hall light flashed a ten minute warning and the crowd queued at the door, where invitations were being checked, an odd precaution for a University gathering. I pulled the engraved invitation from the inside pocket of my linen blazer and reread the handwritten plea tucked inside:

John—please come. You must. We need your help.—H.H.

Randy's second wife Hillary had made the plea. I can't say how many times I'd read it. There I sat in this English taxi, watching the rushing crowd, thinking this note was so strange—Hillary and I had never met. If we needed help, meaning Hillary and Randy, then why hadn't Randy written the note himself?

Hillary's plea made me nervous. I knew Randy's proclivities too well. Had Hillary discovered that her new husband was more of a ladies' man than she had bargained for? Did she want me to tail Randy for evidentiary purposes? But Randy was a very old buddy and I wasn't up for that, and I checked the wording again. *We need your help.* That's what it said, all right, which was why I had come. No decent Hawaiian says no to an old friend, not even to the new spouse of an old friend, and so my intent was, I'd make polite noises to the second Mrs. Haverhill, refer her to someone else, and hit Hale Kava, Honolulu's 'awa bar, until dawn.

I hadn't had a drop of our traditional psychedelic brew in months, and I was out of the loop as far as the rising new talent among our local musicians. When in Honolulu I call upon Soon Amorin to get me around. Soon fills me in on what's happening on the local music scene. I like to crash at my Cousin Duke's hale, his plantation bungalow on Leahi near Kapiolani Park at the foot of Diamond Head, where Duke keeps my vintage Mustang for me in his garage.

My plan was that Soon would take me to Hale Kava after the signing party; I'd crash at Cousin Duke's place until tomorrow afternoon, and then I'd hitch the sunset chopper ride back to Maui with a tour guide company based north of Lahaina at the Kapalua Resort. A few years back I'd nailed a bipolar mechanic before he'd killed somebody and the grateful owner offered me a hefty bonus in the way of free rides for life.

This was plan A, soon to be revised with what I now view as Pele's help; the problem with being a hapa believer, certain messages from Madam P. or wherever, tend to get through to me in a hapa-hazard manner.

THREE

Though I was born and raised in Honolulu, I've lived in Lahaina on the Island of Maui since my late teens, when not otherwise engaged elsewhere, that is. The chopper I'd copped a ride on was late due to the thunderheads we ran into over the West Maui Mountains. No chopper—especially one with a load of tourists aboard—argues with thunderheads.

Thunderheads meant that Madam P. had run out of gin, the pilot said by way of entertaining the tourists, and I thought nothing whatever about this remark, until I had my own mishap, when Soon and I finally reached the unloading zone in front of Jefferson Hall. I was striding backward toward the entrance as I barked at Soon: "Be back here at 9:30 PM. Yeah?"

Soon's eyes went big. He waved his hands and shook his head, but I was intent on delivering instructions and Soon's warning didn't sink in soon enough. Wham! I backed into the jaws of a stone lion that guarded the entry path. Now I can tell you this stone lion was one of the Chinese lions that normally guard Jefferson Hall, each from a tall pedestal; just what that lion was doing down on the ground with its jaws open wide, I have never figured out, even to this day.

Soon leaped out of his black taxi and rushed to my aid. I watched his prehensile lips chew up a laugh and swallow it. "Hey brah. One lion bite you in the okole? You okay?"

"What? A hard-ass like me? Nothing's broken but my dignity." I grinned, hoping to cover the wince I was afraid would show on my face. My abused rump was stinging. "Gotta run, brah. Be here at 9:30 PM. Yeah?" That way Soon and I could make the second set at Hale Kava.

I looked around at the predominantly Asian faces scurrying past. I hoped people would be too busy checking each other out to notice one silly brother making a fool of himself. Unfortunately, I had attracted a cluster of giggling coeds. My face heated up as the two sides of my nature fought for control.

Spyer is an English name. My missionary genes from the stiff upper lip side of me argued for a dignified exit. I could put up my nose and stomp away, ignoring the facts entirely. But I am Mana Hana's boy, a Polynesian at the core. The laugh was on me so I relaxed and went with the flow. I played into the joke, stroked the stone lion's chilly mane and calmed it with a little cat talk. The girls laughed and went on their way, and then a graceful hand took me gently by the arm.

"Mr. Spyer? Mr. John Spyer?" Hula-trained she was, there was no mistaking that feathery touch, and she wore a band of pikake flowers around her forehead, taming a wealth of springy black hair and her black eyes beamed at me and she smiled big. "I'm Lola McCready, a volunteer at the Pacific Rim Institute. Mrs. Hillary is waiting for you."

I studied Miss Lola, a feminine vision if ever there was one, eyes that slanted, lips that pouted, fat cheeks that dimpled when she smiled, and I watched the nuances of her expressive face as she took my invitation from my hand and waved it in the face of the security guard, who motioned us past a line of stragglers still waiting at the door.

Now that Lola McCready has left Honolulu, I suspect that Miss Lola wearing her pikake flower lei wound round her forehead and her clingy Hawaiian-style holoku gown, was in fact Madam Pele in one of her more elegant disguises. Perhaps my clumsy encounter with the lion was a warning from Pele's own lips: *Watch yourself, John Spyer. This Haverhill business will bite you in the okole. Every move you make as a detective will work against the very client you try not to represent. Set foot once more in the Nuuanu, Valley, Spyer, and you pay with the love of your life. You will face down your own ghost. You will put to test one lady you do not deserve. Just who is Maya Menecal to you, John Spyer? Just what will she feel when she discovers who you've been in love with all these years? Ha. Ha. Ha. Ha. Ha. Ha. Yeah?*

Spyer brah? Bring Madam some gin?"

FOUR

It is a fact that Miss Lola McCready has vanished, taking her innumerable talents along with her. Maybe she moved on in order to resume her quiet life? For her sake, I hope so. On the night I first met her, all that I knew about Lola was that she was one beautiful girl, a Pacific Rim Institute volunteer with Randy Haverhill's think tank. I looked around the crowded room. A couple of security guys lurked at the side doors. Such a tight function was unusual for a University gathering. I was impressed. The powers-that-be must have feared that Randy's fans would turn rowdy. The security detail confirmed everything I knew about Randy. He was charisma on steroids.

"I'll take you to your seat and let Mrs. Hillary know." Lola bestowed a dazzling smile upon me, healing my frazzled ego. We started through the crowd, slow going, as people scrambled for their seats, and I trod carefully.

A true holoku, such as the one Miss Lola wore so well, has a train that fans the floor like the plumes of a peacock's tail; Miss Lola's gown had a much shorter train; but I was not about to step on Miss McCready's dress. Play the fool twice in one night? No way.

Lola's dress held a racy secret: it swooped low in the back, deliciously low, a vision I enjoyed as she wove through the crowd with the sensuous hip action of a girl who had learned to hula in toddlerhood. Miss McCready escorted me to a reserved seat in the last row of the second block of seats, not a good location. It was a stretch to see the podium. Since Hillary Haverhill had dibs on any seat in the house, I realised that she had chosen a place where she wouldn't be noticed talking to me.

"I'll tell Mrs. Haverhill you come," Miss McCready said, handing me a program. The lights dimmed and the show began, Hawaiian style, where everybody and all the cousins put in an appearance. Some dancers from Sarawac got the evening off to a rousing start. A Hawaiian priest led the invocation and the blessing of Randy's book, a subtle bow to the constancy of the union of the old religion with the upstart, Christianity.

Praise Jesus, praise Madam, I like to say. After all, in Mama Hana's clan, the elders, all good Christians, never lost their habit of feeding the sharks themselves lest existential harm befall our family, our 'ohana.

A heroic boy scout who had rescued a keiki, a child, from a pit bull attack, led the pledge of allegiance. Then came a distinguished gentleman wearing a linen jacket over a silk aloha shirt of the restrained type. Tori Richards? Tommy Bahama? I could spot the elegance of the garment even from a miserable distance. Our host tried to calm the gathering but the chanting wouldn't stop. The crowd stayed on its feet. Although I couldn't place the gent's long, bony face, we're of the same stock. He had the odd latte' colouring that

I shared with him. We're haoles of the sort whose skin never takes a true tan. Even worse, we're tall and lanky where the average Hawaiian is robust and stout.

I've been out of the loop in Honolulu so long that I confess I had to find our host's name in the program. He was Hillary Haverhill's daddy, Cameron Rooke, CEO of Oahu Land and Cane, one of the power players in Hawaii. His patient bearing at the lectern eventually had a calming effect. As the audience settled down I sat staring at the empty seat beside me on the aisle, wondering what Hillary's father had to do with her new husband's think tank.

I discreetly rolled from side to side in my chair, the better to relieve my tender okole, but this action produced an ominous twinge in my lower spine, the old bullet wound acting up, not a good sign. The fact that one of the most powerful heiresses in Honolulu was desperate to meet the likes of me did not bode well for either of us.

FIVE

It was not until the house lights were dimmed that Hillary Haverhill slipped into the seat beside me. I could see the gleam of her perfect teeth by the stage lights. She had the same long-cheeked face as her father. I couldn't make out the colour of her eyes, but only their long diamond shape. Her blonde hair gleamed like a pale winter moon in the dark, cut in a sleek globe that added width to her long face. She clamped my extended hand between icy fingers, sending waves of apprehension down my spine. Her cool, moist kiss brushed my cheek, bathing me in the minty miasma of what must have been three pounds of carnation leis draped around her neck—a funereal smell, or so it seemed to me.

"John. Finally we meet. Thank you for coming," Her whisper was deep and throaty. She was one of those handsome, masculine-looking women as opposed to a drop-dead beauty such as Miss McCready.

"My pleasure."

"Did you just get in from Maui?"

"Just in time to be bitten by a stone lion," I said, covering myself, in case she'd already heard about the run-in. The coconut wireless we have going in Hawaii happens to be far more efficient than any cell network.

Hillary shrugged her shoulders, tipped her head. A coy grin crossed her face. Sure enough, somebody had ratted me out, Miss McCready, probably. The noise level was such that Hillary leaned close and talked to me from behind her program. "Randy told me about your work with the DEA in Florida."

"Did he?" I tried for a smile; managed a wry grimace. "Yes ma'am, it was loose talk that killed my career."

"Oh." The whites of her eyes went wide in the dark.

"Not Randy?"

"Not Randy." I shook my head. A glory-seeking idiot in my own ranks blabbed to the wrong newspaper reporter. But so what? As the surgeon who removed a misplaced bullet from my back pointed out, better one dead career than one dead Special Agent.

On the stage, Hillary's daddy welcomed everyone and launched into an introduction of one of Hawaii's brightest native sons: Randy Haverhill, Harvard grad, Rhodes scholar, Pulitzer prize winner, economic advisor to politicians, financiers, investment bankers and heads of state, not to mention the CNN TV network. As this litany went on, a few scenes of Randy came to mind.

The time we'd fought in the grass over the fate of a tiny green frog with a red pinstripe on its side; our famous run-in with the ghost dog of the Nuuanu Valley; our secret clubhouse where we sneaked comics and smoked cigarettes.

"After years of phenomenal success on the mainland," Rooke was saying, "Randy returned three years ago to his beloved Hawaii. He founded the Pacific Rim Institute here on the Manoa campus. Randy and his young scholars offer research services to governments and businesses of the Pacific Nations. The Pacific Rim Institute aims to eradicate poverty while uplifting native cultures. The Institute promotes democracy, industry and commerce. It is my pleasure to announce that this coming September, The Pacific Rim Institute will host the Economic Congress of Pacific Nations on United States soil for the first time ever." Rooke led the applause, then let his eyes flow over the rich walls panelled in koa wood waiting for the audience to settle down.

"And now, ladies and gentlemen, reading from his newest work, *Econ Decon*, which the *New York Times* calls "an entertaining and insightful collection of essays,"I give you Randolph Ke-a-LO-ha Bi-shop HAVer-HILLLLLL." Rooke dragged out every syllable of his son-in-law's name as if he were some verbose announcer in a boxing ring, a gimmick much enjoyed by the sports-savvy audience.

Randy came onstage at that point, his dark complexion burnished under stage lights, his black eyes liquid with brilliance, his broad, even features alight with that charismatic combination of intelligence and humility, his heavy build kept in trim with years of rowing in the east, outrigger racing in the west, and the sailing and we'd done as kids.

A master of timing, Randy paused. He let the audience catch its breath. The loops of flower leis piled around his neck swayed as he put the moves on the microphone. Randy's voice, resonant, mellifluous, took on a humble timbre. "Gee thanks, Dad."

This homey gambit brought the audience to its feet once more. People laughed, clapped, stomped, cheered. Above it all I heard a keening more appropriate to a rock concert: I looked behind me. A bevy of university coeds stood at the back cheering and waving banners.

"Randy could run for President," I said to his beaming wife. Hillary's eyes widened. She shook her head. "Never. Randy promised me. He says he'll always do more good being an advisor to heads of state behind closed doors. Let our Punahou brother take the political heat." This, of course, was a reference to our native son and Punahou grad Barack Obama now seated in the Oval Office.

"So?" I said, realising the roar of the crowd would keep anyone from hearing our conversation. "How can I help you?"

Hillary's face twisted. Her shoulders rounded as she crossed her arms over her chest, forming a bodily shield. "We're in serious trouble, John." Her voice cracked. Her body rocked. Her hands squeezed white slashes into her own forearms, marks that I could read even in the low light of a darkened hall.

"I'm at my wit's end," she said. "I don't know what to do. Randy's being stalked."

SIX

R andy Haverhill's gift as a communicator was that he could bring the light of plain speech and common sense to the field of economics, known from the nineteenth century on as the dismal science. As his reading came to a close, the crowd was on its feet once more. Hillary excused herself, but made me promise to meet with Randy after the book signing. It was 8:00 PM already. I feared I'd never make the second set at Hale Kava, but agreed to hang around.

The crowd possessed that learned—and yet exotic—look you see at any university, but at Randy's signing the Asians were the dominant group. There were scores of bright looking young Ph.Ds, scholars from the East-West Center, the women showing off their national pride in the form of exotic jewellery, wraps, bags and such—Thai silks, Hong Kong tailoring, and all that, dividing themselves into the haves and the have-nots.

The haves clutched their copies of *Econ Decon*, with its bolt of white lightening through lines of grey headlines and stock ticker symbols on the cover. The haves headed for an open bay on the ground floor of Jefferson Hall, overlooking the Japanese garden at the back. Hands down this magnificent garden is my favourite spot on the entire campus. Randy sat behind a table festooned with flower leis. A line of fans snaked out the door, a number of them looking disgruntled.

A tall and very thin Asian woman with long black hair and a bustline no doubt invented in some plastic surgeon's office was fawning over Randy Haverhill at the head of the line. The rest of the Asians in line stoically held their places, while the haoles in the same line began to mutter to themselves, shake their heads, and glance at their watches. Hillary and her father worked the room, greeting Randy's readers.

I was among the have-nots. We all headed to an adjoining bay for the lavish cocktail spread, heavy pupu. Roughly translated, this means: hey brah, we got enough stuff here you won't want dinner. I loaded up on imu pork and Japanese appetisers, rolls wrapped in black seaweed parchment and stuffed with various combinations of pasty white rice, fish and veggies.

"John Spyer," a voice wheezed behind me. "What brings you to Honolulu?"

"Putt Jorgenson." I turned around to behold a sight I never thought I'd see. My journalist buddy is a guy who favours limp denim work shirts and tattered ties. But Putt was turned out in a pristine white barang, the fancy kind with rows of pleats down the front. Fresh from the box, the shirt still had fold marks down the sides.

"So, Putt, I see you've gone native."

"Fine invention the barang." Putt fanned his middle with the shirt, banded at the bottom. A barang is never tucked in. "Anything that lets in the tropical breezes works for me." Putt's other hand balanced a small plate heaped with sweet and sour pork on the back of his skinny reporter's notebook.

"So what did you think of Randy's talk?"

"Whooo," Jorgenson's tortoise-shell glasses waggled on his blunt nose. "What a delivery. The dude is a popularizer. He's to economics what Obama is to politics, and a ladies' man just like Bill Clinton. Did you hear those campus lovelies scream? I'm jealous as hell." Putt's dark eyes swept the room. They landed on Eva Haverhill, Randy's first wife, his ex.

Eva, a dumpling of a damsel, wore a short, black A-line dress over sheer black tights, the better to hide her oversize okole and show off her magnificent legs. She teetered on spike heels which had to be miserable, but the shoes gave her instant lift, four inches of much-needed height. Her hair was bound up in a turban which added a few inches more.

"No wonder Eva couldn't handle Randy," Putt muttered, shifting around to face me. Though banned from smoking in the building, Putt used the stem of his unlit pipe to jab the air, underlining his point. Putt was careful to talk about Eva Haverhill with his back turned to her. Putt claimed that Eva could hear through the reinforced walls of a bomb shelter, and he was in a position to know: Eva was Putt's boss on *The Honolulu Gazette*.

Across the room a handsome young male, foxy of feature, brought Eva a plate of pupus and escorted her out to the terrace overlooking the Japanese garden, where some musicians were cranking up. I hoped they were good; it was close to 9:00 PM. Hale Kava was about to be scratched from my personal playlist.

"Who's the lucky guy?"

"Eddie Cooke, Eva's intern and boy toy."

"So Eva poached on your assignment, the better to parade young Mr. Cooke in front of Randy?"

"That's the ticket," Jorgenson said. "Come say hello. Eva mentioned you the other day. We haven't seen you in Honolulu since her Christmas party." As we crossed the room, I found myself looking over my shoulder for Hillary. She and Eva were not on good terms. The last thing I wanted was to get caught in the crossfire between Randy's ex and current wives, but Hillary was off in the adjoining bay, still mingling with the haves in the crowd. I thought I was safe, but Madam P., if she happened to be sober, must have decreed otherwise.

SEVEN

The Japanese garden is a stately pocket park that lies between Jefferson Hall and the Manoa Stream which defines the outer edge of the campus. By daylight the park is the symbolic demarcation zone between the groves of academe and the real world. The scruffy Manoa Hills lie just across the stream.

The garden is kept in manicured natural sans benches and tables. Since it was well after sundown, there was nothing to be seen but a few elegant shrubs in pools of pathway light, but in the velvety air of the tropical night, the blended fragrance of the garden was thick enough to slice. The garden formed a perfect backdrop for the youthful musicians on the terrace, doing the usual aloha type stuff, except the beat was stepped up in a kind of Hawaiian reggae, and a catchy beat it was.

Eva and Eddie Cooke—Mr. Boy Toy—briskly applauded the number. Putt and I joined in and I could see the reason for their enthusiasm. Toby Haverhill was on the program. Toby was a high school sophomore: Randy's only child; Eva's beloved son. Hillary had two daughters by a previous marriage, who were much younger, and the blended family got on just as badly as anyone might expect, considering the fact that Eva detests Hillary.

Toby and a Hawaiian kid were playing guitars for a pixie of a lead singer, a big-eyed shave-head with a match-stick build. A Lorna Luft type of stylist, who all but swallowed her hand mike as she belted out a Broadway via Waikiki tune, shimmying at the finish like a human tuning fork. The fact that Eva was leading the cheering section came as no surprise. Eva may have been a femme fatale, if only in her own mind, but she was an adoring mother as well.

"John, I'm so glad you could hear this." Eva beamed. "You know your music, what do you think?"

"I think that they are good enough to audition at Hale Kava."

"Really?" Eva had a square face dominated by limpid hazel eyes that widened, and the effect was of more eyes and fewer chins than I recalled.

"You ready for Toby to turn pro? I'll pass the word." This may have been a tad of an overstatement on my part.

"I thought they might be ready. I don't know, though, I'm the mom. I wouldn't want them to start in on that drink they pour at Hale Kava."

"Not a chance. Kava's an acquired taste, like poi. To kids like Toby it's like drinking mud."

"If Toby turns pro now, I'm afraid he won't go to college."

"True enough, Eva. Why rush a kid like Toby into a very tough business?"

"You're so right." A wistful expression crossed Eva's face. "At this point, Toby's dealing with a stepmother who hates him and that's stressful enough."

Toby's trio launched into an instrumental; Miss Lorna Hawaii strummed her ukulele, the dancing flea, Hawaiians call it; she held her own against the backup guitars. Then the two boys put down their Fenders and the girl led the three of them in a Hawaiian chant. It was very well done and I joined in the applause as they paused for intermission.

"Who are the other two kids?"

"Kimo and Se Se Chandra. Their mom's half Hawaiian and their Dad's half Malaysian. Gorgeous, aren't they? Kimo is Toby's best friend. Se Se is the love of his life." Eva pulled a face. "It won't last, sad to say. I'm surprised it's lasted this long, nearly a year. Se Se's too mature for Toby, but what can I do but keep my mouth shut? Anyway, Chandra Senior is a sound engineer for Clear Channel. He's putting together a CD for them right now."

Putt cleared his throat and tapped his watch. "Deadline approaches, Eva. Are you coming back to the paper with us?"

Eva took my hand. "I have to run. John. I'm putting the paper to bed tonight. Will you be here for a few days?"

"Not likely. "

"Why not stay?" Eva gave me the big eye. "There's a spare room at my house." That predatory look of hers gave me goosebumps, known locally as chicken skin.

"Thanks, but I'm bunking over at Cousin Duke's place on Leahi."

"What do you hear from Maya?" Eva said. She had hosted a sendoff dinner party for us when Maya came for Christmas. On the morning of the 27th, we had flown to Serenoa, Maya's ranch in Florida, for New Year's Eve. Maya and Eva adored each other. Toby was to spend the summer of his junior year on Maya's ranch.

"Maya's coming in September. We'll do the Aloha Festival and all that."

"Fall for a Florida cowgirl?" Putt snorted. "Makes for sore ears and lonely nights, eh brah?" I ignored this dig although I was tempted to remind Putt that when it came to cowgirls, Jorgenson himself had been dumped by Miss Best Of Show.

"Don't be a stranger, John," Eva said. "Come see us.Toby thinks the world of you." As she slipped into my arms, I realised my first impression was correct. There was distinctly less Eva to hug than there had been at Christmas.

"You are looking svelte these days, Eva. What is it? Exercise? Romance? The exercise of romance?" I cast a glance in the direction of Mr. Boy Toy who had wandered over to the pupu table and was talking to a leggy blonde with big hair.

"Chemotherapy." Eva tossed me a wicked grin."Hell on the system but great for weight loss." She marched out with a rat-a-tat-tat of her spiky heels, beckoning to her intern, who cast a long-suffering look in my direction. The tall blonde blew a kiss at Mr. Boy Toy, who waggled his fingers furtively at her. Eva's intern didn't want her to know she had competition.

I was stunned. I felt sick for Eva, about the chemo at any rate; as for the boy toy, I knew very well that Eva could take care of herself. I didn't know what to say, I hated the fact that I'd played the fool twice in one night after all. I took out my irritation on Putt. I snagged his arm as he brushed past me and yanked him around.

"Why didn't you tell me?"

"About Eva?"

"About Eva." I clamped a vice grip on his arm.

"Hey John." Putt wrenched loose. "I'm sorry about this, but I'm sworn to secrecy. Eva controls her own news." Putt straightened his barang in fussy moves. Shaking his frizzy head of dishwater blond hair, he turned on his heel and headed for the door and I followed him.

The pupu trays had vanished and so had the crowd. It was 9:25 PM. Soon Amorin would be waiting outside. I'd have to toss him a twenty and ask him to wait. I was passing the book-signing bay where at least a dozen people were still waiting. I couldn't catch Randy's eye. I was heading for the main door when Miss McCready came dashing up to me, the train of her gown hitched over her arm.

"Mr. Spyer," she panted, face flushed.

"Lola. What's wrong?"

"It's Mrs. Hillary. She says you must come now, wikiwiki."

EIGHT

Flexibility is the keynote inside Jefferson Hall. Some conference rooms can be opened at the ends to accommodate large crowds or closed down for intimate events. Two long bays adjoined the ground floor auditorium where Randy had spoken. Lola McCready rushed past these and I kept pace with her. She opened a third door to a much smaller room. This had been reserved as a staging area for the event. Evidently Randy shared space with Toby and his musician friends, since various music stands and instrument cases were scattered around. The place was a shambles.

Chairs were flung around the room; guitar cases had been emptied and tossed into corners. Bits of paper were flung around like confetti. The contents of a woman's straw carryall had been dumped on the floor. Hillary Haverhill was down on her haunches, her elegant gown pooled around her, as she plucked glass from a shattered bottle of perfume with her bare hands.

My nose recoiled. My eyes watered. The broken bottle was that Calvin Klein stuff. My friend Susan Kopono wears it. Smells like sex, some say; others, including me, say it hints of death. Eternity, it's called, and that's a perfect name for the stuff. A whole bottle of it, pooled on the floor, was overpowering. "Smells like some dowager had an accident with the bottle," I muttered, "and died."

A smile flitted across Hillary's face. She settled on the backs of her heels for a moment, raking her fingers through her scalp. Her sleek, fashion statement of a hairdo was snarled and falling in her face. "Come on Hillary. You can't do that. There may be fingerprints." I got down on my haunches with her, stared at her.

Her eyes were distant and her voice defeated. "I'm sick of this stuff, John," she hissed. "I can't handle it."

"I know you are. We'll get to the bottom of this, Hillary. I'll help you."

I got to my feet and pulled Hillary to hers, taking a nasty jolt from my back in the process. I heard a small sneeze and turned around. Lola McCready stood sniffling at the smell, back to the door, bracing it against entry, doing her best to hold her composure.

"Lola," I said. "Find Randy Haverhill and bring him wikiwiki."

"Dr. Haverhill's still signing."

"You're one smart girl, Lola. Make excuses. Promise everyone in line a free copy or whatever, but Dr. Haverhill must come here. Right now."

Lola started out the door, then turned back as if to ask if there was anything else, and there was.

I told her, "Find a security guard. Tell him to round up the force and get over here."

Hillary was trembling, teeth chattering. I found her wrap, bundled her in it, turned a chair upright and sat her down. I mounted a chair backwards and got eye to eye with her.

"You okay, Hillary? What can I get you?"

"Nothing, thanks. I'll be all right in a minute."

"Before Randy gets here, fill me in."

She stared at me, face blank.

Realising that she was in shock, her thoughts scattered, I coached her: "How many of these bashes have there been?"

Hillary rubbed the thin bridge of her nose between her closed eyes. "So hard... She shook her head, massaged her temples. "I'm so tired."

"Put them in order for me, Hillary. What happened first?"

"Yes. All tight. The first one was a break-in at Randy's apartment. We were secretly engaged and sometimes I stayed over with him."

"Randy had an apartment?"

"He rented a place down the Pali Highway while we redid his house on Dowsett."

"And?"

"We came home one night after a function. It was a Pacific Rim fundraiser. The apartment was trashed, Randy's manuscripts shredded; the bathroom demolished; some of my clothes were, ah, molested, I guess you could say."

"When was this?"

"Before we were married, so it would have been about nine months ago, mid-October. It's why we decided to elope.

"As I recall from the society pages you were a December Bride.

"We were married on December 21st, the first day of winter." The tension left Hillary's face. Her gaze looked right through me, back to better times. "We did the Las Vegas thing, just a couple of tourists. It was so funky and so much fun. Nobody recognized Randy. When you are brought up a Rooke, you know, things are supposed to be planned to the nth degree, with the formal invitations and all that. Dad was crushed, of course."

I smiled. "I see he got over it."

"He did. Dad loves Randy."

"All right, when was the next time?"

"January 5th, the day we came home." Hillary rubbed under her eyes, wiping at tears in the corners. "I had worked so hard to get the kitchen and the master suite done at the Dowsett house. When we walked in for our first night in our new home, I found my wedding china smashed, the new cabinetry carved up. Randy's study on the main floor had been trashed. All his files dumped, his desk ransacked. Toby's room had been trashed. The new furniture we bought for him was demolished."

"What about the rest of the house?"

"Fortunately, the antiques in the sitting room were untouched, and whoever it was didn't bother with the master suite upstairs."

"Maybe you surprised them?" Hillary shook her head.

"Maybe."

"Anything else?"

"The Pacific Rim Institute's new offices were wrecked shortly after we moved into them."

"In Burns Hall?"

Hillary nodded. "In early March. The Pacific Rim Institute is a new division of the East-West Center. When a professor retired, Randy was offered his suite. I had it totally redone. I found myself doing it all over."

"It sounds as if this stalker doesn't like transitions," I said. "So, we have three incidents beginning back in October of last year; one in January, the next this past March?" Hillary's face crumpled. "They are sort of spaced out. Every couple of months; just when I think this is past us and we can move on."

"Anything else?"

"In mid-April the tires were slashed on Randy's new Jaguar. Our personal papers were dragged out of the office and scattered around in the parking lot."

"That's it?" 1 said.

"Isn't it enough?" She snapped. Then she shook her head. "I'm sorry, John."

"Okay, Hillary, we've got several incidents here, either at home or at the Institute. What other similarities can you think of?"

"Sometimes there's a note."

"A note? Did you find a note here?"

"On the white board by the lectern."

I went to have a look. A few letters, some backward, a childish scrawl. "This is a note?"

"I believe so," Hillary said. "It never makes any sense, but I've seen this sort of thing before."

This so-called note, a jumble of childish, disconnected letters, made no sense but I took a shot of it anyway with the camera in my cell phone.

NINE

A tapping came at the door. Randy stuck his head in. "Hillary? What?" His eyes flashed around the room, took in the chaos. He rushed in, slamming the door behind him. In two strides he was at Hillary's side, drawing her into his arms. Randy was a big guy and there was something about his aura, his presence, that seemed to shrink space. "Oh lord baby, I'm sorry, so sorry about all this."

He held her close, rocking her in his arms. Hillary was tall, Close to six feet. They were a startling pair. Over the top of her head he greeted me with a nod and a wide-eyed stare.

Hillary, rigid in his arms, wasn't buying it. She wrenched free, strode toward the glass slider that opened on the garden side of the room, stepped outside and sent the door along in its track with enough force that I thought it might shatter.

"Whooo," Randy said, shaking his head. "One angry wahine, yeah? One mad woman. But what can I do about it?"

He flashed a grin, tossed me a local style handshake, one shaka, thumb and pinkie extended, middle fingers closed in a fist. We embraced for the sake of old times, and I smiled despite myself at the eminent scholar's lapse into good-old-boy style.

"John brah. Where you been keeping yourself? You never come see us."

"Hillary sent me a note, said it was urgent." I looked around the room. "I have to agree with her."

Randy threw his hands in the air. "Thousands of students on this campus? There's going to be at least one kukui nut in the mix."

"Randy, come on. Face reality. Hillary doesn't think this is any unbalanced student."

His face did contortions as his eyes shot sparks of anger, indignation, self-righteousness, but his mouth had a sly twist that I didn't much care for. *"Professor Randy, he's just dandy with the ladies,"* Randy said, his voice a singsong. "Lotta talk."

"That's not what I've heard from Eva."

Randy snorted. "Tall tales from one short lady."

I sighed. We were getting nowhere. "Look at the facts, Randy. A break-in at your apartment. Your Dowsett house invaded. Burns Hall office trashed twice over. Now this. Your book party in chaos. What are you going to do about it?"

"Come see, John, I've got a new security gate at my house on Dowsett. The alarm system's loud enough to summon the troops off Hickam Field. I had an alarm installed at my office in Burns Hall as well. Tonight?" He frowned, shrugged, shoulders sagging. "We beef up campus security? We check invitations at the door? Look what happens? What can I do? Go into hiding?"

A knock came at the door. I got up to answer it. Toby was in the hall with his musician friends. "Is there some trouble? Is Dad okay?"

"Where did you hear that?"

The girl beside him, the mite of a Se Se, answered: "First I see Lola McCready in the ladies room trying to scrub tears off her face. Outside, Dr. Haverhill, he rushes in here. Spells trouble."

I slipped outside to talk to them, closing the door behind me. "There's been a ruckus. Nobody hurt, but I can't let you in until the campus police arrive. When were you kids last in the room?"

"We had our last break at 8:45," Toby said. "Everything was fine."

"Did you see anybody hanging around the doors?"

"Lots of people outside on the terrace," Kimo said. "Lots of coeds, a few half trashed. They passed along the path that leads over the bridge, toward Hale Kuahine."

"Did any of you notice anything here in Jefferson Hall?" The kids looked at each other. "It was empty," Toby said.

"Is our music okay?" Se Se wailed, staring at me.

"You'll have some sorting out to do," I said.

Toby slipped his arm around her, pulled her close. Se Se barely reached his chest. She had the stature and the shape of a pre-pubescent gymnast. "We'll fix it."

Randy poked his head through the door. "Our security man is here, John. Wants to talk to you." Randy and I traded places. I slipped past him; he stepped into the hall. "Hey kids, I heard about your fine performance. Outstanding."

"Thanks, Dad," I heard Toby say. A good word from this overpowering dad meant everything to a shy kid in a precarious position. No doubt Toby felt like a third wheel in Randy's new life with a new lady—a new lady who was having her struggles with his mom.

TEN

Inside the trashed room, Hillary Haverhill had regained her composure. "John," she said. "Come meet Satch Marshall, head of security. He was very helpful to us last time."

"All right," I said, taking the measure of a slender redheaded haole with a long line of a moustache, straight as a level. Satch's moustache was considerably wider than his mouth. "Toby and his musician friends were in here at 8:45 PM. At that point everything was fine; Hillary sent for me at just about 9:30."

Satch surveyed the room. "Lotta mess made for such a short time. More than one person did this, I'd say."

"No doubt, and these mokes were invited guests."

Marshall's forehead wrinkled. "What makes you say that?"

"Invitations were checked at the door. Randy himself hired the security."

"True enough. Let me check with the guys on the door. Maybe somebody screwed up," Satch said.

"Do that," I said. "Noise would have been made in here, so just where was Randy's beefed-up security? I'd like to know."

Satch checked his clipboard. "We had two men out patrolling the front rooms. One where Dr. Haverhill was signing, the other keeping watch on the party, and two men outside watching the terrace." He shuffled more papers. "Just before 9:00 there was a disturbance down in the garden. A student came rushing up, said somebody fell into the Manoa stream."

"Okay," I said, "That explains it."

"My guys rushed down there, broke up a lover's quarrel. The female accused her boyfriend of two-timing her and tossed his backpack into the water."

"Could this have been a diversion?"

"I doubt it, but I'll check it out."

"This is the third go round for Dr. Haverhill here on the campus."

"Right," Satch said.

"Any similarities?"

"Yeah, brah. Just like any other student pranks we get during finals week," Satch said. "Exams over, they blow off steam."

"Okay, but what about the note on the whiteboard?"

"Whiteboard?" Satch said. "What about it?"

"The scrawls on there. Hillary mentioned them to me."

"There's nothing on the whiteboard, brah," Satch said.

I looked for myself. The whiteboard had been erased, very carefully. I shook my head, muttering my private imprecation under my breath. Jesus Madam. "Hillary," I said. "You saw the scrawl. You brought it to my attention. "

"I did, Satch. It was there. John's got a picture of it."

"Time stamped," I said.

"Okay," Satch said. "I'll make a note of it."

"Ohmigod," Randy said, striding in, making a show of whacking his forehead, a staged gesture if ever I saw one. "I erased that myself. Didn't think anything of it. I'm so sorry. I shouldn't have done that."

"So, Dr. Haverhill. You *did* see something on the whiteboard?" Satch's tone was deferential. He was not about to cross the star professor, though I could read the scepticism on the security guard's face.

Hillary drew in a breath. Her face was ashen. She cast a glacial look at Randy.

"I'm sorry about this, Dr. Haverhill," Satch said. "I can't figure it out."

"Don't blame yourselves. You tried," Randy said.

"We all tried, didn't we dear?" He hugged Hillary who stood at his side, rigid as some department store manikin. "And now, please excuse us. My bride is exhausted and upset. I must take her home to bed."

Randy clapped me on the back at the same time he dismissed me with a self-satisfied smirk. "John, brah. Come see us sometime."

Was this an ego in denial? Or was Dr. Randolph Kealoha Bishop Haverhill involved in some side games he was hiding from his new wife?

PART TWO

ELEVEN

I had taken my vintage Mustang for a spin around Diamond Head. The drive had gone well. I'd done a tune-up in the hope it would resolve the complaints of my Cousin Duke. He garages my car for me, since I'm rarely in Honolulu for any length of time. The disastrous Haverhill book-signing back in June had been my last visit.

I arrived Thursday afternoon on the tourist chopper and worked on the car all day yesterday. Duke had complained that the car had a ghost driver, I have to admit that my cousin is a better Hawaiian than I am, more of a believer, while I'm the better mechanic, and so I'd gone with an under-the-hood solution to the vehicle's crankiness as opposed to Duke's more metaphysical approach.

My lady friend Maya was due in from Florida midweek. I wanted my wheels in perfect shape by then. Maya had emailed me a long list of see-and-dos and the Mustang was sure to be in for a workout. She's a '65 GT350H Shelby, candy apple red with the Le Mans stripes, and she demands constant tinkering. I'd installed new plugs and changed her oil and washed and waxed her. I'd pulled her up the steep driveway, into her stall in cousin Duke's garage.

I was stowing the tools, wringing out the chamois, and looking forward to a shower and a shave. The cool morning trades had subsided. The afternoon would be a scorcher and I was beginning to drip. Duke's cat Kiki sat on the tool bench supervising my every move. I heard a car race up the driveway and screech to a halt. Had Duke returned early from his barge tour? He's a captain for Dillingham Transportation—but tossing his own gravel around wasn't Duke's style of approach.

I poked my head out of the garage and there stood a BMW sports rig straight off the showroom floor. My journalist buddy Putt Jorgenson was at the wheel, his image enhanced by the solid car. Putt looked only half as ugly as he really is. A middle—aged woman was in the passenger seat. Her face was obscured by a big straw hat and sunglasses. What little I could see of her skin was pale as moonlight.

I flung the chamois on the tool bench and went out to admire the vision—of the car, that is. "You finally got tired of driving junkers, Putt? As Mama Hana used to say, a solid car does wonders for one kanaka."

"Eva's new wheels." Putt pulled his pipe from between his teeth. Behind his tortoise shell glasses, his dark eyes shifted toward his passenger. I realised then that the pallid woman beside him was Eva Haverhill. No way was she the same Eva I had seen back in June. Here we were, coming up on mid September. Aloha Week was upon us.

"Eva. You look wonderful." I went around to the passenger side and opened the door for her. I'd adopted a jovial tone to mask my shock. Her once round face was a bony square. She'd lost the last of her chins, revealing a jawline you could hone knives on.

She flung her hat aside, stepped out of the car and into my arms. "John Spyer, you are one charming liar." Once powerful in her bulk, Eva was another woman entirely. Stripped to her essential self, she was all bones, but at least the bones felt sturdy. Even in the stiletto heels she always wore, her head barely reached my collar bone.

"You look like somebody's waif, Eva." As I returned her hug, I could see the top of her pale skull through her thin hair. Nothing was left of Eva's thick, honey-roasted brown locks but a few limp strands that framed a big-eyed face, a child's face. The keiki's face puckered. She burst into tears.

Over the top of Eva's head, I bugged my eyes, threw Putt one fright look. What had I done? How had I offended the woman? Putt-—the coward—wouldn't look at me.

"Hey, Eva, cut it out, now. You are looking fine, one solid wahine for sure. If anybody can beat the big C...."

"It's me." Eva said, wiping her eyes with her fingers. "I know that. I'm one of the lucky ones. The cancer is gone. Now all I have to do is survive the cure."

But Eva was also one of the weary ones. She clung to me some more. I realised she had to get off her feet so I walked her to the porch swing in cousin Duke's backyard. She sank into the swing, stiff as an old woman. Since my back chooses its moments, I wasn't much better. I eased into the swing beside her like some old stiff.

"I'm a survivor," Eva sighed. Her eyes were swollen. "I'm *the* survivor and Randy is gone. Would you believe that?"

"Randy? Randy Haverhill?" I leaped out of that swing as if I'd been stung. I came close to tossing Eva out of it as well.

"We've been trying to raise you for an hour," Putt said. "Randy's dead. Murdered on his doorstep. It's all over the news."

"Jesus Lord and Madam Pele. What happened?"

"Two shotgun blasts. One to the chest, the other to the crotch." Putt's mouth turned down. "Let's hope the chest shot was first, poor bastard." He clamped his pipe between his teeth.

"Who did it?"

Putt raised his palms, shook his head. "We don't know. The cops don't either. I'll let Eva tell you the rest of it, John. She's in trouble. She needs your help."

TWELVE

Putt sat down in the swing beside Eva, handing her a wad of tissue. I took a faded wicker chair across from her. Duke's cat joined the party, jumping into the swing. Kiki is black with white legs and black patches on her knees, cat shin guards. She kneaded Eva's thighs a few times with her paws and curled up in her lap.

"Eva, I am so sorry about this." I managed to croak out the words, struggling to keep a level tone. Eva had no idea. Sorry? Yes, but I was also outraged. I'd tried to talk some sense into Randy months ago at his book party. Randy had brushed off some stalker. He must have assuaged Hillary's fears. She never got back to me. And now this? I was beside myself.

I paced in front of the swing while Putt saw to Eva, trying to get her to compose herself, while I subjected myself to a tongue lashing, trying to explain my own failure to be there for my oldest friend. "I'm damned sorry, Eva. I let it go. I knew about the stalker. Hillary told me there had been several prior incidents that night that the book signing was trashed. When I didn't hear anything more from Randy, I figured he had handled it some way. He was such a capable guy. I thought he'd taken care of it, that maybe he'd found someone else to investigate." I paced around cousin Duke's backyard, working off an urge to punch a few holes through the side of the house.

Eva drew in a weary intake of breath and released a fresh spurt of tears.

"I loved Randy," I said.

Putt got up to pace around and I slipped into the swing beside Eva and put my arm around her and let her cry herself out. Eva dabbed at her eyes and wiped her nose while I went on talking story, making small talk, rushing to fill a painful void. "Randy had his faults, but he was a famous man. One of a kind."

Eva shook her head. "Tch," was all she could manage.

"You okay, Eva?" Putt said.

Eva's face twisted. "Randy *would* diddle around until he got himself killed."

Her vehemence stunned me. I was speechless. Eva made Randy what he was, a famous economist, a talking head on TV, and a Pulitzer Prize winning author. It was Eva, and not Hillary, who had made Randy's career. The trouble was, Randy Haverhill had charisma to burn and it looked as if one of his lady friends had done just that—burned him. That's what Eva meant to tell me. Eva and Randy had a love/hate relationship, no question. But this was too callous, and I was too angry to let this pass, but even so I tried to take it easy on her.

"Now Eva, let's not blame the victim," I said.

"I just know Randy's disgusting lifestyle is mixed up in this."

"But surely not so disgusting that you offed Randy yourself?"

The swing stopped moving. Eva stared at me.

Putt intervened: "Hey, John. That's cruel."

"All I'm saying is, be careful what you say, Eva," I cautioned. "You're ex-family, and that makes you a suspect until you're ruled out."

"John, you have no idea, not a clue," Eva shot back."I have the best alibi in the world. I was in the newsroom all morning with Putt here and three other reporters. It's *Toby* they are going after. They'll arrest *my son* for Randy's murder."

"Toby?" My voice cracked. Randy's only child? Oh yes, Randy also had a pair of young stepdaughters, Hillary's girls, and the blended family wasn't doing so well on the blending, but personally, I had to fault Eva on this. Eva had divorced Randy, after all. It's a haole thing to carry on when your lover takes another; a good Hawaiian accepts the love of the beloved and makes do.

"How does Toby figure in?" I said. Toby was a shy kid. The last time I'd seen Toby, he was playing backup guitar in a band that played at Randy's book signing party. Toby hovered in the shadow of his flamboyant dad. Toby Haverhill couldn't murder a cockroach. Of that I was quite certain.

Eva leaned so far forward in the swing that I thought she might fall out of it. A startled Kiki jumped before she was dumped and stalked off, back arched, tail turned down.

"Toby witnessed Randy's murder. Being there when his father is murdered? That would be punishment enough." Eva mopped her eyes. "To be charged with the crime? Toby is so sensitive this will kill him. I'm afraid he'll try to commit suicide. Right now we can't even find him. You have to help me, John. I beg you."

"Tell me exactly what happened."

THIRTEEN

va stared at me. "I don't *know* exactly what happened. I wasn't *there*."
"You weren't there, Eva. You were in the newsroom. I got that."

Eva ran her fingers beneath her leaking eyes. "I got a call from our police reporter, Mitzi Wong, just after noon. She tipped me as soon as she heard. Putt and I rushed over there. We couldn't get in the house. I asked for Toby but the cop on the door told me he was on the way downtown for routine questioning. Routine questioning? Hah. No way do I want Toby questioned alone. We went straight downtown to H.P.D. headquarters, but Toby wasn't there. The dispatcher said he hadn't come in yet."

This sounded too odd to be anything but a mix-up, so I tried to calm Eva. "Toby was on the scene? The police will want to know what he saw. By the way, what was he doing at Randy's? I thought Toby lived with you."

"Mondays through Thursdays he's with me. Friday evenings he goes to Randy's. On Saturday mornings they paddle at the Outrigger Canoe Club, doing the male bonding thing. They came home around eleven and were waiting for a pizza delivery. The doorbell rang and Randy answered it. Toby was in the kitchen, setting out some Cokes. He heard shots fired at the front door. Toby rushed out and found his father lying on the porch with a knife in his back."

"Wait a minute, Eva. You said that Randy was shot."

"Shot, yes. But when Toby found Randy, he had a knife in his back."

"Shot first, then knifed?"

Eva pulled in a breath and exhaled the details: "Two shotgun blasts—one to the groyne—and a knife in the back. What does that tell you?"

"A spurned lover?"

"That's what I think. Randy drove some woman over the edge. It's obvious to me, and you know it, John."

"Toby was at the murder scene," I said. "He's a witness. The police will want to know what he knows." I refused to go where Eva was thinking.

"Toby got on his cell and called emergency. He stayed right with Randy doing the emergency protocol until the ambulance came."

"How do you know all this?"

"He called me after the medics arrived." Eva wiped her eyes and shredded the tissues into bits. "I warned him not to talk to the police until I got there, but what if he doesn't listen? Meanwhile, I get the runaround from the cops. Something is wrong here. I can feel it."

"How old is Toby?"

Sixteen. He's a baby. He just got his driver's licence."

"It's procedure, Eva. The police will walk him through the crime scene several times. They'll go over and over it with Toby and make a report."

"They'll charge Toby with the murder of his father."

"Why would they do that?"

"Why? To get even with *me*, of course, the tita editor at *The Honolulu Gazette.* That's one way to end my probe of the justice system."

"That's your own paranoia talking, Eva. Don't think like that."

"Mitzi Wong warned me. She says they've got some kind of clue."

"Implicating Toby?"

"She hinted as much. You've got to help me, John. You're a licensed investigator with connections."

I found myself rubbing the stubble on my jaw while I thought this one over. "I'll find Toby for you, Eva. Beyond that, I doubt there's much I can do."

Putt yanked the pipe stem out of his mouth. "Excuse me?"

"I knew Randy Haverhill. I grew up with him. Things might surface that wouldn't be to Toby's advantage." This was the best excuse I could think of on the spur of the moment. It was not smart to let Eva know that I had been talking to Hillary.

"Bull." Putt rapped the bowl of his pipe on the arm of the swing. "It's on account of Maya, isn't it?"

"Maya will be here midweek," I said piously, grasping at a convenient straw that Putt had handed me. "We have plans."

"Toby is at risk for his life and you have plans?" Eva's stinging tone shamed me. I felt myself colour.

"You'll have to pardon my haole-ness, Eva." The fact that the word had surfaced on my tongue meant only one thing. I was out of line, trying to shirk the very nature that Mama Hana had instilled in me. Your Haole-ness Mama would say when she caught me thinking like a white guy. For all the awkwardness of the situation, I could no more ignore the plight of Eva Haverhill than I could slide on a ti leaf off the side of Mt. Lē'ahi."

"Your holiness?" Putt sneered.

"I apologise, Eva," I said, ignoring Putt. "I was thinking from the haole side of my brain. Let's take this one step at a time. Toby will be questioned, but not alone. I'll get right on it. But you have to realise this is a Saturday. I'd venture to say that the lead detective is short-handed, which most likely explains the delay. Who's the lead investigator by the way?"

Eva's fingers flew to her face. "I don't know. I think they told me but..."

"A guy named Tabura," Putt said.

"Telly Tabura? That helps. I know Telly from way back."

"Yes," Eva brightened. "I just knew you could help me, John."

"Tabura is a senior man. Doesn't play games. Nevertheless, Toby was on the scene, which makes him a person of interest. The police reporter hears they have something. Won't say what. If I were you, I'd hire an attorney, just as a precaution. Meanwhile, I'll find Toby for you. I can do that much."

"I've already called Harlan Kawahara, the best attorney in town. He's on the golf course, right there."

"At the Country Club?"

"Harlan is on his way to the house." The Honolulu Country Club is in the Nuuanu Valley, just across the Pali Highway, minutes from the Haverhill estate on Dowsett, our old neighbourhood, Randy's and mine. The Honolulu Country Club is haunted, so say the Hawaiians. For Randy's sake, I chose to give the Hawaiians the benefit of the doubt. Where in the other realm had Randy Haverhill taken himself by now? Was he haunting Harlan Kawahara's tee on the back nine? Or was he hovering in the locker room at the Outrigger Canoe Club?

"I'd go with you, John, but I'm exhausted," Eva said.

Putt helped her to her feet. "I'm taking you home, Eva. Let John find Toby."

F O U R T E E N

Nuuanu: cool high ground. That's the meaning of the word. It was no surprise to me that by the time I arrived at the Haverhill estate in the Nuuanu Valley, clouds billowed over the Pali peaks like the soft folds of a tent, rendering their green pinnacles invisible.

My shirt fluttered on my frame in a breeze flecked with rain. Most of the patrol cars were gone and only one TV truck remained. The ambient sound was the cooing of doves above the reverberating roar of traffic on the nearby S.R. 61, The Pali Highway. A pali, by the way, is a cliff in Hawaiian and The Pali Highway follows an ancient trail through the Koolau Mountains. These days The Pali Highway separates the southern, densely populated coast, including Honolulu, from the spectacular and much quieter bedroom communities to the north.

Tranquility had returned to Dowsett Avenue, but I was out of step with the mood.

I was an hour into the investigation and it wasn't good. I had to account for a shotgun, a knife, some kind of clue, and one missing keiki. I'd dropped by the H.P.D. headquarters on my way up here. I'd gotten a mouthful of the same doubletalk that Eva had run into. The dispatcher told me Toby hadn't come in yet.

Cops will lean on a kid before a parent turns up, but Eva had asked for her son and she knew the ropes. Lead detective Telly Tabura was a seasoned investigator. He'd conduct the questioning himself. Tabura would know better than to allow some subordinate to squeeze a cop car confession out of Toby. Or so I hoped.

I gave my name to the beat guy on the gate and he let me in, seeing as how Telly Tabura is an old friend. Grinning, Telly shot me a shaka shake. He stood at the outer edge of the crime scene tape blocking the entry. No way he'd let me onto the crime scene; I knew better than to offend him by asking. Telly might have the demeanour of a laid-back good ole' boy, but he pays attention to business.

In my mind's eye I saw Professor Randy paddling off in his outrigger, bound for the motherland, headed for Tahiti. I wouldn't let myself connect with what remained of him, lying there in front of me in his canoe club sweats in the columned shadows of his mansion, sprawled face down in a pool of darkening blood. Even in his indignity, Randy still had presence, seemed muscular. Dr. Haverhill kept himself in shape.

Telly had been in no rush to cover Randy, since direct sun wasn't an issue. No doubt the detective was awaiting an official from the medical examiner's office. Telly would be careful to keep procedure up to snuff. The murder of a glamorous academic was sure to attract attention from around the world. Solving it would test the mettle of a justice system that Eva Haverhill and *The Honolulu Gazette* had already taken to task for its altruistic attempts to convict petty crimes on the strength of slipshod procedure.

I stared at my watch. It was close to 3:00. "Hey, Telly, what's taking?"

"Professor got one appointment?" Telly said, with a wry twist of his mouth. "Cancelled, I guess." Telly's grin revealed one missing upper tooth, a hole—a puka—I'd put there myself. A head bump on a wrestling mat, accidental of course. Telly was a champion wrestler from Waianae High. I was a preppie punk from Punahou. Telly, dark and beetle-browed, was a head shorter than I am and three times as wide, with hands the size of shovels. I'd survived many a tussle with my heftier Hawaiian cousins on leverage and speed and found myself ahead on points on the seventh round until Telly pinned me, minus the tooth. The next year I turned out for tennis.

"John Spyer. Long time, brah. You got reason to be here?"

"Representing the family, Eva, the first Mrs. Haverhill."

Telly's unibrow shot up. "Mrs. Eva?" The whites of his dark eyes were yellower than the last time I had seen him, his complexion was grittier and his girth expanded by a factor of too many Hawaiian plate lunches, barbecued pork, gluey white rice, and macaroni salad drenched in mayo.

"The first Mrs.?" Telly's hand swayed. "What she need?"

"Toby Haverhill is Eva's son. She is afraid for the boy. She doesn't want him questioned without an attorney. She's hired Harlan Kawahara. You can understand where she's coming from."

"Toby's gone downtown already."

"Gone downtown? When? What time?"

Telly shrugged. "One hour. Two, maybe."

"Try three, Telly. Eva's already been downtown and so have I. Toby hasn't come in yet."

Telly frowned. His mouth worked. "I'll check on that."

I'd lodged my protest and knew Telly would follow up, so I changed the subject. "Toby was here for the… ah, festivities?" Inwardly, I cringed.

"In da kitchen, back of da house."

"Did he say who did this?"

Telly shook his head, glanced at his notes. Then he looked back at me. Raised two fingers to belt level, a hidden gesture, a fraternal oath in a brotherhood of two. Telly was about to exchange inside information with a trusted brother. Anything Telly said was safe with me. Besides, he owed me.

FIFTEEN

Telly was the insider with an entire homicide team at his disposal; Telly was chief. I didn't qualify as a kahili bearer, a guy to man the fly swatter, so to speak. Nonetheless, Telly and I had a bond. I lifted my fingers, mirroring his gesture. Telly's hand brushed across the dome of his head where his hair used to be. He still had a thick black pelt, but only on the sidewalls, which gave me a perverse pleasure. Telly had won our most important wrestling match but I'd come out on top. The top of my head that is, where I still had ample thatch. Telly leaned across the porch rail, festooned with crime scene tape. His lips scarcely moved as he talked.

"The son was found right there, on the porch with Dad, covered in blood. The EMC team had to pull him off. Toby had a knife in his hand."

I winced. So this was what Eva was driving at. The missing Clue: *Toby had a knife in his hand.*

Had Eva known this when she talked to me? If so, she'd conveniently left it out of the picture. I couldn't say that I blamed her for putting her own English on the scene. Most clients do. "I heard something about a knife found in Randy's back. Nothing about it being in Toby's hand."

Telly's response was one sparing nod. "Knife came from one chock in da kitchen."

"Jesus Madam. You sure?"

"Nobody saw anyone leaving the scene, brah. Got no footprints, no forced entry."

"Wait a minute, Telly. I heard Randy was shot."

Telly's long brow flattened into a glare; his eyes narrowed. He peered out at me through the slits.

"Hey, Telly, it's okay. The police reporter has that, and Eva Haverhill is her editor. Off the record, background only. It won't come out in the paper."

"Better not," Telly drew a slash across his throat with a forefinger. We watched each other, warily. Then Telly broke the tension with a swig from a bottle of Jamba Juice. "Tech found one entry point from da knife. The Medical Examiner may see more, once Professor Haverhill gets his turn in the lab."

"You've talked to Toby. What did he say?"

"Son said Dad was bleeding, said he pulled the knife out of Dad. The knife pinned one funny note to Dr. Haverhill's back."

"A note?" So this was the clue the police reporter had hinted about. "What note?"

Telly frowned. "The note went downtown along with the son."

"Right, Telly. Downtown." This was polite code.

What it meant was, the note was a key piece of evidence. I could see where this was leading. Detective Tabura thought that Toby had written the note. He was leaning on me; Telly wouldn't have told me about it if he didn't want to pass the word that we were in trouble.

Maybe Telly expected that I'd pass the word to the lawyer and get Toby to confess? But I wasn't about to sell out the kid, so I played stupid.

"Got a theory, Detective?"

"Hard to say. We haven't recovered the weapon."

"That's a relief." I muttered.

Telly frowned.

"I was just thinking out loud, Telly. If young Haverhill did the deed, the shotgun should have been right here on the scene, wouldn't you say?"

Tabura crossed his arms and nodded. "Maybe."

"By the way, where was the second wife, Mrs. Hillary?"

"Out in the country on her horse farm."

"Her two daughters?"

"Gone with rnama to ride their ponies."

"Hillary has an alibi?"

Tabura grinned. "Fifty people saw the second Mrs. Haverhill and the girls. They have these horses that dance around. One hula, maybe."

"Dressage "

"That it?" Telly bugged his eyes. "They teach horses to hula at Punahou?"

"Is Mrs. Hillary here?"

Tabura shook his head. "Came and went one hour ago. Second Mrs. arrived with her attorney, answered some questions. Then she rode off with her father in the company limo." An Oahu Land and Cane limo was what Tabura meant.

"I assume that Hillary told you that Randy was being stalked?"

Tabura's eyes widened. "So?"

"So, find the stalker, Telly. There was a nasty incident at Randy's last book signing. I was there."

"We'll talk," Tabura said.

"Aloha and mahalo, Telly. I'll keep in touch. I'll want to view the crime scene when you are ready. How about tomorrow morning?"

Telly shook his head. "Hard to find personnel on a Saturday. We'll be at this all night. Better figure late afternoon."

"No crime is solved before overtime, detective."

Telly punched a button on his phone: "Chief, sir. How can I help you?"

I tossed Telly a shaka and headed for my Mustang. Telly's chief was calling, my cue to return to the H.P.D. If I knew anything about Telly Tabura, Toby Haverhill would soon be delivered into Eva's arms.

Toby would have the protection of his mother and his lawyer. As far as Ron Kawahara was concerned, I had to tip him off about this strange note, not to mention where Detective Tabura was going with this.

SIXTEEN

I loped across Beretania, took the steep steps two at a time. H.P.D. headquarters is perched like a fortress on a vast green mound and the steps are cut into the side of it. The mound hides an enormous underground parking garage. In Honolulu, even the justice system is aesthetically correct.

It was close to 4:00 PM and I had lost ground. I did my best to erase a dark vision from my mind: Toby Haverhill over Randy's back pinning some note to the body with a kitchen knife. Could this nightmare be possible? What was keeping Toby? Where was he? I announced myself to the security officers in their glass enclosed booth and plunked down my SIG, permit and licence, then headed for juvenile intake.

The juvenile unit lies to the Diamond Head side of the headquarters building. A huge teddy bear maintains a security watch at the glass-fronted entrance door. Inside, some kiddy drawings soften the official menace of the place; nevertheless any keiki delivered here would have to be feeling the creeps.

As I entered the lobby, I was relieved to find Eva's lawyer already here. Still in his golf shirt, Harlan Kawahara was badgering the duty officer manning the front desk. This was quite a different Harlan from the white shoe lawyer I know, soft-spoken, polite and self-effacing. Harlan's ropy brows were furrowed and his dark eyes narrowed as he grilled the female desk jockey.

"Young Toby Haverhill. Where is he?" he demanded. "I was told he'd be here two hours ago."

I clapped Harlan on the shoulder and flipped him a shaka in support.

"Where is Toby Haverhill?" I chorused, Harlan grinned at me, and then turned again to the duty lady, who was talking to a patrol car.

"Officer Hime and his partner bring Mr. Toby in," she said.

Harlan pounded his fist into his palm, a resounding slap that made her blink. "Not Hime. The patrol car confessor?"

"Please sit down, Mr. Kawahara," the woman said in a monotone. She was one big lady, taller than Harlan, her stature enhanced by her bulk, her expression blank. She was not about to succumb to bullying from any lawyer, especially one she outweighed by at least fifty pounds. "Officer Hime and his partner bringing Toby wikiwiki.

"Wiki slicky?" I murmured to Harlan. "There's trouble. We've got to talk."

"In a minute," Harlan said, *sotto voice*. He turned back to the duty officer.

Her name badge said she was G. Willing. What did the G. stand for, I wondered. God?

Harlan made a show of staring at his massive Rolex.

"This is an outrage. It is now 4:00 PM. Note the *time* of Toby's *arrival* in your log, madam. Toby Haverhill is sixteen years old. His father has been murdered. He is several hours overdue. If officer Hime comes in with some cockamamie statement from my client, it won't be the first time. I'll be after his badge. Please make a note of what I am telling you, Ms. Willing, and kindly add that private detective John Spyer is here as my *witness*."

Officer Willing's broad dark cheeks flushed, but she wasn't buying the guff. She waved Harlan off to answer another call, and so I snagged Harlan, made sure he knew what Detective Tabura had tipped me to: Toby was indeed the prime suspect in the murder of his dad. Toby was the sole witness to the crime, found covered in blood, holding a knife that pinned a strange note to Randy's back.

"Eva told me it was a shotgun murder," Harlan said.

"A shotgun *was* the murder weapon. The knife in Toby's hand pegged a note."

"Sick." Harlan's lip curled. He shook his head.

"The police haven't found the shotgun but they say the knife came from the kitchen. That's why they are looking hard at Toby."

Harlan grimaced. "Not good, but at this point it won't make a difference. They haven't charged Toby and we haven't seen him, much less the evidence."

Within minutes Toby arrived at last. He came propped between two patrolmen, a burly local, stolid of demeanour, and this Officer Hime, a wiry haole with one of those cute, Ken Doll faces that might be confused with trustworthiness, particularly if you were a teenager in distress.

Toby's face was drawn, his skin blotchy, betraying intermittent crying. His hands shook. He wore an aloha shirt that bagged on him, possibly one of Randy's. No doubt the police had already taken the kid's Canoe Club tee into evidence. His hands and nails were freshly scrubbed. Toby would have been swabbed for gunshot residue and must have washed off the gunk.

Harlan claimed Toby by taking his arm. "Thank you, officers. I'll have a word with my client. After that, we'll be ready for any questioning, which I expect will be handled personally by Detective Tabura." *And not by two clods* is what Harlan meant. Harlan's acid tone to Officer Willing turned syrupy as he asked for a private room where they could chat and they started off in the direction indicated by Ms. G. Willing.

"I need to talk to my mother," Toby said, still shaking.

"She's on her way here, son. She'll be here any minute."

At six feet and then some, Toby Haverhill towered over his lawyer. His height qualified him as a bona fide Haverhill, but Toby was a pale carbon copy, neither as tall nor as dark as his old man. Toby had the same squared features and lantern jaw as Randy, yet I noticed something about the boy's presence that suggested he hadn't quite mastered the part of a Haverhill male. Or else Toby was totally aware of the Haverhill male and was determined to shrug off the Haverhill identity. Where Dad would preen and strut, Toby slouched and shrank. Perhaps Toby was aware of his father's sexual exploits? Maybe Toby was embarrassed by Dad? To be fair, this was not the best time to draw any conclusion, considering what Toby had been through. He looked whipped.

"Hang in there, Toby," I said. "I know it's tough."

"Thanks, John. Have you seen my mom?"

"Putt Jorgenson took her home to get some rest. I'm sure she's on the way."

"Toby and I will have a chat," Harlan said, patting Toby's back. "We need to buy some time to get comfortable with each other. We three need to confer before Detective Tabura gets here."

I'd done what I could, fulfilled my mission. Eva would arrive at any moment and I had to talk to her.

Meanwhile I decided to shadow the two beat cops. Suppose they had taken it upon themselves to squeeze a confession out of Toby?

SEVENTEEN

I caught up with Officer Hime and his partner at the snack shop in the corner of the H.P.D. building. They bought cold drinks. I bought an iced tea. They stood outside to have their drinks and so did I.

"Sonofabitch," the haole, Jim Hime, said to his partner, "If it wasn't for that cockroach of a lawyer, the kid would have confessed."

A cute game. Toby had been on his way to headquarters, all right, driven around and around, talked to and talked to some more, out there on cop turf. None of us, not Eva, neither his lawyer, nor his private investigator for that matter, were there to offer Toby any help or moral support.

Put enough pressure on a disoriented kid and he's likely to join in on speculation on just how the crime might have been done and pretty soon he's confessing under duress. But the courts have gotten wise to such tactics. It wasn't smart for a police officer to question a minor without a lawyer or a parent present.

Nevertheless, some cops—for instance this haole, Jim Hime—were possessed of more ambition than brains. Hime's was a game I could not imagine that Detective Tabura would condone, but it was a Saturday and Telly was stretched thin. He had to supervise the scene. He should have had an assistant to bring the kid in, a detective sergeant he could trust, but maybe the assistant was doing another errand.

A blur whiffed past me.

"How dare you," Eva Haverhill shouted, a terrier to a pair of mastiffs, snarling at the uniforms. "Where have you been all this time?"

Tiny as she was, Eva was a newsroom boss and knew how to play the authority game. Eva took the role of Goddess/Mother/Teacher; she addressed the two beat cops as guilty boys she'd caught in the act of plucking the wings off flies. I had to admit Eva's instincts had been right and this pair deserved a tongue lashing. "If you've tried to wring some bogus confession from a confused boy who has just lost his father, I'll personally see to it that both of you are busted to the dog catcher division."

I took Eva's elbow, pulled her back and the two cops made a run for it. "That's enough now, Eva. Cool it."

Glaring, Eva wrested free of me and stalked toward the door to juvie intake. The clatter of her four-inch stiletto heels raised chicken skin on my arms. The dress she had worn earlier had been replaced by a clingy top and a slim skirt cropped above the knee to show off her chorus girl's legs. Eva had lost weight the hard way and was clearly interested in flaunting her new shape.

She flung back the glass door and marched past the teddy bear. At the intake officer's desk, Eva changed into another role entirely, that of the supplicant mother, pleading for a favour from another woman, a woman whose name wasn't, after all, God. "Thank God you're here, Gina. Could you please help me? My son Toby has just lost his father. He'll be crushed. He's not that stable as it is."

I dragged her aside. "Cut it out, Eva. Don't be talking about Toby's stability in here." *Toby? stability? What was Eva hiding?*

"Sorry, John," she said, flashing her big hazel eyes, made all the more compelling by their dynamic presence in her drawn face, and emphasised by the straw hat covering her wispy hair.

Officer Willing stared at Eva, ignoring me and what I'd just said. Or so I hoped. "Your son is with his lawyer, ma'am. Would you care to join them?"

I stepped in, took her by the arm. "Harlan wants a minute with Toby, Eva. Toby's okay. He's anxious to see you, but give Harlan some space."

Glaring, Eva stared at her watch. "Three minutes."

I found a couple of plastic chairs where we could wait, but Eva refused to sit. She paced the floor in front of me, her spike heels rapping on linoleum tiles. I was amazed at how she'd recouped her energy and mesmerised by her new shape. Gone was her standard black tent dress that once barely covered an outsized okole. Gone were the black leotards she used to wear to show off her stunning legs, replaced by sheer bronze pantyhose that made for a fake tan.

"Calm down, Eva. Harlan has seen to it that Detective Tabura personally does the questioning. Toby has to tell the police what he knows. It's procedure."

"Procedure my ass," Eva blurted. Realising that Ms. Willing was attuned to every word she uttered, Eva sat down and studied her watch. She gave Harlan another five minutes, then had me point the way, but her burst of energy was gone. I had to help her cross the room. I tapped on the door. Harlan emerged, leaving Eva to confer with Toby. As the door closed, mother and son were in a clinch, both in tears.

"How's it going?" I said.

"Telly Tabura will be here in half an hour," Harlan said, "He's not thrilled with the antics of officer Hime but no harm done. Fortunately young Toby took Eva's advice. He stonewalled the beat boys. He pulled the knife from Randy's back because he thought it was hurting him. That's a perfectly acceptable explanation. He's told me what he knows, and it tracks with what he told Eva."

"There's more to it, Harlan. The knife pinned some kind of note to Randy's back. Telly Tabura hinted to me that the note is going to show up in our faces."

"Right. And we have to anticipate that." Harlan glanced at his watch. "So what we'll do now is we'll all sit in with Toby and hope we can calm him down before Detective Tabura gets here."

"Will Eva sit in on Tabura's interview?"

Harlan shook his head. "That's a tough one. Eva's behind a series of news stories attacking our prosecutor. Her presence might be an irritant. I was impressed by how Toby's handling himself. He comes across as a decent kid caught in a tragic situation, but I'll leave the decision up to the two of them."

Harlan let Toby and Eva have fifteen minutes together, going outside to return phone calls. I thought about calling Maya in Florida and decided to wait. Things were looking up where Toby was concerned. I checked my cell phone, hoping to hear from Hillary Haverhill, but there was no message. I hung around as a courtesy to Eva. Harlan joined Eva and Toby in the interview room and it was my turn to pace the floor.

A few minutes later, Eva slipped out the door and stood leaning against the wall, looking defeated.

"Is everything okay?"

"I hope so," she said. "Toby's fine. He did listen to me. Otherwise, there might have been trouble. But now he's siding with Harlan. They don't want me around when Tabura the Great arrives. They're scared I'll lose my temper and give him hell."

I laughed, further annoying her.

"Why, John," she said, eyes wide, tone honeyed. "Could I possibly have misjudged you? I pegged you as a more sensitive male and here you are, reverting to type."

"Why Eva," I said, aping her sarcasm, "if you were half the tita you pretend to be, I'd be quaking. Now let's be nice, shall we?"

Harlan interrupted us. "John? Eva? It's dress rehearsal time."

EIGHTEEN

This is crazy," Toby said, setting down his Coke.

"Yes it is," Kawahara said. "A bad break for you Toby. That's why your mom hired us to help you. Let's sort this out. Now as I understand it, you went over to visit your dad and your step mom on Friday?"

"We get credit for field trips, so Dad picked me up at noon. After lunch we took all the girls to the 'Iolani Palace."

"Your stepmother, Mrs. Hillary included?"

"Usually Hillary and the girls don't do stuff with Dad and me, but this time we were all together, at least until we got to the Palace."

At that point, he explained, the group split up. Randy and Toby buzzed through the palace top to bottom in forty minutes; the women dawdled along, fussing over the furnishings. 'Iolani was tops with Toby because it had electric lights before the White House did, thanks to King Kalākua, one cool dude who travelled around and had the smarts to hook up with inventor Thomas Edison.

There wasn't anything cool about the rest of the evening in Toby's retelling. The family had dinner at home. Afterward Toby took the girls out to play wiffle ball in the Nuuanu Valley Park. Steffie, eleven, repeated something she must have picked up from some dispute between the parents: Why waste prep school tuition on a kid too dumb to go to college? That was the gist of it.

Eva gasped.

Harlan and I exchanged glances.

"Surely prep school tuition is pocket change to an heiress?" she snorted. "How could she..? How could Hillary be so mean spirited?"

"How do you feel about that?" Harlan said to Toby.

"I need the prep school because I'm dyslexic," Toby said. "My mom insisted. It's part of the settlement." Toby's tone was robotic, his posture defeated. He'd been labelled as damaged goods and seemed willing to accept the fact.

"You tend to mix up letters when you write words?" Harlan said.

"B's, ds, a's, and *I's.* Those are my worst. It drives my mom nuts." A sly look crossed Toby's face as he glanced at Eva. Perhaps he enjoyed his own dyslexia in some perverse way? Maybe driving Eva up the wall was kind of fun?

At that point I had a stray thought, and doodled it on the side of my notes. *Handwriting. Note. Often a note. Per Hillary.*

Then Harlan went over what we'd already heard from Eva. I listened to Toby's version of the story, adding new details: *Canoe racing at the Outrigger Club was a summer project. Toby began training in June. Paddling since early July.*

"Paddling is great. It has rhythm," Toby said. "I've gained upper body strength, lost most of my gut—some of it, anyway." Toby flexed his hands, tone animated for the first time. "My fingers are stronger, so it's good for my music, the guitar." Realising there would be no more canoeing with his dad, Toby swiped away tears and Harlan and I pretended not to notice. "Whether I'll continue racing? I don't know."

The routine: *Randy and Toby at Canoe Club 8:00-10:00 Saturdays. Hillary & the girls leave for the farm. Killer cases place? Waits in the house on the day of murder? Pizza order placed 11 AM. Randy shot at noon.*

"What's the name of the pizza place," Harlan said.

"Twice-a Slice-a. "

"Twice-a Slice-a?" I blurted, "been there forever."

"That's what my dad said."

"Is Yodi Noda still running it?"

"Nah. His son runs it most of the time."

"H.B.? He was a keiki when your dad and I were in high school. Was he there?"

"H.B. took the order when I called in."

"Then what happened, Toby?" Harlan said softly.

Toby's face dissolved. He scrubbed tears out of his eyes with his knuckles and answered in a quaking voice. "The doorbell rang...ah...Dad said...Dad said he'd get it...and... then it happened."

"You heard the gun go off?"

"Twice."

"Did you hear your dad say anything?"

"He screamed after the first shot."

Scream means first shot was to the groyne? Revenge killing?

"Where were you by then? "

"I ran from the kitchen, through the hall. Dad was face down on the porch."

"You didn't see anyone at all?"

"I didn't pay attention. I was trying to help Dad."

"Was your father still alive at that point?"

"I think so. He seemed to be gasping for air."

"What did you do next, Toby, do you remember?"

"I went back inside and called 911."

Harlan and I exchanged glances. I scribbled a note and underlined it: *Toby goes off the scene to make the call.*

"What phone did you use?"

"Looked for my cell phone. Couldn't find it. I'd used it to call for the pizza. I thought it was in my backpack on the bench by the front door. Then I realised I'd left it lying on the bench, but I was so upset I'd knocked it on the floor."

"How long do you think you were away from the door, Toby?"

"Five minutes at the most. I kept looking for the cell phone. I found it behind the urn where we keep umbrellas. "

Killer has five minutes to get away.

Toby began to squirm. "I need to call my friend Kimo, tell him I won't make practice."

"All right," Harlan said. "We'll take a break."

"Is it okay to get something to eat?" Toby said.

"I'll take him to the snack shop," Eva said.

I sat where I was, waited for them to leave. Harlan reviewed his notes.

"What do you think, John?" he asked.

"Toby mentioned the knife but not the note."

"Maybe he didn't see it," Harlan said.

"Well Detective Tabura did. He's got the note. Suppose he asks Toby to copy it?"

Harlan shrugged. "If Toby didn't write it, where's the harm?"

"That's right," I said, pulling out my cell phone. "Randy Haverhill had a stalker. I've already alerted Telly Tabura. Hillary Haverhill no doubt filled Telly in on that as well. There was a stalker incident at Randy's book signing. The place was trashed and the stalker left a note that Randy erased, but not before I took a picture of it."

Harlan whistled. "When was this?"

"June 12th. Randy was signing his latest best-seller."

Kawahara grimaced. "I was invited but couldn't make it."

"Hillary knows I took the picture. I mentioned it to the security guy." I scrolled through my phone, pulled up the photo, some gibberish is all it was. I handed it to Harlan.

"What is this?" Harlan said. "It makes no sense."

"Take a close look, Harlan. There's a backwards a in it."

Harlan's face twitched. "Even so, we'll need to turn this over to the detective."

"I offered to tell Telly Tabura what I know, but he wasn't ready to hear it. Maybe there's an explanation for this. It would help if we could see the note Tabura's got."

"Ah," Harlan said. "I see what you are saying, John."

"The way we get a look at Tabura's note is, we allow Toby to copy it."

"But if Toby wrote it, maybe we don't want him to copy it."

"There's the risk," I said. "Outsmart ourselves and Toby's busted."

NINETEEN

Toby and Eva came down the hall, an incongruous pair. Beside her son, Eva looked like the child. On Harlan's instructions, I was to wait with Eva. Kawahara didn't want me to sit in with Tabura. The detective might decide to nail me about the stalker incident, in which case I'd have to mention that I had a note. Where this bit of evidence was concerned, we thought it was better strategy to see what Tabura had first.

"Toby's going to be tied up here for an hour, maybe two, Eva. Harlan will call us if there's anything sticky. How about I take you out for a drink?"

Eva looked at her watch, a chronometer of a thing, dwarfing her twig of a wrist. "I'd love to, John, but it's time for my hospital run. I'd rather not cancel since I have to wait around anyway. It's hard enough to get a chemo treatment set up for a Saturday." Eva's eyes burned unnaturally bright in her fevered face. She rummaged around in her black straw carryall. A flip-flop fell out. I picked it up and she stuffed it back into the bag. "Would you mind driving me?" she asked. "I'm feeling a little faint."

"Not a problem. I'll let Harlan know where we are."

"Chemo is a drag," Eva said. "But what can I do? Doctor's orders. I just have to beat this cancer. I have to survive, for Toby's sake. Now that Randy's gotten himself killed, where would Toby go if I went? Who would be his parent?' She found the signature keys of her grand wheels and dangled them at me.

"Fine by me, Eva. We'll talk."

"We'll talk story," Eva purred, putting the keys through a hula, a sexy smirk playing on her mouth. I offered to bring Eva's car around, but she insisted on trekking through the parking lot in her stiletto heels. To reflect in the glory of her latest wheels? To prove she wasn't yet dead? I can't say, but it was a long haul. We had to stop every few minutes while Eva caught her breath. "Ta dahhh," she sang out as we approached her gleaming silver sports job. "Putt isn't much of a driver. I'm waiting to see what she'll do on Round Top Drive with a NASCAR club champ at the wheel."

I bowed, sweeping my arms wide: "My reputation precedes me."

I stowed her carryall in the trunk, alongside a mound of Toby's high school detritus, books, a guitar case, and a laptop. I helped Eva in, handed her the seat belt to fasten. By the time I'd gone around the car and stuffed myself in, Eva was putting some finishing touches on her makeup. "I can't go in there looking like death, I'm afraid they'll give up on me."

"You look great, Eva."

"For a cadaver. "

"Cut it out. You can beat this. My money's on you. Queen's, I take it?"

"Where else?"

The three blocks from the H.P.D. to Queen's Medical Center wasn't much of a NASCAR track, but I tried to rally Eva's spirits. I suggested putting the top down, but Eva said she had to stay out of the sun as part of her treatment. I sped through the light traffic on Beretania to amuse her. She kept one eye on her cop scanner and the other on the rear view mirror. I hung a right on Punchbowl and swung into the botanical wonderland that marks the entrance to Queen's Hospital a few minutes later, and this modicum of excitement rallied the patient.

Eva's colour was up a notch and her energy was rising. She made a grand entrance, strutting past an enormous antique table in the lobby with a towering floral display on it. Honolulu is big on antique tables with towering floral arrangements. In Waikiki the taller the stalks of ginger and bird of paradise in the lobby, the higher the number of stars in the hotel's rating. Queen's Medical Center, in the heart of downtown, is a pedigreed Honolulu institution, not to be outdone by some upstart resort. Queen's was founded in 1859 by King Kamehameha IV, Alexander Liholiho, and his beloved Queen Consort Emma. When the Hawaii legislature rejected Alexander's health care plan, these young royals personally raised private funding for a hospital meant to serve a Hawaiian population decimated by Western diseases.

We made the long march to the information desk across an expanse of bamboo flooring etched in a filigree that might have graced a ballroom. Eva was no longer waltzing, however, she was wheezing. She deigned to allow me to ask for a wheelchair. Once seated, Eva turned harridan on wheels, she insisted I push her across the lobby so that we could take in a full-length portrait of the hospital's founder, Queen Emma, whose summer residence is a few blocks down The Pali Highway from Dowsett Avenue where Randy Haverhill and I were brought up. Queen Emma is the namesake of my sister Emmalaea and of my Mustang Em. Eva twisted around in the wheel chair and stared up at me.

"How does it feel to be a direct descendent of Hawaiian royalty?"

"I'm not. I'm a shirttail relation. Queen Emma and I have a common ancestor and he was a haole."

"You sure? You have her deep dark eyes and full mouth." She cocked her head. "You got shorted on the colouring, though. Could have used a shot or two more mocha in your mix. And where did you come up with that long bony face? It wasn't from Queen Emma's line, that's for sure."

"Enough, Eva." I gave Her Majesty the nod and pushed Eva through the lobby, into an elevator, and around to the chemo unit on the second floor of the Nalani Tower. Here I was, playing nurse and not detective, and I wonder now how things might have gone if I had not spent so much time with Eva, who seemed so desperate to tell me her side of a startling story.

We'll talk story, Eva had said with that sexy smirk on her face. In Hawaii we talk story to pass the time, so I had no idea that the story Eva was about to tell me in a chemo treatment room would put the fear into me about where we were going in the Haverhill case.

TWENTY

We were buzzed into a huge bay lined with adjustable couches, each with its own IV unit mounted on a and pole and equipped with beeping telemetry you could put into some rocket out of NASA. A few people reclined on couches, while a couple of nurses in white caps passed out their poison in little paper cups. It was freezing. I clenched my teeth to keep them from chattering.

A delicate Filipina nurse ushered Eva to a couch, hooked her to an IV machine and handed her a potion mixed in noni juice. Noni has long been a medicinal favourite in Hawaii, and now some say it can put a dent in cancer. Eva made a face as she drank it.

"If the smell doesn't kill you, the fruit will cure you, as Mama Hana used to say."

Eva rummaged in her carryall and brought out a pashima wrap. "It's cold as a tomb in here. I realise they are trying to prevent infection, but the chill goes through me, right to my soul. I can feel the Grim Reaper breathing down my neck."

"The Grim Reaper won't get you where Madam Pele rules, Eva. You can't let it get to you."

"I have esophageal cancer," Eva blurted, "Randy's parting gift."

I rubbed my Saturday stubble, at a loss what to say. "You can't mean that."

"Oh, can't I?" She dredged her day book out of her carryall and found a dog-eared pamphlet, one of those write-ups about health issues that do-gooders in the medical profession like to hand out. The sort of thing that I would avoid like an outbreak of bird flu in any doctor's office. *Esophageal Cancer and Treatment Options*, it said.

"Catchy title."

"You can skip the carcinoma diagrams. "

"Mahalo."

"Look on the back toward the bottom. I've highlighted the essential fact."

I scanned through mouse print until a yellow highlighted phrase leaped out: *some evidence the disease is transmitted through oral sex.*

"Uh huh." I kept my face straight and tone level, embarrassed for Eva.

"So what did your doc say about this?" I shoved the pamphlet back to her as if it were a hot brick. Too bad it wasn't.

"The cancer doctor said it wouldn't do me any good to dwell on the cause. I have to put all my energy into getting better." Eva shrugged. "The usual horse shit. You men stick together." She inserted the worn pamphlet like a bookmark into her appointment book. No way she'd let go of the idea that Randy's exploits might be the death of her.

"But Eva, isn't it a stretch to connect some obscure medical theory to..?"

"I know that. I just wish I'd divorced Randy earlier than I did. It was bad enough he was screwing every—"

"You *knew* all about Randy's...ah, extracurricular activities?"

"Certainly. Randy made sure of it. He thought his exploits were a turn-on for me. I was supposed to believe it was a privilege to be married to 'The Carl Sagan of the Dismal Science'; Eva lisped, in a dead-on imitation of Barbara WaWa interviewing Randy.

"The co-eds hung around Randy like... like..." Eva nodded off mid-sentence. I stood up, made for the door, but she blinked and sat up and resumed the conversation right where she left off: "...groupies." "Did I mention Sasha Perestroika?"

"Perestroika?" I don't believe so."

"Well, whatever her name was, Sasha was the worst." Eva's voice gathered strength as she resumed her tale: "This happened the time Randy had a six-month fellowship in Russia. Toby was a baby and I couldn't go. Randy was among the young hotshots called in as advisors to the Putin government. He urged our government to do a lend/lease type of deal. We should have done it, too. Now look what they've got. The KGB and a bunch of Mafiosi have hijacked the Russian economy." With a dismissive wave of her hand, Eva consigned the Russian economy to backwater status. "At any rate, Randy got wined and dined everywhere. Vodka'd too, no doubt. So then he carried on with this female statistician. "

"Sasha?"

Eva pulled a face. "Sasha was a social outcast to begin with. She'd never come to grips with communism, and she wouldn't believe anything would get better, either. The usual Russian downer attitude, you know. She saw Randy as a means to get out of the country. When he left her there instead, she'd call our house and throw tantrums on our answering machine, threatening to kill herself. I listened to all that. Then the calls stopped. I lived in fear that she really did off herself. Some turn-on that was."

"I'll bet."

The Filipina nurse came over. "How do you feel Mrs. Haverhill?" she said, holding Eva's wrist, taking her pulse.

Eva glared at her. "Well enough, considering."

"Any nausea?"

"No more than usual," she cooed, "but it really isn't chemo therapy that's bringing me down, at least not today."

TWENTY-ONE

Eva was snoring halfway through her treatment. I went out to the lobby and called Harlan. Telly Tabura was late; the questioning hadn't started. We decided I should drive Eva home. Harlan would drive Toby home when the party was over.

I called Soon Amorin, at Taxi Service Soon. He agreed to come to Eva's house on top of Mt. Tantalus and deliver me back to my Mustang in the H.P.D. parking lot. I spent the rest of the time trying to lose the chill from the treatment room. I flapped my arms, blew on my fingers, and stared at the butterfly prints on the wall. Unfortunately for me, butterflies don't flit around icebergs.

It was after five PM Honolulu time, which was six hours later in Florida. I'd kept Maya up on the phone last night after Putt and I had closed up Hale Kava. We'd made a list of what Maya wanted to see and do. We'd done the no-brainers on her last visit, the Bishop Museum, the 'Iolani Palace, the miles of walking tours through Waikiki and all that.

Maya wanted to see the wildlife sanctuary at Paiko Lagoon, the green sea turtles at Halona Cove, the Makupuu lookout and the Kaupo lava flow, the Kukaniloko birthing stones where the royal women gave birth, and the ancient temple, Ulupou Heiau. I didn't much care where we went. The sight I wanted to see was Maya.

I dreaded calling her with the news that I was up to my ample thatch in a murder investigation. I was afraid she wouldn't come. I couldn't bear the thought that Maya might reschedule her trip. I debated calling her and decided to wait. Toby was safe in the capable hands of Harlan Kawahara. Eva's fears would prove to be unfounded. The investigation would take a different turn and I would be off the hook.

Eva woke up about forty minutes later and had me summoned into the chemo unit. She looked doughy, like malasada batter before it's dropped into the hot grease. Eva gave me no argument whatsoever about trying to walk out to her car. I wheeled her down to the lobby, collected her BMW, tucked her pashima shawl around her, and we drove from downtown Honolulu to the top of Mt. Tantalus.

I rallied her spirits with some banked turns on Round Top Drive, the corkscrew climb up the mountain. Eva had stopped shivering and was smiling big by the time we reached her hale, one of the first homes on the mountain ridge.

Eva's hale perches just below Round Top Drive. It sits on a stone bluff just down the flank of the mountain. There's nothing to be seen of the residence proper but a gated stone wall covered with bougainvillaea and a garage door. I wheeled the BMW down into the garage and parked it next to the space normally occupied by her vintage Jag.

"You traded the Jag for the BMW?"

Eva's eyes widened in horror. "Of course not. The Jag is in the shop. I'm having the engine rebuilt. Since Ford bought out Jaguar, I've been able to get parts. When you have to get to work the way I do, it's important to have spare wheels."

"Definitely."

I helped Eva down the stone steps to her house. She had a part-time nurse who answered the door and took custody of her.

"Where's Toby?" Eva said. "What's taking them?"

"I'll call Harlan and find out. Not to worry, Eva. You get some rest. Toby is in good hands."

The nasty part of esophageal cancer, or so I learned, is that the patient is fed through a tube. This is a dreary procedure that takes ten to twelve hours at a stretch. It was past time for Eva to go on the tube, and so I pecked her on the cheek and headed into her salon. I helped myself to the Drambuie that I favour. Even though I rarely saw Eva, she likes to cater to the men in her life. She kept Drambuie for me in her well-stocked bar.

I dialled Harlan's cell number. He wasn't picking up, so I left a message.

I dialled Soon and gave him Eva's address. Soon promised to be here soon. I rattled ice cubes and sipped and watched the sun sinking out to sea, casting its pink glow on everything, doing a makeover number on Diamond Head. which is a bit dry and scruffy in September. Lights blinked on all around Honolulu. The white surf line took on a purple glow in the afterlight. I had to admire Eva for her guts and her grit and her *joie de vivre* and this small but elegant manse she had found for herself.

Eva lives in a Mediterranean style home she claims she stole from a candidate for mayor who put it up as collateral to finance his run for office, but was then defeated. He had to sell at a loss. From her Round Top nest, Eva gazes down on everything, on Diamond Head, Waikiki, the 'Iolani Palace, the Governor's Mansion, and her newspaper, *The Honolulu Gazette*. She could walk to the other side of the Round Top lookout and peer down on the Manoa Campus of the University of Hawaii. It was there that the newly departed Randolph Kealoha Bishop had had a suite of offices comprising his Pacific Rim Institute in the East-West Center complex.

As I sipped Drambuie and rattled ice cubes, I came to terms with what was bothering me. Eva blamed Randy for her illness. This left me wondering whether Toby knew how his mother felt. Suppose Toby was aware of all this? Eva would never say such a thing outright to Toby. Of that I was certain. But I knew from the crumpled look of it that I wasn't the first person who had seen that pamphlet, and this is Hawaii and people can't resist talking story after all, and stories have a way of coming back to people close to the source.

I wished I'd followed my first instinct, to pass on the trip to the chemo treatment. What Eva had done for me wasn't good for Toby. Eva's theory that Randy's promiscuity had caused her cancer now planted doubt in my mind. If Toby blamed his father for his mother's illness, maybe the kid had one good reason to want Dad dead.

TWENTY-TWO

"Take care," Soon Amorin said as he dropped me off in the rear parking lot at the H. P.D. where I'd left Em, my Mustang. "One mento you after." Nutcase is what Soon meant.

"I'll watch it," I said. "By the way, who's on tonight at Hale Kava?'

"Da Girlas," Soon's eyes crinkled around the edges as he grinned, showing lots of gum beneath his rubbery lips. Soon Amorin loves Hawaiian music almost as much as he loves 'awa.

"Da Girlas? Don't know them."

"You should. "

"That good?"

"Da best. Plus I like watching girlas mo' bettah den guyas. "

"All right. I'll make it."

It was only then that I noticed yellow camera lights trained on some action and realised that something had gone terribly wrong. Toby Haverhill was coming out of the back door of the H.P.D. in handcuffs. The same beat officers, Hime and his stolid partner, marched the boy to a patrol car. I wanted to wipe Hime's smirk right off his Ken Doll face.

TV floods bleached the tan out of Toby's skin. He trembled. Nevertheless there was something of Randolph Haverhill in his bearing. The kid had learned about pride from his father. He gazed straight ahead, wasn't hiding under some coat or towel. He ignored the reporters calling out to him, baying like hounds on the kill. Not that it was a huge press turnout.

It was just after sunset on a Saturday so the press corps was light, but what few reporters there were made up for their paucity of numbers with a roar that reverberated off the side of the building, a pounding sound that made my ears ring. I was shocked to see Eva's police reporter right there among them. Mitzi Wong scribbled in her skinny reporter's notebook and shouted to be heard above the din like the rest of them. Here was Eva's own police reporter doing this number on Eva's kid.

"Toby Haverhill is a minor. There's nothing to hold him on." I shouted at the building like everyone else. I was enraged. Why was Toby being arrested? The police didn't have the murder weapon. The kid was being arrested because of who he was; Eva had said as much and I had to admit Eva had better instincts than I did.

Officer Hime put Toby in the patrol car, making a show of holding the top of his head the way cops like to do, especially if there's a camera around. As the car pulled away I looked for Harlan, caught certain parts of his statement: the words travesty, and *flimsy evidence* whipped on the breeze.

An elbow jammed into my back. I wheeled around and there stood Putt Jorgenson, notebook in hand.

"Christ all to Madam P. You of all people, Putt. I thought Eva was your friend."

Putt stared at me, an absent look on his face. He was in for the kill just like the rest of them. I think it took a minute for him to recognize me.

"Later, John. I have to have a quote from Harlan."

Putt moved past me. Putt, who wouldn't appear on camera, was dressed in cutoffs and a tee shirt and had flip-flops on his feet. He clenched his pipe between his teeth as he marched straight into the fray.

"Mr. Kawahara," Putt bellowed, waving his pipe stem like a baton. This commanding gesture silenced the mob. "*The Honolulu Gazette* and Mrs. Eva Haverhill in particular, have been critical of the prosecutor's office bringing cases on the strength of underwhelming evidence." Putt's reedy voice was elevated. Even Putt was talking for the camera, or so it seemed. "Would you care to comment on that?"

"What need of this?" Harlan spluttered. "This fine young man has lost his father. This is a tragedy for him. Toby Haverhill is left to grieve in a cell? He's not allowed to spend the night beside his father in his coffin? This is an outrage."

"Thank you, Sir." Putt turned away. He shoved his thick tortoiseshell glasses up his nose for the millionth time since I've known him. His muddy brown eyes and thin, lipless mouth focused for a moment on studying the precious quote he had just committed to paper.

Putt came back through the crowd. "Later, John," he said in passing, "I'm on deadline. Gotta get back to da nupapah. "

I had to laugh. Putt was no local, but he did his best to pick up what dialect he could borrow from me or ferret out for himself. He'd won a Pulitzer for his coverage of massive fraud in Miami after the last Florida hurricane and had been rewarded with a cushy tour of duty here in Honolulu. He would spend the next six months helping his chain shape up *The Honolulu Gazette,* its latest acquisition in a string of corporate takeovers of ailing newspapers.

"Just one friggin' minute." I strode right alongside Putt. "What's the deal here? They can't justify this. Toby is a minor."

"Different rules apply in a capital murder case," Jorgenson said, pipe waggling between his teeth.

"This is an arrest," I said, "Not—"

"Arrested but not charged. I know that, John. This story is a perfect opportunity to do an opinion piece. Telly Tabura does have probable cause."

"No murder weapon? No forensics? This is a crock."

"Enough to hold Toby, but risky business. The sort of business in fact, that Eva has been complaining about. That's what I'm addressing in my op-ed piece, leaving Eva out of it, of course." Putt took a long draw on his pipe. A cloud of smoke escaped his thin lips.

"Toby will be out by tomorrow afternoon," I said. "This is politics not police work."

"I'll agree with you there," Putt said, "but just between us, they have a note. That may be what they are banking on. Mitzi Wong is duty bound to keep her mouth shut. Either she knows what's in the note and is off the record or else the police are holding out on her." Putt's pipe went out. He turned his back to the evening trades to relight."The prosecutor's doing business as usual," Putt said on the exhale. "He's an idealistic guy. He believes too many criminals get away and he'll take the risk and arrest when maybe he shouldn't, but on the other hand, what's he going to do? The *Gazette* has been questioning his conviction rate, saying he's wasting public money on no-win situations. Eva has been a thorn in his side. So what's he supposed to do? Roll over?"

I nodded. "But where's your loyalty? Eva's one of your own. "

"Exactly. Runt she is and sick as some mutt, but Eva is a tita, as tough a broad as they come. Eva knows the rules. The press has the story. It's making national headlines. The *Gazette* can't make an exception where one of its editors is concerned."

"Jesus Madam, Putt. You of all people?"

"Read me in da nupapah tomorrow. We have very special circumstances here. I'm on the opinion page. Our police doll, she's doing the straight angle." Putt smirked, his expression salacious: "Mitzi Wong. Work of art she is."

Putt had parked his bug at a crazy angle in the lot and hadn't bothered to lock it. He'd learned to drive junkers in Miami. People would talk to a reporter who drove a shabby car, he once told me. In Miami, the pimps and the drug dealers were the ones with all the fancy wheels.

"Wait," 1 said.

Putt piled into his rattletrap and turned the key he'd left in the ignition. The beast roared. At least the engine was in good shape. Putt poked his head out the open window. "Hale Kava? Midnight? We'll talk." Putt flipped me a shaka shake. They say the shaka sign originated with a friendly guy whose middle fingers were eaten in a cane grinding machine, but that's only one theory. Putt made the gesture his own by drumming his curled middle fingers on the side door of his wreck.

"Midnight? Past my bedtime?"

"I'm gone. Gotta find six-hundred big ones by 10:00 PM." Words, he meant. When Putt got into one of his writing blitzes, it was hopeless to try to reason with him. "You want to talk, let's do it over 'awa."

Putt's nothing of a mouth crimped. He raked his fingers through a thick head of dirty blonde hair that looked as if it had been teased by a cattle prod. He sped off, waggling the shaka back at me through the driver's side window.

TWENTY-THREE

I was heading over to the parking lot to collect Em when Harlan Kawahara pulled up beside me in his Mercedes, wheels the size of a yacht.

"I'm going to the juvenile facility on Piikoi, " he said. "Intake won't be long. Ride with me? Toby should see that we have a team. Besides, we need to talk."

I flagged Soon Amorin and asked him to follow us in his taxi and we took off.

"Why an arrest? Why now?" I settled into the leather seats of what amounted to a luxury liner on wheels. The oyster coloured car was showroom pristine, which figured. Harlan Kawahara was one meticulous dude.

"I told Telly Tabura that he was jumping the gun," Harlan said.

"So Telly himself did the questioning?"

"What there was of it." Harlan's mouth worked. "We respectfully declined to answer most everything."

"Does Eva know about this?"

"Toby called her. She offered to come down. He wanted no part of that."

"Kid must be tougher than I thought."

"This whole thing is my fault," Harlan said. "I take full responsibility."

"How's that?"

"The note did it, our calculated risk." I sucked in a whistle as my own words from earlier in the afternoon came back to haunt me: *If Toby wrote the note that Tabura had, he's busted.* "Toby chose to cooperate?"

"Toby didn't write the note, so why not copy it? That was his thinking. He figured it would put him in the clear. So how could it have implicated him instead?" Harlan pounded the steering wheel. "Damn. I should have known better."

"It's okay, Harlan. It's what we agreed on. At least we've got a copy of what Tabura has."

Harlan needed some space, so I kept quiet and studied the convoy we had going. Right ahead of us was the police car, siren blaring, then Harlan's Mercedes, followed by Soon Amorin in his English taxi. We swept Diamond Head along South King, sidelining motorists, leaving pedestrians gawking from bus kiosks. Poor Toby. If he could distance himself from the horror, he'd enjoy his own bizarre parade. I kept my mouth shut, let Harlan rant.

"Toby writes a backward letter or two and that puts us in the kim chee."

"Did you see the original?"

Harlan shook his head. "Tabura gave us a typed copy for Toby to work from. That's the way these things are done."

"What did the note say?"

"It's gibberish. Some sort of code, maybe."

"Did Toby recognize what it said?"

"I don't think so. He's pretty upset, of course, so I'll talk to him in the morning. Maybe something will occur to him."

"I'd like to be there."

"Fine. I'm sure Toby will be pleased to have you."

"Detective Tabura tells me he'll have the scene processed by tomorrow afternoon. I'll take a look."

Harlan sucked in a breath, bushy brows lifted, movie star handsome now, and no wonder: Harlan was the spitting image of his maternal uncle, Alfred Apaka, the 1970's Honolulu singing sensation, except Harlan wasn't singing *Lovely Hula Girl*. Harlan wanted me to do the singing while he called the tune.

"Don't tell me you invaded the crime scene, John."

I raised my right hand, swear-to-it style. "I did not. No way. Never set foot on it. But nothing's to stop me from being there once the yellow tape comes down."

Relief washed over Kawahara's face. "Mahalo, John. The defence can't risk messing up a crime scene." His eyes returned to the road. The light changed. Harlan hung a right on Piikoi. We drove through a mixed neighbourhood of condominiums and restored plantation homes dotted with restaurants and mini marts.

"Okay, so we've got two serious problems with this note: there's the dyslexic's lettering and the fact that the knife that pinned it to Randy's back came from a set in the kitchen."

"That's what you said, but who tipped you?"

"The wireless. "

"The police reporter?"

"The Tabura wireless. "

Harlan whistled. His face relaxed. "Very good, John. Excellent."

"Excellent that the knife came from the kitchen?'

"Excellent that the lead investigator tips you. How did you manage that?"

"Detective Tabura and I went to the mat a few times in high school."

"And you a Punahou boy, John? Hanging with a local kid from Waianae?"

The question revealed the speaker. This wasn't about Telly Tabura. Harlan Kawahara himself was a local kid from Waianae. I'd been brought up in the Nuuanu Valley, gone to an elite prep school founded by the missionaries. Kawahara was the son of a grocer from Waianae, to this day more of a blue collar place even if it does have fine and famous surf, so much for elite beginnings was what Kawahara meant. His distinguished career has far outshone my own brief tour with the DEA in Miami.

"My dad was an assistant city prosecutor. Telly's old man was a detective," I said. "Our dads went fishing together. Telly and I surfed and wrestled."

Kawahara grinned. "I'll have to remember that."

The backside of the juvenile facility appeared, an obscure place looking like a warehouse or a barracks crouching in the evening shadows. It was surrounded by a chain link fence and none of its clients were anywhere around in the exercise yard. The grounds were kept up but barely so. Harlan drove around to the entrance on Alder, where a bleak neon *love* sign peeking through a window was the only softening touch in a grim picture. There was no huge teddy bear offering solace beyond the glass door. None that

I could see at any rate. Kawahara pulled into a space reserved for officials. The squad car with Toby in it had gone through a back gate.

"As for the knife coming from the kitchen, that's devastating news," Kawahara said. "No doubt that's why Tabura told you. Unless we can find an explanation, this is difficult for our side."

"The knife problem is the first thing I'll work on."

"Please do."

TWENTY-FOUR

Mt. Léʻahi is the highest point on Diamond Head. It knocks me out that when I'm on Oahu, I crash at my Cousin Duke's house on its namesake, Leahi Avenue, at the foot of the Diamond Head Crater and a block mauka of Kapiʻolani park. Cousin Duke's hale is one of the plantation era bungalows you see in the older Honolulu neighbourhoods. The roof is as steep as a coolie's hat; the board and batten siding is now a faded red. There are deep porches and windows on all sides for decent ventilation. Air conditioning we do without. Duke's hale is hidden behind a tall wooden fence in a garden of mango and monkey pod trees. It sits on a bluff above the public flower gardens at the edge of the park and that keeps the place fragrant.

Cousin Duke Shimabuka's claim to fame: he's the best surfer in the family. When Duke surfs Maui, which isn't that often, he stays with me at my official residence, a cane shack on the beach in Lahaina. Here on Oahu, I've got the use of his sleeping porch or maybe the spare bedroom, when it isn't occupied by some California surfer dude over for a tournament. I was lucky. Second week September is way too early for tournament surf and Duke himself was out on a barge at sea.

I drove Em up the steep drive and into her stall in the garage. I turned on the garage light and looked around for any sign that something had been moved in my absence. Duke has hinted a time or two that Em has another driver. My sister Emmalaea comes back from the other realm and takes Em out and over The Pali when Duke is off on one of his barge trips. Or at least that's what Duke said one night and I wanted to believe him. Trouble was we were in the second set at Hale Kava at the time and Duke was well into his third bowl of 'awa. At any rate, I couldn't find any evidence that my sister Emmy had visited the garage in my absence, so I crossed the yard, enjoying the evening air, dense with the floral scents wafting up from the gardens.

Kiki jumped off her perch on the roof and wrapped her front paws around my leg. I picked her up and gave her a back rub and tweaked her ears and talked a little cat talk with her...about mean old Duke going off on his trips and her left all alone to guard the place with only her cat door and her food dish and her water fountain, her scratching post and her radio playing her favourite surfer girl music. Poor Kiki. She yowled when I put her down but I wasn't about to be guilted out by some feline. "Make yourself useful," I told her. "Find a mouse to toy with, babe, a real one."

I went into the narrow kitchen, opened the window to let in some fresh air and found my beer still in the fridge. We each keep our own supply. That's rule number one of our share plan, and Duke is very good at keeping his end of the bargain. The veggie bins were empty and so was the freezer. Reason being, the antique fridge is the type that melts the ice cream and freezes the produce.

I popped the cap on the beer and pondered the mess I was getting into. Eva needed my help, had to have it, and that was that, but Maya was arriving in two days, and on those rare occasions when we get together we treasure our time.

It was then that I heard my cell phone chime.

I checked the call screen, then my watch, 8:00 PM my time, 2:00 AM hers. Maya was on the line. My stalling had put me in trouble.

"Maya love," I said. "What are you doing up in the shank of the night?"

"Well, at least you are alive." She was keeping it light, but with an effort. In a long distance relationship, you learn to listen for every nuance and I read from the strained timbre of her voice that Maya was frightened for me and not happy about feeling that way.

"Who told you?"

"I heard from Putnam Jorgenson first thing this morning."

"Good old Putt. Ever the journalist, first with the news." *Jorgenson, damn him. Double damn. Was Putt trying to scope out what I knew about Toby by calling my lady friend? A pox upon his acne-pitted hide.*

"Better than Spyer being so late," Maya said, forcing a laugh. When she called me by my last name, things were on a downhill slide.

"I meant to call, Maya. You know that."

"Of course you meant to call," Maya said, "I do know that. I also know you are out after some loco who has murdered the famous economist. It's all over the TV, every five minutes."

"FOX?"

"FOX. CNN. MSNBC. What the TV does not say is where is John Spyer?"

"You could call Putt Jorgenson for regular updates."

"Thank you very much for the teep," Maya said in snippy Cublish, what I call her Cuban-style English. "Aloha, Mr. Latte'. "

Mr. Latte' was how Maya referred to my wishy-washy, hapa haole colouring. Usually she does this in fun, for instance when she one-ups me with a better tan. Under the circumstances, however, I took the moniker as a dig, her put down of my wishy-washy attitude.

The phone bleeped in my ear and I knew I'd gone too far. Why hadn't I called her first thing? I knew all along that I should have called her. I hadn't figured on Putt Jorgenson butting in, but what was I thinking?

Jorgenson, my old buddy from my DEA days in Miami, first my enemy, the guy who printed the anonymous tip that broke my cover. Jorgenson, who begged me to forgive him from my hospital bed is now my friend...and Jorgenson loves Maya.

It was Putt who introduced us, Putt who persuaded Maya to hire me when her husband was murdered and the government seized her Serenoa ranch. Was I being too harsh? Was I paranoid? But Putt could have called me before he talked to Maya. Or at least tipped me off that he had spoken to her.

I took the rickety stairway up the side of the house to the view deck over the sleeping porch. I redialed Maya's number.

"You have reached Serenoa Ranch in the Okeechobee country. The office is now closed. For reservations at the hunting lodge, press or say one. For the quarter horse farm, press or say two. For cane and rice dealers, press or say..."

I pressed six, Maya's private line, the number that wasn't in the spiel. "Maya, my love. My sweetheart. My hula princess. My salsa darling. I'm prostrate with grief over here in Honolulu. I'm grieving because the sun has splashed down one more time and you weren't here to watch it with me and wait for the green flash. Yes there is such a thing as a green flash and you'll come to Oahu and I'll show you, I guarantee, and yes, I should have called you the instant I knew Eva Haverhill was in such trouble. Toby has been arrested for his father's murder, Maya. Eva Haverhill is a friend of yours, of course. She's a sick woman. She has a nasty case of cancer. I just couldn't say no to Eva and didn't want to worry you."

There was no response. I pictured Maya in one of her snits, pacing the room, winding her thick black hair through her fingers. I could see her fine-boned face, the shape of it, the undulating curves, in at the temples, out over the cheekbones, in again below the cheekbones, out at the jawline.

Maya's face has the carved shape of a fine instrument. Think of a face with the curved shape of a violin and you have the idea. But when Maya gets upset her face freezes into a mask, her changeable eyes go black, her pillowy lips freeze into a thin line. This is Maya in despair, and despair is the flip side of Maya. Despair is when Maya is not in passion. With Maya there is no mood in between. She's mercurial in the extreme. This much I have figured out. Times when Maya is inconsolable, it helps when I talk to her. Or so she has said; I talked some more.

"Frankly, I didn't call you because I wanted to see you so badly." I paused, waiting for Maya to pick up the phone. When she didn't, I kept on talking story: "I couldn't stand the thought that you might change your mind about coming." More silence. "Or maybe you already have." I waited on the line some more. Then I hung up the phone.

TWENTY-FIVE

SUNDAY SEPT. 11

Daylight hadn't improved the looks of the Juvenile facility. The grounds were parched and bleak, the chain link fence was severe, and the neon *love* sign that I'd noticed last night was turned off. I pulled Em up next to Harlan's boat of a Mercedes and caught up with him as he was being buzzed in through the security entrance. He had a briefcase in one hand and a paper bag from McDonald's in the other.

A guard showed us into a broom closet of an interview room and then fetched Toby. He arrived dressed in garish orange jail garb, drawstring pyjamas with flip-flops on his feet. He was bleary-eyed, his skin had broken out and his chin sported some fuzz. The kid was a fuzz face, a teen with every advantage. Here he sat, reduced to pyjamas, facing the ruination of a promising life. Could Toby possibly have done this? Of course. Kids like him pulled dumb stunts every day. Nevertheless, I had to set aside my doubts; I remained steadfast in my belief that Toby was innocent. Harlan handed him a Big Mac, fries and a whopping Coke, which brightened his mood considerably.

"They don't feed you in here?" I said.

"We had mush this morning, lumpy and cold."

As Toby ate, I studied the slit of a window toward the ceiling, four chairs and a battered table. That was it, one small cell, one big stink: a miasma of fast food grease, Harlan's stinging aftershave, Toby's teen testosterone, and the refried ozone stench from an air conditioner that clanked like a cane grinder. Under the table, I felt the tremor of Toby's crazy leg.

"How is my mom?"

"I spoke to her this morning. She's on her feeding tube for another hour or two. Then she'll be down to see you," Harlan said.

"When do I go home?"

"Not today, son," Harlan replied. "We go before a judge tomorrow morning. The police bring their charges, if they have any. And we hope that doesn't happen."

"I have to spend another night here?"

"I'm afraid so."

"This is nuts."

"Yes it is," Kawahara said. "A bad break for you, Toby. That's why your mom hired us to help you sort this out."

I sipped vending machine coffee that tasted like spit. Toby slouched in his chair. He stared at the table as Harlan reviewed the notes he had made yesterday on his yellow legal pad.

"I have a few more questions," Harlan said. "We'll wrap this up before your mom gets here. All right, Toby. This knife in your dad's back. When did you first see it?"

"I was on the phone, waiting for the dispatcher to answer. I pulled the knife out of his back before she got on the line." The table began to vibrate. Toby's crazy leg was on the move.

"You pulled out the knife? That was it?"

"I thought it was hurting Dad."

"What else did you do?"

"I pulled up Dad's shirt and used the tail of it as a compress."

"You are doing this while the dispatcher is talking to you?"

Toby scrunched up, ear to shoulder, aping how he'd managed this.

"All right," Harlan said. "Did you see a note under the knife?"

"I don't remember any note," Toby said. "Is that what I copied out for the detective?"

"That's right," Harlan said.

"They think I wrote the note? I never did. I swear."

"Not to worry, Toby," Harlan said. "Handwriting is no exact science. We'll sort it out, but for now let's just go over it some more. What happened next?"

"Then the lady came."

Harlan tossed his pen on the table. He stood up, paced the short stretch of the room and turned back, thick brows drawn together. "Wait a minute, Toby. What lady?"

"I forgot about her until just now."

"Perfectly understandable, son. That's why I like to go over things with my clients time and again," Harlan said. He stood behind Toby's chair and massaged his young client's shoulders like some fight manager prepping the kid for the next round.

"Excellent, Toby. This is good news." He patted Toby's shoulder, sat down once more and poised his pen over his legal pad. "All right, Toby. This is important. This is a witness. She may have seen the shooting. We have to find her."

"I didn't see her except for a second. She said she would run and get a towel."

"Run and get a towel?" I said. "Run where?"

"I don't know. The dispatcher was talking to me and I couldn't concentrate."

"You are doing fine, son," Harlan said. "Can you describe this lady?"

"I hardly saw her. She had on big sunglasses and a rain cape over her head."

"A rain cape? Was it raining?"

"Not right then, but… " Toby shrugged.

"The Nuuanu Valley gets three-hundred inches of rain a year," I said. "It could pour in ten minutes and dry out in ten more."

"Right," Harlan said. "Skin colour?"

"Sort of golden. "

"Asian?"

"I guess."

"Dark as I am?"

"Lighter."

"Filipina?"

"I don't know, pocho, maybe." Pidgin for Portuguese. "She seemed like a local, that's all."

"Describe what you saw of her," Harlan said.

"Her face was broad but her chin was pointed and what I could see of her hair was blonde."

"So where did she go?" I said. "Across the street? Next door?"

"I can't say. I was down on my knees trying to talk to Dad and I thought the lady would come back."

"Then what happened?"

"The EMS came instead. A woman was with them. She took me inside to see if I was upset. Then the police came and they talked to me. I never saw my dad again."

"All right, son," Harlan said. "That's enough for today, unless you have questions, John."

"Let's go back earlier, before the shooting," I said.

"Okay."

"When you and your dad came back from canoeing, are you sure you were alone in the house?"

"As far as I know. Hillary and the girls were out in the country. Hillary doesn't like me. She takes the girls and goes somewhere else whenever I'm around."

"Was anybody there that morning? A newspaper boy?"

"A delivery, I guess. Dad took the *Gazette*."

"And you called Twice-a Slice-a?"

"I did."

"Did H.B. call back to confirm the order?"

"Nah. We ordered every Saturday at the same time." H.B. knew what I'd order."

"Which was?"

"It was my turn, so I ordered the Hula Girl."

"The Hula Girl?"

"Chopped ham with Maui onion, roasted red peppers, sun dried tomatoes, black olives and pineapple. It's their top of the line, sprinkled with flowers."

"Those little orchids?"

"Some other flowers. Edible, they say." Toby grimaced. "I never liked eating flowers, so I'd save the blossoms for the girls to put in their hair. "

"Okay, Toby. We know it wasn't the pizza delivery when the doorbell rang. Did Twice-a Slice-a ever make the delivery?"

"Yes."

"When did the pizza arrive?"

"I can't say."

"Maybe it was never delivered?"

"It was. I saw it in the kitchen. I was too sick to eat. Some of it was gone, though."

"The police ate the evidence?" Harlan said, pocketing his pen.

"Evidently," I said as I reviewed my own notes and scrawled a list of marching orders to myself:

Knife in R's back from kitchen?
Find the witness in the rain cape.
Call on Twice-a Slice-a.
Where is the shotgun?

Harlan's cell phone rang. He checked the call screen. "It's your mom," Harlan said to Toby. Take the call, son, Then let me talk to her."

We left the room so Toby could have some privacy.

"You'll go to the Dowsett house today?" Harlan asked.

"This afternoon. I'll get in if Telly keeps his word."

TWENTY-SIX

When I got back to the Haverhill estate on Sunday afternoon, a beat cop was pulling down the crime scene tape. Detective Telly Tabura was out on the porch. His face had the slack look of the sleep-deprived. His same aloha shirt from yesterday was rumpled over his bulk. His pants sagged below his gut. His eyes were bleary as a Sunday morning drunk's. His hands shook as he took a pull from a bottle of that green Jamba Juice that made me turn green just to look at it.

"Long night, Telly?"

"I'm too old for this stuff."

"One quick walk through and I'm done."

"You owe me when this is pau." Tabura chopped the word into the air with the side of his hand: Pau. Pow. *Done.* His weary grin revealed the hash mark of our ancient combat, his missing tooth; although it was an accident, I felt a pang of guilt.

Randy Haverhill was pau. The crime scene investigation was pau. Though the tape was gone, we gave the dark stain and the chalk outline of the body a wide berth. As I climbed the steps I noticed bloody shoe prints leading to the front door.

"Toby's?"

"We have a match on the kid's shoes."

"So? The kid tracked the blood in when he went to call 911."

"That's his story," Tabura said, peeling off his latex gloves and opening the front door.

Against the bright day, the hallway was as dusky as a cave. "Mind if we turn on the lights?" I said. Tabura obliged.

The hallway took on the slightly reddish hue of its koa wood panelling. The chandeliers were the old-fashioned wrought iron ones from Randy's parents' day. Murals of early day Honolulu were painted on the walls above the koa wainscoting, the sailing ships in the harbour, the fish ponds of Waikiki, outriggers paddled, hulas danced.

The painted scenes were all that remained of the stately setting. The rest of the rooms were askew, with cushions stripped from antique sofas, the contents of drawers dumped on tables, paintings and photos yanked from walls, carpets rolled up.

"You really did a number on the place, Telly."

"I had good help," he said, exposing his missing tooth.

"I hope you guys realise that that sofa you've mauled once belonged to King Kalākua,"

"The red one?"

"Hattie Haverhill found it at a hotel auction."

"Kalākua was a man of the people. If he could nap on it, why not me?" Tabura scrubbed his fingers through his single long eyebrow.

"Did you search upstairs?"

Telly shrugged. "Knife in Professor's back came from the kitchen. The son is the only witness."

"So I'll do the whole tour."

I borrowed Telly's gloves and headed upstairs for the master suite, which had been enlarged as Randy's father grew progressively more ill. As a gay young couple, Walter and Hattie Haverhill had collected art, loved music, travelled Europe, and wined and dined with Honolulu's social elite. Then tragedy struck in the form of Walter's debilitating illness, multiple sclerosis.

Walter Haverhill was CFO of the Bishop estate. He continued to work for the next ten or fifteen years, but the Haverhills became more and more isolated and reclusive as Walter's illness progressed. Walter had been confined to a wheelchair and then to his bed and the once vivacious Hattie Haverhill became a humourless martyr.

The massive four poster bed and the hoist that lifted Walter from it were gone, however, replaced by a Cal-king bedstead and matching dressers and nightstand all hand carved from some pale local wood, tamarind, maybe.

There was a new master bath with a Jacuzzi tub and double sinks. Past a short hallway between his and her walk-in closets was the second Mrs. Haverhill's study. The master suite had been snooped through and meddled with. Beyond the disarray, however, one thing was apparent—there was nothing to be had in the way of trace evidence. No signs of violence. Nothing left behind to suggest that fingerprints had been lifted or blood trailed along the floor.

I went out on the wide deck off the master bedroom. This was added after Walter's illness imprisoned him upstairs. Hattie designed the deck so that Walter sitting in his wheelchair could fish the Nuuanu stream which ran through the property. The lower level of the house had been reinforced with poured concrete to keep the house from collapsing into the stream.

Meanwhile, Hattie had turned the acreage behind the house into a botanical wonderland, the park that Randy and I—and my sister Emmy—had adopted as our own. The Cook pines with their shaggy bark and ropy needles were now enormous. The kapok tree was still there with its superstructure of above-ground roots providing kid-sized fortresses, and the cannonball tree was in bloom.

Here was a sight to add to Maya's list. She'd love the cannonball tree, its grotesque clusters of earthen red blossoms with their hairy centres and purse-like mouths. I'd call her again and leave a message. There were times Maya was too disconsolate to talk, but when her moods hit bottom she would still be listening. I'd tell her how the cannonball tree dropped an arsenal of kid-sized ammunition every year, its dark nuts ranging in size from hand grenades to bowling balls, and how Randy and I had fought off the ghost dog of the Nuuanu valley with..."

"Hey John, you ready?" Tabura shouted.

"Be right there." I glanced at the rest of the rooms, the bedrooms of the little girls. Even these were askew.

But where was Toby's room?

TWENTY-SEVEN

Detective Tabura was waiting for me as I hurried down the staircase. "Been here twenty-eight hours," he said. "Couple more, I be one ghost detective."

"I'll do this wikiwiki. Where's Toby's room?"

"Off the kitchen."

Compared to the rest of the house, Toby's back bedroom was spartan. There was a dresser built into the walls, a small closet, a single bed, a desk. There were a couple Hawaiian botanical prints on the walls and an old chenille bedspread. Notably absent was anything personal. No posters, no photos.

"Looks like a hotel room," Telly said.

"This room was trashed. Hillary Haverhill must have told you about the earlier stalkings." Tabura stared at me. He wasn't going to tell me what he knew just yet.

"The new furniture they bought for Toby was destroyed. There was a whole series of incidents," I said.

The adjoining bath was primitive, with white chicken wire tile on the floors, a wash stand and a claw bath tub. There was nothing in the medicine cabinet.

"What did Toby have here?"

"This is it," Tabura said.

"No extra clothes?"

Telly shook his head. "Boy kept nothing here. He said he forget a bag his mother packed with extra clothes."

Tabura looked at his watch and gave me the evil eye.

"The kitchen," I said. "I have to see it."

The old dining set, the chairs with rush seats where we'd find spiders lurking, was now in the kitchen. The new dining table was a fancy polished thing. The chairs had skirts. Randy's mother would never have allowed such frills. The kitchen had been redone, had an island in it with upscale granite countertops. Hattie Haverhill would be spinning in her grave.

A wooden chock nearly full of kitchen knives sat on the counter. The sight of it raised hackles on the back of my neck. *This is what I had come to see.* The investigators had taken quite an interest in it as well. I could see fingerprint powder smears on it.

"A knife is missing from this set?" I said.

"No worry," Tabura said. "One knife turned up in Professor Randy's back."

"So you say."

"Toby's fingerprints are on that knife."

"So?" I said, struggling to keep my tone level, not quite succeeding. "Toby pulled the knife from his dad's back."

Telly pulled a photo out of a packet he had under his arm. A rule lay next to the blood-smeared knife. It was a seven-inch utility. The blade was shorter than the handle.

"Toby pulled the knife," I said. "He admits that, but denies he put it there."

The next photo was of the wooden chock with the suspect knife stuck into the empty slot. "Knife fits," Telly said.

"Wait a minute," I argued, showing him the photo.

"Look closer, Telly."

"What you mean, Spyer?" When Telly called me by my last name he didn't like what I was saying.

"Look at the picture. The knife in the photo—the one from Randy's back—is *flat* along the top of the handle. The other knives in the chock are *rounded* at the top."

Telly stared, shook his head. "So? The blade fits in the chock."

"The blade fits the chock for length," I said, "but it's not a *match* for the set."

Telly rubbed his chin but said nothing and I realised I'd made a dent in his thinking; I also knew I should get off it, so I went on: "The knife was not the murder weapon, it was a peg, a means of delivering the note."

"The doorbell rings," Tabura said, "Dad go down da hall to answer. Toby has one shotgun hidden behind one door. Follows Dad to the door, knife in hand, shoots and stabs father."

"Why would he do it right out in the open?"

"Yesterday boy was in a fury, doesn't care who knows it."

"He doesn't care? So why is he now denying it?"

"Yesterday he was in a rage." Telly swigged some Jamba and smacked his lips. "Today he is in shame."

"Toby is one busy boy."

"Convenient, brah?" The theme song of the old Magnum P.I. TV show rang at Telly's side. He retrieved his cell phone with a flourish.

I laughed.

"Birthday present from my kid," Tabura said. Cell phone at his ear, the detective headed outside where the reception was better. I put on the gloves, started working through the pile of kitchen utensils arrayed on the counter and dumped from drawers: a couple of corkscrews, a garlic press, several wooden spoons, a few turners, an ice cream scoop and then a pile of knives. Bread knives, a few cleavers. And there, right in plain sight, was what I wanted. It was the short utility, the one with the rounded handle. *This* was the knife that belonged with the set.

"Praise Madam," I muttered to myself, as I took a photo of it.

I heard the detective coming back down the hall. I put the knife down. Harlan had to know about this right away.

Tabura looked at his watch. "Time to go. I got one meeting."

"Let's go grind. What do you say to a pizza?"

"One Hula Girl?" Tabura said, patting his gut. He took the photo of the knife he'd shown me and deposited it in the envelope.

"Ham? Pineapple? Edible flowers? Gourmet fare, Telly."

"Gourmet gas," the detective muttered, bugging his eyes. He turned out the kitchen lights. I followed him down the hall right past the bench where Toby's backpack had been, where Toby had scrambled for the cell phone. The bench had been dusted for fingerprints, there were also smeary signs along the wall and on the floor right behind the front door.

"Is this where Toby was supposed to have hidden a shotgun?"

"One theory," Telly said.

"Right here?" I waved at the space beside the door. There was a scant foot of clearance. The door opened against the corner, clearly lighted by a tall, narrow slice of a window that ran the length of the door. There was nothing in the corner except a ceramic umbrella stand and a couple of umbrellas. "A shotgun left here would have been obvious to anyone approaching from the hall. Professor Randy would have seen it as he walked past."

"Why not?" Tabura said, grinning. "Maybe Professor's own shotgun."

"Toby Haverhill says Randy Haverhill wouldn't have guns in his house on account of Hillary having two young girls. As I see it, Telly, your whole scenario has one big problem: If Toby did the shooting, where's the gun?"

TWENTY-EIGHT

I stood in the circular drive of the Haverhill estate watching Detective Tabura drive away. I was talking to Harlan Kawahara on my cell phone. "We've got a break here, Harlan. The knife from Randy's back was not from the set in the house. Yes, the knife fits the chock here in the house for length. Right length but wrong handle."

"So where is the right knife?" Harlan said.

"On the kitchen counter. It's in a bunch of stuff dumped from drawers during the search."

"Fine. That means it's been photographed. It's in evidence already," Harlan said. "A real break for us. Nice going, John. I'll follow up on that."

It was 3:45. So I had another fifteen minutes to kill before heading down The Pali Highway to Twice-a Slice-a. The pizza place was about twenty minutes from the Haverhill house and didn't open until 4:00 PM on Sundays. Toby put the pizza order in yesterday, around eleven. Yet the delivery had taken—what? At least an hour. Why?

I clipped my cell to my belt, and looked across the street. There was a loop of bougainvillaea trained over a gate where Lopeka Street ran into Dowsett. My sister's friend Melissa Tan had lived there. Lopeka was where Randy and I had had a run-in with the ghost dog of Nuuanu Valley one night. I turned back toward the Haverhill house, still much the same, though I couldn't get used to the new colour scheme, peach with cinnamon trim. What would Randy's mother think? Hattie Haverhill was a missionary's daughter. Hattie clung to whitewash.

I started down the front walk, a walk back in time, and found myself staring at a ti plant that had been in the yard since I was a kid. I cut across the Haverhill lawn, veering a little to the left of the front steps. The yellow and green ti plant leaves were enormous—primitive boards to the keiki of Hawaii—and dappled with brownish red blotches. I sprang away from the bush, appalled. The ti plant I'd known so many years ago was spattered with Randy Haverhill's blood.

What I was seeing was a scene out of our past. An exquisite green frog sat on the ti plant leaf. It was maybe an inch long, and it had a red pinstripe along its side. I must have been about nine. Randy plucked the frog off the bush and squeezed it in his bare hands. There was something off about the grin on his face as the frog began to struggle.

I don't know what got into me. I guess I didn't like the odds for the frog. I jumped on Randy's back and wrestled him around in the grass, which, as I think about it now, was an accomplishment. Randy was way bigger than me and five years older. He was somehow related to the right Bishops and three quarters

Hawaiian from his mother's line, descended from generations of three-hundred pounders. Me? I'm a hapa haole, also descended from Hawaiian royals, but much less gloriously, a hapa haole whose genetics were dished out backward, or so it seemed to me at the time.

I was a skinny runt who inherited the wiry English build from the Spyers and not the heft of Mama Hana's line. I was the runt among my Hawaiian cousins, who seemed the size of banyan trees. I'd been forced to learn, for the sake of my own survival, that I could land a punch or two if I was mad enough. At any rate, I was thrown on the ground and Randy straddled my scrawny body and…

Then I remembered something else, *the storage shed*. It was around from the front porch behind a lattice screen that covered the lower front of the house. The storage room had been constructed when Walter's fishing deck had been added onto the house. There was a shed door, set in behind a cascade of ivy trained into the latticework. In our boyhood days, the shed had functioned as a playhouse. We'd drag junk food down there and cigarettes and comic books. Randy's mother wouldn't allow comic books in the house. Spider Man she considered a corrupting influence.

I slipped around the corner of the porch and there was the untrammelled green ivy wall. Not a leaf was out of place. I found the old way behind the green cascade without much trouble—and there it was, the narrow door. I dug the gloves I'd borrowed from Telly out of my hip pocket and peeled into them. The door opened easily. The hinges squealed, but the simple gate latch was no problem. I found the light cord in the low ceiling that had served forever to illuminate the place and took it all in.

Our hideout was now a potting shed, filled with the limey stench of various fertilisers and bug killers. Yet one side wall was different, covered with neglected sporting gear, low tech tennis rackets, a clumsy old surfboard, some dusty snorkelling gear, and a few fishing rods. And there it was—what I didn't want to see—propped in a corner.

Best to get out of there, best go call Harlan.

I doused the light, shut the door. I ducked past the ivy curtain and started toward the stoop. I was eye level with the crime scene. Resting there on the stoop were two black regulation oxfords. The toes seemed to be staring right at me.

"Find something, Spyer?" said the voice overhead in a neutral tone, a professional, indifferent tone. My friend Telly had drawn his gun on me.

"Professional courtesy, Telly?"

I opened my hands broadly, shoulder high, palms out, made it a casual shrug. I wasn't going to give him the satisfaction of lifting them as if I were some criminal caught in the act.

"I had a few minutes before Twice-a Slice-a opens."I said. "I grew up down the street, you know. I remembered a shed under the house."

The detective's unibrow raised, his mouth relaxed.

He holstered his weapon.

I lowered my arms. "Checking up on me, Telly?"

He laughed. "I got down da road and no knife chock. Twenty eight hours I been at this, no wonder. I come back to get it. Coming out the door, I hear noise. Scared the hell out of me. I thought the killer come back, wanted to clean up something. So? What you find down there, Spyer?"

I shrugged, hesitated, considered. It wasn't the best deal for Toby, not good at all, possibly devastating, but I couldn't sell out my detective friend, couldn't crib on evidence. Do that and I'd lose my pipeline to the investigation. If I didn't come clean, Telly would go poking around where I'd just been. It was best to throw a bone to Tabura, make him look good.

"There's a storage shed under the house. Randy and I used to hide out there. It was our playhouse. Now it's a garden shed. I don't believe you guys searched it."

"No? Find anything?"

"Maybe. There's a shotgun in there."

TWENTY-NINE

Nuuanu Avenue is the main cultural artery of Honolulu. It follows an ancient trail from what is now Honolulu Harbour, up and over the spine of the Koolau Mountains through a gap, The Pali. This route has been in use for centuries, even though foot travel was precarious. Early day autos heeded wind warnings or were blown off the road. A modern highway has long since been tunnelled through The Pali.

A strategic bluff where the defenders of the Island of Oahu gathered to battle King Kamehameha I lies along Nuuanu Avenue, now the site of the Royal Mausoleum. It's no surprise then that the main business of the Nuuanu Valley is culture in its myriad forms. There's an endless assortment of churches, temples, schools, consulates, charities, The Hawaiian Cultural Center, Queen Emma's Summer Residence, and then there's the shrine of the business world, the Honolulu Country Club.

Lower down toward the harbour, near the foot of Nuuanu Avenue lies an unassuming strip mall on the corner of Nuuanu and South. The mall supplies the fuel for all the rest of the activity. It's the hi-octane stuff: yoghurt, sushi, a Hungry Lion, a Subway, the Bon Koch Chef and the granddaddy of them all, Twice-a Slice-a, sheltered beneath an enormous banyan tree. The colourful Hawaii Chinese Buddhist Society is right across the street.

The Twice-a Slice-a was originally a dark hovel plastered to resemble a grass shack. The shack has been replaced by a plantation style villa set into a wooden deck built around the banyan on the makai corner of the mall property.

Yodi Noda—Uncle Yodi—was presiding over the Sunday afternoon crowd when I walked in.

"You haven't changed a bit, Yodi," I said. The old man smiled. I thought he was an old guy then and he still was, but Yodi had changed, of course. He was more grizzled, more scooped, shorter, wider.

"Hey, Johnny Spyer,' Yodi said. "You the one changed on me. I used to look down on you. Now you look down on me." He laughed. His big square face was covered with brown blotches. His head was crowned in white fuzz. "Nice to see you, boy. It seems like yesterday, you two boys. You and Randy drank Cokes and waited while sister Emmy finished her shift." He teared up. "Now there was one beautiful girl. "

I nodded, cringing inside. It was always that way. My twin sister Emmy had been a radiant star. Just as beautiful as Princess Ka'iulani. Just as beautiful as Hawaii's last princess and just as tragic, people said, after Emmalaea disappeared, taking my own youth with her, and I didn't like to go there, peeking into the abyss.

"You've expanded the place," I said. "It looks wonderful." It did: a pizza place turned old-fashioned fern bar.

"We added the decks outside. You see more of the inside, now we be smoke free," the old man said. "Now we got the healthy food, the salad bar. He picked up a menu. "You sitting inside today? Or out on the deck?"

"Wherever, Yodi, but we need to talk."

"Okay, brah," Yodi said, eyes downcast as he shook his head. Yodi knew full well what we were going to talk about. "Let me get someone out front. Find a place in the back."

I picked out a dark and ferny corner, slid into a booth, cracked a menu. So few lunches, so many pies. A girl came by. I asked for the favourite drink of my youth, POG---pomegranate/orange/guava juice over ice.

Yodi set down a tall glass of iced tea and slid into the booth. "A terrible shame what happened to Professor Randy. Terrible."

"Did you know his son Toby?"

"Oh yeah, sure, sure. The professor bring Toby in on weekends. Maybe professor one famous hotshot, but he was Randy boy to me and he used to sneak smokes in here where his mama couldn't find him. Oh, I'd rat out one professor to his boy Toby and they would laugh and have one good time, the father and the son."

"You didn't see that they had any issues?"

The old man shook his head; With a wave of his hand he swatted any such idea right out of the park.

"Yet Toby was found over his father's body."

"I read."

"What do you think?"

"Do I think he did it? No way. Never. Toby loved his old man. He could no more do it than little Lani could."

"Lani?"

"Laniki. Lani. Randy's niece, Toby's cousin."

"I didn't know Randy had a niece." The social isolation of Randy Bishop Haverhill was an amazing feature of his life. Randy was an only child and didn't seem to have an extended family; or if he did, perhaps the severe Hattie Haverhill drove everyone away. Everybody in Hawaii had lots of cousins. I had lots of cousins, the haole ones and the Hawaiian ones. My problem was I was more like the haole ones. but a Hawaiian cousin wannabe. The Hawaiian ones were not only bigger, but also they had more fun.

"Oh yeah. Lani is Toby's cousin by way of his first wife, Mrs. Eva."

"That explains it."

"Lani—she's one lovely girl. She is also bright. She wanted to study economics like her uncle Randy. This made him very proud, you could see. He always tell me how she studies economics every time he bring Lani in here."

"When was this?"

"Been a few years now. I don't see Lani but when she comes out on break. She's studying at one big university, Stanford, maybe. Professor Randy got her one scholarship."

Yodi's son, H. B. came in. He was a good-looking, dark-eyed boy with a bed of gold coloured spikes sticking out of the top of his flat black head. H.B. is short for Honeyboy, though I have no idea how he got the nickname. H. B. was slim and poised for business in a splashy aloha shirt graced with a brawny black kukui bead lei. We exchanged pleasantries about how H.B, was eight years old when Randy and I were hanging out at Twice-a Slice-a and how he loved sneaking us refills behind his daddy's back.

"Toby tells me he ordered pizza around 11:00 AM Saturday."

"Yes sir," H. B. said. "The last pie before one professor is pau." He shook his head, eyes downcast.

"The doorbell rang just about noon. Professor Randy went to the door, thinking it was the pizza delivery."

"Oh, man. I didn't know." H. B. spun clear around as if taking a hail of buckshot himself.

"Wait a minute, H. B. I'm not implying Twice-a Slice-a had anything to do with this."

"It's all right, Johnny," the old man said. "You were Randy's friend. You do your job. You got to look out for Toby."

"I need to talk to the guy who delivered the pizza."

"Markham," H. B. said. "Elihu Markham."

The father rolled his eyes. "We let him go. Yeah?"

"You fired the pizza deliverer?"

"Markham, he's one cousin of our other guy, Tomas. Elihu filled in for Cousin Tomas now and then. Elihu was not much on learning routes."

"Did he say anything to you that day?"

"He ran behind at least one hour, maybe more. I had orders calling, threatening to cancel. I had to give out credit. Freebees. We had good business in the house here, or I'd have lost my okole, I tell you."

"These orders, were they scheduled behind the one to the Haverhill house?"

"That's right. Elihu said he got delayed by the ambulance and the cop cars."

"But you fired him anyway?"

"It was in the paper?" Yodi said.

"What was in the paper?"

"Time of Professor's death. Elihu doing his job, he should have come and gone *before*." The old man's expression turned fierce.

"*If* he was doing his job?"

"Dad thinks that if Elihu had run on time, maybe he would have seen something," H. B. said. "Maybe he would have saved the professor."

"You got an address for Markham"

"Naw. He just fill in for his cousin Tomas."

"So where does Cousin Tomas live?"

"I'll find it for you," H. B. said.

H. B. went out front and came back with a name, a phone number and an address.

"Cousin Tomas, he will know how to find cousin Elihu."

"What does this Markham guy look like?"

"One skinny haole, thin face, gold-tipped dreds. "

"Blond?"

"Dark brown hair, about five seven or eight."

"How old?"

"Twenty-two or three, maybe. Got a college degree."

"And he's delivering pizza?"

"Just a fill-in on weekends. He's got a day job somewhere, some book store, maybe."

"Mahalo, gentlemen," I said. "I'll find the guy."

"You don't be no stranger no more," Uncle Yodi said, and we clinched.

I'd forgotten to leave Em's window cracked open. I opened the door to let out the blistering heat and put in a cell call to Tomas, Elihu's cousin at the number H. B. had given me. Tomas didn't answer and I didn't want to leave a message. I checked my messages and got Eva's voice, sounding tired.

"John, please come when you get this. Harlan called and left a message. He said he'll by this afternoon. When the lawyer comes to you on Sunday afternoon it can't be good. I'm afraid they are going to *charge* Toby. I just can't believe this. It's all directed at me. What else could it be? The prosecutor knows I'm sick and this is his way of delivering the *coup de grace*, please come wikiwiki. I'll serve you Drambuie. I'll make you dinner."

The fright in Eva's voice gave me chicken skin. My gut felt hollow and my back seized up. I had to shuffle around in the parking lot until I could get my spine to loosen up. The cops had the shotgun, just what they needed to charge Toby with murder.

No doubt Eva would grill me, but I had to go see her. What choice did I have? I'd found the murder weapon. I'd handed Telly Tabura the weapon he needed to charge my own client's son with the murder of his father. I climbed into the hot seat, closed the door and took a roasting, let the sweat roll down my face. What had I been thinking? Why had I taken this case? *Some things might surface that wouldn't be to Toby's advantage.* I tried to tell Eva first thing. Why hadn't she listened? And why hadn't I heard the sound of my own voice?

THIRTY

Putt Jorgenson answered Eva's door, my old buddy, my old score. Though we had settled our differences years ago, I was pissed that Putt had upset Maya. I needed to have a chat with Putt about her, but now was not the time.

"Spyer, brah. What's happening?"

"Eva called. She sounded upset."

"She's very worried about Toby. We think charges are coming down. Mitzi Wong tipped Eva this afternoon. I'm on my way out. I dropped off some copy for Eva to review. She's on the phone, distracted for the moment, thank God. She's been a basket case all afternoon." Jorgenson rolled his dull brown eyes and his thin mouth stretched to one side as he ushered me down the hall. "Eva's on the phone with her Austrian boyfriend. You should see the rig she's wearing just to whisper sweet nothings to Mr. Edelweiss. Do you suppose they have phone sex?"

"Austrian? Somebody new?"

"Deter? No, no, no," Jorgenson said. "Eva and Deter have been at it for years. He was a postdoctoral student of Randy's."

"There's one way to get even with Randy."

"I would guess that's the appeal." Putt drummed a table with his fingers for emphasis. Putt is a first rate drummer, frequently invited to sit in as a guest at musical shindigs at Hale Kava. "Have a seat, John. I'll pour. What'll you have?"

"Drambuie rocks."

Jorgenson made a face. His blunt nose twitched, "I doubt that Eva has…"

"She's got Drambuie. On the top shelf."

Jorgenson's Afro lite disappeared as he looked for the bottle. "Oh. Right. Here it is." Putt found some ice and handed me my drink in one of Eva's cut crystal glasses. Eva lived in the grand southern belle manner her mother, an Atlanta blueblood, had instilled in her. At Eva's house we drank from crystal, not coconuts.

I stirred my own drink and downed a shot, thinking about Eva's European connection. Then I recalled that she had another love interest. "So what happened to Eva's other squeeze? The newspaper intern?"

"Ed-die Co-oke," Putt said. "Mr. Boy Toy. Started his second internship in June. Didn't make it through the August staff cuts. Not to worry. He starts law school this fall. He's the well-connected son of some big shot attorney here in Honolulu. Or so I found out. Eddie avoided entanglements, much to Eva's chagrin. She considers him gutless. We disagree there."

I sucked in a laugh, rattled the cubes, took a sip.

"How goes the investigation?" Putt said.

"So so. Some good news and some bad news."

"Off the record?"

"More than one knife fits in the chock on the murder scene, and that's good."

"How good?"

"The knife in Randy's back was not from the kitchen. It was delivered by the shooter, brought to the scene. That's what we'll argue if we wind up in court."

"Wonderful," Putt said, fingers riffing the sweating sides of his Coke can. "No jury will buy the pap the prosecutor's office is leaking about Toby and that knife. It's so ridiculous I'm thinking Honolulu justice really is after Eva."

I nodded, sipped some more. Strains of Jack Johnson, surfer dude turned songwriter, filled the room. Eva had the hots for Johnson big time.

"What else?" Jorgenson said, ever the journalist. He was never satisfied with one tidbit of info. He was always ready to wring more out of me.

"Our latest problem is a shotgun that was found on the premises."

"Lord save us, Madam Pele," Jorgenson said, with a sly turn of mouth. He loved putting his own twist on lingo he lifted from me. "The murder weapon was right there on the scene all along?"

"About twenty feet from where Professor Randy was shot." Though I believed I could trust Putt, I didn't tell him exactly where the gun was found, and certainly not that I had found it, and I didn't intend to tell him anytime soon.

"How could the cops miss that one?"

"Thick foliage."

"Or thick heads?"

"Now Putt. I didn't say that."

"Well," he replied, a droll expression on his face, "You found a ringer knife for Toby. So why not come up with a ringer shotgun?"

THIRTY-ONE

Eva made her grand entrance, tripping into the room on her elevator heels. She was a costume drama of one in a Chinese silk brocade dress with a mandarin collar, the type slit up to here along one thigh. She'd topped off this rig with a thick blonde wig, one of those eighteenth century big hair jobs. Or was the wig something straight from sexpot singer Dolly Parton's closet?

"Jesus, Madam." I blurted.

"I knew you'd like it, John," Eva cooed.

I rose to kiss her cheek. "You are lovely," I lied. "Blue silk brings out your eyes."

Eva's grey eyes went lavender against the dress. She had plastered on rouge to hide her sickbed pallor.

"I haven't gotten into this dress in seven years," Eva said, smiling big. "Chemo is good for weight loss, that's for sure. My friend Deter will be thrilled. He loves this dress. He bought it for me when we were in Hong Kong." Eva flounced up the hall in a credible imitation of the loose-jointed model's stroll.

Putt clapped and whistled and I sucked in a laugh or two. Surely Eva's sheer exuberance would keep her in remission.

"Deter will be here on Friday for the Economic Conference of Pacific Nations." Eva flopped into a wing chair, crossed one leg over the other and swung her foot like a pendulum. "Deter is presenting a paper on European fiscal policy. Randy set the conference up, you know. He had no idea Deter was coming. I intended to strut in on the arm of a much younger scholar." Her mouth puckered. "Now we'll be tossing flower leis on Randy's grave, instead. Deter loved Randy. It's so sad." Eva's husky voice trembled and she blinked back tears. "And now *this*... this *thing* with Toby. This is a *travesty*." Eva's face crumpled.

Putt cleared his throat and stared at his watch.

"Go. Run with it," Eva said, swatting Putt out the door with one hand.

With an ironic turn of his head to me and a nod over his shoulder at Eva, Putt grabbed the bundle of marked copy he'd parked on Eva's liquor cabinet and dashed out.

Eva yanked the wig and tossed it into a basket of old newspapers. "Damned wig is too hot." She curled into the wing chair, drawing her legs up under her. A tray of pills stood on the table at her elbow. Sans wig, Eva's weariness seemed to reassert itself.

"You look stressed, Eva. I've heard stress isn't good for..."

"What's stress to me? Eva snarled, "I don't get stress, I hand it out."

"Can I fix you a drink?"

"A chardonnay, please. Dr. Kojimura said I can sip. Now there is a lonely man. Did I tell you we read philosophy together? Last time I saw him, Dr. Kojimura personally walked clear down the hall to the nurses' station to get me some pills. I do think that signifies interest, don't you?"

"Definitely," I said, gritting my teeth.

Eva raised her glass and clinked mine. We sipped. "John—we have to talk."

"What's up?"

"I'm worried to death. I'm wondering if I shouldn't fire Harlan."

"Why do that?"

"Toby has been in jail for a whole night. Why? Where's the evidence?"

"Coercion would be my guess. The cops may have arrested Toby because they think he knows something he isn't telling. There's a very short window—about twelve hours—that's as long as they can hold him. For some reason, Telly Tabura is stubborn. He's going to hold Toby for every hour he can get."

"More sloppy work by the prosecutor," Eva said . "It's just what we've said in the paper all along. This prosecutor's conviction rates are terrible. It's because he pulls shit like this." Eva smacked her drink on the table. Fortunately the crystal didn't shatter. "Toby is a decent, tender-hearted boy who has never been in any kind of trouble."

"I know that, Eva, but…"

"But *what*? Toby is disconsolate. He's just lost his father. He's crushed to think anyone would believe he had anything to do with Randy's murder."

"These things take time, Eva. Firing Harlan would only slow things down."

"I suppose you're right."

"How were things between Toby and his dad, by the way?"

"Randy adored Toby. They spent Friday nights and Saturdays together. I very often let Toby stay over Sunday, as well. I'm working terrible hours now that I've got a major series on corruption coming out. Randy might have been a philandering bastard but he did make time for Toby. They went out canoeing every Saturday morning and came back for pizza."

"An established routine?"

"A ritual."

"And this was just dandy with the second Mrs.?"

"Hillary?" Eva blew off the second Mrs. Randy through puffed cheeks: "Pfhhh. Hillary may be an old-line blue blood and a trust fund babe, but she's one shave ice of a bitch. She made Toby miserable and her spoiled brat daughters took their cue from Mom."

"Uh huh. Family went their separate ways on Saturday mornings, a routine set in stone. It was a ritual," I said. "Who knew the routine better than the second Mrs. Haverhill? Eva stared at me. I thought she'd pick right up on this, no love being lost between the two Mrs. Haverhills, after all, but Eva merely shook her head.

"It wasn't Hillary," Eva said.

So who was it? Did Eva know?

THIRTY-TWO

Eva sat in her wing chair, head flung back, eyes at half staff. Her lips worked silently to Jack Johnson's tune, *Wrong Turn*. When Jack got to the part about it being the worst hour of his day, I couldn't have agreed with one brother more. I got up, helped myself to the Drambuie.

"Can I get you something, Eva?"

"No more wine," she murmured. "I'm afraid to drink these days. I might have some of that noni juice I'm supposed to drink. I hate it, but I promised."

In the kitchen, I sipped Eva's poison on the tip of my finger. Pure gaak. I put some fresh ice in the blender, frappéd it, poured the noni over the ice, added nutmeg shavings and a vanilla swizzle stick and served it in a tall glass. It looked so good Eva had no choice but to pretend she liked it, and so she sucked up a straw full and smiled.

"Lovely, John."

"What an actress. Okay, Eva, let's get back to work, back to Saturday. Randy and Toby were doing their bonding number. Does that explain why the second Mrs. and her daughters were out of the house when the gun went off?"

Eva stirred the noni concoction with the straw and drizzled a glob of it onto her tongue. "Hillary has been so mean that I considered cutting off Randy's parental contact. But Toby badly needed a strong male influence." She set the glass on the table. That was it for the noni. "When Randy and Toby were together, Hillary retaliated by taking her daughters out to shop. You'd think she'd find something intellectual—or at least athletic, but of course, she's a bit too shallow for that. I recommend you go see her. I'm sure she'll tell you as much."

"About how shallow she is?"

"Please, John," Eva said. She drew herself up and sighed big time, but she looked fragile, hunkered in the cocoon of her wing chair.

No doubt it had killed Eva when she divorced Randy and he promptly turned around and married an heiress with Hawaiian roots as noble as his own. Hillary's father Cameron Rooke owned vast tracts of Oahu real estate, including office towers, shopping centres, housing developments, and resorts. All this the Camerons and the Rookes had acquired through the generations, thanks to the intricacies of a lease holding system of land ownership borrowed from the British.

Not one scrap of these blue-bloods' holdings was ever sold outright. Leases were negotiated for a leisurely ninety nine years. Buildings built upon the estate lands reverted to the landlord. And so, over the generations, Oahu Land and Cane had acquired immense holdings. The corporation also farmed vast acreages in sugar cane, pineapple, produce, flowers, and cattle. Oh yes, and they bred fine horses.

"So Randy and Toby had their ritual and Hillary and the daughters had theirs. A well-established ritual?"

"Why do you say that?"

"A stalker will know the victim's routine."

"That's true. Toby started paddling at the beginning of last summer. He's one of those tall boys who wouldn't play basketball. Paddling? That was different. Toby loved the rhythm of it. He's quite the musician, as you know."

"How's his group?"

"Shattered. Se Se's on the mainland. She broke up with Toby when school was out. I just knew it wouldn't last. He's too immature for her."

"Is he sticking with the music?"

"It's his lifeline," Eva said, stirring her drink with the straw. "He was depressed over Se Se before this happened, and now this? Toby is devastated. I've told him to turn to his music. Right now, it's his only solace. Toby's in a private high school for performing artists.

He has a wonderful ear. Written language is confusing to dyslexics. They often compensate by learning to listen really well. Toby and Kimo have a guest gig with a military band coming up, an Aloha Week thing. Toby's just a baby. He's in jail, could be there for life, and what's he worried about? Playing his gig at Aloha Week, and I thank the dear Lord for the diversion. You'll take me to hear him, won't you? Putt can't come. He's on the night desk this week."

"I'll be glad to." On the stereo, Jack Johnson went into high gear. I got up, added some ice to my drink and drizzled Drambuie over it.

"The Canoe Club was my idea," Eva said. "Toby loved being one of the guys. Here was something athletically challenging that Toby was good at. He was badly out of shape so I got him a personal trainer until he was good enough to be on a team. Toby could develop a weight problem if he doesn't watch it. He's lost twenty-five pounds since he started and feels great, but now he won't touch food. I'm afraid he'll turn into a skeleton."

"Toby started paddling last summer. I got that. Now about this season. He was about how many weeks into this new ritual?"

"Twelve or thirteen. Is that important?"

"Maybe. "

"Maybe why?"

"Maybe Mrs. Randy the Second didn't care for the switch in the routine."

Eva Looked Incredulous. "You don't think Hillary did this?"

"Hillary has one fine alibi, but alibis can be arranged. "

Eva rose, paced on the rug and turned back. "No, I can't believe Hillary did it."

"Maybe Randy was more of a handful than she'd imagined. Maybe the honeymoon is over."

"I can't stand Hillary, but she just wouldn't…"

"Why not?"

"What would be the motive? Passion?" Eva smirked. "Hillary wouldn't know the meaning of the word."

Eva went to the French doors that opened onto the patio. I joined her to watch the sun splash down. The air was fresh, infused with raindrops. Scruffy Diamond Head went golden in the afterglow. As seen from above, the crater had a leonine shape, like one giant Sphinx.

"Let me tell you something about Hillary, just so you know," Eva said, resting on the railing of her lanai. "After I'd had enough chemo to shrink the tumour, I went in for surgery. I had to be hospitalised for several days. Randy stayed with me the first night. He slept in a chair by my bedside."

"Decent of him."

"Randy was crushed when I divorced him," Eva said. "He never got over it, not for a minute. Hillary was furious. She told Randy that she knew he loved me above all. She said she knew he'd see me in his mind's eye when he drew his last breath."

"Randy told you what Hillary said?"

Eva smiled through tears. "It was Randy's way of telling me he still loved me."

"So? Hillary's pissed that she's not number one in her new husband's life," I said. "Suppose Hillary arranges to let Randy draw that last breath? She finds somebody to waste Randy while she and her daughters are off at the horse show. The event is rigged so Toby takes the blame."

Eva shook her head. "I can't stand Hillary, but I can't believe she did it. Hillary's too cold. She wouldn't murder Randy. She'd cut off his allowance. Passion was something she saved for her horses."

We watched the colours change in the afterlight, doing an array of pinks and silvers, a mother-of-pearl sort of evening it was. Jack Johnson was still going at it on the stereo, singing about the water and the sky and the clouds crying, and it rhymes when brother Jack does it, and Eva got teary-eyed as her head nodded along. She asked me to get her pashima wrap so that she could stay out and enjoy the heavy floral scents in the warm evening air. As I draped the shawl over her, Eva slipped an arm around my waist, her head barely reaching up to my shoulders, her face drawn. In that instant I glimpsed the fright behind her jaunty mask.

"A cancer in the windpipe is a rare one," Eva said. "My odds aren't even twenty percent. Dr. Kojimura finally told me. These doctors know the statistics, but they don't like to use them around the patients. I wormed it out of him."

"That's the journalist talking," I said. "You're no statistic, Eva. The big C has nothing on you." I wrapped her in my arms and felt her solid bones. I took heart from her stout underpinnings and her ferocious will. If anybody could beat cancer it was Eva.

"Thank you, John," she said, slipping out of my arms. "I needed that. I need hugs and moral support. I've been put on the list of a lot of prayer groups. I do have a following among my readers, you know. It all helps. I am a winner, one of the lucky ones, except in love, of course."

The doorbell rang. I released Eva and went to answer it. It was Harlan. His face was ashen.

"John. Am I glad to see you."

"That bad, Harlan?"

"Worse."

THIRTY-THREE

By the time I arrived back in the living room with Harlan in tow, Eva had slipped out of the Chinese rig and into a fancy muu muu with matching slippers and turban. She waylaid us in the hallway. "Harlan," she laced her arm through his, "you must be beat."

"It's been a long day," the lawyer said, kissing her cheek. Eva seated us in the dinette in the kitchen. The chairs were antique wicker, the cushions a colourful Tahitian print, reflecting Eva's exquisite taste. Eva invited Harlan to shed his jacket and loosen his tie. She twisted some lime into a drink and handed it to him.

"A lawyer's Mai Tai?" I said.

"The Poet's Truth, a sake drink. Harlan loves them. Don't you, my dear?"

Harlan nodded. The look on his face made me wonder whether he wasn't another of Eva's conquests.

"Will you have another Drambuie, John? Or one of these?"

"A Poet's Truth? How could I resist."

"You've got it."

"Time you sit down, Eva. Allow me. Just clue me what to pour."

"The recipe is on the tray," Eva said, obviously grateful that I was giving her the opportunity to get off her feet. It was getting stuffy, so I opened the door onto the lanai. Then I made myself busy blending sake, dry vermouth, and a twist of lime, maintaining a low profile. I knew the news was bad and I wanted Harlan to have the space to break it to her gently.

"Thank the dear Lord, Harlan. I've been waiting all day. Tell me..."

"They're charging Toby. They found what they needed, the murder weapon, a shotgun in a shed on the property."

Eva's jaw went slack, her colour drained. "The bastards. They *planted* it," she moaned, shaking her head. "It's me. This is all directed at me." Energised in her rage, Eva paced in the narrow space between the table and the kitchen counter.

"We can't say that at this point, Eva," Harlan said, keeping a level tone. "Frankly, I'm a little surprised. They don't have all the forensics in. They have the shotgun, but can't prove Toby pulled the trigger. This is risky business. My theory is, they pressed charges because Toby is a minor. This is another tactic to pressure Toby. There's a very short window before the judge demands Toby's release unless..."

"Unless they charge him? What could they charge him with?"

Harlan stared, shook his head. He wasn't going to say the *M* word.

"What case?" Eva cried. "What case could they possibly have?"

"We're okay on most things," Harlan said. "The knife? We have good defence on that. The note? That's a hard one for us. We can find our own handwriting expert. There has to be an explanation. It all comes back to this shotgun, found at the Haverhill estate. That's what the prosecutor's hanging his hat on."

"Shotgun?" Eva said. "Where was it?"

Harlan shot a conspiratorial glance at me and then crafted an answer that left me out of it. "This afternoon the police found a shotgun in a storage shed under the house, not twenty feet from the porch steps."

Eva sank into her chair. "Toby couldn't have done it. Toby never fired a weapon in his life. I'm against guns. I wouldn't have it."

"What about Randy?"

"Not interested in shooting," Eva said. "Not that I know of, and I've known Randy since he was sixteen."

Then she looked at me, on the sly. "Well, fourteen, fifteen, somewhere in there." It was that look she gave me that jogged my memory. Harlan was laying out the case. He turned to me.

"What about you, John? You knew Randy as a child."

"My dad taught my sister and me to shoot the summer we turned ten. We shot skeet and had to qualify for safety certificates. For once, Randy was beside himself with jealousy, so my dad talked to his parents. They had a country place and Randy's grandfather lent him an old shotgun."

Harlan gave me a look, but said nothing, but I knew what he was thinking. Perhaps it was this same shotgun that I had found in the storage shed.

"The prosecutor would never call John," Eva said.

"Lot of people knew Randy, grew up with him. We have to be prepared," Harlan said. "But look at it this way, Eva, Toby will be out on bail tomorrow, sleeping in his own bed."

"What's the bond?" I said.

"One point five."

A million and a half? " Eva drew a deep breath."Outrageous."

"A slap at Eva and *The Honolulu Gazette*," I said.

"I couldn't agree more," Harlan said.

Her voice, though trembling, was controlled. "Does Toby know?"

Only that we'll be going to court, that we'll deny any charges, and that he'll be home in the afternoon."

"I spoke to the warden. I had Toby put on a suicide watch last night," Eva said.

"Do you think that's overkill?" Harlan said.

"When Toby doesn't speak to his own mother, he's despondent. I have the medical records to… you'll have to trust me on this. I reminded the warden that if my own son made a foolish attempt...well, it wouldn't be the first time it happened there, and I'd sue the entire juvenile justice system and name him personally as a co-respondent. I'll insist a matron keeps watch on him tonight."

"All right then. You take care, Eva. Best you arrange the bond this evening. I'm sure that John can drive you."

"Right, counsellor," I said. "What bondsman do you suggest we use?"

"Monica Fat, I should think."

I sucked in a breath. "Bondsperson Fat." Monica Fat was a dragon lady to be sure, but discreet.

"She's at the opening of the Bishop Museum show tonight," Eva said. "She's on the board. My publisher will be there as well. Monica's quite the collector, you know."

"Let me put in a call," I said to Harlan. "I'll have Monica meet with Eva tonight in her salon." Monica Fat was such a class act that she had her office behind her antique shop right next to the ritziest building in Chinatown.

Eva walked Harlan to the door while I found Monica's number in my cell directory and left word for her to call. There were dark circles under Eva's eyes when she returned. "We have a couple of hours, John, and I did offer you dinner."

"I'll rustle up something. I want you to rest."

"Rest? There's a good one. I have to track down my publisher right now...There's some fresh 'ahi. I was going to grill it for you. "

"'Ahi I can handle."

"Oh thank you. This may take awhile."

Eva's eyes watered and her mouth drew down. "I have to pull myself together and summon the courage to resign."

"From the paper?"

Eva shook her head. Her eyes wandered away. "A job I love—my series—all gone."

"But Eva, this isn't your... "

She brushed off my protest with a wave of her hand. "You don't understand, John. I have to resign. I have no choice. A journalist must resign when she starts making the news."

Eva flounced out of the room leaving me to start dinner. I couldn't get that odd look of hers out of my mind. And then it clicked: Eva said she had known Randy since he was fourteen years old? If so, why hadn't I heard anything about her back then?

THIRTY-FOUR

I put Eva's good china and linen napkins out on the dinette, fresh candles in holders, my cell phone on buzzer mode and Jack Johnson's *G. Love and Special Sauce* on the stereo. Eva came in looking drained. I seated her.

"Were you able to reach your publisher?"

"Oh, yes. Dan called me right back. It was intermission. It's pau."

"The opening?"

"My job." Eva struggled to control her puckering mouth, wiped her eyes on a napkin, then tossed it aside, squared her shoulders and glared at me. "Dan is putting me on medical leave."

"Better than a resignation, Eva."

"My series is pau." Her head revolved slowly, side to side. "I have to turn it over to Wayne Hinkley, the bastard. I wanted Putt Jorgenson to have it, but Dan said no."

"That's too bad."

Eva made a face. "Oh, I'll have my name on it, I'll get to sign off, but it's finished. Wayne has all the guts of a gecko and half the brains. Honolulu is full of politicians on the take. I had hoped we would put the worst offenders in the slammer."

"Your publisher is sensible, don't you think?"

"Yes, I suppose so, but it's going to look as if this thing over Toby has laid me low."

"Jesus, Madam, Eva. Are you in denial, or what?"

"Death by denial," Eva said. "It's the story of my life."

I passed a plate to her. "It smells wonderful. What is it?"

"Special sauce, Eva. Caramelized Maui onions over grilled 'ahi, accompanied by fresh mango chutney and saffron rice. Chardonnay?"

She grimaced. "No thanks."

I'd frappéd more ice and noni juice in the blender, poured it into a champagne flute, and added a slice of lemon for a chaser. Eva shuddered in disgust as she sucked it up through a straw. "This stuff tastes like toothpaste. Dr. Kevin made me swear I'd drink some with every meal. He says my diet is killing me. All those sulfites in the meats we journalists live on. I'm not telling him sex is killing me. I wouldn't give him the satisfaction."

I put down my napkin. "Dr. Kojimura said that?"

Eva shook her head. "Dr. *Kevin*, my son, Toby's half brother; he's an intern in neurology at Stanford. He'll be coming to Randy's funeral."

"I didn't know Toby had an older half brother."

"He has two. Both thirty-somethings. Bart's a rocket scientist based in Houston, works for NASA."

I stared at Eva. "You have sons in their thirties? I don't believe it."

"I always did look young for my age. I got asked for my I.D. in lounges until I was thirty-five." She laughed. "Toby's older half brothers are my sons by my first marriage to Nelson Akala Sneddon. The Akalas are old line Honolulu with all sorts of business interests, but Nelson was different—very intellectual—or so I thought." Eva made a face.

"You divorced him when you found out he wasn't?"

"We married too young. I wanted to get out of the house—away from my mother. She never got over being an Atlanta debutante, and here was Nelson, one big hunk with an athletic scholarship to U.S.C. and an intellect on top of that. Then along came Vietnam and we were history."

"The separation did it?"

"Politics," Eva said. "I believed in the cause and so did Nelson—at least at first. Then he went over there and got on pot. He went liberal, turned against the war and became bitter, and I didn't, at least not at that time."

"So you parted company?"

"And I fell in love with Randy." Eva sipped at her noni juice. "Nelson and I separated and he thought I'd come back to him. He was crushed." Her fingers worked the curves of the crystal. "Poor Nelson. I treated him shabbily. I've written to apologise. One of the good things about having cancer is, you reflect on what's gone wrong in your life. Anything happens, I don't want Nelson on my conscience."

As for my gourmet 'ahi, Eva took a polite bite or two of her dinner, which is all that her doctor allowed. I wound up eating most of it myself. I could have done with a side of two-finger poi, but Eva had nothing so native in the house. By the time we got to the raspberry sorbet I'd found in Eva's freezer, conversation had dwindled.

"What's eating you, Eva? It's a cinch your mind isn't on my meal."

"It's not the bail. The newspaper has insurance. They'll take care of that for me. What bothers me right now is that damned note pinned to Randy," Eva said. "They had Toby write out some words. They'll find some handwriting idiot to swear Toby wrote it. That must be what their case is based on. What else could it be?"

"That isn't strong evidence, Eva. If that's all they've got, it isn't enough."

"And that shotgun. What if Toby handled it? Just out of curiosity?"

"Do you have any idea whose it is?"

"l never allowed any weapons in my house. I don't know about Hillary and her tribe. If I were you, I'd ask her."

"I fully intend to. I'll get to Hillary. When's the funeral?"

"Friday morning. Hillary agreed to hold off a few days. Friday is the opening day of the Economic Conference. That way Randy's colleagues can come. Randy has—*had*—an international reputation, you know."

"Question is, a reputation for what?"

Eva shrugged off my jest. She wasn't in a joking mood, so I switched subjects. "So these older sons of yours are coming for the funeral?"

"Oh, yes. We need to have a family conference. We have to decide who will look after Toby when I... if I....if something should happen to me." Eva's voice trailed off. "Poor Toby. The choices are all wrong. Kevin in medical school has no time for a kid. Bart in the space program is more spaced than his rockets. Rhonda, my sister-in-law, has fallen apart after the death of my brother. She's on meds for depression."

I picked up her plate, set it on top of mine, adjusted the spoons and watched her carefully as I asked what I had a hunch was a loaded question: "Speaking of family, there's your niece Lani."

Eva blanched. Her eyes widened as her head revolved slowly side to side. "Lani? What about her?"

"You tell me, Eva."

THIRTY-FIVE

Eva rose, shoved back her chair and began to pace in the kitchen. "Lani was fifteen years old. *Fifteen.* Do you hear me?"

"Loud and clear."

"Lani is my sister-in-law's youngest. My brother was dying of…"

"It wouldn't be cancer, now would it?"

"Eldon's was colon." She drew a line down her own centre. "Along the same pipeline. My nephews stayed with their mom that summer, but my sister-in-law Rhonda thought Lani was too young. She wanted Lani away from home for the summer. The boys had started to notice her. She's tiny, with a perfect figure, graceful, poised, a beautiful cocoa complexion with pale grey eyes. A gymnast, you know."

"With a Hawaiian name?"

"Part Hawaiian, one quarter on my sister-in-law's side, but brought up on the mainland. Rhonda hoped Lani would come back to the islands and find her roots."

"But young Lani connected with Randy instead?"

"He took Lani and my boys to an exhibit of cultural artefacts from the Cook expeditions. The paper did a wonderful account of it. Brilliant, even if I do say so. A project of mine, by the way. I was very proud of it. We won a national award for features." Eva drained her juice, stirred the slush and drank again. It took her so long to say anything more that I realised this was a dodge. Eva meant to choose her words carefully.

"Laniki—Lani—was smitten with Randy. She wanted to study economics and archaeology, both Randy's fields of interest. Lani hung on Randy. Girls of a certain age will do that, and it didn't bother me. After all, her own father was too sick to be there for her." Eva headed for the sink and flung some dishes around. From across the kitchen counter, I watched her face do contortions. "Lani took care of Toby while I worked. He was three at the time."

"Wait a minute," I said. "I thought you and Randy came back to Hawaii just three years ago."

"This was twelve years ago. Randy's father was very ill. His mother was frantic. So Randy took a teaching fellowship with the University here, and got a healthy advance to write his second book. I filled in three nights a week on the copy desk at the *Gazette* and snagged the Cook project in features."

"Lani took Toby to the beach every day. My baby was in heaven. And then, all of a sudden, Lani wanted to leave. I thought she was homesick. I never suspected a thing. Lani was gone for two days when I got a furious call from my sister-in-law. Rhonda wanted to know what the hell was wrong with Randy."

"He molested his own niece?"

"It never got that far, but not for my dear husband's lack of trying."

I didn't know what to say. There I was, hand over mouth, literally. Finally, I made a half-hearted joke. "Well. You know what they say about the Polynesians."

"Fuck the Polynesians," Eva spat, and we both had to laugh, though our mirth was of the hollow variety.

"My own niece," Eva said. "I had no one to blame but myself. I was a damned fool. I had been hearing for *years* from various friends about Randy's exploits. Randy was with this student and fooling around with that one. I heard the rumours, but I let them roll right off my back. But this... this was *Lani*. This was family."

I rubbed my forehead, dug at my eyes. Images of the Randy I knew flooded my mind. *Randy the popular. Randy the articulate. Randy the guy the girls hung on. Randy the guy who would manipulate. Randy who had man-handled the frog...*

"Well, that was the end of it for me," Eva said. "I'd gone on and on with Randy and his women. Here is this brilliant professor who thinks he is invincible, fucking anything that walks, blithely unaware that to certain kinds of women he's a trophy to bag; but to some others? Randy's actions were viewed as predatory or worse. By this time there's AIDS and he's doing lectures on economics. He's in these Asian and African places and he takes no precautions. None whatsoever. And then he tries to meddle with Lani? That was the end for me. I just freaked."

"You never reasoned with him?"

"Did you ever try to reason with a genius?"

I felt my mouth crimp on the left, the twitchy side. This rang true. Randy always did have a way of twisting any argument around until he was on the winning side of it.

"I figured that anybody who'd won a MacArthur Genius Grant should be able to figure his flaky behaviour out for himself."

I was clearing the plates when my cell phone buzzed on the table, doing a hula. I checked the caller ID. "It's Monica Fat."

"I'd better go change," Eva said.

"Just find a wrap, Eva. Don't bother to change out of your fancy gown. Monica will be dressed to kill."

THIRTY-SIX

Monica Fat, bail bondsperson to the Honolulu elite, is famous for where she's not. She's not located in one of those tacky places near the courthouse with the red neon signs. Monica's place is in Chinatown. We sped past the Gateway Plaza, the stately hi-rise condo that bridges the gap between the grand merchant plazas of downtown Honolulu and Chinatown proper, with its low-rise brick buildings topped with gingerbread trim. We had arrived in a different cultural space, one that hailed from an earlier century.

Luckily, I found a parking place right in front of the elegant Consuelo Zobel Alger Foundation building on North Hotel. A glazed green tile roof is studded with oriental gargoyles and slathered with symbolic trim. It gleamed in the night light. Fat Antiques and Imports is next door. Monica had trimmed out her shop to match the grand Consuelo Alger building, so that the first impression is that Fat Antiques is a vast establishment.

Eva had bundled up in her pashima shawl and girded herself for battle with the bondswoman. In her long gown, matching turban and stiletto heels, she was a head taller than nature intended, and feisty as you please. The balmy night air revived her spirits. Eva's latest defeat was behind her. Eva Haverhill had lost the last battle, but she was not about to be defeated in the war.

Eva surveyed North Hotel in both directions, assessing the risk to her precious new convertible. She glanced Diamond Head. The Honolulu P.D. Downtown Substation was a reassuring half block away in the Dan Liu Building, its elaborate trim played up in a green, tan and cream paint job shiny as so much lip gloss under the street lights.

"Leave the top down," Eva decreed. "We'll be fine. We're a shout from the H.P.D. and parked in front of the bail bond palace. Who would dare touch us? Any thief who happens by will figure us for drug moguls."

We rang the bell and waited to be identified, no doubt through some hidden camera. Eventually there came a tumbling of locks and then Monica opened the door to her antique shop. Bride of the bonds people, Monica wore a spectacular white lace gown. Her thick black hair framed her round face in one of those severe, helmet-style haircuts. She had delicate pale skin and bee-sting lips. Her obsidian eyes, magnified behind lenses as thick as soda bottles, were all business.

The women sat down at an antique black lacquer table. Monica offered Eva hot green tea and lemon from a silver service. With a certain delicacy of gesture, she slid the paperwork across the gleaming surface for Eva to sign.

I stared all around at the various antique pieces. Crossed swords on the walls. Suits of chain mail. Samurai gear, vases, screens, paintings, Polynesian artefacts carved from vonu, ironwood or hau, hibiscus, inlaid with mother of pearl. Monica had priceless uli uli shakers trimmed with feathers from extinct birds, not to mention trays of curlicue fish hooks carved from bone—some no doubt human. To Hawaiians, the fish hook is a symbol of power. Over the centuries beautifully carved fish hooks segued into an important art form. Under the circumstances this was very intimidating.

Monica Fat had the reputation for appraising the antiques and the art collections of high profile miscreants and then using them for collateral to raise bail. Then, after they had gone to court and were short of cash, Monica would acquire the art on the cheap. Monica and Eva sipped their tea as Monica explained the terms to Eva. The paper's insurer was putting up one hundred fifty grand against a bet of a million five that Toby wouldn't skip town.

Eva pulled herself together and discussed the whole matter as if it weren't her son's life they were talking about. It was the tone they would use bartering over one of the Ming vases in Monica's shop.

"Interest to accrue at the rate of ten percent."

"What percent?" Eva said. "Isn't that rather high?"

"The court sets the rates," Monica murmured. With a lacquered claw, she tapped the line Eva had to sign.

"If the *Gazette* had no insurance, the rate would be more."

"Just sign, Eva," I said. "It's the best you can do."

Eva stared at me. I didn't think she'd heard what I said.

She signed with a flourish and threw down the pen.

"I tell you, Monica, I was always afraid of something like this. Always. My genius of an ex hadn't a lick of sense where his prick went wandering, and now look at this. Look what he's done to his own son."

"I am so sorry, Mrs. Haverhill," Monica purred. "But not to worry. Your son come out okay."

Then I witnessed something I thought I would never see. These two titas stood and embraced in a consoling hug. I got Eva out of there before she cracked.

We were downtown, so I offered her a nightcap in the Aloha Tower.

"You choose where," I said.

THIRTY-SEVEN

Honolulu Harbor was once the crown jewel of the city's tourist economy. Fleets of cruise ships plied the harbour during the roaring twenties and well beyond. Now that the airlines dominate the tourist business, the cargo containers rule in the harbour.

The Aloha Tower, built in the twenties to welcome tourists, is now the centrepiece of a classy shopping mall. We took an escalator to the second level where two of my favourite local watering holes are right across from each other. I glanced at Eva, waiting for her to make her choice. Turned out it had nothing to do with the prawns in salt at Gordon Biersch or the pizza on surfboards at Don Ho's. Eva's choice lay with a more delectable entrée: Men.

Her face lit up when she a row of sailors in dress whites lined up at Don Ho's bar, not that she mentioned the attraction outright as we entered. Eva was too classy to do that. She focused on the thatched roof, the split bamboo ceilings, and the tablecloths made from pareau wraps before she let her eyes rove over the sailors sucking up the Mai Tais that Don Ho's is famous for.

"Hawaiian kitsch at its finest," Eva said. "I met Don Ho once at a benefit. The *Gazette* co-sponsored it. "The man was drop-dead gorgeous with charisma that wouldn't quit, even in his seventies. People forget that Don Ho was an Air Force pilot before he became a famous singer—but that's why military guys feel so comfortable here."

I waited for a table as Eva worked her way down the row. In three minutes she had the sailors laughing; in five, they were on their feet, kissing her cheek, as she waved farewell and flounced toward me. Five minutes of flirting had turned her life around.

Meanwhile, I'd found us a table out on the water's edge, ordered a Drambuie for myself and a chardonnay for her. I studied a school of fish darting around a patch of coral spotlighted in the lights from the bar.

Eva's face glowed as I seated her. "Three of them are submariners from USS Cheyenne….fired one of the first Tomahawks in Operation Iraqi Freedom. Two of them are from the destroyer O'Kane. Those boys launched nineteen Tomahawks in the Shock and Awe Campaign. "

I shook my head. "I should have known you went in for war, Eva."

"My dad was a ship's electrician," Eva said. "We've always supported the troops, even when we didn't go along with the politics."

"So you didn't go along with the politics?"

"Don't get me started," Eva snarled. "We can't fault the military for the debacle in Iraq." She syphoned a few drops of her wine onto her tongue.

"You were a school teacher, Eva. How did you get into newspapers?" I had switched to what I thought was an innocuous topic, unaware that I had just grabbed the third rail in the Haverhill case.

"I started on a suburban daily in Pennsylvania," Eva said. "Randy was winding up his doctorate at Wharton, a fabulous opportunity—one that I had engineered for him, by the way. But Penn is a nation unto itself. There was nowhere for me to work. So I took this newspaper job. I never had such fun in my life. In three years I was managing the newsroom." Eva said. "The paper did these personnel seminars on how to avoid stress. I was supposed to attend. I refused. I don't *get* stress, I hand it out. That's what I told them." She sipped her drink, musing. "Now I can't believe I said that. Maybe the Big C is payback."

"Don't be so hard on yourself, Eva."

"My star reporter was Sally Wightman. Sally is now the political beat reporter for the Washington Bureau of the *Wall Street Journal*. Sally would never be there, except I wrote her this glowing recommendation. It was my way of saving face." Eva *made* a face as she said this. "Sally Wightman. There's a tita for you."

Eva sipped her chardonnay and shuddered. "I was this rising star on a suburban daily and Sally was fresh out of college. Sally was jealous of me. She wanted my life...and she got it. I had it all: a husband people admired, a power job, sons who were academic superstars, a period home in the elite section of town. Little did Sally realise that this brilliant guy I was married to was a faculty philanderer."

I reached across the table and patted the back of her hand, trying to calm her down, but Eva ranted on: "I brought Sally to Honolulu the first time we were here. I thought she was following *me*. I was so flattered she'd leave the mainland for *me*."

Eva set her wine glass on the table with a flourish. What I read in this move was, she felt like throwing it, but was too classy to do anything so operatic. Her delivery was operatic enough: "How dare they do it to *me? Me* of all people."

"Randy?" My gut pinched.

"Randy and Sally," Eva said. Pain stained her face. "That bastard. Randy was nothing before I met him. He was a prep school dweeb. I was Randy's social studies teacher. Oh yes, he was brilliant, but he didn't have it together. I divorced the stick I was married to and eloped to Reno with Randy the day he turned eighteen. I was thirty two years old at the time."

"Wait a minute." I was stunned. My back stabbed me at its weak point, a wakeup call: *Madam P. you've tricked me. You old tita, you've been tricking me for my whole life.* I swallowed a shot. Drambuie. One big icy sweet cold shot: I let it sear my gullet as it slid down. Maybe I wanted it to numb my nervous system? My good friend Randy Haverhill had paid for his brilliant career with a family life that had to have been a shambles? It took awhile before I could say anything in response.

Finally, after my vocal cords had warmed up enough such that I could speak again, I said to Eva: "My sister Emmy and I...we were five years younger than Randy. We hung out with Randy when he'd let us. We thought he never dated. He said his parents were so out of it they wouldn't let him. Meanwhile he's *doing* the teacher? And you, Eva, were his *teach*?"

"It's okay, John. It's all right." She reached across the table, patted the back of my hand. Obviously, she'd read the shock that I thought I'd kept off my face.

"That's what the other kids would have said." Eva took another sip of her wine and she was through, except to toy with the straw she'd asked for. "Randy was in an exclusive group of five students I prepped. I got all of them outstanding scholarships at big mainland campuses. I got Randy into Harvard as an undergrad and then into Wharton."

Eva looked around to see if anyone was listening, then continued: "But way before that, I tutored Randy in the most *liberal* of the arts, I admit it. Randy was a very fast learner on that score. In no time he was calling the shots in our sex life. He wanted to play. He was into sex toys and filmy lingerie. I went along with his fantasies, mostly what he read about in *Playboy*, but that stuff was never a turn-on for me."

I was aghast. "Eva, do you not realize that if you had done such a thing these days, you might well have wound up in *prison*?" She waved her hand, swatting away my protest. In her own mind Eva's own case was nothing like that of Mary Kay Letourneau. Or any other of the latest school teacher/seductress cases on tabloid TV.

"Oh yes, I was Randy's lover," Eva said. "And his teacher." In the dark bar I couldn't read the colour of Eva's eyes, but I could clearly view the earnestness in their expression. "I admit it, yes. But you have to understand. I also *mothered* Randy. His own mother spent every drop of energy she had nursing his father. His father had M.S., you know, and at the time there was absolutely nothing they could do."

I found myself nodding my head. "Henrietta Haverhill was a saint. Hattie Haverhill was devoted to her husband. That's what Mama Hana said of her."

"Hattie Haverhill was devoted to her husband at the expense of her son. Randy was a lost boy, starved for attention," Eva smirked. "I gave it to him, and how."

"But still, I can't see how you got away with it. Honolulu's a tropical fish bowl and the Haverhills were golden koi."

"Oh, there were rumours." Eva took an abstemious sip of her drink. "In fact, I insisted Randy take out a girl who invited him to the prom. He swore to me he never did anything after the dance when Miss Melinda made a grab for his zipper." An odd look crossed Eva's face. "In hindsight...maybe Randy was two timing me even then?" Her voice trailed off. She thought about it, shook her head. "No, I can't believe it. I won't. I believe Randy was true to me. That's what is so wonderful about the love of a young man. A young man loves with his whole heart."

Eva looked weary then. I signalled for our check. We sat in strained silence listening to the wash of waves on a beach bleached white in the lights from the bar. Or at least Eva did. I was busy running through the implications of what she had said. Suppose Toby knew all of this? Suppose the police already knew? Here was the motive for murder straight out of some Greek tragedy.

The check came. I tossed some bills on the table. "Ready, Eva?"

She pouted then, a big-eyed keiki in a dress-up turban. "I hate to leave, John. I have nothing to look forward to but a long night on a feeding tube worrying about Toby."

I checked my cell phone again. No message from Maya. It had been twenty four hours since I'd heard from her. She had to be in one royal snit. "You call it, hon. I'm okay. Harlan hasn't buzzed me with more orders. I'm good for another drink if you want one."

"Eiswein," Eva said, brightening.

"Never heard of it."

"Gordon Biersch will have it," Eva said.

THIRTY-EIGHT

Gordon Biersch is the Honolulu rendition of the West Coast microbrew chain. Biersch's combines sixteenth century German brewing techniques with twentieth century steel tanks. The décor leans to the utilitarian as well, what with the exposed piping and the industrial lamps. In The Aloha Tower establishment, the industrial leanings are softened by the tropical ambiance, the native woods, the plants, and the sea air blowing in. Fearing that Eva might catch a cold on the deck, I suggested that we take a seat inside, but she nixed that, made for the deck bar instead, and snuggled into her pashima wrap.

"What do you have in a white eiswein?" she asked the waitress.

"Riesling or Vidal Blanc."

"The Riesling, please."

I ordered a Marzen, brewed on the premises. Pure beer the way German law decreed: malted barley, hops, yeast and water. No additives.

"Fill me in," I said.

"I'm certain that Randy didn't make a move on her." Eva had a faraway look in her eyes. She was gazing into the distant past.

"The waitress?"

"*Melinda*," Eva snapped. Her tone suggested I was a dullard who couldn't keep up with the plot in Eva's soap opera. "Melinda couldn't figure out why Randy didn't have the hots for her. That's how we got caught."

"Ah, yes, Melinda." We were back in prep school, Randy's Punahou days, which, as it turned out, were way hotter than mine had ever been.

"Randy kept telling Melinda that I picked him up for the tutorials because I was the dutiful teacher saving his mother the trip. Finally, Melinda got suspicious and followed us. She ratted us out to Randy's mother. The Haverhills had a hissy fit and went to the principal. But you know these high schools. They weren't going to oust the academic coach who was getting such results."

Eva adjusted her wrap. A group of tourists in flower leis settled at the next table. Eva lowered her voice and continued. "My students loved me, even Melinda, the nosy little tita. I got Melinda a full scholarship to one of those seven sisters schools where half the students were lesbians even then. Melinda's parents were so busy looking at the full ride I got their daughter that they had no idea what I was really doing to her." Eva closed her eyes. Her face was suffused with pleasure.

"It was sooo…hasty with Randy. So intense. So dangerous, The secrecy of it. That made it all the more…" Her eyes popped open. "But let me assure you, it wasn't just the sex. Randy had this beautiful mind and it was such a pleasure for me to groom him for bigger things, for the grand things that I could see would come to me." Eva paused, eyes widened. "Did I say *me*?"

"Maybe you viewed Randy as your ticket to bigger things, Eva."

"I believed in Randy's potential. I risked my relationship with my own sons because I believed in him."

"How so?"

"The Haverhills. They couldn't very well publicly expose my relationship with their precious son. So they went to my husband Nelson and tattled. They offered to back Nelson in court if he moved to take my boys away from me."

Our drinks arrived. Eva's eiswein was served in an aperitif glass. She took one sip and set it down. "Perfect," she said, eyes closed. "I first discovered eiswein while we were on ski trips to the Alps when we lived in Paris. "Have a taste, John."

I sipped. "Intense," I said.

"Bliss in a bottle, the Germans like to say."

"What is it?"

"Eiswein is made from frozen grapes. The best eiswein has some acidity to it. The acidity accounts for the crisp finish."

"Uh huh," I said. When wine buffs went on about *finish*, I was done for. Fortunately, my Marzen arrived. I could indulge my sweet tooth on the stuff. "Marzen," I said, waving my stein. "Mildly butterscotch in flavour with a banana *finish*. Try it, Eva?"

"Later, maybe. I'm afraid I wouldn't taste my eiswein." She was radiant, face glowing in the dusky light of the deck lamps. "Eiswein is my idea of what the ancients meant when they talked about ambrosia."

"Ambrosia," I snorted. "The drink of lesser gods. Now Madam Pele, she's the real thing. Madam prefers *gin*." Eva laughed and took a hearty swig of her eiswein. Then she returned to her moment.

"You have to realise, John. You have to know that if Nelson had done as the Haverhills asked, that would have been the end of Randy and me. My children came first, always have." Eva took another sip, rolled it on her tongue and we sat silently, contemplating the crackle of the surf. By the light of the bar on the water, I watched a school of tiny fish holding a formation in the backwash while Eva's racy memories imposed dramatic tension on a placid scene.

"I have to say this for Nelson. He was decent about it. He told the Haverhills he would never do such a thing to the mother of his children. He told the Haverhills to go fuck themselves. Nelson was very hurt when I divorced him. He didn't understand it. He never understood me. I eloped with Nelson at age eighteen. He was headed to the mainland to play sports. I think he could have been a pro golfer, but Vietnam got in the way. Nelson's number came up. He could have gotten a deferment in thirty seconds but Nelson had to be a patriot. He wrecked his knee in the Mekong Delta and that killed his athletic career."

The waitress came around. I asked for our check.

Eva went on: "Nelson was your typical embittered veteran. He chose to come back here to Honolulu and went into auto sales. I just couldn't stand it. Nelson had no ambition other than to make a lot of money selling cars and to hang out at the country club. I wanted Nelson to do something with his life. He could have gone into politics. His family was well known. He wouldn't hear of it. Fuck the country club. I wanted to be in the world of ideas."

Eva's face was haggard. I felt guilty. I'd let her stay too long. I took care of the tab and walked her out and She leaned on me on the escalator ride down to where a valet brought her BMW around. I checked my cell phone. Not a word from Maya. It was close to 10:00 PM Honolulu time, but the sun would be rising on the Serenoa Ranch. Would a wakeup call be in order? By the time I dropped Eva off on Round Top drive, I'd have time to decide.

THIRTY-NINE

We headed Diamond Head along Ala Moana Boulevard, but on a whim, I swung into the parking lot of the Maritime Center next door. We sat looking at the Center's pride tied to the dock, the magnificent relic, the Falls of Clyde, the only completely outfitted eighteenth century four-masted sailing vessel left in the world.

"Isn't she gorgeous?" Eva said. "I first brought Toby to see the Clyde when he was six. Then we read Robert Louis Stevenson together. Toby was ecstatic." Eva was silent for a time. We watched the romantic sweep of the rigging under the city lights. I tuned into KINE, the Hawaiian music station. Keali'i Reichel was doing a number from one of his greatest albums, *E O Mai*, combining the sonorous Hawaiian chant with contemporary sound.

"Fabulous, isn't he?" Eva sighed. "Toby adores him, has every one of his albums."

"Every time I hear that lilting voice of his, I feel it," I said, rubbing my arms. This was no exception. I let the music play softly and the singer's passion stirred more of Eva's memories. Her voice became a riff on the music. "Oh, I adored Randy and he loved me. I am sure of it. In our early days together, I possessed Randy's whole heart, don't you know?"

"By the time we hit the academic big-time, Randy had already done post graduate work at The Sorbonne in Paris. I had a side job translating Baudelaire into English, Randy began to win academic accolades and got published. I edited everything for him. I helped him develop his writing style."

"I didn't realise."

"His editor tried to horn in, but I wouldn't have it." She sighed heavily. "We spent four years in Paris and soon Randy developed this European attitude toward marriage: it's okay to fool around on the side. He'd take me to nightclubs in Paris where couples copulated in nets over the heads of the diners and the cum fell down on our heads." Eva made a face. "Disgusting, but the French? Hah. They think we Americans are prudes. Maybe so. Maybe I am a prude, but Randy loved that kinky stuff."

"Problem was, it was never a turn on for me. Randy fucked a black whore on our seventh anniversary and I was really weary of his antics, but I loved the life we had. We were invited to A-list parties. We dined at The White House. If I needed to verify some policy question I could call up the Chairman of the Council of Economic Advisors and get an exclusive. I met Samuelson himself. I didn't want to give up on the marriage because it meant the loss of a high profile lifestyle."

"So the marriage lasted how long?"

"Way too long." Eva stared out over the water. Laughter was drifting toward us from a couple on the sidewalk closer to the vessel. "I knew I would have to divorce Randy, but I took my time getting out. I produced Toby at age forty-nine. I knew we had to have a child together. How else could I lay claim to Randy's assets?"

I stared at Eva. She had to be in her mid-sixties.

"Eva you still look like a keiki," I blurted.

She brushed away tears. "Fucking bastard, ruined my life. He'd have been tenured at Columbia by now. Or maybe a department chairman at Wharton or Yale. I'd have been on *The New York Times* or maybe *The Wall Street Journal.* Instead? We're right back in Honolulu. Nowhere. Right where we started."

"Yes, but what about the Pacific Rim Institute?"

Eva rolled her eyes. "The Pacific Rim Institute was a setup." She shook her head. "A graceful way to kick a famous economist out of Eastern academia."

"Yes, but Eva. Randolph Haverhill returned to Hawaii to lead the building of a new economy on The Pacific Rim," I said, "He aimed to forge an alliance between the U.S. and Asia that would set the tone for the decades ahead."

"Who said that?"

"I read it in your paper. In Randy's obit."

"What would they know?" Eva closed her eyes, listened to Reichel, his voice soaring like a tern on the trades. At the station break she shifted in her seat. "I negotiated a cushy settlement. I never had to go to court. If I had, Randy's career would have been over right then. I left Randy so little to live on that he had to marry that shave ice of a Hillary for her deep pockets. Her daddy is right there to bankroll the Pacific Rim Institute. I can't imagine Randy married Hillary for their sex life. Hillary isn't his type."

"So your own paper didn't do any digging?"

"Hah! When I came in as city editor I had to kick their asses into gear. They hadn't seen a Pulitzer in twenty years when I arrived. Now we have two. I'll tell you all about Randy B. Haverhill, the story the paper *didn't* print: Randy wasn't tenured because he seduced the wife of the president of...well, never mind. Let's just say that the president of this major Ivy League university is a great academician. I adored him. A decent man as well. He found Randy the Pacific Rim deal. I'm sure he wouldn't have bothered except the university shares in the royalties on Randy's three non-fiction best sellers."

Eva tossed the turban she'd been wearing into the carryall at her feet and ran her fingers through her bedraggled hair. "Oh, Joan, I wish you could feel this air as I do, this fresh breeze, the sweet night chill. There's nothing like a major illness to make you live, really live again, these small pleasures, I have to tell you." She was quiet for a time, seemed lost in the beat of the music, then she said: "I'm the executor of Randy's literary estate, by the way. I got a call from the publisher this morning. He offered his condolences and a contract. They are rushing out a three volume edition. Hardcover. Foil stamped dust jacket. That rotter Randy Bishop Haverhill is now a literary icon. Did you see his obit in *The New York Times?*"

I shook my head.

"*The New York Times* never said one word about the fact that nine women came forward in support of my divorce action, including the mother of my niece Lani. Nine women I had lined up to testify, including my own sister-in-law. Nine women were prepared to swear in court that the big shot professor and renowned economist had hit on every one of them."

I stared at Eva.

"Oh, don't you go giving me that look, John Spyer. He wasn't getting any at home. Is that what you think? Well, I can assure you, that simply was not the case. If it were, I wouldn't be sitting here with throat cancer right now."

"For a tita who never made the A team, Eva, you sure do play hardball."

"Damn right," Eva said. In the rearview mirror, enough moonlight beamed down on Eva that I could read the smirk on her face: "Not only did I clean Randy out of his academic salary and benefits, but I also have his literary royalties. Hillary doesn't. She has no claim on the best part of Randy Haverhill. The best part of Randy is his brain."

I fired up the BMW. The music pulsed and I stared at Eva.

"*Was* his brain," she corrected herself.

By the time we hit Round Top Drive, Eva was snoring. In repose her sharp features had lost their fierce expression, gone skeletal. Just looking at Eva gave me the shivers and the stories Eva told reverberated through my head, and as we hit the sharpest curves, a scratchy voice leaped into my head.

"Oh yes, John Spyer. Eva Haverhill made Randy what he was. Every which way, brah. Ha ha ha ha ha. "What Eva makes, she also destroys. Yeah? Spyer, son? Bring Madam some gin?"

FORTY

I t was after ten when I arrived back at Duke's place on Leahi. I gave Em a shot of gas to encourage her up the steep driveway, and then I caught something not quite right about the place. A light was on in the kitchen. I didn't leave the light on in the kitchen. Why would I leave the light on? Cousin Duke must have come home early. That was it. But as I rolled Em into her stall in the garage, Duke's car wasn't there. I left the garage door open and took it easy heading to the back door.

The shades were drawn and this was disconcerting. Maybe I should have drawn the shades, but I hadn't. And then a shape bobbed behind the blinds and I heard music playing. Duke and a girlfriend? It just had to be and then the shadow of a shapely arm swept across the blind and the torso twisted in a language all its own, the language being Cublish.

I tried the back door. It was locked from the inside. I rapped on it, gently, not to frighten her, to let her know I was onto her.

"Maya?" The salsa beat halted. The footsteps approached.

"John? You there?"

"I'm here and so are you, love. Praise Madam."

She opened the door, stepped back, gave me that glance she does so well, sidelong it is, the tease, the come on. "Well, *alo'*, Mr. Spyer, I thought you never might get here." She raised her arm as if to study her watch. "Some date you are."

I had to laugh. She slid into my open arms and we rocked each other around in the miniscule kitchen and I pulled her off her feet as she clung to my neck and I buried my nose in her thick hair. Maya's heavy hair has a mind of its own and it smells fresh as sun-baked laundry on a line. My fingers played the hollow in her throat so that I could feel her voice, feel her laugh, training my fingers to remember this, how she felt when she talked.

"The airline was so nice when I *esplain* how I had to come quickly."

"Uh huh," I murmured. I waltzed her into the living room and put her down on the sofa and got busy tasting her explanation, forcing her to talk around my lips.

"There has been a terrible murder of my friend the economist and maybe the airline heard of this on CNN?"

I pulled back, laughing. They waived the change fee on the ticket?"

"Decent of them," she said. "It helps to be the flyer of the frequency."

"Why didn't you call me?"

"Why didn't you call me?" she mimicked, making a face. "Talk to Puttnam Jorgenson you said, and so I did."

I picked her up, carried her to the bedroom. "If we are going to bicker, Maya, we'll have to do it on the horizontal. It has been a rough couple of days."

Maya and I were in the same bed, and this was bliss, and if I'd had my way we'd have stayed there until starvation set in. But as it happened, we shared the bed but not the time zone. Maya's internal clock was hours ahead of mine, which is why she awakened me too soon.

"John, you have to come now," Maya pleaded, shaking me.

"Come back to bed, Maya," I murmured, my tongue thick with sleep.

"First you get up," Maya purred, "just for a few minutes and then we'll see about a little nap."

She sat on the edge of the bed, her fingers cajoling beneath the sheet. She gave me a squeeze where it got my attention and I made a grab for her but she was gone, giggling, and the chase was on. I seized a towel and charged after her. Maya raced out the back door upsetting Kiki who stood up in her cat bed out on the sleeping porch. Kiki spat and yowled and hunched her back, tail curled down and I couldn't blame Miss Kitty her hissy, not one bit.

I followed Maya up the weathered stairs barefoot taking care to step lightly. The old stairs were full of slivers. My skin rippled in the brisk predawn air. The morning was black as a bruise, illuminated as it was by the glow of Honolulu's city lights.

Maya had been up for a while. The buttons on her cell phone glowed on the small table beside a deck chair. She must have called her ranch in Florida already. She'd also made a pot of Cuban coffee. When she handed me a small cup of it, the milky whiff combined with the bitter black beans woke me up, let me tell you.

"Café con leche? In Honolulu?"

"I brought it with me, silly," she said. "Spyer loves thee café Cubano. No?"

I tested it with the tip of my tongue, having scalded it more than once on prior occasions. Finding it perfect, I proceeded shamelessly to drain the teensy cup.

"Ah," Maya said. Now you are awake, no? So take a look here, I want you to see."

I stared out to sea, where dawn had come up like the proverbial thunder and saw it through Maya's eyes, the angry haze on the horizon. The sea was purple at the horizon line, blending into striations of azure closer in shore. Long white combs of waves came foaming in, and Maya was right. It was weird, and it was spectacular in an ominous sort of way.

Maya wore a midnight blue satin kimono that barely covered her okole, and I put down the cup and pulled her close to me and copped some feels under that skimpy slick rig. The top of her head fits neatly under my chin. Her thick black hair tickled my bare chest and her warmth was a comfort in the sultry morning breeze.

"I never saw such a morning, ever," Maya said. "This, I hope, is no hurricane?"

"Ah ha. Not to worry, my dear. This is no Katrina, but you are right, it is special. The surf is way up, and when the surf foams like this on our side of the island what you are seeing, my love, is the opening of the winter season on Oahu."

"Winter? In *thee* middle of *Septiembre*?"

"*Exactamente*," I said. 'It'll be rough as hell on Waikiki. Every sane surfer knows that on a morning like this the place to be is back in bed." My ploy fell on deaf ears. I should have known better. *Sane* is not a word to use around Maya.

"So?" A wicked grin rearranged her face. "What do the crazy surfers do?"

FORTY-ONE

Within minutes we headed out of the house in our jogging togs. We cut through the public gardens across the street and trotted along Kapi'olani Boulevard, joining a throng of early risers who must have felt the special energy of this day. We looped the enormous Kapi'olani Park with Diamond Head, a skulking dark shadow hovering at our backs. As we reached the Outrigger Canoe Club, I slowed down to explain to Maya that this was the place where Randy Haverhill and Toby had had their last morning together.

"Madre de Dias," Maya murmured, crossing herself, Though she'll sometimes rail against the established church, Maya is a devout woman. She stopped right at the Outrigger's modest entrance where the tiki torches flickered in the dawn's purple light and murmured a prayer for the newly departed.

We resumed our trek along the sidewalk atop the seawall and quickly absorbed the energy thrown off by the pulse of the heavy surf beneath our feet. Our strides lengthened and our steps matched and Maya's face glowed, suffused with sea spume as we watched the shoreline where youngsters with surfboards appeared; but these were local kids, savvy enough to give the big surf its due. Mostly they stood in awe, like sentries, boards pointed upward like spears.

The story was quite different in the heart of Waikiki. Conditioned surfers with decades of experience stood down out of respect for the waves, watching green tourists take the plunge. Already the lifeguards were at work rescuing the unwary. For a moment I was back there with them riding herd on the tourists as the three of us had done, Randy, cousin Duke and myself, back in our glorious beach boy days, and that was how Maya managed to slip out of my grasp.

She dashed for the surf and leaped in and there was nothing to be done but to go after her and we had our few minutes of body surfing before I could feel a tremor in the water. I looked around. An enormous wave was coming in and I shouted to Maya, who, fortunately, is a powerful swimmer. We swam furiously before it slammed us and dragged us under and we took a good grinding before we were tumbled around like two pebbles and spewed out on the sand.

I found Maya down the shoreline streaked with mud and her hair in her face and pulled her to feet. My back spasmed and I gritted my teeth and tried to hide it, but Maya read the look on my face and rushed into my arms. "*Perdon*, John, So sorry. I shouldn't have done that. I don't know what got into me."

"I don't know what gets into you, either, Maya." I kissed her forehead and released her, not feeling so friendly.

We had to shower the mud off ourselves at the surfboard wash stand and it was time to head back. Maya kept mum all the way as far as the snack bar at the edge of the park where we stopped for coffee and malasadas. It was time to consider what to do with the day.

"Don't feel you have to entertain me," Maya said. "I want to see all of it, the museum, the gardens and make *thee tors—*"

I kissed the raw patch on her shoulder to make it better. "Tours? I said. "First we'll drive up The Pali Highway. You'll see the Haverhill mansion in the Nuuanu Valley, mine and Randy's old neighbourhood."

"You're sure I won't be in the way?" Maya said. "You have to save this Haverhill boy. You are still a beach boy at heart, still doing the rescue *nombre*. No?" She tossed me that sideways glance and I was her slave once more.

"I'm taking you to meet a real Hawaiian tutu, Maya, a wise old lady. She lives next door to the Haverhill estate. I'm hoping she'll help us find a woman who may have witnessed Randy's murder."

Dowsett is a horseshoe of a street with two entrances off The Pali Highway. I took the lower leg, where Queen Emma Preschool is situated in an old mansion on the mauka side of the street. The Haverhill estate was up the road a block at number 68. I parked next door at number 54, a cottage by comparison.

"Is this where you grew up?" Maya said, reaching for the windbreaker that she'd brought along at my insistence.

"This is Lia Manalolo's hale. Tutu Lia's house."

"Tutu Lia Manalolo? From Honolulu?" Maya's voice went singsong and her fingers fluttered in a mock hula.

I pulled her close and knotted my hands in her shoulder-length hair. "Okay, doll. You are too funny. I forgive you your stupid surfing tricks."

I parked on the road, careful not to pull Em too close to the curb. That's because there are no curbs to speak of, seeing as how the Nuuanu Valley stream meanders through the neighbourhood. Deep channels are carved along Dowsett. I knew better than to put one of Em's wheels over the edge and I warned Maya to be careful when she got out of the car. We had already had our spill for the day. Maya was feeling no pain but my back was burning.

Tutu Lia's hale is a two-story, cream-coloured affair with blue trim sheltered under a sprawling banyan. Her property is set off from the Haverhill estate by the enormous cypress hedge that surrounds the compound.

The Haverhill manse can't be seen from Dowsett, or anywhere else in the neighbourhood, for that matter. It's a parcel of some five acres. Tutu Lia's lot and several others are part of the original Haverhill land, sold off by the Haverhills, probably to pay Walter's medical bills.

"I don't see Lia's car. She's not back from church yet, so we have time for a tour of the hood," I said.

A hint of rain arrived on the breeze; there were clouds on The Pali. The sun was high but not onerous as we walked along, hand in hand, listening to the cooing of the doves above the echo of traffic drumming on the impaling green spires in the distance.

"This is so lovely, John. Is this the way it was when you lived here?"

"Pretty much." We arrived at the corner of Dowsett and Lopeka. "See that house with the bougainvillaea over the front gate? That was where my sister Emmy's friend Melissa Tan lived. Lopeka was the street where Randy and I came face to face with the ghost dog one dark night. It was in the fall around this same time of year. I remember the marbled clouds and a full moon."

"A ghost dog?" Maya's eyes widened and her lips stretched down.

"A ghost dog runs in the Nuuanu Valley, as any Hawaiian will tell you. Tutu Lia used to warn us about it when she had us over for cookies after school. Ominous things could happen to boys who crossed paths with the ghost dog, which was why boys ought to stay home and not go sneaking out at night after their parents were in bed."

"So you had to sneak out to find the ghost dog?" Maya said, smiling big.

"I don't remember what we were doing that night, but I do remember the dog. Randy and I saw this ghost dog come racing out of Lopeka. It made straight for us."

"Did you jump in the stream?"

"We made for the Haverhill driveway. It wasn't gated back then. We raced down Randy's drive and hid in the backyard, behind the roots of this big kapok tree. The kapok tree has enormous roots above ground like the flying buttresses on a cathedral. We hid behind one of the big roots and fired grenades from the cannonball tree at the ghost dog until it ran away."

Maya was giving me that look of hers. "Ghost dogs and kapok and cannonballs. One big story, *no es?*"

"I kid you not, Maya."

We followed Dowsett and listened to the burbling Nuuanu stream. Where Dowsett curves into Alika, I was home, a couple of blocks away from the Haverhill place.

I pulled Maya close as we stood in front of a two-story plantation house with deep porches all around set way off the road in a monkey pod grove. I stared up at the second floor dormers. Emmy had had the room that looked over Alika, and I had the one at the other end, facing into The Pali peaks. Not much had changed at our old place. The most recent owner had freshened the pale grey paint. The banyan near the street had been trimmed but the koi pond was intact, fed by the Nuuanu stream, which meandered through the yard as it always had.

I looked up at the window where Emmy's room had been. A curtain fluttered there and I felt my forearms ripple, but I turned away, not wanting to see what wouldn't be. Emmy would never stick out her head and toss the shaka sign, which would have meant she had gathered her gear and was on the way down to wherever we were going. She would not dash down the stairs and sweep through the garden gate and would never again insist on driving. Emmy would never again jump behind the wheel of Em the Mustang and I could not bring myself to stand around and see how this scene would never unfold...

"What is it?" Maya said. "John? Are you okay?"

"Tutu Lia must be home by now. We need to get going."

FORTY-THREE

I rang Tutu Lia's doorbell, setting off torrents of barking within the house. Finally came a shuffle of steps behind the door. A shadow fell across the peephole. The door opened a crack. A wizened old lady edged the door open. Behind her a one-eyed white mongrel whined, wagging his tail.

"Tutu Lia? It's me. John Spyer."

The old lady beamed, her ruined face all smiles. "Well, Johnny." She flung the door wide, engulfed me in an enormous hug and stepped back to look up at me.

"I haven't seen you since when." She peered around me at Maya with a startled look on her face.

"Tutu Lia Manalolo, this is my friend from Florida, Maya Menecal."

Tutu Lia embraced Maya as well. "Please forgive me staring, Maya. For a moment you reminded me so much of…. "

Tutu Lia caught my warning look but had her say anyway. "When I saw you I thought I was seeing John's sister Emmy. Now there was one beautiful girl."

Maya stared at me and I shrugged. Tutu Lia was an astute woman. She had nailed us in an instant, Maya and me. There was something of my sister in Maya, and this was why I found her so compelling—and so exasperating. But why was it that I had not seen this for myself? I was speechless, could not respond and so Maya covered for me.

"Emmy must have been lovely," Maya said lightly, "being John's twin."

The dog nudged Maya's knees. "*Alo'* pooch, and who are you?" Maya said, stooping down and letting the dog lick the back of her hand.

"Hone! Your manners," Tutu said to the dog.

"Hone?" Maya said, much to the dog's delight. What means Hone?"

"Sweet," Lia said.

"Think of honey," I said.

"Hone is my sweetie," Lia said.

Maya got down on her haunches. She rubbed behind the dog's ears and combed his back with her fingers, then held his head still between her hands as she surveyed his damaged eye, sewn shut. "What happened?"

"Hone's eye gone to cancer," Tutu said.

"Hone, I'm so sorry," Maya said. She gave his head a rub and stood up. "Will your doggie be okay?"

"I hope so," Tutu said. "Hone and I been together a long time. I don't know what I'd do without him." She waved us inside. "Please come in, sit awhile. I got something in the oven."

In keeping with local tradition, we slipped out of our shoes and left them on Tutu Lia's doorstep.

Tutu's thick hair had gone grey and she wore it in one long braid down her back. She was wearing one of the long muu muus she favours and it swayed gracefully as she listed along on her stiff knees aided by a cane with a bottom like a tripod. Tutu Lia took Maya's arm and the women went down an entry hall festooned with photos of youngsters. Tutu Lia had been a widow ever since I'd known her. She had den-mothered various nieces, nephews and cousins from the outer islands come to Oahu to get their education.

The kitchen was the traditional sort with a big table in the middle covered with an antique oil cloth cracked here and there. Hawaiian quilting with its stylized floral designs blanketed every small appliance. As usual, the kitchen was overheated and the house smelled of fresh baking.

"Coconut macaroons?" I said hopefully.

"Macadamia nut."

Tutu got a pitcher of her lilikoi lemonade out of the fridge and pulled a tray out of the oven. "I bake for the Women's Shelter every Sunday," she said.

"You need a taster, Tutu?"

She laughed. "This one was the operator," she said to Maya. "He would never beg for a cookie. Not Johnny. He would offer his expertise. Sit down, sit down, you two."

Tutu passed a plate of the macadamias, and Maya, effusive in her praise, asked for the recipe.

Tutu Lia rambled on to Maya about Mama Hana and Dad, the assistant city prosecutor. How the loss of Emmy changed his life.

"We all changed," I said.

"And now we lose Randy Haverhill," Lia said. "I don't know what this world is coming to."

"I'm helping Toby Haverhill," I said.

"The police came by. They asked me about Randy's boy. I couldn't help them."

"I need to find out about a certain shotgun, Lia. It seems to have been in the Haverhill house. Toby and Eva both say it wasn't Randy's."

"It was probably Walter's. I think the Haverhill men used to hunt birds on their country ranch. Walter wouldn't have done any hunting after he got that disease, yeah? Walter had M.S. for years before he became an invalid. Hattie devoted her time to Walter's care. She didn't have much energy to devote to little Randy. The boy became very bookish at an early age."

"And then Eva came along?"

"Hattie thought Eva was wonderful for Randy. She was a mixed blessing, I guess." Lia poured out the lemonade, sat down, and passed a plate of cookies. "Eva told Hattie that Randy was brilliant. Eva took Randy under her wing. She tutored him for the college exams. Hattie had no idea what else Eva was tutoring her boy in, of course. Today, there are laws against such things."

"What did Hattie do?"

"Once she found out, she went to Nelson, Eva's ex. She tried to get Nelson to take some action. She told Nelson that Eva's behaviour was bad for Randy and bad for her two boys as well. It was, too."

"Eva's boys have done well enough," I said, "One rocket scientist, one medical doctor."

"Careers," Hattie scoffed. "That's haole talk, John Spyer. Careers are not the whole man. Those boys were extremely embarrassed about their mother's behaviour. They resented Randy."

"Eva told me that Nelson wouldn't bring charges."

"To tell you the truth, Nelson needed a nurse himself. He wasn't about to take over as father to his own children. He wasn't physically capable of doing such a thing," Tutu Lia said. "It would have been hard to take those two boys away from Eva at any rate. It just wasn't done in those days, especially not in this state. The Hawaiian tradition, you know, take love where you find it. Eva might have been a strange one in her love life, but she was an attentive and good mother to her children."

"An attentive and good mother to Randy as well."

"Eva knew that Randy was emotionally needy. She told me that herself."

"I didn't know you talked to her."

"Oh, goodness yes." A puzzled expression crossed her face. "I know you forget those days, John. Once Emmy was gone? We didn't see much of you after that. You spent most of your time on Maui, over Lahaina way with your Mama Hana's family, yeah?"

I took a pull on the lilikoi lemonade. "Truth to tell, my old man banished me to Lahaina," I blurted out. "Emmy was gone. I was doing lousy at Punahou. All I was good for was ti leaf sliding off the side of Mt. Tantalus in the rainstorms."

"Thrill seeking," Tutu shook her head. "One good way kids get killed."

Maya stared at me. "John. You didn't."

"Not consciously," I said. "Try to find Emmy in the other realm? Not really. I was too confused. We all hoped she was still alive somewhere. Besides, I didn't have the guts."

"*Que es?*" Maya asked Tutu Lia, rattling the ice cubes in her glass. She was covering for me, saving me from any more awkward revelations.

"Lilikoi—passion fruit juice," Lia said.

"*Delicioso,*" Maya said, tapping her glass and we chuckled politely and then sat in awkward silence, finally broken by Tutu Lia, resuming her tale.

"Randy come by see me nearly every afternoon and you too, Johnny, sometimes. Randy would hang around my nephews and nieces. They'd treat him like a little brother. We had a normal household going over here. It wasn't like one sickroom his mama kept next door."

"Eva came around to pick Randy up for tutoring?"

Tutu nodded. "Randy was a junior, maybe. Eva was his social studies teacher. At first Hattie didn't think anything. Randy wasn't the only one Eva coached. So when Hattie found out about them and went down to the school and raised a ruckus, nothing happened. At least at first."

"At second?"

"Walter and Hattie hired a private investigator. They got the goods on Eva. She went out on the quiet. Eva took a job at another private school until word got around. Then Eva was out of teaching for good. After Eva and Randy eloped to the mainland, Eva went into the newspaper business."

"She turned out to be very good at it."

"Even with all the pressure, Eva and Randy carried right on with each other," Lia said. "They seemed to thrive on the disapproval from their families. Randy graduated at the top of his class, gave the graduation address and got a scholarship to Harvard."

"Eva takes credit for the scholarship," I said.

"She wanted Randy all to herself," Tutu Lia said. "Randy turned eighteen a month after graduation and the next thing you know, they eloped to Las Vegas and stayed on the mainland. Randy's mother never got over it. Hattie felt that Randy should have stayed here and gone to the University of Hawaii. She needed his help with Walter. That was what she wanted. So it was no wonder she disinherited Randy. Of course he did inherit the house from his father, being the only remaining Haverhill." Tutu Lia got up and refilled the plate.

I did tasting duty and ate some more.

Tutu Lia went on: "I used to get Christmas cards from them, for the first six or seven years they were married, but Eva outdid herself. Randy became this very famous scholar and... "

"And he went all out for the ladies, shall we say?"

"Such a handsome man. A spellbinding lecturer. The coeds fell all over him. It can't have been easy for Eva."

"I guess not." I shifted in my chair.

"That old bullet wound?" Tutu said.

"I'm sorry Lia. I have to keep moving or it crimps up on me." I rose, explained my mission. "Toby mentioned that someone rushed over to help the morning Randy was shot. A woman in a rain cape. We have to find this woman."

"It wasn't me, I am sorry to say. Hone was having eye surgery Saturday morning. It was a case of the eye going or the dog. We didn't have a choice, did we, pup?" The dog put his head in Lia's lap. She stroked his head. "I was sitting in the waiting room in the animal hospital. I saw the awful news on the TV."

"Toby said this woman had a garden spade with her. She said she would run home for a towel. Do you have any idea who that might be?"

"It wouldn't have been anyone on my side of the street. The Matsudas are on the mainland and Sara Nelis would have been at work. But let me think about it."

"Would you mind if I look around in your yard?"

"Go ahead, John. "You won't find anything where a hand trowel would be of any use, I'm afraid."

"How's that?"

"My plumerias, my cypress, all grown big. Like my children. No keiki coming, even among the plants."

"No grandchildren ready for college yet?"

Tutu made a face. "All the girls, they got careers. Taking their time on the babies."

"They'll be coming, one of these days."

"I hope so. Hone and me, we getting lonely."

"I don't suppose anyone in Randy's household did any gardening?"

Lia shook her head. "It wouldn't have been Hillary, her and her horses. And not Randy, neither. What gardening was done was the garden service. Now Randy's mother, she was the one."

"Into bedding plants?"

"Oh yes, the impatiens, and all those botanicals in the back. That was Hattie's recreation. Hattie would garden while her husband napped. It was the only pleasure Hattie allowed herself."

"Well, Toby must have seen something. He's into guitar picks. I can't believe he'd invent a garden spade."

Tutu Lia struggled to her feet. "Toby is a sweet boy, or seems to be. I never met him, you know."

"That's odd, isn't it?"

"Once Randy married Hillary, things changed. I didn't see no more Randy, no Toby. Oh, Randy did stop to chat sometimes, if he saw me out in the yard; but that was it. They all kept pretty much to themselves over there. Randy may not have wanted Hillary finding out too much about the role Eva played in his past, yeah?"

I pushed away the plate of cookies and set down my drink. "I'm going to take a look around your yard."

"You go right ahead, Johnny." A sly look crossed Lia's face. "That way I can bore Maya with all the old stories."

FORTY-FOUR

I slipped out Tutu Lia's front door, stepped into my loafers and found my trusty flashlight in Em's glove box. Maya stayed on to visit with Lia. From this side of the cypress hedge, the Haverhill house was invisible. At the base of the cypresses on Tutu's side was a woody hedge featuring fat leaves and small white flowers, but Lia was right. There were no small plants that would benefit from a garden spade anywhere on her property. However, someone in the Haverhill house did do some gardening, more so than Tutu realised. I'd seen the garden stuff in the shed under the house when I'd found the shotgun.

I pushed through the woody hedge and made my way through the cypress trees, crossed the Haverhill yard, went up to the stoop and got down on my haunches, taking care to avoid the bloodstain. If Toby was crouched over his father's body, he would have peered through the wrought iron railing. The stoop was so high, the woman who spoke to him had to be tall, as Toby had said. *Going after a towel* this woman had said to Toby. Toby thought she went toward Lia's, and she might well have done that without being seen, since Lia herself had not been at home.

And yet this neighbour lady never returned with a towel. So what was she doing? Then this thought occurred to me: Suppose this neighbour lady was the murderer, having a look at the scene? Suppose she was the stalker? If she'd been having a fling with Randy, perhaps he'd had her at the house. Maybe they trysted in the garden shed. Suppose she took a special glee from using the family shotgun to kill Randy, and then ducked back into the garden shed and put the shotgun back. At that point she picked up a garden trowel from the shed. But why do that? As a way of staying on the scene? Or was it for some other reason? Supposed she had a mission?

I walked back across the lawn, searching. There wouldn't be any tracks to be seen in the thick turf. If this person with the trowel was in fact the murderer, would she have hidden somewhere in the cypress hedge watching the chaotic scene?

I went back to the street and started along the Haverhill side of the hedge, working my way to the back of the yard. The piney smell made me sneeze. I studied the vantage from the cypresses, hunkered down and all but crawled from one tree to the next. Overhead, about sixty feet up, the pointy trees impaled the midday sun. At their bases, the thick foliage harboured cobwebs that plastered my face as I crept along making my way with my flashlight. The beam of light illuminated nothing so sharp as a buried memory deep in my own brain.

I recalled the time Randy and I hid out in this hedge, fleeing Hattie Haverhill's wrath. We'd been wrestling around in the hall and upended a bedpan on the floor runner and the usually distant and distracted Hattie turned wrathful and came after us with a fly swatter.

I arrived at the last cypress tree that was still in the line of sight to the stoop. This was it: the final place where an observer could watch the festivities. It offered a fine view of the show: the arriving ambulance, the TV cameras, the cops guarding the crime scene. Since the cypress hedge was so thick, the observer could not have been seen from the street—or from the murder scene.

I lasered the flashlight beam through the dusty gloom and when I did, there it was, a garden spade. I slipped out from under the hedge, scrolled down to Telly Tabura's number on my cell phone. Telly's gravelly voice bristled onto the line.

"Hey Telly, where are you?"

"Downtown. Doing paperwork."

I asked him to drop everything, come wikiwiki and bring a crime scene tech. I also called in a favour. This was the time. I told Tabura I had something hot and told him what I wanted in return.

"I knew there was a reason I would never get home to bed," he growled.

As I waited, I went to the back alley, along the trail of tall cypresses. Would the police have searched back there? It was likely. If they did, and took pictures, perhaps a car was back there. It may well have still been on the scene while the police assumed the getaway vehicle was parked out on the street.

I made a note of all the vehicles parked there. Lia's decrepit Falcon. A fancy horse trailer. A pickup truck filled with buckets of horse gear. Randy's new Jaguar.

Detective Tabura made it in fifteen minutes, driven by a beat officer. A crime tech and a police photographer came. They took photos; they ran a tape measure from the spade to the stoop. The tool hadn't simply been flung there. It was stuck in the dirt. There was a slight mound, a depression beside it.

Telly paced and swigged his Jamba green as the tech used another garden instrument, a hand fork, to rake through the small mound. He made a few passes before reaching pay dirt. He pulled out a tightly wadded roll of red plastic and shook it out. It was a rain cape.

"So this woman in the cape is no witness—she's the murderer," I said to Telly.

His eyes flashed. For the first time, he seemed to agree with me.

"Maybe," Tabura said. "If there is one woman in one rain cape."

"What's your explanation?"

"Toby didn't talk about no woman such as this in his statement."

I nodded. I knew what Telly was driving at. Suppose the woman in the cape was Toby's invention? Toby might have buried the cape himself.

The tech stowed the rain cape in a paper bag and labelled it.

"Come on Telly, let's go grind. On me."

"Where we going?"

"Twice-a Slice-a. Where else?"

We ordered Toby's ritual pizza, one large Hula Girl. Maya had declined to join us. She had gone with Tutu Lia to some benefit for the Women's Shelter. It was being held at Queen Emma's Summer Residence just down The Pali from Dowsett. Since Queen Em's summer digs was on Maya's list, I told her I'd pick her up after lunch.

"Hold the flowers," Telly said to the waitress, which was how I knew he was in a good mood and he beamed at me. I'd done well. I'd handed him a clue. Telly had come up with the murder weapon in the garden shed thanks to me. Now he had turned up a garden spade and a rain cape. That's how headquarters would perceive the news. In my camp, what had I done for Toby? I'd turned in evidence that got my own client busted, but at least I'd found the rain cape and the garden trowel, supporting Toby's statement about a witness at the scene. But if this witness had buried the rain cape with the garden trowel Toby had seen in her hand, then she had something to hide, and the way I made it, she had to be the murderer.

The detective and I had found a corner out on the deck, under the banyan's shady sprawl. Telly worked on the Jamba. He took a long pull on it and smacked his lips and flicked his damp fingers at little birds standing on the railing staring at us, waiting for crumbs.

"Green slime?" I said. "Algae bloom?"

"Jamba Juice Matcha Green Tea Shot," Tabura said, pushing the label at me. "My son insisted I try the stuff. Some Japanese green tea in it. Intense stuff. A little O.J., a shot of caffeine and some other stuff. My boy said it would revive Dad. It works. I feel less dead than Professor Haverhill."

"Great, Telly." I kept the wince off my face. Hawaiians consider certain seaweed a delicacy, but the colour of this stuff made my molars ache. I couldn't wait to change the subject. "So we know the murder weapon was the shotgun found in the garden shed right on the Haverhill property. We know that Toby saw this woman with the cape over her head and the garden spade in her hand."

"If it was a female," Tabura said. He swirled the Jamba Matcha and chugged down some more.

"Well covered, wearing sunglasses."

"A woman maybe," Tabura said.

"Okay, Telly. Maybe." I said. "At any rate, we can eliminate Toby as a suspect."

Telly's mouth twisted. He dismissed my play with a wave of his hand.

"Think about it, brah," I said. "Toby is on the phone with the dispatcher. He's found hunched over his dad with the knife. So how is he going to bury some rain cape with a garden spade?"

"An accomplice help out," Tabura said. "Kids do crimes with other kids." Telly looked around, tapping his knife on the table. When he saw that no one was on the deck to hear us, he shot me a real zinger: "Or maybe they act out a crime under one parent's influence."

I stared at him. "Eva? You aren't suggesting?"

"Not suggesting. Maybe we got one tip."

"No way."

"It's a lead, Spyer. We follow da leads."

"Never give up, do you, Telly?"

"One slice-a, John?" Tabura said, magnanimous now that he'd aced me again. I took the slice, trying to be gracious, but I had tested too many of Tutu Lia's cookies to be hungry. I had a few bites of the Hula Girl pie and we ate in silence. Telly topped off my irritation by smoking in front of me and I squirmed at his enjoyment as he sucked in the precious smoke and I tried to picture it shrivelling my companion's lungs, but even that didn't relieve my discomfort. Nevertheless, I hid my impatience, waiting for Tabura to have his fun.

Finally, when he'd snubbed out the cig, I called in the favour he owed me. "Okay, Telly, I found you the garden trowel and the rain cape, so where's the photo of the note?"

"Thought you'd never ask, Spyer," Tabura rumbled.

He pulled a brown clasp envelope from a folio he'd brought and handed it to me.

I slipped a pair of glossies out, eight by tens, and stared at a line of gibberish that might have been written by a fourth grader, but this was not the time to focus on the note. I thanked Telly profusely, and left cash on the table. Out in the parking lot I opened Em's windows and punched in Harlan Kawahara's number as I waited for the Mustang to cool off. When Harlan's voice asked me to leave a message I told him to be prepared for a shocker: the police had a tip that Eva was involved.

FORTY-SIX

Maya and I were sitting in Cousin Duke's garden just before sunrise, dining on papaya and café Cubano. It was the morning of Randy Haverhill's funeral and I was awaiting a verdict on the day. Within minutes I knew. The skies were clear. The bruised looking purple sunrises of a few days ago with their strange green striations had given way to soft shades of pink and brass. The surf was calm. The paddlers who would bear Randy's ashes out to sea were in for a pleasant ride. As the pink rays rolled back the blue-black night sky, the grassy flanks of the Diamond Head crater stepped into the shoreline.

Maya's cup rattled. "Mt. Lē'ahi, thee ring of fire?"

"All right, hon. You got it," I said, running my hand up her bare thigh. Maya and I had had a delicious two-day respite from the case, thanks to the fact that Harlan Kawahara was in court and Eva was busy with her sons from the mainland. We had a wonderful time despite the fact that Maya is one of those exasperating tourists who takes field notes. She took dozens of photos of mango, kukui and monkey pod trees to remind herself which was which.

At the Ka'elepulu bird refuge in the town of Kailua, Maya identified every feathered friend in the guide. At the Kaupo lava flow she latched onto some tour guide who thought she was cute. He nattered on about pillow lava, formed into cobblestones underwater, and Maya swam through the water photographing the stones.

I feigned interest in all this minutia while I took mental snapshots of my own: Maya's face elegant in repose under the Manoa Falls as streams of water ran down her face; Maya's lean legs scissoring against a ferny background on a Nuuanu Valley hiking trail; Maya's struggle to get the hang of the vagaries of Hawaiian speech as we stood on the Diamond Head lookout. Diamond Head was misnamed in the eighteenth century by sailors who found calcite crystals in the crater and mistook them for diamonds. That's why many Hawaiians favour the traditional name for the highest point of the crater, a name which Maya was determined to master.

I'm in the camp that prefers Leahi, "ring of fire." What better name for a dormant volcano? On the other hand, Lé'ahi, pronounced with a long vowel and a glottal stop, means "forehead of the 'ahi," a yellow fin tuna. Legend has it that a goddess approaching Oahu from the east thought that Diamond Head looked like one big catch.

"So?" Maya shrugged. "Maybe she was hungry."

I drained the coffee, finished my papaya and took the last of the fresh malasadas when Maya declined it.

"We've got time for a jog through the park before we have to get ready for the ceremony," I said.

Maya put down her cup, came round behind my chair. Her strong fingers massaged the back of my neck sending thrills down my spine.

"This funeral is important to you, John. For me? No. I don't want to go."

I turned around to face her. Maya's face, bathed in the pink glow, made me catch my breath. I read her sadness, her torment. "All right, Maya. There's no need."

"The grand funeral," she said bitterly. "It would be like burying my David all over again."

I rose, wrapping her in my arms, pulling her close. "Maya, it's all right. You don't have to explain anything to me." As I kissed her forehead I could see tears leaking out from beneath her closed eyelids. "I'd beg off myself but... "

"Please, John. Go. You must. You must find your friend's killer. I don't want to be in your way."

"You aren't in my way, Maya. Never. It'll all be over early this afternoon. I'll take you to the beach, surfing, sailing, anything you want."

"What I want is to fly to Maui to visit your Mama Hana. Do you mind?" She caught me with her sidelong glance. Hell yes, I minded, but of course, being Hawaiian, I could not mind. It was against code. We are gracious people. Above all, we accept the wishes of those we love.

"You talked to Mama Hana?" I struggled to keep a light tone, I felt betrayed.

"Today Mama Hana will uncrate a shipment of Tahitian art. I can help her in her shop. Would you mind very much, John, if I stay for a few days at your place on the beach?"

Speechless, I could only smile and nod. "Enjoy Mama Hana," I said. "She is a trip." My girlfriend and my mother getting thick? Why was I not thrilled? Then it came out, what was bothering Maya. "Tutu Lia believes I am your sister Emmy reincarnate, no?"

"No!" I blurted. It couldn't be. This would be Madam Pele playing tricks on me. My sister Emmy was my soul mate, not my bed mate.

"Tutu said that when your twin sister Emmy disappeared you never recovered," Maya said. "I'm so much like sister Emmy, Tutu thinks maybe you are seeing a ghost."

"You two must have had quite a talk." I said. *Tutu Lia, you old troublemaker* is what I meant.

Maya gave me one of her looks that went from worry to resolution in the passage of seconds. I could just make it out in the rising dawn. "So?" Maya said, smile now flirtatious. "We will see what Mama Hana has to say about all of this."

FORTY-SEVEN

The funeral service for Randolph Haverhill began at 10:00 AM in downtown Honolulu at the church known as The Westminster Abbey of the Pacific: the Kawaiaha'o Coral Church on Punchbowl. It was close to noon before the funeral procession arrived back in my territory at the Outrigger Canoe Club. The burial service was conducted in English and Hawaiian on the beach in front of the club. Beside me, Putt Jorgenson was turned out in his barang and he fanned it at the bottom, muttering: "I don't know why they don't sell these shirts at The Gap."

The mourners fell into two main groups. The newcomers were either too pale or too sun-burned, their business dress stiff in the tropics. Then there were the tanned kamaaina, the locals in the fancy silks, the flowing dresses and flower leis. Arms raised, the priest said the benediction and the Hawaiians repeated it in the sonorous chant that thrills me every time I hear it. The Hawaiians had no melodies until the missionaries came and that may be why I find the ritual chants so compelling and so powerful.

"Where's Maya?" Jorgenson said, blotting his brow with a starched handkerchief. Putt with his pitted complexion looked greasy in the heat.

"She changed her mind about coming."

"Too bad for you." Jorgenson craned his neck, studying the crowd. "Have a fight, did you?"

"Hell no," I said. "I took her on my personal tour."

Putt grinned. "Your signature Girl from Mainland Package?"

"With plenty of side trips," I said. Why bother Putt about any of this? I let the images flash through my brain and kept my mouth shut. Maya was gone. I was baffled and lost.

"I can hardly wait..." I said aloud. Putt thought I was talking about the funeral and I let it go. What I meant was, I could hardly wait for Maya to return. What would happen? The dilemma Maya hinted at was too painful to share with Putt, who would, I feared, make light of it.

"Look at this turnout. It's phenomenal," he said. "There's the new chairman of the Council of Economic Advisors, flanked by three of his underlings. His Eminence is talking to the head of the Senate finance committee.

"Who are the others?"

"The university crowd," Putt said. "The schools send their superstars on a paid junket to Hawaii, lured by a chance to hula with the fiscal elite in the tropical heat."

I scanned the crowd, feeling out of sorts. "Maya said she had had enough of posh funerals when she'd buried her husband. She flew to Lahaina this morning to visit with Mama Hana."

Putt pulled his pipe out of his pocket. I envied him the pipe and hated that I envied it. Putt took his time lighting up. "So you told Maya that you didn't mind, but you did."

"Maya said she didn't want to distract me. She wanted to stay out of my way."

"Makes sense." The smoke drifted in my direction. I had to remind myself that this was not the time for me to light up.

"That bothers me, Putt. If Maya can't face up to the funeral of a man she didn't even know, then maybe she isn't ready to move on."

Putt's face disappeared in the smoke. "Looky there. See that doll with the microphone? That's the current cute number from FOX."

"You some celebrity stooge, Putt?" The dig was deliberate. I was ticked. Putt had changed the subject. It was his way of agreeing with what I'd just said. What I wanted from my friend was commiseration. I was stuck with acknowledgement. Putt had boxed me in. There was nothing for me to do but put a lid on the box.

FORTY-EIGHT

va Haverhill smiled and waved at us, a picture of studied reserve in a navy lace dress. Creamy leis of tiny, pungent pikake flowers were mounded around her neck, Chinese jasmine, the flowers Princess Ka'iulani named after her pet peacock. A wide straw hat hid the absence of Eva's hair. She leaned on the arm of a tall, nice-looking guy. Eva was a head and a half shorter than her date. She seemed to expand beside him, to appear taller and sturdier than she usually did. Perhaps Eva fed off his energy. Or was it simply one of the good days cancer patients enjoyed at random? At any rate it was clear that Eva kept the big C at bay for a day.

I nodded back, wondering whether she had any idea that the police suspected she had a role in Randy's murder.

"That's Deter, Eva's European love interest." Jorgenson conveyed this info with only the slightest movement of his lips. Putt didn't want his boss to see us talking about her and her boyfriend. "He's the one Eva dolls up for just to talk to him on the phone."

"I figured."

"Deter is Eva's main squeeze. He was one of Randy's post graduate fellows. Deter is Eva's payback, her way of reminding Randy that she made him what he was."

"Eva does say that, Putt. But let's not forget that Randy was from a powerful Hawaiian family. He'd have done well in any case."

"Oh, sure. Randy would have been a player on the local scene, but an intellectual superstar who wrote his own ticket in the academic world? I doubt that."

"It's interesting that Randy happens to be murdered on the eve of his economic shindig, don't you think?" *Eva's final message to Randy?*

"It's too bad Randy wasn't here to see this," Putt said, dodging what I'd just said. "Randy brought The Economic Conference of Pacific Nations to Honolulu for the first time ever. Usually it's held in Hong Kong or Beijing."

"Have you seen Mrs. Haverhill the Second?"

"Over there in the kamaaina crowd. The black straw hat towering over all the other women."

"Hillary must be a good six inches taller than Eva."

"Six inches taller, twenty years younger and wealthier by millions." Putt snickered. "Hillary is much closer to Deter's age. Maybe Hillary will steal Deter from Eva."

"So Hillary outclasses Eva in every sense of the word."

"You got it, brah."

"Speaking of financial interest, there's Daddy."

"Cameron Rooke," Putt replied, drawing on his pipe. "He manages to stay off the lists of the world's wealthiest people. Got his bucks tucked away in vast tracts of real estate classified as farmland. Hillary's old man's money is the principal force behind Randy's foundation."

I stared at Putt. "So I heard."

He shrugged, waving his pipe "Eva had me check the whole foundation out."

"Randy Haverhill was bought and paid for?"

"Eva's right about that." Smoke painted sideburns on Putt's pitted face. "Eva viewed Randy's marriage as a sellout to filthy lucre."

"Except Eva dumped Randy. Or so she told me."

"That's true," Putt said, "but it killed her to do it." Putt sucked on his pipe. "The Rooke family money wouldn't impress Eva. She would, however, admire their old line pedigree."

"The Rookes go so far back that the family adopted Queen Emma," I said.

"There you go," Putt said. "That's just the sort of pedigree that would impress Eva. Pedigree was what Eva saw in Randy in the first place."

"That Randy was a Bishop."

"Exactly. Eva's true to her roots in that respect. Her parents were transplanted southerners from Georgia sod." Putt took a drag on the pipe. "Southerners respect breeding. Randy had breeding—so, incidentally does this Austrian guy Deter. He's descended from titled Europeans. There's nothing snootier than an Austrian, you know. Eva likes to collect pedigrees. Same thing with the newspaper kid, the summer intern she was flirting with."

"Edmond K. for Kaiser Cooke," I said.

"Eddie Cooke. A kid with an old family name who is also a Kaiser, and the son of some big shot lawyer. Eddie's here somewhere with a girlfriend." Jorgenson's cheeks puffed like a bellows as he relit his pipe and shook out the match. "You have to remember. Eva may have divorced Randy over his predatory ways, but she taught him the rules. She's a player herself."

"Eva moulded Randy into the predator he became?"

"Maybe," Putt folded his arms and tapped a rhythm on his own collarbone with his pipe stem. "Of course I'm no psychologist, but that's how it looks to me."

FORTY-NINE

The wind shifted. Floral and sea scents wafted over us and it was another beautiful day in paradise. A burly Hawaiian blew the pu shell horn as the outrigger was launched. The paddlers moved 'ewa along the edge of Kapi'olani Park. Scores of mourners lined the shore, witnessing the spectacle. The outrigger headed for the sacred Tahitian stones fenced into an enclosure in the heart of Waikiki. From there it would turn out to sea for the scattering of the ashes. In the ancient days Randy's bones would have been buried up The Pali, hidden in some cave, the better to keep enemies of his clan from stealing his bones and carving them into fish hooks.

The mourners tossed flower leis after the departing canoe and gathered under a tent set up in front of The Outrigger Club for Randy's last luau. The group fell into two camps just as Putt predicted, Eva's contingent on the left, the pale teacher types and the economic heavyweights. Weather-beaten field researchers were trailed by gaggles of respectful students.

Meanwhile, the bronzed and monied Hawaiians in their slacks, aloha shirts, blazers or barangs and mounds of flower leis drifted to Hillary's camp on the right, where she was flanked by her father and her daughters in matching pale dresses, patent leather shoes and anklets.

I watched the crowd disperse. The second Mrs. Randy left her two daughters with her father and wandered off by herself. She found a stone seat at the edge of the lawn. It was time I paid my respects.

"A magnificent service," I said.

"Nice to see you, John. Yes. Randy would be proud." She wore a simple black sheath piped in white; a straw hat draped with a black veil sheltered her face.

Hillary sat dumping sand out of her sandals as she glanced up at me from her bench.

I realised this was the first time I'd seen Hillary in daylight, up close. She had a strong, chiselled face, and her father's long cheekbones and high oval forehead. Her eyebrows rose, sculpted brows perched proud as banners above eyes that were pale blue and slightly turned up at the corners, revealing a trace of a Polynesian influence somewhere in her genetic past. This was no surprise, considering how long the Rookes had been power players on Oahu. Yet, I found Hillary startling until I realised what it was: there was a hint of a younger Eva inside her. Hillary had succulent skin. Fruity, peaches and apricots, very hard won in the tropics.

"I'm sorry this happened, Hillary."

She turned her face away from me. When she turned back, tears leaked from the corners of her slanted eyes. "It's all my fault," she said. "I insisted Randy deal with the stalker. He told me he had taken care of it. He insisted. I should have gone to the police myself. I should have called you again." Hillary's mouth twisted, revealing a vulnerable touch, a short and thin upper lip topping a thick and pouty lower one, betraying a sensuality that was kept under wraps? She patted a place beside her on the stone bench.

I sat down. "I'm helping Harlan Kawahara investigate Randy's death."

"I'd love to help you, but I don't know how. Detective Tabura talked to me for hours. We went over that awful day, minute by minute. I was away. My girls had riding practice."

"Paniolas?" I said, using the Hawaiian word for cowgirl, face straight.

She smiled, brightening, removed her hat and brushed back thick brownish blonde hair that had grown out since I'd last seen her. Her hair winged its way down from the crown of her head and curved around her narrow chin.

"Dressage," she said.

"Oh yes, with the crops and the riding coats." My tone was light, hiding my own opinion of a sport that was a holdover from our British colonial days.

"The girls rode in a practice meet. That left Randy and Toby some time to themselves. Toby needed some one-on-one time with his dad. Toby's tied to Eva's apron strings, which you must realise."

"What was his relationship to Randy?"

"Improving, I think. "

"And—forgive me for asking—with you?"

"Toby was beginning to feel more comfortable with me. He tended to be a bit sullen and resentful when we first tried to blend the families. I bought him a pony, but he wasn't interested because Randy wasn't. I was crushed." She stared at her feet, long bony toes working the sand, an unpretentious gesture I found attractive in this immaculately turned out woman. "After the fiasco with the pony, I tried to stay in the background," Hillary said, working the sand with her feet. "Toby didn't lack for mothering—some would say smothering—and so what did he need from me?"

"Eva seems to think you were jealous of Toby's relationship with Randy."

Hillary shook her head. A fleeting smile crossed her sombre face. "Poor Eva. She does love Toby, loves him to death. Eva feared Randy's attachment to my two daughters. Randy did adore the girls and Eva sensed that. She may have worried that Toby would be pushed out of his father's affections. I would guess that's natural, if you have cancer. Eva wants a future for Toby. I suppose I'd be as paranoid as she is if I were the one battling a terminal illness."

"Terminal?"

Hillary grimaced, lips turned down. Her fingers brushed across her mouth. "I shouldn't have said that. What do I know? Eva's very determined. She could beat this, but she has one of those erratic types of cancer. There have been cures in the survival literature, of course, but the statistics aren't good. I happen to know all this because I work as a Cancer Society volunteer. My mother died of breast cancer, you know."

"I'm sorry to hear that." Hillary nodded. "Eva is getting the best treatment and her tumour was found early, but her chances are not even fifty-fifty. She'd be the first to tell you that."

"My money is on Eva. She's a survivor."

"Yes, that's right. Attitude is everything. Despite what rot Eva spouts about me, I'm on her side and not just for her sake, but for Toby's. Now that Randy is gone, Toby needs Eva desperately." Hillary brushed the sand off the bottoms of her bare feet and slipped them back into her sandals.

"And if something happens to Eva?"

"My home is Toby's home. I intend to make that clear to Eva, once we have time to talk. Now is not the time. Eva seems to believe that I think Toby murdered his father."

"What *do* you think?"

Hillary swung her head around, eyes flashing, pale as mirrors. "Of course not. I don't suspect that for a minute. It would mean... It would mean..." Her eyes watered. She turned her face away. When Hillary had composed herself she turned back to me. "It would mean that Toby would have done it out of resentment over me. I can't put my mind around any such idea. Her eyelids fluttered as she struggled to hold back tears. It's just that... the police... .they... "

"Detective Tabura? He's a friend of mine. "

"Well then, you know how he thinks."

"We talk."

"That knife in Toby's hand? That note with the funny lettering? Of course I've seen Toby mix his letters up. But the note is written with a marker pen. I'm no handwriting expert and they tried to get me to say I'd swear that the note was from Toby's hand. I refused, of course, but I could see some similarities. Any fool could see that. I'd prefer you don't mention that to Eva. She'll take it the wrong way."

"The note might implicate Toby, but it surely won't convict him."

Hillary shook her head as she rose and I remembered what a big woman she was, at least five ten, square of shoulder, spare of build. "That's not the impression Detective Tabura gave me," she said.

"He wouldn't. That's not his job."

Hillary shook her head. "I don't have a clue how these things work."

"Now tell me. The murder weapon turned up."

"The knife?"

"The shotgun."

"Oh. That."

"Did Randy own a shotgun?"

"Not to my knowledge."

"Yet the gun was found in the garden shed under the house."

Hillary stared at me. "That's inside information."

"Correct. Investigators' privilege. We keep that to ourselves."

"That shed back of the stairs?" Hillary said. "Someone could have waited for Randy. Someone who knew the pizza routine."

"Does anyone come to mind?"

"The stalker, of course," Hillary said. "The one I told Detective Tabura about."

FIFTY

The funeral crowd was breaking up. I was on my way out. A woman was shredding paper into the water in the wake of the canoe. The outfit she wore, a simple wrap dress, a pareau, pegged her as kamaaina. The wrap showed off her broad shoulders and cupped her boyish fanny. She had muscular legs. Maybe she was one of the surfer girls who keep a board at Waikiki. She wore a hat and dark glasses; I couldn't get a look at her face, but she had one of those golden tans that suggested some Asian strain somewhere in the genetic mix. Pocho, Toby had said of the woman in the rain cape with the garden trowel in her hand, which is why I kept watching her.

The petals had accumulated in a small tide pool left as the tide receded. I worked my way closer and picked up a few. The petals weren't petals. They were bits of paper. I looked around to make sure I wasn't being watched, and then scooped up what I could of the shreds and sifted through them. I couldn't make out anything on them, but I stuffed them in my jacket pocket.

Jorgenson caught up with me and handed me a business card. "This one. Enid Stearn. Dr. Stearn. She's quite the researcher." Putt had replaced his pipe with a notepad.

I studied the card. Stearn was an adjunct professor of economics at the University of Hawaii, Manoa campus. She was also a senior advisor at the Pacific Rim Institute.

"Enid knew Randy from back east," Putt said. "She was his first graduate assistant. She said Randy came onto her. She was flattered because he offered personal assistance on her graduate thesis. She soon realised it was her other talents he was attracted to."

"How so?"

"She got the idea when he put his hand down her dress. Claims she steered clear of him after that. Says their relationship was strictly business, and has been all this time, but she noticed Randy going after another doll."

"And who might that be?"

"I don't see her right now, but another case is here as well...a beanpole in a pareau. I've seen her somewhere before."

"A pareau?" I asked, patting the damp shreds of paper in my pocket. "I'll keep an eye out for her."

"Gotta run," Jorgenson said. "Got to file a follow-up on the funeral."

On the way out, I was trying to catch up with the woman in the pareau, the one whose shredded message I had in my pocket, when I passed a pair of stocky young men and a woman, small, dark and a beauty. I pegged the male sartorial misfits as part of the mainland crowd. The young woman was in one of those power suits with flower leis piled on. I glanced at her as she passed me, noticing the startling pale eyes in the lovely dark face.

"Lani?" I smiled big, opened my arms, as if to someone I knew. The ruse worked; the party stopped.

"Have we met?" A puzzled smile crossed her face.

"Aren't you Eva Haverhill's niece?"

"Yes, I'm Lani, but I don't recall that we—"

"John Spyer. I'm working with Toby's attorney, Harlan Kawahara? I was hoping to have a word with you."

"Of course. Anything I can do to help Toby. He's a wonderful kid. It's absurd that he—"

"We'll collect the car and come back to pick you up," one of the young men said, his tone stiff.

Lani took the hint. "Mr. Spyer, I'd like you to meet Eva's sons Bart and Kevin Sneddon."

I extended my hand to the speaker, whose handshake was distinctly unenthusiastic.

"Bart Sneddon. "

"Dr. Sneddon?"

"I'm Dr. Sneddon, Kevin Sneddon," the shorter of the two said. In contrast to Toby, Eva's sons took after their mother. They were both a head shorter and a width stockier than their younger half brother.

"Pleased to meet you," I said. "Your mother is very proud of you both."

The pair nodded curtly. A real pair of puppets, these two.

"I'd like to talk to the two of you as well."

"However much we'd like to help Toby, I doubt we'd know anything useful," Dr. Kevin said.

"Maybe that's something I should decide."

"Fair enough. We'll be here through the weekend, spending some time with Eva."

"If Eva has time for us," the older one—Bart—said with a sardonic laugh. "Our mother has unexpected company from Europe who seems to be monopolising her time."

"Well then," I said, "you may have some time to help me out."

"Whatever," Kevin said.

"Now, Kevin," Lani said. "We owe this to Toby."

"You'll have to pardon my brother," Bart said. "He's the typical intern in his second year of sleep deprivation and suffering from jet lag on top of that. Of course we'll help you." Bart handed me his card. "You can catch me on my cell number. We'll be staying with our mother."

Kevin yanked Bart away, but I caught a part of the interplay as they headed toward the street: "Maybe you'll stay under the same roof with the Austrian Golden Boy, but count me out, Bart."

"Don't mind Kevin," Lani said. "He'll come around. It's very difficult for an intern to break training even for a family emergency, and in a sense, Randy isn't really family anymore."

"Obviously Eva's friend Deter isn't popular with the Sneddon sons."

"They came all the way over here to Honolulu to show support to Eva. Then they find their mother fawning over a man younger than they are. I love Aunt Eva to death, but I know how she is. Not interested in having Deter join any cosy family gatherings. He'd pick up on their true age difference."

"That would be upsetting."

"Don't get me wrong. Eva's sons love her, despite the fact that they view her romantic interests as... " Lani raised her eyebrows and her mouth pulled down.

"Over the top?"

"Yes, you could say that. The boys did make a special effort to come to Randy's funeral, which they would not have done otherwise, except for Eva's illness. You know about Eva's illness, don't you?"

"I do. I'm sorry. But if anyone can beat cancer it'll certainly be Eva."

"That's how I feel about it," Lani said. "Meanwhile, the heat is getting to me. Do you mind if we find some air conditioning?"

"My pleasure."

We went into the Outrigger Club. I looked around for a dark corner where we could talk. The waitress came around. Lani ordered a frozen mango daiquiri. I asked for a Maker's Mark over ice. It was 2:00 PM, on the early side for Drambuie.

FIFTY-ONE

The Outrigger Club feels hunkered down, with its low ceilings and its series of step-down bays flanking the beach. My favourite touch is the arbour with the vines trained over the top, beside the sand volleyball court. Normally, I like to sit there, but the coolest and darkest spot was the corner by the bar. Lani studied some early photos of the club hanging on the wall while our drinks were being poured.

"Look at this," she said. "This place started in a grass shack."

"They should have kept it," I said. "Trouble was, the grass shack couldn't hold a weight room, a rowing tank and various dining rooms." I found seats for us in a secluded corner. I didn't want anyone tuning in on what was apt to be a very private discussion.

Lani lapped at the daiquiri with her tongue and used the bar napkin to wipe her forehead and cheeks."It's been years since I've been here. I'm not used to this heat."

"You were here at age fourteen or thereabouts?"

"Fifteen, actually," Lani said. "I'd stopped competing in gymnastics. I grew about four inches and began to... mature."

I grinned. "And nicely, too."

She blushed. "Mahalo."

"Eva said you scared your mother to death."

"That's right," Lani laughed, showing very pretty teeth. "I guess I was boy crazy that year. Mom was busy taking care of my dad. He declined quickly and I was too self-absorbed to notice, I'm now ashamed to say."

"At any rate, you came to Honolulu and stayed with Eva and Randy."

"Just a couple of months. Uncle Randy was writing his first book. Aunt Eva found him a publisher."

"Eva called the shots?"

"She was very good at orchestrating my uncle's career," Lani said. "She had a way of doing it without being obnoxious." Lani stirred the thick drink and tossed it down as if it were a shave ice, closed her eyes and clutched her throat. "Ohhh, it's so cold. I didn't realise."

"You okay, Lani?"

"I just about froze my windpipe," Lani said. "At any rate, Eva got Randy a summer teaching stint here in Honolulu and a grant to finish his first book. This was a long time back. Toby was a toddler. I was in high school. They needed to be here because Randy's father was dying. I had an opportunity to do some of the research, mainly checking references. I wasn't qualified to do any of the original research. It was a fantastic opportunity for me nonetheless. It was my first exposure to economics. Aunt Eva got a promotion at the newspaper and worked days. I took over care of Toby. It was wonderful for me. I took him to the beach every day and let him crawl around in the sand while I worked on my tan and checked out the lifeguards."

"And Uncle Randy?"

Lani blushed. "I adored Uncle Randy. He was the most interesting talker. He took me to concerts and museums. He had all sorts of interests. He loved anthropology and the geology of the Pacific Islands. He broadened my mind. He really did. I would not have pursued an academic career if it were not for my uncle."

"Yet you pulled the plug on the summer and went home early."

"Yes I did."

"May I ask why?"

"It was time."

"Eva said there was some trouble between you and Uncle Randy."

Lani's face worked and she glared at me. "Well then. So you know."

"I want to hear it from you."

"What does this have to do with Toby?"

"I can't answer that yet, but there's some evidence that your uncle Randy was one randy fellow. I'm hearing that maybe one of his conquests may have done this."

"Ah," Lani said, nodding. "Maybe."

"Something you remember, Lani, maybe it will help me fill in the blanks."

"Okay, I get it." She fanned herself with a bar menu. "It was obvious that Eva and Randy were both absorbed in their careers. They always got on together in a civil fashion. There was no arguing at home. But I soon realised a lot of young women, college students were hanging around my uncle and I'd hear them talk."

"It wasn't just talk, Lani. Randy came onto you."

"My mother warned me about Uncle Randy," Lani's tone grew heated. "In fact, we thought he'd be away from Honolulu on a field trip, but somehow that fell through. My mother said that some men—even in one's own family—sometimes do inappropriate things. So I was forewarned. But when it really began to unfold, when Uncle Randy found excuses to take me out—alone—to museums and ruins and all—and then he began to fondle me—or try to, well I just knew it was time to go home."

"And Uncle Randy's treatment of you became an issue in the divorce."

"Well.. .not exactly. My mother…she recognized as soon as I got home that something had happened. I told her nothing truly bad happened, but my mother wasn't satisfied until I'd been examined by a doctor. She told Eva about Uncle Randy's behaviour. She couldn't understand how Eva would put up with it. She felt it was so demeaning to her sister. I don't believe my mother ever recognized that maybe the reason Aunt Eva didn't do something about Uncle Randy was her own..." Lani's voice trailed off. She lowered her chin, raised her eyebrows, and shrugged.

"Pursuit of other interests?"

"I don't know. I never saw any such behaviour at the time. But I do know that Aunt Eva was way older than Randy, that Randy was a mere five years older than Bart and seven years older than Kevin. Both Kevin and Bart were furious with Eva for divorcing Uncle Nelson and taking up with Randy. They suffered terrible embarrassment over it."

"What about their dad?"

"Uncle Nelson?" He was a perfectly nice man. A college athlete of note. ROTC guy, called up. Went overseas. Just one of those stories where he came back a changed man, embittered and stressed out. Took a military discharge and disappeared into the family business. Wasn't Aunt Eva's style. She was very ambitious. She couldn't stand that. She'd married Uncle Nelson early in life. My mother always said that Aunt Eva did it to get away from their mother. Aunt Eva was the oldest."

"What about Eva's mother?"

"Also very driven. She was an antique dealer and decorator. She specialised in helping upper crust Hawaiians track down pieces from the British colonial days and finish them out with quality Hawaiian artefacts."

"And Eva's father?"

"Easy going, handsome, a real charmer. He made an excellent living as a ship's electrician. That's why Eva's parents moved to Hawaii, for government contracts during the Second World War. He was a drinker, though. There was tension in that family."

"Eva says now that she loved your Uncle Randy. She blames his behaviour as the cause of the divorce."

"That was a major issue, I am certain of it. But you have to remember, Aunt Eva was more than a wife to Uncle Randy. She was also... " Lani looked pained.

"She was also his surrogate mother."

"Yes, that's it," Lani said. She'd finished her drink and looked at her watch. "Bart and Kevin are waiting for me by now, I expect."

"Of course. I'll see you to your car." We were on the walk to the street on the Kapi'olani Park side of the building when I saw Ms. Pareau leaving the party on the arm of Eva's ex-fling, Mr. Pecs, Eddie K. Cooke. He was here at Randy's funeral with the same big-haired woman he was talking to the night of the book signing. They were about the same height, maybe five six, five eight, and I wanted to stop and study them but with Lani in hand this wasn't practical.

"Did you keep up your ties with your uncle?" I said to her.

"Oh yes," Lani said. "I'm doing research for my doctorate. I had to apply for a grant. My uncle reviewed my proposal and made several helpful changes. He was brilliant. I loved talking shop with him. His brain was by far the best part of him. As for the women and all that?" She grimaced and turned her head away.

"Do you know anything about your uncle's life with Hillary?"

"He was settling down. I believe he missed having a normal family life with a woman who didn't... "

"Seem like his mother?"

"Yes. I did talk to him about the time he went for tenure and was rejected. It had to be humiliating. I called to console him. And you know? Uncle Randy took it very well. I really believe it was to satisfy Eva that he'd pushed to stay in the Ivy League. He was sick of academic politics. He thought that the Pacific Rim Institute was a great opportunity and he loved the idea of coming back here to Honolulu."

"And how did Eva take it?"

"I never talked to Eva, but my mother did. She said Eva was crushed. She came back, got a job on the paper and started divorce proceedings."

"Using Randy's kinky sex life as an excuse."

"It wasn't an excuse. Uncle Randy really was out of control, but my mother never could understand why Eva hadn't done something early on to rein Randy in."

"Maybe Toby got wind of this and took revenge on his father."

"No way," Lani said, eyes flashing, mouth drawing a determined line. "Toby couldn't have done it. He may have been ignored by his father for years but he was thrilled when Randy began taking an interest in him."

"Toby didn't think his father's escapades had caused his mother's illness?"

"What? That's crazy. It's so bizarre. I never heard one word from Toby about such a thing."

"Swear to that in court?"

"Of course I will."

What do you know about Randy's involvement with Dr. Enid Stearn?"

Lani drew in a breath. She shook her head. "Enid Stearn is a respected scholar. I never thought she liked Uncle Randy. Now I know why."

"Could your uncle have been stalked?"

"A stalker? Ohmigod. That's news to me."

FIFTY-TWO

The Sneddon boys were waiting at the curb. I helped Lani into the backseat and waved them off. Lani smiled and waved. The brothers in the front seat stared straight ahead. The Outrigger Club is such a short walk back to Duke's place on Leahi that I had left Em home to chill in her garage. I was all set to cross Kapi'olani Park and enjoy a walk back to home base when a hand clamped on my shoulder. It was Detective Tabura.

I tossed him a shaka. "Enjoying the funeral, Telly?"

"Some send-off, yeah?" The detective talked around a toothpick in the corner of his mouth.

"I'm heading across the park. Want to stretch your legs?"

"Wife's waiting. I gotta take her to a baby luau."

"Hey, I found some leads for you. Here's one: Enid Stearn, a respected scholar who worked at The Pacific Rim Institute as Randy's assistant. She might know something."

Tabura removed the toothpick and looked at the name. "We talk to her already. Got lots of women to check out."

"You found the professor's little black book."

Telly grinned. "Not so little."

"How you doing on the stalker?"

"You got to the second Mrs. Randy?"

"I was on the scene, Telly. There was a nasty incident at Randy's signing. I told you about that and so did Hillary. The security guy for the University has a report on it."

The detective waggled his hand. "We can't find."

"You have no idea who the stalker is?"

"Nothing to go on. Mrs. Hillary say this about the stalker. Professor Randy's tires slashed. His office broken into. House trashed. All this from her, after the professor is pau. We never hear this before."

"There was never a police report?"

The toothpick waggled, a tiny baton, as Tabura shook his head. I was stunned. Randy Haverhill had sold us out, Hillary and I, and Randy Haverhill had paid for his arrogance with his life.

"That is odd, Mind if I work on that?" *As if I hadn't been working on it all along.*

Telly shrugged. The whites of his eyes were yellow in the daylight. "Can't hurt."

"You done working the professor's office?"

"I wouldn't be here if I wasn't."

"Mind if I check it out?"

"It's a free country." Tabura"s unibrow lifted and he plugged the toothpick back into his mouth.

"Thanks, Telly. Anything I can do for you, let me know."

"You gone wading?" Telly said. He stared at my damp pants cuffs.

I patted my jacket pocket, also soggy. "Lady seemed very distraught. She was tossing scraps of paper into the water. Some message meant for Randy, maybe. I was just curious. I want to know what it said."

"What it said?"

"I found nothing on the shreds."

"You find something, you pass it along, Spyer." Tabura's smile was friendly but the unibrow thickened over his eyes as he gave my shoulder another squeeze. I knew then that Telly Tabura might well have been watching that strange woman in the pareau. Or else he was watching every move I made. A fancy Toyota convertible swept past. I recognized the hat, the pareau lady, and Mr. Pecs, Eddie Kaiser Cooke, with his sharp chin and wolfish nose. Telly Tabura and I looked at each other and laughed.

As I think about it now, the laugh was on us.

FIFTY-THREE

Randy Haverhill's new think tank, the Pacific Rim Institute, fit right in with the objectives of The University of Hawaii s East-West Center. A thousand foreign students from the Pacific Rim nations are admitted to study every year on scholarships paid for to the tune of millions by the U.S. State Department. The East-West Complex is a campus within a campus with special student dorms and a hotel for visiting faculty. The centrepiece of the complex is Jefferson Hall, where Randy had held his book signing back in June, but the faculty offices are in Burns Hall makai on East-West Boulevard.

I'd called Hillary last night after the funeral. I told her the police had no record of the stalker, but Hillary insisted that after the fiasco at the June book signing she had made a police report, which she had told Detective Tabura about. She was shocked when I told her Tabura hadn't found it. We agreed it would be best to find her copy of it. I figured that Randy Haverhill, off paddling his outrigger in another realm, wouldn't mind if I copped his parking space. However, his widow had the same idea. I found Randy's white Jaguar gleaming like a bathtub in the director's space. I headed humble Em into a lesser stall reserved for Pacific Institute staffers, whose stalls were empty. They would be at the Economic Conference sessions mauka on East-West Boulevard in Jefferson Hall.

For years Mama Hana had been a docent at the East West-Center Gallery in Burns Hall when she wasn't teaching hula kahiko, an ancient form of the dance, classical hula you might say. I must have been to dozens of the EWC gallery's openings. I glanced through the tall glass doors mounted in koa frames to see that dance costumes and musical instruments from Sarawac were the exhibit du jour.

Unfortunately, the exhibit du jour on the third floor wasn't nearly so artistic. The double doors of the Pacific Rim Institute were festooned with yellow crime scene tape. Hillary Haverhill stood waiting in the hall, dressed head to toe in denim. She was gaunt and leggy and paced in long strides talking on her cell phone. She waved at me and went on with the conversation. She was polite but firm, demanding that someone from the East-West Center security department come let us in.

"How are you doing?" I said when she got off the phone.

Hillary shook her head with the dazed look of someone who'd gone to bed too late and awakened too early. "I took enough sleeping pills to knock out one of my horses and finally got some sleep. I'm spaced today."

That killed our conversation. I left Hillary to stew while I got on my cell phone and located the scholar Putt had mentioned. Dr. Enid Stearn was teaching a class at Saunders Hall until 10:45 AM.

Some people's feet do not march unless to music and the security guy was one of these. We could hear him come whistling down the hall on *Tiny Bubbles*, only in his case the bubbles had gone flat. Hillary smiled, extended her hand as this tuneless haole arrived.

"Satch," she said. "I'm so glad it's you."

"Mrs. Haverhill," Satch said. "I'm so sorry about the professor. Such a nice man." He hugged Hillary.

"Satch, you remember John Spyer. He's a private investigator. He's helping us find out who did this."

We shook hands. Satch was that lanky redhead with the moustache wider than his mouth I'd met at Randy's signing-turned-trashing back in June. Satch yanked down the crime scene tape and unlocked the door. We stepped inside.

The desk lamp light had been left on. It beamed a murky pool of light on the blank spot on the desk where a computer had been. Somehow the air seemed rank with crime tech effort. Hillary pulled back the blinds and opened the sliders to a small lanai to let in some breeze. I looked around at a suite of offices that had that upscale, money-can-buy-it look, Hawaiian variety. Various art objects as good as anything I'd ever seen in the EWC gallery downstairs were mounted on the walls. Papers and books were slung here and there. Fingerprint gunk was smeared around door handles and the reception desk.

"When did the police search here?" I asked Hillary.

"After I mentioned the stalker to Detective Tabura." Hillary's face was pale, devoid of makeup and her dark blonde hair was gathered into a clamshell of a comb clamped at the back of her head.

I went into Randy's inner office, panelled in koa, cushy in linen and leather, with an outsized ego wall.

There were photos of Randy with Oprah, Larry King, Bill Clinton, Barbara Walters, Teddy Kennedy and Barack Obama, of course, plus various Congressmen, women and heads of state. On the desk, where Randy's computer had been, lay an Ethernet cable smeared with fingerprint dope. I tried his desk drawer. The lock had been broken. The files were askew. I was about to go through them when Hillary came in.

"I remember filling out a report. I thought I had it at home but couldn't find it. I looked in the general office files in the outer office. It isn't there."

"It's probably here," I said.

"Let me look," Hillary said.

I left Hillary to her search and went out to talk to the security guy. Satch was whistling in front of the elevator when I caught up with him.

"A shame," Satch said. "How can I help you?"

"Hillary has always maintained that Randy was stalked. "

"That's a tough one." A corner of his mouth twitched. His outsized red moustache, straight as a level, moved to the side of his face.

"Did you make a report on the business after Randy's signing?"

"I did. I not only reported everything we talked about, but I gave a copy of the report to Detective Tabura. Say the word if you need a copy."

"I'll pick it up before I leave."

FIFTY-FOUR

Hillary closed the sliders and pulled the blinds at the Pacific Rim's offices. "It's going to take a week to put the place in order, but now is not the time."

"Did you find your copy of the police report?"

"I did." Her tone was weary. "There on the desk."

I picked up the form and glanced through it. It was very detailed. It even mentioned the odd note on the whiteboard and referred to all the prior incidents.

"The dates were as accurate as I could recall," Hillary said.

"Right," I said, sitting on the edge of the desk.

"You made this out and signed it."

"That's right." Hillary sank onto a small couch and rummaged through a leather tote. She extracted a pack of cigarettes and a lighter, took a look at what she was doing and shook her head. "I'm woozy enough without this." She tossed the unlighted cigarette in a waste basket. I restrained an urge to grab it and light up.

I waved the police report. "You turned this in to the H.P.D.?"

Hillary massaged her temples. "Randy took care of that."

"Uh huh." I stared at her.

"That's what he told me." Hillary read my tone.

Her fingers dropped into her lap. She had long, skeletal fingers and a way of moving her hands so that every remark she made took on a theatrical quality. She stared at me, her face blank.

"What if Randy didn't file this?" I did my best to squeeze any hint of accusation out of my tone.

A defeated expression washed over her face. She sighed. "I took what Randy said about the stalker at face value," she said, evading my question. "I knew all about his exploits. Everyone did, even my father."

"Speaking of Dad, you say they got along?"

"Famously. My father respected Randy as an economist. Randy loved archeology as well and that's one of Dad's passions. They talked by the hour. I'd listen in, spellbound. It was Randy's intellect that I loved."

"Poor Randy," I said. "Loved for his intellect alone."

"Well it's true," Hillary said. Her hands swept outward, expanding the space around her. "When he invited me out, I tried to keep it just for fun. I teased Randy about his reputation. I told him I didn't want to become just another of his... "

"Groupies?"

She smiled. "We became close, but not lovers. I think that's what Randy found attractive about me."

"You were no easy conquest."

"I was not."

"So what about this stalker?"

"Randy wasn't keen on reporting it, but I insisted. I had had it. We had this Economic Conference on the agenda and didn't need any more trouble. Dad was a close friend of the chancellor of Harvard. He knew all about Randy's... "

"Proclivities?"

"Randy was a charmer. He had Dad convinced that most of what he'd heard was the gossip of jealous colleagues."

"Even though Randy had been caught diddling with the president's own wife?"

"I knew the lady in question. She'd been a graduate student in one of Randy's seminars. She was a trophy wife to start off with. So what, really, could The President expect?"

"It wasn't all Randy's fault."

"It takes two."

I nodded.

"Randy was fairly young to become tenured, you know, and he admitted to me that Eva pushed for it, but he didn't expect it."

"About his supposed reform. Do you think Randy fed your dad a story?"

"I believed Randy at the time," Hillary said. Her long fingers rubbed at her temples, then pressed against the sides of her head, containing her anguish, maybe. "I sincerely believed he was sick of all the..." Hillary's voice dropped off.

In the ensuing silence I watched her struggle to compose herself.

She finally said: "I'd seen for myself his charisma at work. I never saw him chase women. They fell all over him."

"Randy's so circumspect, how come he's stalked?"

Hillary shook her head, hugged her arms around herself. Her eyes watered. "Randy took what precautions he could and shrugged it off. The games seemed to be pranks." Hillary's voice quavered. "After I wrote out this report, made it as detailed as I could, nothing happened, which is why Randy never wanted to bother in the first place, I suppose." Hillary's long fingers swept the issue away. "I would guess things like these had happened to him before."

"Are you sure Randy took the report to the police?"

Hillary stared at me. Her eyes widened. "Wait a minute, you don't think…"

"I'm going to take a copy of this, if you don't mind. Detective Tabura told me he couldn't find…"

"I don't believe this. Randy promised me."

"Maybe he did file this," I said, "But there's no tracking number on it, no time stamp."

Hillary wrapped her arms around her own middle. She rocked from side to side. "I knew it. I should have taken it in myself. Randy insisted on taking it. He said it wasn't seemly for me to have to…." Hillary's chin wobbled. She wiped the damp corners of her eyes with her forefingers.

Suppose Randy wasn't so interested in finding the stalker?"

Hillary stared at me. She nodded.

"Suppose Randy was playing one of his side games?"

Tears flooded Hillary's eyes and ran down the sides of her nose. "At first I couldn't believe such a thing."

"But now?"

"But now, I'm thinking that maybe Randy didn't follow through because..." She dropped her cell phone and her lighter into her tote, hoisted it onto her shoulder and stood up. "I've got to run, I'm sorry," she said, wiping her eyes. "I have to pick up my girls."

"Because why, Hillary?" I said, taking her arm.

"Maybe Randy never cared to pursue the stalker's identity because he knew who it was all along."

FIFTY-FIVE

S aunders Hall is mauka of Burns, straight up East-West Boulevard and a left on Maile Way. It was about 10:30 AM. on Monday. I peered through a glass window on the door. Dr. Enid Stearn was halfway through her lecture. She was an Amazon of a woman with a spiky shock of black hair. She was chalking some inexplicable formula on a board with such force that I could hear the rap of the chalk from outside the room.

Whatever she was talking about, it must have been good. There were at least twenty-five students in the room, paying attention. No doubt it helped that most of the students were respectful Asian types and not a bunch of haole smartasses.

I found a bench across the hall and got busy on my cell phone. Harlan was in court so I left a message telling him I'd found a police report to back up the stalker as a suspect. Harlan would be thrilled. Every defence lawyer needs other suspects to point the finger at.

I called Telly Tabura and reminded him about Hillary's police report. I read off the date and asked him to look for it again, if he hadn't already done so. Though I hated to admit it, I had to be straight with my detective friend. "Hillary left it to Randy to file the report. Maybe he did. Maybe he didn't."

Telly grunted in response. I pictured the unibrow rising on his face.

"If Randy didn't file the report, it could have been because he knew who the stalker was," I said.

"Maybe Mrs. Eva."

"No way."

"Mrs. Eva one sick woman."

"So it's a good thing she has an airtight alibi," I said, reminding him that Eva was in a newsroom meeting when Randy was shot.

"One late police report," Tabura scoffed, "very late."

"So what's the status on the shotgun?"

"Ballistics says the weapon fired same buckshot that killed the professor." Telly's tone turned jovial. "You find the murder weapon, Spyer, I thank you. The department thanks you."

I winced over this one. If the shooter and the stalker were one and the same, this was one organised stalker. The murder would have been done not simply out of passion, but premeditated passion.

"Anything on who owned the gun, Telly?"

"Hard to say with such an old weapon."

"Okay, Telly. I'll see if I can be of any help." I looked at my watch. Dr. Stearn's lecture was ending, but I still had a few minutes, so I got Eva on the line. I had to run the stalker business by her.

"How are you feeling, Eva?"

"Fine, John. I had a wonderful weekend. We made love."

I laughed, shaking my head.

"Deter was wonderful."

Tell me about it. "I've got some new information, Eva. I need your take on it and Toby's as well."

"Toby is out with Bart and Kevin. I'm sending all the guys to a show at the Hilton Village. I needed to buy some time alone with Deter. Drop by around four. I'll have to go on the friggin' feeding tube and I don't want Deter to have to see me like that."

The doors to R. 436 flung open and students hustled out. I bided my time while Dr. Stearn, who towered over some stragglers, answered questions.

I fell in beside her as she came out the door, striding to her next class. She had to be six feet tall, big boned, with mannish features and a ratbite of a haircut. Dr. Enid Stearn was devoid of any feminine charm that I could see, except when she glanced at me, she had fabulous brown eyes, glowing with warmth.

Nevertheless, I couldn't fathom a guy like Randy putting his hands down this Amazon's dress. What, after all, would have been down there? When I explained my mission she paused, batted those big browns at me and said she would love to cooperate.

"So what do you teach?"

"Statistical modelling and the limits of same."

"One of Randy's interests?"

"Oh, yes. I was involved in the field before he was."

"Congratulations. "

"I chose it as my graduate thesis. Dr. Haverhill was to be my tutorial advisor."

"And?"

"Statistical modelling became the basis for our book. I was listed as his major researcher."

"Dr. Haverhill stole your idea?"

"Not exactly. He offered to be the co-author. I'd be the lead person. Then we got a publisher. It was the publisher's idea to list Randy's name first. I went along with it. Dr. Haverhill had published more than I had. He had a name and I was a nobody. We split a healthy advance, money I needed desperately to pay off my student loans."

"Where was this?"

"Harvard. It's where I earned my doctorate."

"So what brought you out here?"

"The opening of the Pacific Rim Institute."

"I heard that the Institute was a put-up job, a consolation prize."

She looked away. "When Randy lost his footing, mine wasn't secure, either."

"Pardon my asking, but were you ever involved with Randy?"

"I was not." The head swung back; the chin came up; the eyes flashed. "Oh yes, he tried with me. He thought he was God's gift to women and maybe he was, but I wasn't interested. My ambitions were academic. It was obvious to me from the outset that any woman who let herself become involved with Randy in a significant way would be miserable."

"He was married to Eva when you first knew him. Did you know Eva?"

"Oh, yes. I admired Eva. She stood up to Randy. She held her own with him."

"It was Eva who made Randy's career. That's my understanding."

Dr. Stearn's expressive eyes flared. Did I detect a spark of resentment? "Eva was the consummate faculty wife, that's for sure."

"Are you aware of how they met?"

She shook her head. I told Eva's tale; she was a school teacher seductress who snatched Randy right out of high school and made good on an unlikely setup. Enid stared at me, the soft eyes thoughtful now, as she shook her head. "I had no idea. Are you sure?"

"Eva told me so herself."

"That would make Randy a product of... " She started, "...could that account for his..." She shook her head. "But what does it matter now?" She glanced at her watch. "I'm ten minutes late. I must run. I don't like to keep my students waiting."

I took her briefcase and we picked up the pace.

"Randy was stalked. Do you know anything about that?"

Enid Stearn stopped, looked around, making sure no approaching students heard what she said. "There were a number of incidents. I was very concerned."

"What did Randy do about it?"

"He shrugged it off. That's what I thought." She craned her neck warily and lowered her voice another notch. "It wasn't a healthy situation," She said. "Dr. Haverhill's status was a distracting factor. It took away from our work. I soon decided to look for a teaching position and took the first opening I could find. I love teaching, you know."

She turned those big brown eyes on me and melted my scepticism. I found myself loving this teacher who loved to teach, and I called Harlan the minute she was out of sight. Enid Stearn was a very credible witness who recalled the stalking incidents. Since Telly Tabura had already talked to her, he had to have known as well, and I was stumped. It made no sense that he clung to Toby as the main suspect.

FIFTY-SIX

It was close to 5:00 PM by the time I arrived at Eva's Round Top hale. I lingered outside the front door enjoying a mist of raindrops in the air. It took awhile before Eva's son Bart answered the door, invited me in, and invited me out at the same time. "I'm sorry, but my mother isn't well."

"The cancer?"

Bart shook his head, a woeful look on his face. "The boyfriend. Eva had a fight with the Austrian and she's been sick. Kevin and Toby went after a prescription."

"Too bad. Eva told me just this morning that...uh...Deter had done great things for her health."

Eva's voice preceded her down the hall. "Deter. You've come back?" Her gown was flowing, but her demeanour was strained and she couldn't hide her chagrin at seeing me: "Oh, John. It's you."

I sucked in a laugh. "Such a welcome."

"You wanted to see me. I forgot. I'm sorry." She ran her hand through her dishevelled hair and straightened the long skirt of her muu muu. "Please come in, won't you? I've something to show you."

"Mother," Bart said. "You've been upset all afternoon. Don't you think... ?"

"Hush, Bart dear."

Eva ushered me into her huge inner sanctum, her bedroom, study, and library, all rolled into one. Volumes of textbooks were strewn around. A huge leather folio was flung open, the pages scattered. "Please excuse the mess," Eva said. "Deter and I had a hissy." There was a fevered look in her eye.

I stared around the room. The medical gear was gone. "I see you've cleaned house."

"That's right," Eva snorted. "I'm sick of being sick. I shoved the IV tree and the pump into a closet and gave the nurse the weekend off. She tattled on me to Dr. Kojimura so I fired her. He called me and I took care of him. We had an intimate chat about *The Road Less Travelled* on the phone." Eva paced around the room as she talked. "Deter and I needed some time together, so I sent all the boys out to see a Polynesian show at the Hilton Villa. Fantastic women, wonderful dancers. And did you ever see their lead male? A Fiji islander. He's got yards of tongue. Seeing that tongue always makes me wonder what else he's got."

I leaned against the doorframe, laughing.

"For Heaven's sake, sit down, John, you make me nervous." Eva indicated a leather chair.

"Cushy," I said, sinking in. It was a big chair. Way over limit for Eva.

She poured me a Drambuie. She sipped on a noni juice frappé. "Dr. Kevin made this for me. He's so sweet. To tell you the truth, I think it might be working."

"Something must be. You're looking lively, Eva."

"Poor Deter. I nearly tore him to bits," Eva said. "It's been way too long. Once I've finished this course of chemo, I'm heading for Austria for some R&R, I tell you."

"I thought you two were on the outs."

"Yes, It's this. I wanted you to know about *this*." Eva waved her arms at the muddle of books and papers. "Randy's library. Here I was," she said, patting her enormous bed, "surrounded with candles and incense. Deter was supposed to join me, but I must have dozed off. When I woke up, I went slinking out, looking for Deter. I thought he must have fallen asleep. What do I find? Deter was flipping through Randy's old textbooks. He was going through them book by book, looking for what the great man had underlined in the texts. Can you believe it?"

"If you say so."

"Deter was Randy's student. He was deliriously happy, just looking at the footnotes the genius had left behind." Eva stood arms crossed in front of the mound of books flung on the floor, a fighting stance. "Well, I was pissed," Eva said. "So what else was an artefact the great man left behind?"

I was at a loss. I spread my hands.

Eva closed in on me, stared me in the face, her angry, slate-coloured eyes bored into mine. "I was. I was an artefact. I was a castoff."

"Eva. You can't think…"

She pulled back, satisfied. "Deter said the same thing. He was mortified, but I was in a rage. I was furious. So I showed him the other great works penned by his idol."

Eva picked up a handful of papers and threw them at me. They were letters.

I stared at her. "These are addressed to you."

"So? Have a read, John. Go ahead. "

"Dear Eva," I read aloud: "Another dreary day in the threadbare salons of the Kremlin. The bankruptcy of the communist regime is everywhere evident. I went to the theatre with a state-appointed minder who with hand signals passed comment on the performance that he couldn't otherwise… "

"Skip the political shit," Eva said. "Go to the next page."

"Dear Eva, my desire for you burns on the page. Though we cannot be together, think of your hand as my instrument. Find your hand as if guided by mine. Through your hand feel mine stroking your… your…" I stopped, glanced at the paragraph ahead and felt myself colouring. "I get the idea."

"The great man," Eva said. "That was Randy. He'd spend his days writing out his grand theorems in classrooms. Then he'd come home and write me this pornography. His ambition was to be a writer of erotica on the scale of one of the literary geniuses of the Victorian era. The Victorians passed around pornography in their drawing rooms, you know."

At that point it dawned on me what Eva was driving at. "So what did Deter think of all this?"

"Deter is a conventional man. He makes love like a regular man, which is what I prefer. I didn't have to dress up in ridiculous garter belts and do it on the kitchen table the way I'd do to satisfy Randy. In the end, kinky sex was never a turn on for me. Neither was any of this garbage. " She raked the letter out of my hand and swept it into the pile on the floor. "Goddamn Randy. Why did he think he had to be a genius about every single thing?" Eva sank to the floor, flinging the letters around, a frenzied expression on her face.

"Enough, Eva," I said. I pulled her to her feet and wrapped her in my arms and let her cry it out. "Calm down. You can't carry on like this. It'll kill you. It's over. Randy's gone. You've got a normal guy. Deter loves you. It's all right."

"I went crazy," Eva mumbled into the middle of my chest. She pulled out of my arms, staring up at me. "Deter was appalled. He couldn't take it. He can't stand scenes. He fled."

"He'll be back Eva."

"I don't think so. I called his hotel. He's checked out." Eva sighed, slipped out of my arms and settled in a slipper chair. "I'm sorry, John, I didn't mean to freak out. You wanted some help? What was it?"

"Did Randy ever mention a stalker to you?"

Eva stared at me. She shook her head. "A stalker? He never said a word about it to me. He wouldn't have, but it fits, as I've maintained all along."

"Hillary knew about it. She said Randy ignored it."

"Two shotgun blasts and a knife in the back," Eva said. "A crazy lover did this. That's who Tabura the Great should be looking for. Instead, he harasses my innocent boy."

There was a knock at the door. Bart poked his head in. "Kevin and Toby are back with your prescription, Mom."

"I'll get out of the way, Eva," I said. "Do you mind if I talk to Toby for a second?"

"About what?"

"The shotgun found at the Haverhill estate. Toby might know who owned it."

"It couldn't have been Randy's," Eva said. "He wasn't into guns."

Toby and I hovered in the doorway. Eva perched on the edge of the huge leather chair as her son Dr. Kevin took her pulse. "Toby. Get my stethoscope, would you?"

"Never mind, I'll get it," Bart Sneddon said.

"Mom, you have to get a grip," Kevin said. "This tachycardia of yours. It's becoming a problem. The stress you put on yourself won't help your heart. It's racing out of control."

"I'm just upset." Eva yanked her wrist out of her son's grasp. Big brother Bart arrived with a stethoscope. Dr. Kevin moved the instrument over his mother's milky breast.

"Kevin. Where are your bedside manners? This thing is cold."

"Sorry, Mom. We've got to slow your heart rate."

"I need to call the airport. I have to find Deter."

"You are going to bed."

"I'll call the airport," Bart said.

"I must apologise. I treated poor Deter so shabbily." Kevin plumped the pillows, raised the covers and stowed his mother in bed. "I'm warning you, Mother. You are working on a heart attack. I'm calling Dr. Kojimura."

"Dr. Kojimura should have caught this cancer earlier! Instead we're busy reading books together." Kevin turned his face away, hiding his exasperation from his mother.

Toby sat on the edge of the bed and pleaded with her. "Mom. You have to do what Kevin tells you."

Eva squeezed Toby's hand. "If anything happens to me, you'll be okay, guy. I'll see to it." Toby spun away.

"John is here to see you, Toby. He needs to ask you some questions. He's okay. Trust him." Eva sank into the pillows and closed her eyes. "Play something for John, would you, Toby?"

"But Mom. He wouldn't want..."

Eva's eyes popped open. "Do it for me, Toby. Just do it, please."

Toby led me across the hall and I found myself in his long, narrow bedroom. There was a single bed in the corner mounded with bedding, books, and a tangle of clothes. Paddles and boating gear in one corner. Family photos. Randy and Eva and all three boys. Randy looking like a big brother, Eva looking like a keiki. No wonder she had managed to pull it off as Randy's wife.

Toby played a chord progression on his guitar and I noticed for the first time that he was left-handed. "I can't sing. I don't have a good voice. My friend Kimo, he's good."

"When's the performance?"

"Saturday, the Aloha Week festival. Kimo and I are filling in with the Infantry Band. Want to come?"

"The Downtown Mele? 0kay!" I'd watched scores of meles. Mama Hana's dance troop would perform. Emmy would do a number. I'd be called upon to man the uli uli shakers or set up mama's portable dance floor.

"We have rehearsal in an hour."

"I won't keep you, Toby. I just have a couple of things. It won't take long." Toby strummed idly as I began. I made him go through the whole scene, trying to get him to repeat everything he had said earlier. We went through it all from the moment the doorbell rang. When we got to the part about the witness, I added some new thoughts.

"This lady you talked to. What makes you think she was a neighbour?"

"The rain cape, I guess. It rains a lot up there." He wouldn't look at me.

"What about the rain cape, Toby?"

"I've seen them around somewhere."

"You'd seen the rain cape before?"

"Maybe." He fidgeted, his crazy leg shimmying. "Anything else? I have to rehearse. Kimo's part is awesome, like a Hawaiian chant set to music."

"I can't wait to hear it." I tossed the shaka sign. "Saturday evening. I'll be there. I'll bring your mom. By the way, Toby, about the shotgun, found in the tool shed."

Toby nodded, his face blank.

"Was it always kept there?"

"On a gun rack. It was next to the paddles."

"Whose gun was it?"

"I don't know."

"It didn't belong to your dad?"

"Dad wasn't into shooting like I told you. Neither was I. Mom was against weapons of any kind."

"No cowboys and Indians?'

Toby frowned. "I was never allowed to play with guns, not even toys." He got his guitar case out of a closet, opened it, chucked some music in and closed it. He stood holding the case. "I have to go now."

On the floor, a framed photo had slipped out from under the bed. Afraid that Toby would step on the glass, I plucked it up. Toby and Kimo were on either side of Se Se, her forehead crowned with a band of maile leaves. She had sloe eyes and lush lips and a bit of a double chin. The three wore matching aloha shirts and flower leis.

"Your group," I said.

"We used to play together."

"I thought you still did."

"Se Se's gone, gone to the mainland. It's sad, sad and bad." Toby snatched the photo out of my hand and shoved it back under the bed. "I'll be late if I don't go now." As we left Toby's bedroom, Dr. Kevin was closing the door to Eva's room.

"How is she?"

"l gave her a sedative. She'll sleep for a while."

"What's the prognosis?"

"What can I say? It's cancer," Kevin said. "Her body is stressed to the max. She's gone into tachycardia— her heart is racing—and her doctors can't get it to slow down."

I let myself out but wasn't ready to ride, not quite. I took a walk along the stone wall that flanks Round Top Drive, staring down over the city and out to sea. The day had brightened. The purple haze was off the horizon, there was no surf to be seen and Honolulu hummed below. I paced along Round Top's stone wall, thrilled by the breeze, mulling over what Toby said.

He had seen the rain cape before. But where? I made a mental note to check with Hillary. Did anyone in the Dowsett house have a rain cape? As for the shotgun, the murder weapon, Toby must have known it was there all along. This really bothered me. I thought about Toby, the pained expression on his face as he chucked the photo of his friend Kimo and Kimo's sister Se Se under his bed. Bad and sad, Toby said, and that sized up the general situation as well.

I respect Round Top Drive enough that I never start the corkscrew ride down the mountain with a cell phone in my hand, so I checked the call screen. Harlan had left a message. We were to meet in his office downtown on Monday afternoon. It was time to confront Eva with Telly Tabura's suspicions. It had to be done, but considering her heart condition, it was a risky move.

FIFTY-EIGHT

Bishop Square in the heart of downtown Honolulu is manicured to such perfection that a stooped Japanese fellow scurried around with a long-handled dustpan, sweeping up errant white petals blown off tall plumeria trees. Eva, her physician son Kevin, and I, were on our way to Harlan Kawahara's office in the Pauahi Tower on the mauka end of the square, a meeting that I dreaded.

Harlan and I had decided to hold off for a while on confronting Eva with Detective Tabun's suspicions about her role in Randy's death. The questioning would put further stress on an ailing client. Nevertheless, Telly's hints that he had a tip, and his insistence on Toby as the shooter were so disturbing that this issue had to be answered. Harlan's solution was to call Dr. Kevin and ask him to accompany his mother to this meeting.

We were early. Eva wanted a breath of fresh air. She took a seat on a sun-warmed marble slab at the edge of one of the enormous reflecting pools, one of a series that grace a site sloping gently downward toward Honolulu Harbor.

Kevin and I took places on either side of Eva. I put down the brown envelope I'd brought, a courtesy gift from Telly. The breeze was brisk. I found myself enjoying the radiant heat of the marble on my okole. I studied white clouds swimming across the face of the inky pool, lined with dark blue tiles. Although it was close to lunch time, and scores of people were in the plaza, it was serenely quiet. Perhaps it was the Asian influence, but Honolulans prize their solitude. Unless it's party time they don't go in for loud talk, radio blare, honking horns or tire screech. Consequently, it is possible for a pedestrian to sit in one of the scores of public places the city offers and listen to one's own thoughts or enjoy a quiet conversation.

Eva put her pale face to the rays, eyes closed. "By the way, where's Maya? You haven't brought her by to see me."

"She's on Maui, helping Mama Hana. They are rearranging Mama Hana's Hui Handicrafts top to bottom as we speak. I'll see her over the weekend."

"Bring Maya by for drinks, won't you?"

"Will do. And how goes *your* love life?"

Eva's eyes snapped open. "Bart tracked down Deter. He was at the airport trying to get a flight out. I apologised profusely. We went to the country for two glorious days. I'm exhausted." Eva smirked. "Satiated, but exhausted."

I glanced past her and caught Doc Kevin's sullen expression.

"My mother has tachycardia," young Dr. Oedipus said. "I can't emphasise it enough. Her physicians are trying everything they can think of to get it under control. She has no business traipsing out to the country for some..."

"Tryst," Eva said. "Just say it, Kevin dear." She pulled herself up, raised her chin and directed her next remark to me. "My son would prefer that I take up some other interest. Gardening? Quilting?"

"How about something meditative?" I said, trying for droll. "The *Kama Sutra*, perhaps?"

Eva laughed outright. Kevin looked as if he wanted to shove me into the reflecting pool.

"Please, Mother. For the sake of your health."

"My health, darling, or your overly-developed sense of propriety?"

Kevin winced but said nothing. He didn't have to. His embarrassment was obvious.

"Don't be such a stick, sonny," she cooed, hugging him, then said to me, "Kevin here has been an old man his whole life. He resents Deter, my dear friend, Deter, so gentle. So what I'm worn out? It was a very satisfactory workout."

Turning her back on Kevin, Eva rose and took my arm. From the way she clung to me, I could feel that she was paying for her burst of energy. "Deter is on his way back to Vienna. I'll be off my second course of chemo in June. He'll have the summer off from the university. We'll have six weeks together."

We set off up the square. We rode the escalator to the mezzanine where an art exhibit was in progress. We were confronted by a wire sculpture of a woman, her knees bent, a grimace on her face. She wore a ti-leaf cape draped over her shoulders like a stole. A leather handbag with a bone rattle in it hung off her arm. A tiny infant was visible through her wiry womb.

Eva studied the sculpture momentarily and rendered her verdict on the piece: "The poor lady is wondering whether she'll get any child support."

I punched a button for Harlan's floor and when the elevator arrived, the door opened directly into his lobby. Harlan Kawahara, DJS, was an enormous firm that took up the entire floor. The reception area was a windowless cave lined with leather-bound law tombs.

Slant-backed, armless leather chairs were neatly posed on oriental rugs. Pools of light reflected off koa panelled walls. Japanese wahine in dark dresses hovered over their tasks, so quiet as to appear painted into the scene.

Plush as it was, this cave-like sanctum gave my gut a twinge. For some reason I've never cared for enclosed spaces all that much. I'd guess because my ancient ancestors hid out in caves.

I walked Eva to one of the chairs. We all sat down, whereupon she proceeded to needle her son: "I want to tour the Greek islands with Deter. Maybe we'll do them all. And there's always the Spanish Riviera..."

Harlan dashed in, late from court. He ushered us into his office, offered tea and I felt better. The outer world was now visible. Harlan had an amazing view of Honolulu Harbor. The horizon line was its normal silvery hue and not the odd purple it had been for the past few days, Praise Madam. A good omen, I thought, as I fingered the brown envelope in my hand.

FIFTY-NINE

Black rings appeared under Eva's eyes. Kevin wanted her to lie down on one of Harlan's leather couches, but Eva insisted on sitting up in a wing chair. Kevin found the matching ottoman, lifted his mother's legs onto it and covered them with his jacket. He jockeyed a straight chair into position beside her and sat down. Eva pulled her son's arm into her lap and sat stroking it. Kevin's face relaxed. He felt Eva's forehead periodically and fussed over her as I brought them all up to date.

"I made sure that Detective Tabura found the garden trowel and the rain cape on the Haverhill grounds. Toby's tip led us to it. Detective Tabura made good on an earlier promise. He gave me the police photos of the note on Randy's back. He also passed along a photo of the note that Toby wrote out from a typed copy. It would help if this note meant something." I passed the brown envelope to Eva.

She pulled out the photos, stared at them, and laughed. "You can't imagine the relief." She handed the photo to Kevin, who smiled as he tossed the glossy pics back to Harlan.

"Toby didn't write this. No way," he said.

I stared at them, first Eva, then Kevin. Mother and son both radiated candour, confidence and relief, and I found myself tossing a shaka in the air.

"Please explain," Harlan said, rocking back in his leather chair, hands on his head.

"Yes the reversed letters are similar to something Toby *might* do," Eva said. "Any dyslexic might reverse a letter or two. It's very much in character. But if anything, this note is a setup. Someone who knows Toby might have made such a mistake. But there's a huge difference here. The letters in the original note are joined. They are in cursive. Now look at the second photo, the one Toby wrote. None of the letters are joined. You'll notice the general slant is different as well. That's because Toby is left-handed. I don't know who the police used as a handwriting expert, but whoever it was should have caught this."

"May I see those?" Harlan said. He took a magnifying glass out of his desk. "Of course, Eva. I see that now. Let me call for the handwriting expert's report. Perhaps the expert mentioned this but the prosecutor overlooked it." His mouth twisted. He shook his head and we heard his sigh clear across the room.

"One of those convenient errors that prosecutors make?" I said.

"That's right," Harlan said. "It's our job to find the holes in the prosecution's argument."

"Slipshod procedure," Eva said. "It's what I've said about this prosecutor all along." Eva wilted in her chair. "It was my fault, all of it."

Harlan and I stared at each other across the silence. Was Eva about to confess?

"The note, Eva?" Harlan said, waving the photos.

"Not the damned note. I'm talking about the cursive Toby refused to write." Harlan and I breathed a collective sigh of relief.

"My first two sons were academically gifted children," Eva said. "Bart set the pace and Kevin fell into line. I never had to worry about them for a minute." I looked to Kevin for a reaction. He was glowing by a factor of two-hundred watts.

Eva went on: "Toby was different. Toby was my challenge as a mother. Thank goodness he wasn't my firstborn. I'd never have known how to handle him, his dyslexia. Toby had no confidence whatsoever at school. He had a bellyache every morning and didn't want to go. I did all the wrong things. He had a hard time with writing in second grade and I tried to force him. I am ashamed to say it now, but I was frantic. I went so far as to take Toby to a hypnotist. Toby stood up to me, though. He flatly refused to write cursive, hypnotist or not, and won't write cursive to this day. I realised I was on the wrong track and had to change my strategy with him."

Well, that's fine, Eva," Harlan said. He tore his handwritten notes off a yellow legal pad, stapled them and inserted the notes into a file.

Eva was staring at him. "Wait a minute, Harlan. Do you think *I* wrote the note that wound up on Randy's back?"

Harlan tapped his pen on his desk blotter as he framed a judicious answer. "I apologise, Eva. When you first said that it was your fault? For a moment there, I wasn't following what you meant."

"Do you think I'd stoop to murdering Randy? That son of a bitch? I wouldn't give Hillary the satisfaction."

"Careful, Eva," the lawyer said. "Suppose Randy's reckless sexual escapades resulted in your illness? There's a motive the prosecutor could use to advantage. Not that I..." Harlan's voice faltered. The pen pecked away on the blotter. "The prosecutor could use that angle very effectively. You do see that, don't you, Eva?" The pen paused. Harlan's tone was level, his face bland. I admired that.

"I see. I believe Randy gave me cancer, so I *off him* out of revenge?" Eva shook her head. "Oh, yes, I did say that, early on." There was a nervous tremor in her laugh. "But Dr. Kojimura, and I, we are now reading an old classic, *The Road Less Travelled*. I've learned to lighten up. A more likely scenario is that there's cancer in my family. My brother died of colon cancer. It's along the same pipeline."

Eva turned on me, disappointment on her face. "Ratted me out, did you, John?"

"It wasn't me, not at all. I had lunch with Telly Tabura the other day. Telly hinted to me that somebody tipped him. The police have some sort of lead. Could you have told someone else this same thing?"

"John called me about the tip," Harlan told Eva. "We have to follow up on this. Otherwise we could be blindsided in court."

"I'm guessing that you hadn't made it any secret how you felt," I said.

"Oh, that's true, John." Eva's hands flew to her mouth. "Stephanie Clayton, the medical writer. I did mention it to her. In fact I gave her one of those medical pamphlets and asked her to research it. I don't think I told her outright just why I was looking into it, but. ..but..." Eva flopped back in the chair and stared at the ceiling, her face drawn. The rest of us sat eyeing each other, waiting for Eva to say something else.

"What is it, Mom?" Kevin prompted. "You have to tell Harlan."

"Come to think of it, Stephanie Clayton was thick with Freddie Seligman."

"Freddie Seligman?" I said.

"Fred Seligman was city editor before me. I got him busted for sexual harassment. Of course the paper rigged it to look like Freddie was being promoted."

"All right," Harlan said, scribbling furiously on his yellow legal pad.

"I got Freddie Seligman busted to some nondescript weekly in Bemidji, Minnesota. Freddie is now *the publisher* of a nothing paper where he'll freeze his ass to death."

"Sexual harassment?" I said, careful to wipe the incredulity off my face. Eva got somebody else fired for sexual harassment? And Eva herself was messing around with a summer intern? This was rich.

"Freddie Seligman thought he was funny, sending me these hot e-mails. He'd post them on our internal memo system. Other reporters saw them. I could document everything."

"You won, Eva," I murmured.

"Damn straight," Eva said. "Eddie Seligman hated me, did his best to sabotage anything I wanted to do."

"All right," Harlan said. "Eva's newsroom battles are beyond us—not the issue."

"Here's the issue," Eva said. "When I was first diagnosed, I found it in the literature, my kind of cancer might come from a sexually transmitted virus. This does fit my case. My ex husband's flagrant sexual irresponsibility could be the cause of my cancer. However, Dr. Kojimura convinced me that I can't focus on any negatives. I can't afford to. But the idea that I would put Toby up to murdering his father? Is that what they think?"

"Forgive me, Eva," Harlan said, steepling his fingers. "Let me play devil's advocate. Hawaiian jurors want a story. The prosecutor might well use a tale like this very effectively."

"Detective Tabura hinted that there was some anonymous tip," I said. "Maybe it came from the medical reporter. Or maybe brother Seligman made a phone call from Bemidji."

Eva rose, flinging Kevin's coat off her legs. Kevin protested. "Mother, for the love of... Can't you contain yourself?"

Eva strode across to Harlan's desk, a little shakily. A bit wobbly on her pins, but nonetheless energetic. Hands on the edge of the desk for support, Eva let her lawyer have it. "Pre-*POS*-terous, Harlan."

The lawyer's face lit up. "Tell me why, Eva."

"I would never kill Randy, never would have, Toby needed Randy. Once Randy started to take notice of Toby, my son began to shine. Toby needed Randy's male influence. It was my idea that they take up paddling together," Eva explained. "I insisted that Toby spend time over at the Dowsett house. I had to push Toby into going. Hillary didn't make it easy, let me tell you."

I watched Harlan. His hands were clasped under his chin. As Eva made her plea, Harlan closed his mouth and sealed it off with his clasped hands. He stared intently at Eva, wanting her to say the exact words chat would make her case.

"Toby is my *baby*," Eva said. "Why would a woman in my position, a woman with a potentially fatal disease, murder the loving parent of her baby? I'm a *mother* first, a mother above all. Toby comes first in my life."

"Very good, Eva," Harlan said, writing furiously now.

"*Men*," Eva said. "I do admit I prefer the company of men, but in my life, the pursuit of men is a distant second. My sons—all of them—come first."

"A wonderful sentiment, Mother," Kevin said under his breath. I caught the sarcasm in the son's tone and glanced at Harlan. Fortunately, Eva's lawyer hadn't heard the caveat.

SIXTY

It was a half hour drive from Harlan's office in Bishop Square up the mountain to Eva's domain on Round Top. I followed Eva and Kevin in Eva's silver BMW. Brother Bart was at the door as we arrived.

"Come on in, Mom," Bart said. "Toby and his friend have a surprise for you."

"It can wait," Kevin says. "Mom needs her—"

"Nonsense, Doctor dear, I'm fine, I'll be alright." Eva took Bart's arm and beckoned me in. "Come on, I think you'll enjoy this."

The furniture in Eva's salon had been rearranged. A tower of amplifiers dwarfed the credenza. Music stands and guitars awaited in a cleared area in front of it. Toby and his pal Kimo played a couple of numbers. Kimo was the lead singer. Toby backed him. Eva gave them her rapt attention. Energised, she stood up, applauded, cheered, and demanded another number. Brother Bart and I joined in the hearty applause.

I looked around. Dr. Kevin was not in the room. I slipped away to the kitchen and found him serving up more of his noni juice concoction.

"The next wonder drug?"

"I wish."

"Your mother seems to be doing well today."

"Let's hope she doesn't pay the price tomorrow."

"Will you be staying for a while?'

"I fly out tomorrow night."

"That's too bad."

"I'm going to try to get Mom to pack her bags and come along. I'll look after her. We've got a top cancer unit at my hospital."

"What about Dr. Kojimura?"

He's a gastroenterologist, barely out of medical school. Of course my mother would choose youth over experience."

"Your mother seems attached to him."

Kevin grunted in distaste, and did a mocking imitation of his mother: "'Dr. Kojimura and I are reading *The Road Less Travelled together*.' Dr. K. is another of Mom's imagined conquests, I'm afraid. I met the guy."

"And?"

"He's a decent sort. His treatment follows the protocols from what I understand. I've asked Mom to obtain a copy of her medical records. I'll have them reviewed by someone at Stanford. Dr. Kojimura was treating her simple indigestion for eight months, before it occurred to him to order a biopsy. It seems to me he should have gotten wise sooner. If things don't look right, I'll demand she come live with me."

"That might be hard for her—unless we resolve this thing with Toby."

Kevin stared at me, a short doughy haole, balding, with a pudgy face. His arms and cheeks were pink with sunburn. "This prosecutor can't be serious. It has to be that the police haven't found anyone else to blame. Randy was a high profile victim, after all." His voice rose. "What did Toby do? Toby found his dad and tried to save him. He called the emergency network before he made the first move."

"Eva gives you the credit for that."

Kevin nodded, expression softening. "I drilled everybody in the family on the medical basics. Toby might be dyslexic, but screw that. He's a hell of a good kid and he's got sense."

In the next room, the young musicians were launching into another number.

Kevin set the noni drink on a tray with a pitcher of ice water and pills in a slotted dispenser. He checked the time and made some notes on a chart on the kitchen counter.

"Pretty official."

"I'm leaving notes for Mom's private nurse. Mom doesn't want to accept the fact that she's got to maintain a regular schedule. The worst part of esophageal cancer is that she can't eat. She wants to get off the feedings whenever she feels like it. In the long run, that won't work." Kevin opened the fridge. He took out a couple of bags of saline solution and some milky looking stuff. He had his hands full.

"Can I help?"

"Thanks. Bring that tray on the counter and follow me."

We went to Eva's bedroom. It was dark and stuffy. Kevin asked me to put the tray on the desk and set about raising the shades. He flung open the French doors onto the deck and sniffed the air. "This is more like it," he said. Breezes rustled the mound of papers piled beside Eva's bed, long printouts slashed with red markings."No need for the place to smell like a sickroom," Kevin muttered. He rolled the hospital pump out of the closet and opened the doors to the hall. Strains of *The Wind Beneath My Wings* floated in. "Mom's favourite song," Kevin said. "The tears will be flowing by now." The intern looked at his watch then waved me to the big leather chair, while he settled into a smaller one.

"So what do you think?" I asked. "Could Randy's recklessness have caused your mother's cancer?"

"Who knows?" Kevin said. "That's one of those anomalies of medical literature. Studies show that this or that is a risk factor for cancer. People love to apply that stuff to their own case. It's helpful to think, 'Why me?' Personally, I think Mom's diet may have equal or greater weight. She lives on this packaged food, full of sulfites."

"So you wouldn't blame Randy."

Kevin's whole body twitched. As if he'd been struck. "I was eleven years old and my brother was thirteen when my mother eloped with Randy. We saw our dad on weekends. He was devastated. He couldn't cope."

"And Randy? Was he any kind of a dad?"

Kevin stared at me, incredulous. "You don't seem to get it, John. Picture a pair of school kids. Mom brings home a guy who's just turned eighteen. She says they are married. We were stunned. She acts like Randy is God's gift to creation. What we see is a dude going off to college. The only difference between Randy and us is, we've still got zits."

"And Randy gets to sleep with Mom."

Kevin stared at me. "Thanks."

"Sorry. I shouldn't have said that."

Kevin waved his hand. "Forget it."

"So Randy never tried to become a dad to you guys?"

"Nah. He became big brother, the kid with the special privileges." It was the bitterness in Kevin's voice I heard, and I understood the intern's sense of displacement.

"So you were demoted from the baby of the family to a distant third?"

"You could say that."

"So what did you do about it?"

"Me? I took up with Pamela Fong."

"Found your own girlfriend." Although I knew better, I simply couldn't resist needling Kevin. He was such a stuffy bastard. "Or someone to mother you?"

A salacious grin crosses the intern's face. "Hell no. Pam was a brilliant girl. One of those girls who does everything right, the cheerleader, the scholar, the athlete. Pam had it all and she loved to do the nasty."

"You were how old?"

"A teen going on middle age just like big brother Randy."

"What did your mother do about it?"

"She raised hell a time or two, but I had her cold on that one."

Toby stuck his head through the bedroom door.

"Kev, can you come?" he said. "Mom's having a spell."

SIXTY-ONE

We rushed back to the living room. Eva lay slumped on the sofa. She laboured under ragged breaths. Kevin put a stethoscope to her chest.

Toby hovered behind the sofa, hand on his mother's forehead. "She's all clammy."

"Bring the pills off the kitchen counter, would you, Toby?" the intern instructed. "And Bart, find a pillow and a blanket. She'll be all right."

Toby's musician friend Kimo grabbed his sheet music, shoved it into his guitar case and threw the shaka shake. "See you, Tob. I hope your mom is okay."

"It's cool," Toby said.

Kimo bounded out the door, thick hair flying.

Dr. Kevin lifted Eva's legs onto the sofa, settled her head on a cushion and tucked a blanket around her. He whipped his cell phone off his belt and speed dialled. "This is Dr. Sneddon. Find Dr. Kojimura. Stat. My mother's tachycardia is flaring up again."

"Dr. K's out on *The Road Less Travelled?*" I said.

Kevin glared at me, which was my cue to exit.

"Hey, Toby," I said. "Let's talk, brah."

"Yeah, sure, John," Toby said. "But do you mind if I make a pizza? I haven't had anything to eat today."

We headed into the kitchen. Brother Bart was reading about the latest moon probe in *The New York Times.*

Toby was a kid who could fend for himself. He assembled his own pie, Toby's Surf Rider, a doctored pepperoni and swiss, adding Maui onion, pineapple, olives, zucchini, red pepper and avocado, topped off with a storm of fresh parmesan cheese, not the stuff from a can, but shaved right off a brick he stored in one of those graters you see in the pasta palaces.

"Your music sounds good, Toby, What's your inspiration?"

"I'll hear the theme in my head," Toby said, "I fiddle around on the strings until I get the right chord progressions. I have to learn it by rote. I'm no good at formal composition. I wind up getting the notes backward or else in the wrong place on the staff."

"Got any gigs lined up?"

"Kimo's father has an in at a karaoke bar. They let us play on slow nights. He got us our Aloha Week gig with the Tropic Light military band. A couple of their regular musicians from the Hickam air base were transferred."

"The Downtown Mele?"

"You coming?"

"Of course I'm coming. I was brought up on Aloha week. "

"My mom is researching which colleges have the best music programs."

"Has she picked any out?"

"She's looking in California. That way I'd be near Kevin."

"Not Manoa?"

"Mom doesn't want me staying in Honolulu. She says I need to learn how to function on the mainland."

"Might be good advice."

Toby looked at his watch. "I have to head off to rehearsal in a half hour."

"Right," I said, "so let's get down to it. Let's see what the killer meant by this note on your dad's back."

We seated ourselves at the wicker table in the kitchen. Toby wolfed down pizza. I got out the envelope with the photos of the notes.

"You've already seen the originals."

"Sure. I wrote that one."

"This other one. Did you see it?"

"Not when I wrote my version. Detective Tabura gave me a typed copy; but look at this first one. It's written in red marker pen."

"And you didn't write it?"

Toby's forehead wrinkled. "Of course not. I don't own a red marker pen."

"Why not?"

"The teachers at my school use red. Students use black. I don't use college ruled paper, either."

I looked at the original note. Toby was right about ruling on the paper.

"What would you use?"

"Intermediate school rule." Toby measured off the between his fingers. "We don't use college rule. It's not allowed."

"That's great, Toby. That helps us." I took a minute to think about what I'd say next. "Now about these letters. A-D-I—T-C-H... A Ditch?" I said. "A jealous girlfriend, maybe, a ditch, as in 'I was ditched.'"

Toby dismissed the suggestion with a swat of his palm. I suppose. How would I know?"

"You might know more than you think. Suppose we guess what the killer meant?"

"Mom says the killer scrambled the letters on purpose. To get me into trouble."

"Why do that?"

"She thinks the killer didn't like Dad spending time with me."

"Jealousy?"

I handed Toby a pen and my pocket notebook. He wound his hand around the pen, the way lefties tend to do. "Suppose we play around with this word?"

"Okay. But it's easier for me to write on something bigger. Do you mind?"

"Whatever. "

Toby rummaged some lined paper out of a school notebook. He sat down and copied out what he'd done before, and held it up. "The *d* was little when it should have been a capital and I got the *a* backward, That's how I did it when I wrote it for Detective Tabura."

"Does this mean anything?"

"Not to me."

"So let's try to make some sense out of it. Let's say the person who wrote this is trying to imitate the way you would write."

"I am dyslexic. If I don't think carefully, I'd maybe write a word like "first." It might come out "frist.""

"So let's do that with this word."

"It would be AIDTCH," Toby said. He had all the caps right in this test write.

"So, now we have a word. AID. But does TCH have a meaning?'

Brother Bart joined in. He stared over Toby's shoulder. "TCH stands for Transportation Clearing House, a fleet management system for truckers. A lot of our sub contractors use their facilities."

"All right," I said. "But would this have meant something to Randy?"

The scientist shrugged. "Dr. Haverhill needs better gas mileage" We all laughed.

"So what else can we do with this, Toby?"

"The other way I'd write wrong? I'd reverse the first letters. I'm a lot more careful now, so I hardly ever do it anymore."

"Show me."

Toby wrote, laboriously, his hand crimped awkwardly, then handed me the result. "DAITCH."

"Daitch? A name, do you think?"

"Do we know anybody named Daitch?" Bart said.

"Nobody I know," Toby said. He picked up the photo of the original.

"Wait. See how it's written? There's a little space after the second letter. Maybe it was meant to be written in two words."

"That would fit," Bart said.

"But that isn't how the word is spaced," Toby said.

"Okay, Toby. Write it as you see it, brah."

"I reverse the first two letters, so AD becomes DA." Toby held up his handiwork, spaced, childlike letters like the work of a second grader. I guessed that the kid was capable of better writing, but perhaps the rebel ruled, forever rebelling against Mom.

"Pidgin," I said. "DA was pidgin for *the* and the next word was *itch*.

"Da itch?" Bart said.

"That works," I said as I felt the vibration of the cell phone at my hip. I used the call as an excuse to stand up, to stretch. My back was feeling gimpy again.

"John Spyer."

"John. It's Hillary."

I looked around. The brothers were staring at the words on the paper. "Let me call you right back," I said. It wouldn't do to reveal to the first Mrs. Randy's family that the second Mrs. Randy was on the phone.

"Please. It's urgent. I need your help."

"I'm on my way."

"Come right here to the house." Her voice was breathy. In the background I could hear shouting and doors slamming.

"I'll be there in twenty." I stowed the phone on my belt. "Something has come up. I've got to run. Mahalo,

Toby." I grabbed up the photos and slapped him on the back. "I don't know what this means, but maybe it's a start." I shook Bart's hand. Kevin came in. "Doc. Nice to meet you. You've been a great help to Eva. Have a safe trip home."

I was out the door in three, loped up the steps, stiff in the back, piled into Em and headed off Mt. Tantalus, down Round Top Drive, the corkscrew road. The words Toby had scrawled were running through my mind. *Da itch.* It was a Pidgin corruption of the Hawaiian for the Anglo Saxon term, sex. The Polynesians weren't being coy. They simply did it without making any big Puritanical deal about it. Doing it was so natural it was beneath notice and therefore needn't be named, except by its urgency, the itch. Viewed in that light da itch was a Polynesian in-joke.

"Okay, Em," I said, talking to the Mustang. I learned the habit from my mother's family. They talked to their appliances. When Mama Hana replaced her refrigerator after twenty years, she would go down to say hello to the old refrigerator at the second hand appliance mart. She didn't want her old fridge to feel slighted.

"Da Itch. It fits the profile. It fits the crime," I said to Em.

A Hummer came at me, hogging the centre of the road. I swung Em hard right and screeched into a turnout just before a narrow bridge and grabbed my cell phone. I pulled up a photo, the one I'd taken back in June. There it was, the same sort of note, a nearly identical lineup of the same batch of letters. The *c* was backward rather than the a, and the letters had the same slant—Da itch. It fit, but what in the name of Madam did it mean? Was Professor Randy's murderer a local? A Hawaiian? Or maybe a hapa haole like me?"

All I knew for certain at that point was that Randy Haverhill knew exactly what that message meant, which was why he had been so quick to erase the note on the whiteboard from the book signing. My hands shook on the wheel and I eased onto the road very carefully because I happened to be on a blind curve at the time.

SIXTY-TWO

Hillary stood in the front yard of the Dowsett house, leaning against the trunk of an enormous banyan tree, with one booted foot propped against the trunk. She wore faded jeans and a plaid shirt, and swabbed her face with a handkerchief. The evening breezes had slacked off.

A gaggle of blue and whites were parked in the street. A swarm of officers had invaded her house. Telly Tabura was standing on the stoop directing the search, a bottle of that green Jamba drink in his hand. He hadn't noticed my arrival, or at least I hoped he hadn't.

"Oh thank God," Hillary said. "I'm so glad you've come, John. Look. They are trashing my house." I stared at her, taking her measure, that unusual face, long in the cheekbones, softened by that short, thin upper lip and the pouty lower one. Her eyes were diamond shaped, so outsized as to seem painted on, appearing lidless and topped by the high flown brows. I could see how a connoisseur of women like Professor Randy would have found Hillary so appealing.

"I want this circus stopped right now."

"You were served with a warrant?"

She nodded, mouth framing a grimace.

"Then it's legal. They have a right."

"They tore the house apart already. Why are they here again?"

"Could be they've found new evidence?" *A garden trowel. A rain cape.* "I'm sorry but I don't think I can help you, Hillary. I can't represent everybody."

"So? I'm not everybody. I'm just one—"

"Poor little rich girl?"

She stared at me.

"Sorry, Hillary, that wasn't nice."

"You were Randy's friend, John. Eva trusts you to protect Toby. So I feel I can trust you, too."

I stared at her, right into those troubled eyes. "Call your lawyer."

"Who would I call? I haven't a clue."

"Come on, Hillary. The daughter of Cameron Rooke? Surely your daddy has a law firm on retainer."

"That's just it. Anybody who represented me would be working for Daddy."

My hand moved over my mouth as I pondered this.

"Some things you'd rather Daddy not know?"

"My father loves me dearly. I adore him. But..." She turned clear around in little stamping moves, hands flapping at her sides. It was a silly manoeuvre for such a big woman.

"Daddy loves Barbie? Is that it? Not the real Hillary?"

"I never argue with my father. I'm incapable of doing that."

"In return for which, Daddy let you do pretty much as you pleased?"

Hillary threw up her hands. "Forget it, John. I can't see where this is getting us."

"I agree. Good luck, Hillary." I turned, headed for Em. Police reporter Mitzi Wong was coming through the gate. I stepped back into the shadows. A hand clamped over my arm.

"Why, John," Hillary purred. "You can't be seen by the police reporter for *The Honolulu Gazette*. Eva wouldn't like it." Her tone taunted me from the lower registers. She stroked my bicep. I wondered what technique she had for bad backs.

"Call Daddy."

"Daddy can't help me."

"He can't do much with this, I agree. Not right now. Best he can do is damage control. But what choice do you have? How's Daddy going to take this when he reads it cold in tomorrow morning's headlines?"

"I don't have my cell phone," she said. "Let me borrow yours."

"Dad would track me in a minute. I have to stay out of this one, at least while I consider the options." A cold nose pressed into my hand. It was Hone, Tutu Lia's maimed dog. Yellow matter was leaking out his closed eye. Through the thick cypresses, I could hear Tutu Lia calling: "Hone. Hone, come home, keiki. Come to Lia's hale."

"Come on, Hillary. Tutu Lia's baby has gone missing. We'll return him and you can make the call from her house."

SIXTY-THREE

I parked my loafers on Tutu Lia's front doorstep. Hillary wriggled out of her riding boots. I rapped on Tutu's door, returned her dog, and introduced Lia to Hillary.

"I am so sorry for you, Mrs. Haverhill," Lia said. "Professor Randy was one boy of mine, part of Tutu Lia's 'ohana. Yes he was."

Lia beckoned us into her kitchen. A sweet nutty smell radiated from her oven.

"Macadamia nut?" I said.

"I bake for the Queen's Hospital fundraiser. You like to try?" she said to Hillary, proffering fresh-baked cookies on a platter,

"Fabulous," Hillary said. "I must get the recipe."

I stared at her. For some reason, I couldn't picture Hillary Cameron Rooke Haverhill slaving over cookie dough. If she dealt in handicrafts at all, it would be money folding, shaping green bills into artsy birds and paper aeroplanes the way Hawaiians love to do.

"Randy told me how he loved you, Tutu Lia," Hillary said. "He also told me all about these famous cookies."

I let the women natter. Randy this and Randy that. I made the phone gesture behind Lia's back a time or two and when Hillary wouldn't pick up on it, I realised she was stalling and took matters into my own hands.

"Sorry to interrupt this trip down memory lane, Lia. Hillary has an important call to make. She has to do it right now."

"Oh? Yes? Why you not say something, Hillary? Come on. I show you the phone."

Lia left Hillary in the next room, then returned to the kitchen. "A lovely woman, Mrs. Hillary. Good for Randy. I believe he truly loved her."

"Indeed he must have." *Maybe well enough to have gotten himself killed.*

There was a tap at the kitchen door. Hillary peeked in. "Excuse me, Tutu Lia. I need to consult with John."

I slipped into the hall. We were in close quarters and Hillary was plumeria fresh and the whites of her diamond eyes glowed at me in the dark, and I found myself with my hand on her shoulder, a brotherly gesture, of course. Hillary stood there with the receiver in her hand, waving it as if she couldn't figure out how to dial it.

"Have you forgotten Daddy's phone number?"

"What should I tell him?"

"Tell him the truth."

"Knowing Daddy, he'll send someone right over—if he can't come himself. Somebody from Oahu Land and Cane will throw the company weight around, lean on the police."

"So? Is that so terrible?" I gave her a reassuring hug, but her eyes shifted away and I knew something really nasty was bothering her and I also realised I had better find out what.

"Make that call, Hillary. You have to."

"And then?" she murmured.

"And then we'll talk."

I ducked back into Tutu Lia's kitchen. She handed me a cup of mango tea and more of the cookies and I took my time to sip the tea and enjoy the macadamias. After a few minutes, I pecked Tutu Lia on the cheek.

"Duty calls," I said. "Tell Hillary she'll find me out in the yard."

If Hillary thought I was dodging her, so what? I didn't want to be caught dangling on the end of her arm when Cameron Rooke's lawyers in their leather shoes showed up—which undoubtedly wouldn't take long.

SIXTY-FOUR

Speaking of shoes, I'd left mine at Lia's front door. There was a pile of rubber flip-flops on Tutu's back porch. I put on the biggest ones I could find, but even so they were small. My toes hung over into the grass. I flip-flopped through the cypress hedge, emerging across from the garden shed on the Haverhill property, curious to find out whether it had been searched a second time.

"In front door, out the back, eh brah?"

I glanced over my shoulder. It was Telly. He must have come round from the rear of Randy's house, and he must have known I was around all along.

"Detective Tabura. Good to see you."

"Come to da search party?" His unibrow raised in a quizzical arc. He waved the Jamba Juice in his hand.

"Had my scanner on. Recognized the address," I said. "Just curious. You make our garden trowel as coming from the tool shed?"

"Could be." His mouth curved upward on the left side, ever so slightly and his eyes flared, by which I read the news on the coconut wireless. It was a yes. They had linked the garden trowel to the shed—or the house, or were convinced they had, and this was not good for Hillary.

"And how's the trowel doing? Been cleaning it off in a luminol bath?"

"Clever boy," Telly said. "John Spyer knows everything. Except where he keeps his shoes."

"I left them next door at Tutu Lia's. Her half- blind mutt was out. I took him home."

"Dogs and damsels, brah?"

"Mrs. Hillary you mean?" My faked surprise didn't sway Telly, who stood with his hands on his hips, his expression stolid.

"She wanted to use the phone."

"Call her lawyer, yeah?"

"Maybe."

The slam of a car door caught Telly's attention. A black Lincoln, the graceful swirl of an orchid stencilled discreetly on the front doors. So huge a conglomerate on so small an island was overbearing enough was how it came off. Two figures emerged, haole, white shirts, jackets, ties, real shoes.

"The official visit," I said. "See you, Telly. Let's go grind again."

"In a day or two, maybe."

"Good evening, gentlemen." I strolled past the arriving lawyers. Unfortunately my curled-toes shuffle in the short flip-flops earned me notice.

"John Spyer?" the taller of the two lawyers said. He was a clean-cut guy with a thick head of hair bleached white, striking against his ruddy face.

"That's right. "

"Charles Cooke." He extended his hand.

"Pleased to meet you." I shook his proffered hand. No doubt Cooke never flipped a shaka in his blue-blooded life.

"We've met before."

"I'm sorry?"

"The Jacklenen case. You were an expert witness."

"Oh, yes. And how is Mr. Jacklenen?"

"Out of jail, thanks to you." Mr. Cooke Esquire said something to his partner, something I didn't catch. The partner went on ahead. Cooke had neatly arranged to have a private word with me.

"You are working for Eva Haverhill."

"So to speak."

"Some tita she is." His face darkened.

"Excuse me?"

"She was quite out of bounds with my son."

"Ahhh," I said. "Mr, Cooke, Sir. You are Eddie Cooke's dad?" *So Eddie Cooke, the boy toy intern on Eva's paper, was the son of this high profile lawyer, working for Hillary's father's law firm. In other words, foxy young Cooke had his fingers in all the pies—in all the pizza pies, where the Haverhill case was concerned.*

"Eddie handled the matter discreetly," Cooke Senior said. "He chose to leave the paper. This was all to the good, as far as I was concerned. I didn't want Eddie in journalism. What kind of living could he make? And so, it all ended well. However, had Eddie chosen differently, he might have found himself filing a harassment suit."

"With Daddy as his lawyer? How very convenient."

Cooke didn't like that. He scowled, ruining his pretty face. "No need to get huffy. I was merely trying to warn you about this Eva Haverhill of yours."

"You have issues with Eva, I'd suggest you deal directly with her. I'm not representing Eva per se. I'm helping out her son."

"I might have a talk with her." Cooke Senior said through narrowed eyes. I suppressed an urge to laugh in his face. A lawyer for Oahu Land Cane? Get into a scrap with a senior editor of *The Honolulu Gazette?* Not in this century.

I returned to Lia's front porch, found my loafers and noticed that Hillary's boots were missing. That was lucky. I wanted more space to think things out before I got entangled with…

"Oh there you are, John," the velvety voice said. "I've been looking for you."

"Later, Hillary," I said. "Your daddy's team has just arrived. I suggest you go say hello."

"What should I tell them?"

I raised my open palms in exasperation. "You don't have to tell them anything. They'll know what to do."

"Good, " she said. "Help me out here, John. Suppose the police find something I wish I didn't know about?"

I massaged the inner corners of my eyes as I mulled this over. *Hillary was hinting she was in serious trouble. She knew too much.* "Look Hillary, I couldn't represent you. But I suppose I could hear you out, maybe help you find someone."

"Thank you, John. That's why I trust you. It means you care about doing the right thing. So do I."

"I've got a meeting scheduled downtown and I'm running behind."

"Maybe you could rearrange your schedule?"

"And disappoint a lady? Sorry."

"A girlfriend."

"A psychologist, if you must know."

"Have you gone into counselling?"

"I wish I had–years ago. Nope. I'm just getting some background on the case."

"Good for you."

"Meet me in Waikiki. The Surfrider, four o'clock. The search might be over by then. Do me a favour. Try to scope out what's missing. Bring me the receipt the cops give you for what they take. It might help to know what the cops collect."

SIXTY-FIVE

I studied Susan Kcpono while Susan studied the two photos I'd handed her. I stared at the photos on Susan's desk, encased in frames covered in tapa cloth, Susan's tots ages two and four, or thereabouts. Her kids were dark. They took after their dad.

Susan was haole, a tall woman with one of those scooped out, pointy noses that look to have been manufactured in some plastic surgeon's office. I can't say. Susan's been a friend of mine for years, but part of being a friend is, some things you don't ask. Susan's coarse blonde hair was out of a bottle, too. That I knew because her roots were showing. Susan has beautiful brown eyes, though, and these limpid pools are for real.At least I think they are. I don't think Susan's empathetic eyes are enhanced by contacts. Middle age had been kind to Susan as well. She had kept out of the sun. Her face was unlined. Her kids would be what now? Twelve and fourteen?

When she was finished, she took off her glasses and pushed the black and white glossies across her desk. "I'm no handwriting expert, but even I can tell that the same person didn't write this."

"Maybe our prosecutor needed a suspect."

"I hate to hear that."

"The backward letters bother me," she said, " suggesting that the killer was trying to frame Toby."

"Sick, isn't it? But I'm not surprised."

"So maybe my hunch isn't off the mark?"

"Well, this whole scenario. It's bizarre. The killer pins the note on Randy, using a knife. A grisly message to the world. I see this as the killer's weird justification, a way of explaining behaviour that's totally out of bounds." She threw up her hands. "These wackos don't realise they're so far over the top that the rest of us don't get the message."

"You've seen this kind of thing before."

"I've seen it? Hah! I've lived it, as you well know."

Susan herself had been the victim of a stalker, so what she knew wasn't just some babble out of a psychology textbook. I had tracked down the client who had turned on Susan. It was one of those deals where the therapist becomes the client's love object.

"So give me your informed opinion, Susan. What went down between the professor and his conquest?"

"It would only be guessing. "

"Educated guessing."

"All right, On the phone, you told me there were incidents." Susan rocked in her high-backed chair as I described them, the slashed tires, the trashed apartment, the fiasco at the book-signing, the police report filed by the fiancée.

"Hillary Cameron Rooke. I read it in the society section." Susan's arms butterflied as she clasped her fingers on top of her head. "But this was a while back. A year or so?"

"That's right."

"There was way more intervening contact between the killer and the professor. That would be my guess." Susan's arms came down to rest on her desk. Her fingers were long and graceful, her nails manicured. "How so?"

"There are a couple of ways that people wind up victims of stalkers. In both cases there was some sort of relationship. Then the stalker, being a stalker, wants total possession of the lover and the lover breaks it off."

"Which serves to enrage the stalker."

"Right. So how does the victim react? In one of two ways. In the most common scenario, the victim tries to let the lover down easily."

"Let's always friends?"

'Yes, and that doesn't work. The stalker misreads the message, views the lover's friendly overtures as attention.

"The stalker thinks the lover might come back?"

"That's right, and sometimes the lover makes a fatal mistake."

"Do you think this is what happened to Professor Randy?"

"I doubt it,"

"Why?"

"Randy Haverhill was a common sexual stereotype, the charming professor that all the girls fall for. It was a game for him. Maybe he felt energised by the romance?" Susan said. She rolled her chair forward at her desk. "In fact, there are new studies that indicate that the *chemistry* we talk about between lovers really *is* chemical. Maybe Dr. Haverhill believed that his sexual appetites fueled and refreshed his creative imagination."

I inhaled a laugh. "If chemistry is chemical, maybe he was right."

Susan shrugged. "You got it."

"Did you ever run into one of these professors?"

"I went to college, didn't I, not to mention grad school? This is so common I'd venture to say there's at least one of these predatory professors on every campus."

"Men of Randy's intellectual calibre?"

"John, you are a keiki on the rock, sometimes. Look. I was on the campus at Princeton when a certain famous physicist was there. Whoa. Did he do a number on the women? I was at USC in Los Angeles. The prof of the day was a visiting historian. His lectures were so brilliant that he routinely got standing ovations, just like Yo-Yo Ma or some famous singer. At the end of one of his lectures, the prof rushed off the stage and into the arms of some sleek chick. She was about twenty-two to his fifty-five. They groped each other right in the lecture hall with the lights on high. We're liberal at that age—or stupid, maybe—so nobody ratted on The Don to his wife. At least I didn't, and I was the one who called the lady with her husband's travel arrangements."

"All right. So Randy wasn't particularly unusual."

"He was a type."

I glanced at my notes. "You don't think Randy was trying to let this stalker down easy?"

"No, I don't. Not based on what little you have told me. I think it may well have been the other type of behaviour. I'd look there first."

"What other type of behaviour is that?"

"Professor Randy was not anxious to file any police reports."

"He was in a tenuous position. He'd already been eased out at Harvard."

"Maybe he couldn't afford another scandal, but it may well have been something more." Susan's elbows rested on her desk blotter. She clasped her hands beneath her chin. She gazed at me, fully engaged in the puzzle and I soaked in the warmth of Susan's brown eyes.

"This second type of behaviour, you mean?"

"Maybe Randy was looking for new thrills. Perhaps he encouraged bizarre behaviour in the stalker. Maybe he enjoyed the game."

"Only he lost it all?"

"In the end, it became a control issue. The stalker and the professor battled for control."

"And Randy lost," I said. "That must have been the shock of his life."

"Or his death," Susan said.

SIXTY-SIX

I sat in my favourite spot at the Monkey Pod Bar in the Surfrider Hotel in the heart of Waikiki, taking in my nutrients, sucking up a Scorpion, orange juice with a kiss of brandy and a splash of rum. I was mulling over what my psychologist friend Susan had said. Susan Kopono did a thriving business in her Fort Street office in the heart of downtown Honolulu, not far from Bishop Square. I found this very ironic. Even in a place of such beauty, there are all these troubled souls.

Hillary Haverhill was late and I was enjoying the fact. There's something to be said for Hawaiian time, after all. Why worry? Enjoy the stolen moment. Seize the time to absorb the special energy of Waikiki. Our local cynics believe the billions spent by the last mayor to upgrade his cash cow at the expense of the rest of the city were wasted, lulling visitors into believing they are in a time warp, a paradise, a pleasure dome, but I'm a Polynesian, at least a hapa one, and I'll take money spent on pleasure, even municipal money, over potholes anytime.

During the last renovation, four sacred stones blessed in ancient days by Tahitian priests were rounded up from their forgotten locales. These are now preserved with honour behind a wrought iron fence in the heart of Waikiki. Stones emit vibrations, or so the ancient ones believed. Good vibrations, in my opinion, account for the enduring popularity of Waikiki, and so I sat in the Monkey Pod bar soaking up the vibes. Yes, the Haverhill case would be resolved, and soon. Young Toby Haverhill would be exonerated, and I'd be off the hook where my mishandling of his case was concerned.

The Surfrider is one of the oldest hotels in Waikiki, built to accommodate travellers from the steamship era. It's a tropical version of the southern mansion. Tall French windows on both sides of the building bring in the sea air; ceiling fans stir the breeze. The hotel is filled with so much antique bric-a-brac that guests can take in history lectures about the establishment. I love it all: The koa wood rockers on the porch, and the lobby equipped with newspapers from around the world.

I was in luck: My favourite seat in the Diamond Head corner was available. I sat working on my Scorpion while I watched the lovelies on the beach, thinking shallow thoughts. Bathers with air mattresses and plastic tires gambolled on the beach just beyond. Dowagers in bathing suits with dried, striated hides from years of heavy sun rattled their newspapers on the veranda. In a grassy courtyard to my left, a wedding bower had been set against a picket fence. A lovely Japanese bride in her white gown smeared cake on the face of her Japanese groom in his wire-rimmed glasses. A tall woman, an anorexic local with long black hair, played and sang the wedding song on a hand-carved ukulele. Her jumping flea had carved wings like a bird.

So many troubled ones amidst such beauty. I had to admit that this was why a visit to Waikiki was a sop for my own malaise. I had to admit this when I saw the flower seller sweep by. My unease had to do with the glossy ripple of her hair, flowing down her back, the red hibiscus flower over her ear, the mound of pikake flower leis reeking with sweetness; I smelled Princess Ka'iulani's peacock flowers as the flower seller wafted by, giving me a megawatt smile.

For an instant I saw the flower seller as my sister Emmalaea, Emmy alive again, glowing in her beauty, strolling past, inviting me into one of her adventures. I rose, followed the flower seller as she passed among the sunbathers around the swimming pool, wending her way through a sea of grey green iron lounge chairs arrayed on an ocean of flagstone tile. All the cushions and the draperies over the bar were done in creamy tropical whites of the Ralph Lauren variety.

Finally, I caught up with the lady.

"Miss," I said to her. I wanted to see her face, but when she turned to me, she was not my sister, not Emmalaea. Emmy had had startling eyes, light blue, nearly colourless. This woman was lovely but her eyes were black and glossy, kukui nut black, not Emmalaea's eyes; and I stared at her, at a loss. And for an instant I understood the legend, the story of Madam Pele, the woman in the red dress who stands along the roadside waiting for a ride, the woman who vanishes when you pull over, stop the car, fling open the door.

"Sir? Can I help you?" the flower seller said, a quizzical expression on her face.

"Lola?" I stammered. "Lola McCready?"

Her eyes widened and she smiled and I knew for sure. "Oh, yes. Mr. Spyer."

"John," I said, kissing her cheek. "Please call me John. What are you doing here?"

"I'm the flower girl for the hotel."

"Are you still volunteering at the Pacific Rim Institute?"

"Oh, no," she said, eyes big, head sweeping side to side. "After the book signing I never went back. I like to stay away from trouble, yeah? So much better being the flower lady." She held out her basket. "What do you like today?"

"Ah, an orchid, please."

She held her basket out to me. "You choose?"

"I don't know. Which is your best?"

"This one, yeah? Special."

I paid for the orchid and she gave me her card with my change. "Miss Lola McCready," I said. It was one of those Hawaiian cards for a Jill of all trades, only it didn't say so. Instead it said: hulas danced; luaus arranged; massages given; shirts ironed, gardens weeded, houses sat, dogs walked and on and on.

"Massages given? Is that right?"

"Why not? I'm licensed."

"Certainly, Miss Lola. I have to say, you do look exactly like a cure to my bad back."

"I do massage by appointment," Lola said.

"My place?"

She tilted her head, sizing me up, then smiled. "Maybe," she said, and I watched her float off on her leggy stride.

Deflated, I ordered a second Scorpion, toyed with the orchid, and checked my watch. Hillary was a half hour late. I checked my cell phone. There was a call from Eva. I debated whether to call her back.

I remembered what young Dr. Kevin said about putting his mother on a schedule, and so Eva would be hooked up to a feeding tube by now. I decided to wait. I sent Maya a hot text message reminding her that the Aloha Festival was on come the weekend and that if she hurried back from Maui, very good things awaited her.

"John," a whispery voice said as I sent my message to Maya.

"Hillary." I sucked in a whistle through my teeth as I rose to seat her. The princess had arrived and I have to say that Hillary Haverhill cleaned up nicely. Nicely, indeed.

SIXTY-SEVEN

Hillary arrived, looking very Tori Richards, Town and Country tropical, that is. Her pale blue blouse had one of those big floppy collars that yaw in the breeze and her silk skirt was the length of an old fashioned tea gown and swirled gracefully around her long legs as I seated her. She wore a wide brimmed straw hat and long strands of priceless puka shell beads.

"Sorry I'm so late. The police search dragged on and on."

We sat down at my table. Hillary ordered a Manoa Lemonade, lemonade and Chambord. I presented her with the orchid.

"A vanda. The chocolate and the white? How lovely."

"A what?"

"The orchid. A vanda."

"You a gardener, Hillary?"

"Sometimes. A little."

"Orchids?"

"I have a few on the back porch. The police were meddling with my orchids. Would you believe that?"

"I'd like to see them sometime," I said, careful to keep a straight face. *So that was it, the garden trowel, the one I'd turned into evidence. The police were trying to nail Hillary to her own garden instrument, and this, for her, was not good. Not good at all.*

"Are you an orchid fancier, John?" She watched me, measuring, questioning, and I let her question hang on the sultry air a moment too long and her head turned and her lidless eyes produced a blink, my cue, and I took up the beat.

"A connoisseur of beauty? Certainly. Also truth." Corny, I know. I'd become a talking Scorpion.

Hillary sighed and our moment was gone. "Truth is, I'm in trouble."

The power, the sensuality was gone, the healing energy of Waikiki had flown off on the breeze. Hillary evaded my eyes, focusing on the orchid, turning it round and around. *Hillary's mind must be reeling as well.*

I reached out and stilled this tiny, dizzying motion. "Look, Hillary, I'll try to help you, but advice is all I can give. I can't represent you."

She set the orchid down carefully. "Daddy warned me. I wouldn't listen."

"About Randy?"

She nodded. "The *women*. The other *women...that* I could handle." She stared past me, out to sea and it struck me then that Hillary Cameron Rooke Haverhill was one of us, the troubled keiki of paradise.

"Other *women*? Wait a minute? Are you saying Randy was māhū?

"I think, maybe."

"Who?"

"Someone in the paddling club."

"Was this the first time?"

"I can't say. I think Randy was mostly attracted to women, but he hinted that he'd at least tried it out with certain guys."

"The Outrigger Club? I thought Randy went there with Toby."

"He did." Hillary shrugged. "Some guy, one of them, found a lot of excuses to call Randy at the house."

"Okay, that's worth checking out. What's his name?"

"Eddie Cooke."

"Wait a minute. Cooke was *Eva's* love interest."

"Really?" Hillary said. Her lidless eyes widened.

"Eddie Cooke was a summer intern on the *Gazette*, twice over. Eva made a play for him. That's my understanding. Eddie is also the son of one of your dad's lawyers, the white-haired haole who was there today."

Hillary covered her eyes with her hand and shook her head. "Typical, isn't it?" Honolulu is such a small town." A breeze played on her floppy collar. She pinned it down with her hand, crossing her neckline, massaging her throat.

Hillary was in serious trouble, whether she recognized it or not. The garden trowel most likely came from her potting shed. The killer used Hillary's garden trowel to bury the rain cape, which was probably spattered with Randy's blood. Of course Hillary was not on the crime scene when the murder happened, but maybe the neighbour lady in the rain cape was an accomplice of Hillary's. Or at least that might be what Telly Tabura was thinking. I sat pondering the mess she was in. I'd found evidence to extricate Toby, only to get Hillary Haverhill in trouble.

"Eva," Hillary said, grimacing. "That would explain it. Eddie Cooke was working as *Toby's* trainer. Randy hired him to help Toby get into shape."

"Cooke started last summer. Before you were married? "

"That's right. Things went along fine that first season, but earlier this year Eddie started calling the house and pestering Randy a lot about something. So Randy let him go."

"I remember Cooke was at the book signing party, interning for Eva."

"That's right," Hillary said. Randy fired him sometime after that."

"We need to nail that one down," I said.

"I'm too tired to do it tonight." Hillary said. "Is it important?"

"It could be that Eddie Cooke was the stalker."

Hillary's face crumbled. "First Eddie Cooke. Now the photos."

"What photos?"

"Randy took about a million shots of my orchids. I thought he was interested in micro photography. Then I found a strange bag."

"When?"

"A few days ago. I was sorting through his things."

"And?"

"I found a black bag, an aeroplane carryall. It was wedged behind some other luggage in the back of the closet. The police must have missed it in the first search. I thought nothing of it. After all, who uses bags like that anymore?"

"Locked?"

"I found the key in his desk." Her chin wobbled. I put my hand over hers and anchored her to the table.

"Tell me. It won't go any further."

"Inside, all these pictures. Little children."

I was shocked. She sobbed silently, tears streaming down her face. I tossed some bills on the table and took her arm. "Come on, we'll get some fresh air."

I surfed here for years as a kid, so I knew a side trail down to the beach and a stone bench mossy with age. By the time we got there, Hillary was sobbing openly. I put my arm around her and let her cry on my shoulder.

"What happened to the bag?"

"The police took it. They'll see those pictures."

"Randy's household computer?"

"They took it off his desk."

"All right now. It's done. It's gone, a police matter. Just to be on the safe side, get your own lawyer, Hillary, and it better not be Eddie Cooke's daddy."

"Dad. He'll find out."

"So what if he does?"

"He'll blame me. He'll say it's my fault."

"Why? Would he think you were in on it?"

"I don't know." She wiped sooty trails off her cheeks. "You see, the problem is, my daughters. They are in some of the pictures."

The news hit me like a punch in the gut. All I could manage was a tense grunt. I sat shaking my head. Finally I managed to respond with something halfway intelligent. "Surely Randy wasn't posing your daughters?"

Hillary shook her head. "Nothing went that far, at least I don't think so. The photos were portraits. I have some of them in the house."

"Praise Madam for that."

Hillary stared at me. "Tell me what to do. John. I'm so unstrung I can't think for myself. What should I do?"

"Let me get you home. I'll drive you right now. We'll decide."

SIXTY-EIGHT

I left Em the Mustang in the parking garage at the Surfrider. I put in a call to Taxi Service Soon. My buddy Soon agreed he'd pick me up at the Haverhill house on Dowsett and drive me back down to Waikiki in his English Taxi. I was anxious to get home. I wanted to talk to Maya again. As far as I was concerned, she was taking too long on Maui.

The gates swung open on The Dowsett mansion and we arrived at sunset when the shadows deepened and the air took on the depth of the floral scents—so heavy that you could bottle them—especially here in Hattie Haverhill's garden. I parked Randy's Jag in front of the house, tripping security lights that ushered us across the deep porch.

As Hillary put her key into the lock, a torrent of yapping commenced behind the front door. When she pushed the door open, a toy Maltese appeared and not the man-eating bear I expected.

"This is Kahuna," Hillary said.

I picked up the dog. It shimmied my arms. Kahuna's short white hair felt scruffy. The toy dog reminded me of some child's worn teddy bear, loved to death.

"You'll have to excuse Kahuna. He has terrible asthma and a bad heart."

"Maybe Kahuna has trouble living up to his name."

"He's an alpha male. The animal shelter where I got him said Kahuna would cow Great Danes in the exercise yard."

"One big kahuna." I scratched Kahuna behind his ears and set him down. He ran circles around my legs.

"Attitude counts in the animal world." Hillary said, smiling now, though her face was blotchy from crying.

"Shall we talk, Hillary? Or would you rather get some rest?"

"You can't go yet, John," Hillary said, beckoning me in. "The house feels creepy to me. All those people pawing through our things? And what am I going to do?" Hillary shivered, turned on the hall light. Nothing seemed out of place.

"The bag you found. The kiddy porn?"

"Way at the back of the hall closet."

"Let's have a look."

Hillary opened the closet door and turned on the overhead light. "What a mess." Clothes had been pulled off hangers and were heaped on the floor. A mound of boxes and papers had been rifled through and shoved onto the top shelf.

"I can't bear to look," Hillary said, stepping aside so I could do the honours.

I went through the muddle on the floor. It was all clothes, piled on top of empty luggage. No bag. "Gone."

"They took that awful bag," Hillary said, wiping at her eyes. "They'll see my daughters' pictures in there with all those other children. Those poor kids."

"I'll try to find out who tipped off the police."

"I think I need a drink," Hillary said. "Join me?"

"A short one," I said, "It's been a long day."

Hillary led me straight down the hall to the kitchen at the back of the house. She wore the right clothes, I noticed, but her bearing was off, not the prowling stroll of the fashion model, but the listing gait of the horsewoman. The kitchen had been put to right since I'd last seen it. The fingerprint dust was gone and so was the knife holder.

"A nightcap?"

"Drambuie, if you have it."

She made a face. "I don't. Brandy?"

"Fine. "

Hillary poured us snifters of cognac. Her nails were square and unpolished, the working hands of a horsewoman, or maybe even a gardener. She plucked a pomegranate from a bowl of fruit, tore off the rind and sucked the red fruit. The juice spattered her ritzy blouse, but Hillary was too distraught to notice.

"So, Hillary. Do me a favour. Show me your orchids. I wouldn't know a vanda from a panda." I figured if I could get Hillary in motion, it might help clear her head.

She laughed. "John, sometimes you are just too cute."

She turned on a light and opened a set of French doors onto a patio, partially sheltered by the long eves of the house. Her orchids seemed to rise up out of the shadows as the light came on. There were maybe a dozen pots set out on a bench.

"As for a panda vanda, I'll have to find out who bred the one you gave me. The colour is so unusual, but we have orchid breeders right here on Oahu who could produce one." She plucked a spent bloom off a limb and struck something in the shadows underfoot. "Oh, look. Somebody knocked this one over. The soil is all over the floor. You'll have to excuse me for a minute. I can't let this poor plant suffer." She opened a nearby cupboard and brought out a bag of potting soil. "My garden trowel. It's gone."

I examined the side of the prone pot and found fingerprint smears. Hillary returned with a dustpan and broom. She swept the odd-looking soil off the floor and picked pieces of a shattered pot out of her dustpan. No doubt the crime scene tech had already taken a pinch of the soil in tweezers and stowed it in an evidence bag.

Hillary set the orchid upright, scooped soil out of the dustpan and distributed it into the pot up to the level where a v-shaped piece was missing on the side. "That should do it for tonight. I'll repot her tomorrow."

"Her?"

We went back into the kitchen but left the door open. Hillary washed up at the sink.

"Amazing. The house seems exactly as I remember it," I said.

"Randy wasn't eager to change it. This home was a grand manor of its day. The deep porches and all, they still catch the breezes. But now?" She shook her head, smiled crookedly, with half her mouth. "That's Eva's call."

"How so?"

"The house. It's now Toby's. Eva is his guardian. Except for a quarter million Randy left to the Pacific Rim Institute, bequests to Kevin and Bart, and a legacy to me, the rest goes to Toby, Randy's only child. Another drink, John?"

I didn't need it. My lips were numb. I stared into the glass, considering. "A splash."

Hillary returned to the living room and I trailed after her. We sat opposite each other on big squishy sofas, covered in white duck that had been soiled and clawed upon here and there.

Photos of Hillary's daughters stood on the end tables. I picked one up. "I hate to bring this up, Hillary. I know it's distressing. Did Randy take these photos of your daughters?"

"Lovely portraits, just like these," Hillary replied, "I swear I never suspected…"

"Don't blame yourself, Hillary."

"But how would that bag wind up in the closet?"

"We don't know yet, and we won't, at least not for a while. If Randy did have a thing for youngsters, though, his fingerprints will be all over the contents."

"Oh. My. God." Hillary moaned. "I touched that bag. My fingerprints will be there. Maybe they'll think I had something to do with…"

"You'll be questioned, Hillary. Just tell them the truth."

"I was sorting through Randy's things, getting ready to move," Hillary said. "I never saw that bag before. Never. It was locked. That was what got my attention. Randy didn't go around locking things. I came across the key in his desk. When I opened it and saw what it was? I couldn't close it fast enough."

"Let's hope that's the end of it," I said, fearing that for Hillary, this was the beginning.

The second search of her house seemed to be the opening move in a case against her. It wasn't difficult to see where the police were going with this. Hillary was the owner of the garden trowel that was buried with the rain cape. This made her a person of interest, despite her tight alibi. The crime scene tech had taken a snippet of her orchid soil, no doubt in order to match some residue found either in the garden shed where the shotgun was found, or else on the garden trowel that I had found in the Haverhill yard.

That was bad enough, but the discovery of kiddy shots in her closet was the final blow. If Randy was messing with Hillary's daughters, her motive for offing him had just gone into evidence.

Our eyes met across the room. Hillary's eyes were empty pools in a pale face turned ghostly in the shadows. I couldn't bear to point out the obvious. I drained the cognac, warming my gullet, and sought a less threatening topic.

SIXTY-NINE

We had left our shoes at the front door and were barefoot, chilling our feet together on the cool tiles of the salon floor. I gazed around the room at the old paintings and photographs of grass shacks and Hawaiian royalty.

"Where will you go, Hillary?"

"Out in the country, to the farm. It's Dad's property. but I have a bungalow there. I'll add a wing for the girls. Nothing elaborate." She tossed her head, ran a hand through her hair.

"Looks like Eva's won, doesn't it?" I said, watching for her reaction.

"l don't mind, really. I wouldn't want to stay on here, not without Randy. The girls will be fine. They love their horses and the farm." She swirled her drink, drained it, washed her lips with her tongue, and set the glass down. "Eva and Randy," she said with a wry smile. "Now there was a strange relationship."

"So I've heard."

"From Eva?"

"From Eva and from Dr. Kevin."

I talked to Kevin at the funeral," Hillary said. "He's so bitter and it was so obvious to me. Yet Eva and Randy seemed oblivious to the way the boys were hurt."

"Dr. Kevin said Eva treated Randy like another of her sons."

"Eva moulded Randy. She made him what he was. She was an intellectual stage mother."

"Mama and lover, rolled into one."

"The incestuous overtones?" Hillary grimaced "No wonder Randy had his problems."

"And Eva seems to have hers."

"Eva must have been terribly frustrated over the choice she made. What she wanted from Randy was *not* to be Mama. She wanted to be his beloved."

"And never could be, because she was also Mama."

"So, what resulted was, they became competitors. It was a contest."

"To see which one could land the latest conquest?"

Hillary stared at me, her eyes flaring. "You said you knew, John. I hope I'm not talking out of turn."

"You saw Eva's squeeze at the funeral?"

"Deter? Handsome isn't he? And way more acceptable than…"

Her face faltered as I finished her thought: "The intern at the paper, Mr. Boy Toy. Eddie Cooke."

Hillary's mouth crimped as she shook her head.

I stared at Hillary. "I thought you didn't know Eddie Cooke."

"Son of Dad's corporation counsel, of all things, and I never put the two together. He comes from a staid Honolulu family. His parents and grandparents were mortified when they heard about Eva. They expected Eddie to marry one of the local heiresses," she said. "I checked him out this afternoon. I called Dad's administrative assistant."

The air was turning sultry. Hillary opened the doors off the living room. A scent of lilikoi blossoms wafted in on a welcome breeze. "Come outside. Sit with me," Hillary said, inviting me to share the porch swing in the fresh air.

"I have to go, but before I do, could we take a look at Randy's study?"

"Of course. "

The study was in a small alcove off the kitchen. Randy's books had been pawed through and his computer and monitor were gone.

"Wait," Hillary said. "Randy also had a laptop. The police couldn't have taken it."

"Why not?"

"It's been in the repair shop for two weeks."

"Go get it tomorrow."

"What would I do with it?"

"On second thought, let me pick it up."

"Would you turn it over to the police?"

I pondered that one for a moment. "It will have to go into evidence, but first let me think about the best way to turn it in."

"Computers No Ka Oi on Nuuanu. I'll call them in the morning and tell them you'll pick it up."

I looked around. The room was piled with boxes. Hillary was packing for her move.

"When is Eva moving in?"

"I haven't heard," Hillary said. "I hope she's well enough soon. I really do. Toby needs a mother, and from his attitude, I don't think he'll be comfortable with me."

"It would have been alright with you, though?"

"Difficult, maybe, but I'd have been willing to try. There's young Dr. Kevin, but he's such an angry man. As for Brother Bart, I doubt he could distinguish Toby from one of his science projects."

Hillary picked up one of Randy's books. "He was so brilliant, intellectually. So stupid in his private life. He really loved Eva, I think…and I think she loved him as well. If they just hadn't…Oh well." She walked me to the door.

"Goodnight, Hillary. One more thing, if I may?"

"Ask me anything you want, John. I'll be straight with you."

"You once told Randy—you told him that you knew it was Eva. That Eva was the love of his life, the woman he'd see in his mind's eye at the moment of his death."

"Did I? Well, there you go," Hillary said, dissembling. Her admission was in the cold pain etched on her face in the moonlight. Kahuna snuffled at her feet. She ignored him. "A few times, when Eva started chemo, she was hospitalised. Randy would sit all night with her. He'd sleep in a chair at her bedside."

"So you *did* say that?"

"I did. I was angry. I didn't think it was right. But then I realised Eva was no threat to me. A sick woman? How could I have been so petty?"

Hillary stood for a moment, her hand on the doorknob, the dog watching her, waiting to be picked up. "But you know, John, I find it so interesting…" Her voice was so low I strained to hear her. "Randy repeated an intimate conversation between us to Eva. Then Eva repeats the conversation to you." Her mouth twisted as she fought for control. "Don't you see? This is just how it was between them. They couldn't let each other go. Eva is something, isn't she? She's still playing Randy's game. Randy is dead and Eva is still keeping score."

SEVENTY

The moon was high as I said goodbye to Hillary and Kahuna, the tiny dog with the big Hawaiian name. I was wide awake, getting a second wind and I wanted to walk because walking helps me sort things out. I headed downhill along The Pali Highway toward Honolulu Harbour, beaten silver in the distance. It was one of those balmy evenings where you want to walk forever. I planned to walk down to Twice-a Slice-a, a stroll of twenty minutes or so, then call Soon Amorin and have him taxi me over to the Surfrider to pick up Em.

I took Nuuanu where it branches off from The Pali Highway and I had gotten as far as the Royal Mausoleum. I stopped to stretch my legs on the railings of the black, wrought iron fence enclosing one of the most sacred pieces of ground on the island. This is the bluff where the defenders of Oahu rallied their defence against the upstart Kamehameha I and his ten-thousand warriors as they came paddling into Honolulu Harbour, bent on conquering the island.

The Oahu defenders did not save themselves, even though they had British weaponry. Forget the bats lined with shark teeth. The various chieftains all had their mortar and their cannon and their hired haoles to plan their war strategy. Kamehameha's military advisor, John Young, is said to have engineered the pincer strategy that defeated the defenders. Kamehameha's warriors drove Oahu's chief and three-hundred of his finest up and over The Pali cliffs high in the pinnacles behind me. Or else, the brave Oahu warriors fought a final battle to allow their compatriots to flee; it depends upon who is telling this tale.

At any rate, Randy Haverhill and I both have ancestors buried in the Royal Mausoleum, and I stared through the glittering gold-tipped fence at the layout. I'm distantly related to John Young, or so Mama Hana says. Young was a canny Scottish seaman held hostage by Kamehameha with a fellow sailor, so that the pair could not inform their captain that Kamehameha had seized a British sailing vessel. Left behind in Hawaii, Young proceeded to make himself useful to the ambitious Kamehameha, who aimed to defeat his warring rivals and unite the Hawaiian Islands into one kingdom. Young introduced Kamehameha to the Western ways of religion, politics and the art of war with modern weaponry, guns and cannon.

In the Battle of Nuuanu, which happened right on this very bluff, Young manned the cannon that took out a treacherous chief who betrayed Kamehameha. Young was rewarded for his loyalty with royal wives and estates on all the islands. When Kamehameha left Oahu to put down a rebellion back on the Big Island of Hawaii, he left Young in charge as Governor. John Young is buried around back, behind the chapel, and his importance in the greater scheme of things is that his granddaughter was Emma Rooke, Queen Consort to Kamehameha's grandson, Alexander Liholiho, King Kamehameha IV.

In my case, what's left of the John Young legacy Mama Hana gave to me, Young's Hawaiian handle, Oluhana, referring to the boatswain's call, "all hands," that Young used to call his native crews to work. In my days as a beach boy, I must confess I was known by my surfer buddies as "hands."

Randy Haverhill is a Bishop, distantly related to Charles Bishop, the haole who had the audacity to woo and win the hand of Bernice Puahi. Bernice was a great granddaughter of Kamehameha the Great, betrothed in childhood to her royal foster brother Lot, who was destined to be crowned King Kamehameha V. Over the strenuous objections of her powerful family and political advisors, Bernice rejected Lot and took a haole husband. Mama Hana tells me that Bernice had good reason. She was Lot's friend at the Royal Boarding School in Honolulu, where she and Lot and a dozen other high born young men and women were groomed for royal duties.

As Mama tells me, Bernice would have known that Lot was madly in love with his royal cousin Abigail Maheha. Hapai with Lot's love keiki at a tender age, Abigail was banished to her home on the Island of Kauai and forced to marry a family gardener.

Lot, crowned Kamehameha V, upon the death his younger brother Alexander at age 29, rebelled against this early injustice; he neither married nor produced another heir and so, upon his death, an election was held among the eligible royals, won by Lot's cousin the immensely popular William Lunalilo, beating out the more conservative David Kalākua; Lunalilo reigned for a year before dying, whereupon Kalākua was elected king, defeating the Queen Dowager Emma, who ran against him.

As for Charles Reed Bishop, he was a New Yorker by birth but a naturalised Hawaiian citizen and the newly appointed customs commissioner for Hawaii. The Bishops were a loving couple who produced no heirs. Mama Hana tells me that none in Bernice's immediate circle would offer her a child to adopt out of fear something would happen to the child. Suppose Bernice was cursed? Randy's ancestor, Charles Bishop, from whom he descends in some way, however indirect, rests with Bernice in a well-cooled spot in the front yard beneath a tree.

The black iron fence is tipped in gold and the royal fence flickered like fire in the moonlight and the beauty of it raised the hackles at the back of my neck. Ghostly in the moonlight were the elaborate markers of the Honolulu cemeteries flanking the Royal Mausoleum. That's Honolulu for you, a city of commoners lying cheek by jowl with the kings.

When headlights washed over me I realised I was being followed. I doubled my pace and the driver stayed on me, so I ducked into the first side street I came to, the entrance to the city cemetery. I took up a position behind one of the taller monuments, heart pounding. But as the vehicle passed under a streetlight, hung a left and came right at me, I realised it was one of the pizza delivery trucks, and the driver's door flung open.

"That you, John?"

I was breathing heavily and felt my back crimp, a pain brought on by an adrenaline rush. "H.B.?" Honeyboy, Uncle Yodi Noda's nephew. Though he was working late, Honeyboy still looked spiffy in his starched Aloha shirt and his kukui bead necklace.

"Hey. I didn't mean to scare you. Can I give you a ride?"

I climbed into a van that smelled like a pizza oven, laughing my scratchy laugh.

"My imagination working overtime, H.B."

"Hey, no problem, John. One last delivery and we're done," H. B. said.

We pulled into a condo complex a few streets further down Nuuanu. As the lights came on, inside the van, I was startled and also relieved: *A couple of rain capes and a floppy hat or two were hung up in the van by their strings.* These were the same type of rain cape as the one our mysterious female witness had been wearing, the same type I found wadded up and buried in the yard. *This explained why Toby said he'd seen the rain cape before. I would soon break this case. Praise Jesus. Mahalo Madam P.*

H. B. left to deliver his order, returned and climbed into the van. "Nice guy," he said of his customer. "Draft pick for the NFL. Good tipper, too."

At Twice-a Slice-a, H. B. locked the doors and left a few diners to finish their pies. "Is Uncle Yodi around?"

"Yodi's off tonight. Can I help you with something?"

"Got a slice?"

"One cheese, one Surf rider."

"I'll have that."

The Twice-a Slice-a slice wasn't as fresh as the one Toby had made me earlier in the day.

"How about a beer?" H.B. said.

"Got any iced tea?"

H. B. came back with the tea and a mug of beer for himself.

"I noticed some rain gear in the van."

H. B shrugged. "For rainy season. It never fails we get a rash of orders right in the middle of the afternoon downpours. We pack the pizzas in padded wrappers and outfit the drivers with the rain gear."

"Makes sense," I said. "This the pizza Toby always ordered?"

H. B. grinned. He had perfect teeth. "If Toby did the order it was always the Hula Girl. It's our banquet special. We sell Hula Girls for weddings and baby luaus."

"People order pizza for their weddings?"

H. B. shrugged. "Beats a five grand catering bill."

"As I understand it, this guy Elihu Markham delivered."

"That's right. You wanted to talk to the guy."

"I haven't located him. Has his cousin Tomas shown up?"

"I think he worked earlier tonight."

"I need an address and phone number for Markham."

"Tomas's number is all I got. I gave that to you."

"Next time Tomas comes in, find out where Elihu is." I gave H. B. my card. "It's important."

"Hey, no problem." He unlocked the front door, let out one customer and then the next. "Your taxi's outside, John."

"What do I owe you?"

"For you, on the house."

"Come on, H. B."

"I can't write the check. Got carpal tunnel." He laughed. His eyes were a liquid black and sweet as his manner.

Soon Amorin poked his monkey's face in the door. "You ready, brah?"

"Right now." I dropped bills on the counter as I went out.

Amorin's radio was tuned to KINE, Hawaiian music. Falsetto singers and slide guitar. I rolled down the window and let the balmy air bathe my face as I thought about what I'd seen in the van: the rain capes and the floppy hats. No wonder Toby said he had seen the rain cape before.

And the pizza driver, this guy Markham, arrived way late? But suppose he hadn't arrived late after all? Suppose he had been lurking around the scene all along? I had to lay hands on Markham, find out just what he knew. I was feeling fine, high on my new leads, Elihu Markham and Eddie Cooke. I was high enough that I thought I could carry a tune as I hummed along with a slack key instrumental playing on Soon Amorin's fine sound system. I felt wonderful, yeah. Until I got to the carnage down in the parking garage of the Surfrider Hotel, that is.

<h1 style="text-align:center">SEVENTY-ONE</h1>

I knew something was wrong when Mike the Surfrider's night doorman told me that Harry Pang wanted to see me. I took the winding staircase up to the mezzanine floor, and knocked on a certain unmarked door. Harry let me in.

"Hey, John," he said, pumping my hand, motioning me into a chair across a cluttered desk. Harry is chief of security, operates out of a shoebox of an office, a squat guy, doughy face, no neck to speak of.

Harry offered me some of the wicked black tea he claims keeps him going all night. Two swigs into the stuff and I second that. He waved me to a seat in front of his small desk. Behind it hung a scroll on the wall:

When the enemy comes, welcome him.

When he goes, send him on his way.

"I haven't seen you in awhile," Harry said, raking a brick of a hand through thick black hair spiked into points. Harry kept his muscles tuned and attitude adjusted with weekly bouts of Judo. He was retired H.P.D., several degrees into his black belt.

"What's happening?"

"Your Mustang. She's not in good shape, I'm afraid."

"Jesus Madam. My car?"

"Took a beating."

"Where?"

"Right where you parked."

"Let's go."

We rode down in the elevator reserved for the house service staff.

"That's a Shelby Mustang isn't it?"

I nodded. "A '65. My dad's first car. Dad was a task-oriented guy. When he didn't have his nose stuck in a law book, he had it under the hood of a car. When he gave that car to Emmy and me on our sixteenth birthday, it was already a classic, in mint condition.

"Worth what? A quarter million?" Harry whistled through his teeth.

"Fully restored, maybe," I said. "Not that I'd consider selling Em. I'd let her go once and found her again. Found her at a classic car show right here in the city. Same vin number. Em the Mustang was 'ohana to me. We got out on the lower level where I like to park, since it's an easy walk to the bar. There were no other vehicles on the floor. The entrance was blocked off. The hotel wouldn't want other drivers to see Em and when I did, I could hardly blame them. There she was, tawdry and greenish in the yellow light, windows smashed in, door panels caved.

I walked around and around her, a way of containing my fury. My sister Emmy disappeared and we never found her, but there were rumours. It had to do with a major drug dealer Dad was prosecuting. Dad figured I'd be next. He sent Mama Hana and me to Lahaina and I finished high school at a prep school upcountry and went to U.C. Berkeley. A couple of years into law school, I dropped out. This was after Dad dropped dead on the sidewalk on the way to court. A heart attack, the doctor said. A heart broken Mama Hana said.

Too much baggage, brother, the Dean of the law school said. Take some time off. Get your head together, man, and so I got on with the LAPD as a beat cop until I learned I had not only a talent for acting but a passion for scoring on the drug trade, which is how I wound up with the DEA in Miami, a different sort of paradise, but at least not a haunted one.

I knew that finding the Mustang was a message from Emmalaea, from the other side. She was telling me she was happy. She had made the adjustment. I'd just cut ties with the Miami DEA, unhappy with the P.R.work they had assigned me after I was shot in the back. Emmy was telling me to find some direction, get on with my life. I wanted to kick something, throw something. A violation of Em the Mustang was a violation of Emmy all over again.

"How?" I croaked.

"This level serves the downstairs shops," Harry Pang said. "There's not much traffic after happy hour. We figure the perp came out through the door to the parking garage and went back into the hotel the same way. The man on the security camera caught the...er, bashing of the car, and alerted the force. We cordoned off all exits, but we were too late."

"Did you file a police report?"

"Just need your sig." Harry said, "if you insist on being official." This was the hotel, all right. They would prefer to handle everything internally.

"Sorry, Harry, I've got to file with the H.P.D. This could be related to something I'm working on. I'll call the general manager and explain the situation myself."

"Understandable," Harry mumbled. "Would you like to review the tapes? Or would you prefer to get some rest?"

"Hey. Whoever did this got my attention. I'm wide awake."

The Surfrider was an antique of a place. The cameras had gone in during the last facelift. The monitors were on the second floor, on a balcony overlooking the lobby in an annex that once served the ballroom. Harry tapped at the unmarked door and waited to be let in.

He introduced me to the camera surveillance cop, a guy named Dutch. He was so beautifully tanned he disappeared into the dark. I pegged him as one of the surf-above-all crowd, guys who work nights to spend their days on a board. The place was claustrophobic, a dark room lined with monitors and no space to turn around. Dutch was a smoker. The air was thick with a delicious pungence and I began to sweat and to salivate as well.

"What time did you leave with Mrs. Haverhill?"

I stared at Harry for a moment. Did I say I was with Mrs. Haverhill?"

Harry smirked. "One of the employees reads the society pages."

"Or maybe Miss McCready recognized her," I said.

Harry nodded. "Maybe," he said, choosing the cover of professional amnesia.

"Fair enough. I had a drink with Mrs. Haverhill and we left about six."

"The car was bashed just before seven."

Through the tobacco haze, I watched the beating of Em. The perp was in a floppy hat with big sunglasses and what do you know? He emerged from the door to the hotel in a Twice-a Slice-a rain cape. I sucked in a whistle. Harry stared at me. I shook my head. I could have a bout of professional amnesia just as well as Harry Pang could.

It took him about three minutes to destroy Em. The perp looked around. Rather than running down the exit ramp, which anyone off the street would have done, he went right back through the door into the lower level of the hotel.

"Did the camera inside pick up anything?"

"The one right in the entrance. The one in the passage between the lower lobby and the parking garage was blank, taped over."

Then we watched the tape of the action from another camera, at the far end of the lower level. A fair-skinned woman with a mop of blonde hair strolled past, carrying a huge shopping bag. She took her time, studying the merchandise in the windows of the shops. She tripped across the lobby on spiky heels and took the staircase up to the main lobby.

"She's the perp," I said. "She blanked off the camera in the passage and used it for a changing room."

"That's how I figure it," Harry said.

"She's a he."

"One māhū," Harry said, "or a pretender. He's mastered the high heels, but in action he's all boy."

I had to agree. It would be hard for a woman to swing a bat with such viciousness.

It was not until I was back on fragrant Leahi, sitting on the porch swing of Cousin Duke's hale, still jazzed on Harry Pang's high-powered tea, that I confronted what I subconsciously knew. *The basher of my car was Randy Haverhill's killer.*

I called Harry back. I asked him to bundle up the evidence, told him I'd take it to the H.P.D. myself. Then I called Telly Tabura but he was off. Catching up on his sleep, no doubt, but I left a message with Telly's voice mail: "Hey brah. Let's grind tomorrow. Twice-a Slice-a. I got one special gift for you, very special. I can guarantee this is one lunch you won't want to miss."

SEVENTY-TWO

It was the lull before lunch hour at Twice-a Slice-a. Detective Tabura had arrived ahead of me. He'd commandeered our space beneath the banyan, the one away from the action, out at the end of the deck. I had my package with me and set it down with a thump, not that Telly noticed, which was just as well. I had a gift for Telly, but I needed a favour first.

"Look at this, brah," I said. "Hula Girl. Topped with edible flowers."

"Mahalo, John. I pass." Telly's long brow flowed across his face like the crest of a wave, "Must have been da plumeria blossoms I washed down with my beer last night. Gave me indigestion. I'm doing pepperoni and cheese."

We placed our order and got our salads. Tabura dove into his usual two scoops of macaroni salad. I stuck to the greens.

"Sorry about your Mustang." Telly shook his head. "One Shelby, yeah?"

"One Shelby she is. If I wanted to make a career out of restoring her, she might bring a quarter million, but that car is 'ohana."

"Tch," Telly said, shaking his head. "I remember when your dad gave you that car."

"Sister Emmy and I. Dad gave it to us on our sixteenth birthday. We thought we were so hot. A Shelby Mustang was an item even then. The downside was, Emmy was the popular twin, the compliant one, so she got to drive it way more than I did."

"Got any idea how it happened?"

"I was having drinks with Hillary Haverhill. She was very upset so I drove her home leaving poor Em at the Surfrider. This was no coincidence. This was a warning."

"Hillary Cameron Rooke Haverhill?" Telly bugged his eyes. "Heavy duty."

"Hillary may be a suspect," I said, letting my eyes shift to Telly's face, "but she had nothing to do with the murder. Any of it."

"The second Mrs. Randy? One nice lady. All kine people saw her at the horse show exact time one shotgun scratch one professor's big itch."

I sucked in a laugh. "So you figured out the note on Randy's back?"

"Da punishment fit da message."

"So we've arrived at the same page."

"That so?" Telly said. The pizza arrived. Tabura scooped up a slice. I'd ordered the Hula Girl out of respect for the dead. "Maybe the second Mrs. Randy found out it took too much itch to satisfy one new husband," Telly said.

"Yet Hillary has one fine alibi."

Tabura shrugged. "Going rate on one rub is pocket change to somebody like that." He took a mouthful of pizza. "And maybe Mrs. Hillary have one solid reason."

"Maybe." I kept my face straight, knowing full well what reason he was referring to. I sipped iced tea and swatted at a tiny bird hopping around the table. "Mrs. Hillary noticed you seized one funny aeroplane bag. Lotta nasty pictures."

"Is that so?"

Telly stared at me. "I do you one favour, Spyer. I don't ask what Mrs. Hillary tell you already. Not yet." His tone was heated.

"I'll tell you when you are ready to ask," I snarled back. The brown bird stood beside the pizza box, staring at this interchange with quizzical twists of its head.

I laughed, breaking the tension: "Give me some rope here."

"We go back long ways, brah. I trust you. But remember, too much rope might hang one boy."

"Let Hillary tell you what she knows," I said. "You'll get the story straight."

"Maybe she's telling some investigators right now."

"She'll cooperate. Hillary has nothing to hide." The Hula Girl was cooling off. I wolfed down a slice, which gave me a chance to digest Hillary's predicament. I stoked myself on more salad and made my move.

"You seized Randy's computer at his house."

"Maybe," Tabura said.

"I know you did. Hillary told me as much." I washed down the Hula Girl with iced tea and took a stab in the dark. "The computer you seized was in a study off the kitchen of the Dowsett house. Anyone in the house had access to it."

"So?"

"That's why it's clean."

"How you know?" Telly blurted.

"Gotcha," I said, grinning.

Despite himself, Tabura laughed along with me.

You got me," he said. He swigged his favourite grass-coloured drink.

"If Randy Haverhill liked child porn, he wouldn't have put it on a computer that his family could get into. He was too smart to do that."

"You got other ideas?" Tabura said.

"He had a laptop. I know where it is."

Tabura's fist slammed on the table, ejecting the bird into flight. "You withhold evidence, Spyer?"

"Not at all. I've discovered the whereabouts of this laptop. I haven't seen it yet. That's why I need a favour."

"What now?" Tabura said, eyes rolling skyward. The bird had returned. It stood at Telly's elbow, pointing its beak at me. "When did Spyer not need one favour?"

I laughed outright at his theatrics. "Hey, Telly. I'm offering evidence I haven't seen. Maybe there's kiddy porn on it, but I don't think so. I have a hunch there's something else."

"All right already."

"The laptop is in a repair shop. We pick it up together. I get a peek at the contents in your presence."

Telly's palms joined beneath his chin. He dipped head at me in a mock salute. "Okay brah, fair enough."

"Wonderful," I said. "You are one decent guy, Telly, even if you are a cop." We toasted the deal, Jamba to iced tea. Telly shoved aside his plate and got out a cigarette. He offered me one and I took it. I just had to. I was feeling so fine. I pushed the bundle toward him. "Here's a little something for you, Telly."

He fingered the package.

"Don't open it here."

"No?" Telly's thick fingers drummed on the brown wrapping. "Do I have to wait 'til my birthday?"

"I'd recommend you look at it soon as you are back at your office."

"Got one hint?"

"It's my gift to you, Telly. It's the Haverhill case, wrapped up and tied with string."

Tabura sat speechless. Finally he said: "You didn't eat your flowers."

SEVENTY-THREE

The crowd had thinned at Twice-a Slice-a. What few diners there were had opted for sunnier spots. The luau music coming from the speakers masked our conversation.

Telly grinned, revealing the puka where his tooth used to "Talk one good story, Spyer. Maybe I give you a raise."

"In that package are my police report and a tape from the hit on my car. It all fits together." I looked around to make sure nobody was tuning in. "The Haverhill murder began as a stalking case, but Randy was either in denial or playing games. You never got a police report from him. He failed to file it, but we do have the report that Hillary made out. Hillary has said all along that Randy got into a power struggle with the wrong lover and Eva seconded the motion."

"So who da stalker?"

"The pizza guy did it," I said, waving at a final slice of the Hula Girl pie, "and he had help."

"You saying the professor was māhū?"

"I'm saying he liked fooling around."

Telly pulled his notepad out of his shirt pocket. "What's his name?"

"The pizza guy is Elihu Markham." Unfortunately, he wasn't popular in the workplace. Uncle Yodi here at Twice-a Slice-a canned Markham the day after the murder. You'll find in your own crime scene report, Telly, that the pizza was late to be delivered to the scene."

Telly shrugged. "We questioned Mackham. He had one good reason for late delivery: too many police cars. We let him go."

"The pizza was cold. That's the point. I pinched strings of cheese off my final slice and put it in my mouth. "Go back to the scene, Telly. Randy and Toby ordered their Saturday pizza. Same time, place, and pizza, always from Twice-a Slice-a. They can tell you, it was a family ritual. Markham knew about this because he worked the Saturday shifts when his cousin took the day off."

Tabura cleared his throat and reached for his Jamba.

"Professor Randy opens the door, expecting the Hula Girl pie," I said. "Instead he takes a hit in his itch."

Tabura's yellow eyes were wide. At least I had his attention.

"You'll find in there a photocopy of the order book right from this establishment. Delivery was set for noon. Markham's on the scene all right. He gets the gun from the shed, then hides there after he's done the deed. He's wearing a rain cape from the pizza van and goes prancing out, passing himself off as the neighbour lady."

"Why take da risk?"

"Curiosity is killing him," I said. "Markham wants to make certain that Randy is dead." Tabura made notes, read them and added a thought. "He finds da garden trowel in da shed. He wads up his rain cape and buries it."

"Right. He's driving a pizza van with a bunch of rain capes in it, just like the one he's wearing. He's posing as the neighbour lady after a towel as a way to approach Toby. But Toby has his hands full. He doesn't see where Markham goes. Markham ducks into the thick cypress tree hedge and uses the garden trowel to bury the rain cape."

"Then returns to da pizza van and delivers da pie when da police arrive," Tabura said.

"You got a good look at Markham?"

"One haole." Tabura said, "skinny, messy dreds. Golden tone to the skin. "I signed for the pizza."

"Thin face, right?"

"Right." Tabura looped his fingers.

"So you put a wig and sunglasses on this thin face and you get the witness Toby saw. Pocho, Toby said, this accounts for the golden tone to the skin. This same guy's on the security tape from the hotel. It's Elihu Markham, dressed as one māhū when he bashes my car, and for your convenience, I've put the tape of the bashing into the package."

"Murder delivered at noon," Telly said, scribbling on his notepad. "The pie we had came cold. Slice-a cold, flowers wilted."

I had to laugh. "It's okay, brah. You testify, the prosecutor will never ask whether you ate a slice of the evidence. What was Markham wearing when you saw him?"

"Company tee shirt."

"Exactly. That's because his rain cape was in the ground."

"Not raining that day."

"It wasn't. That's my point. Here's the deal. Every pizza van owned by Twice-a Slice-a is equipped with several rain ponchos and big floppy hats. They are hung on pegs in the back of each van. Standard procedure, so drivers can deliver during downpours."

"Rain poncho. I got that."

"You also have Toby's testimony. He said this neighbour in a rain cape came by and offered to go for a towel. She had a garden trowel in her hand."

"Toby say this?"

"He told Harlan and me on Sunday morning. You'd put him in juvie to jog his memory, and it helped. A transcript of his interview is in the package."

"Why didn't he tell me?" Tabura growled.

"I think he was so traumatised by the murder he didn't remember."

Telly tapped his notebook with his pencil. "Go on."

"Markham parks away from the drive. He gets the shotgun out of the shed, blasts Randy. Plants the funny message on Randy's back with a knife he's brought with him in a pizza box."

"Knife in back fits the chock in da house. "

"The knife in Randy's back is a ringer for the one in the house. I found the knife that really belongs in the set in a kitchen drawer, remember?"

"You turn in as evidence?"

"I didn't have to. That knife is in your own crime scene photos."

"Go on, brah."

"Before Toby hits the front door, Markham is back in the shed."

"We're shy on forensics."

"Process the van Markham was driving."

"Lot to do," the detective said.

"But not far to go," I said. "We have to find out exactly where the pizza van was. It may well have been parked right in plain sight all along. What we need is the outtake footage from KITV. They were early on the scene."

"They fight that," Telly said. "Assert their constitutional rights and make a nice story for the liberal reader."

"Or the criminally inclined, anyway," I inhaled a laugh. "I'll ask around the neighbourhood."

"We'll do that," Tabura growled.

"Wonderful. Let the beat guys do the work. It's all the same to me." I stood up, stretched, eased my back.

"Toby should see the tape of the car bashing. We see the same guy, in the same gear hitting on my car."

"Why bash your Mustang?"

"My guess is, he's warning me to back off. This mento's so far over the top that we can't decipher what he views as a straightforward message."

Tabura laughed. "Here's da message. Markham never went for a towel, went for a garden trowel."

"Here's a case forensics will love. They'll have to do studies on the cooling rates of pizza pies so they can present a credible timeline in court."

"Eat your flowers," Tabura said.

I scooped them off the empty platter and stuffed them in my pocket. "Later. I prefer them with my afternoon tea."

Tabura rose, shook my hand, "Mahalo, Spyer. I thank you. The department thanks you." He grabbed my check. "Today I buy." We walked out to our cars.

I was driving a borrowed gas hog, a black Chevy pickup with the detail posted in the rear window: Convertible 2 door, as/is no warranty, $47,000. "A loaner from Akamai Guy's dealership. Any time I'm pressed for wheels Guy finds me a loaner. I try not to abuse the privilege."

"The auto dealer whose cars kept going missing?"

"An inside deal," I said. "An enterprising general manager was running a ghost sales operation off the books. He thought Guy wouldn't care. Guy could claim insurance."

Tabura waited while I climbed into the truck. No doubt he wanted to see the cushy interior. I opened the window, sensing Tabura had something more to say.

"Fancier than one Mustang."

"Yeah. Nice wheels, but too thirsty for me," I said. "Besides, Em is family."

Telly tossed a shaka shake my direction. "We find this Markham, process the van he was driving, and have Toby in to see the tape. I got one problem with it."

"What's that?"

"The shotgun in the tool shed. One hard place to find, this shed. How would one pizza guy know about it?"

"That's where Markham's accomplice comes in," I said.

"What's his name?"

"Eddie Cooke, Eva's boy toy and Toby's personal trainer, He has a part time job at The Outrigger Club. We saw Cooke and Markham together at the funeral."

"Cooke the foxy guy?"

"The one we saw driving by with the blonde in the fancy car. The blonde was Markham in drag."

"One māhū" Tabura said, grinning. "Now we getting somewhere."

"And I'd better be getting over to Eva's. I'm taking her to the Downtown Mele tonight. Toby Haverhill's playing a gig."

SEVENTY-FOUR

When I arrived at Eva's Round Top castle, Tutu Lia greeted me with Hone wagging his tail at her side. Eva's latest nurse had tired of her antics and quit. I suggested to Eva that Tutu Lia would make a great nurse.

I kissed her cheek. "How's the new job, Tutu?"

"We love it here, Hone and me. Eva loves Hone, but I don't know. I bake everything for her, but she won't eat, no macaroons, no macadamia nut."

"It's not your cookies, Lia. It's her treatment."

"Really?" Lia's frown relaxed. "That's what Eva say. I thought she made it up, not to hurt my feelings." Tutu Lia ushered me into Eva's bedroom where she was reliving the past. A breeze was blowing in through the French doors, riffling the pages of the high school annuals flung on the bed.

"Here's Nelson Sneddon in his tracksuit," Eva said. "He was also a star of the swim team."

"Nice looking guy. Your sons have their daddy's jaw line."

Eva stared at the photo. "I guess you are right, John. I never noticed. Nelson abandoned his boys when I divorced him."

"You said you married Nelson to rebel against your mama."

"That's why it didn't work. Nelson came back from Vietnam. I didn't know him. He'd gone hippie and I hadn't. He did dope and I wouldn't. I believed in the government's case for war. I still did. I was late to turn against the war. I admit that now." She flung the book aside. "Would you believe I was going to be an aeronautical engineer? I tested for it. The good old boys made sure I couldn't do it. I switched to political science."

Eva left the albums scattered on the bed. I went out so that she could shower and dress. I sat in the living room flipping through one of her college annuals. Eva had short, conservative hair and wore a white collar and pearls. In those days, you were expected to look like an adult. The whole generation was adult.

Eva appeared in new, skinny jeans and a clinging zippered jersey, her thin hair combed up. She had a baseball cap on her head and her pashima wrap in hand. She did one of her entrance routines, swaggering down the hall, shaking her okole at me.

"I'm now a size six, except at Chico's where I'm a zero. Isn't that wonderful? Tutu and I went shopping. She's such a trip, John. I can't thank you enough for recommending her. Dr. Kevin did his best to spoil it for me. I talked with him on the phone last night. He had the nerve to ask me why I would shop for new clothes when I have cancer.' Her face flashed a mixture of pain and grief.

"He didn't mean it the way you took it, Eva."

"So what did he mean?"

"He meant you need to conserve your energy to fight the cancer, and not tire yourself running around in the Ala Moana Center."

"Well, I forgive him then. I'll call him tonight. He gets off shift at 4:00 AM mainland time; it'll only be 1:00 AM here. I'll be on the tube. I'll call him and we'll gab through the wee hours."

"I thought you spent all your time talking to Deter."

"Deter is on a junket to the backwater villages of Nepal."

"No cell phones?"

"The only power is a generator. It runs the refrigeration and that's it." She was teetering on platform wedgies. She fingered an ivory fish hook charm around her neck.

"Toby bought this for me. It's a heart, don't you see? The carving represents the healing of the heart." Eva blinked back tears. "Toby is such a thoughtful son. Doctor Kojimura insists I've got to check into the hospital. They can't get my heart to stop racing."

I examined the charm. "This is a genuine piece, Eva. Carved from the antique whalebone that the good carvers use, a finely worked piece."

I got down some wine glasses for her. Eva favoured stemware at least as tall as her heels. She poured herself a chardonnay, all for show. We sat down at her wicker dinette set in the kitchen.

"There's something I have to share with you, Eva, but you can't pass this on. I could lose my link to the investigation if you say anything to anyone. I am an outsider."

"And I am a newspaper editor. You don't hear me blabbing about who we are going after in our investigations, do you?"

"Is yours going well, Eva?"

"Without me? Hah. It'll be all piss and rainwater by the time my replacement wimps out. You wouldn't believe how business is done here. Politicians meddling around in business, taking cuts. It isn't right. You'd think Honolulu was third world."

"Keep after them, Eva. Put the bastards away. At any rate, here's our deal. The police have seized some incriminating stuff on Randy."

"Smear the victim. They always do."

"Now, Eva."

"Thank God I divorced Randy when I did. I had so much stuff on him, so many women lined up to testify."

"What kind of stuff?"

"Randy hitting on them."

"Any rape?"

"Rape? Why would Randy have to rape anybody? Women fell all over him."

"Yes, but the niece."

"Lani? She was borderline, old enough but not old enough. We don't know what Randy would have done. One of those Lolita affairs, maybe. I'd hate to think he was that depraved, but in those days I was firmly in denial."

"What about Randy and little kids?"

"Children?" Eva's face paled, which was something. She was sheet white to begin with. "Absolutely not." She took a big hit of the wine and grimaced. "Chardonnay tastes terrible now." She pushed her glass away. "I don't dare get sloshed on Toby's big night."

"Don't worry, Eva. You can lean on me." Something predatory rose in her face, making me nervous. The last thing I needed was to get into Eva's sexual crosshairs.

Eva struggled to her feet, went around the bar counter and poured her wine down the sink. "Randy and little children? Who said that?"

"Nobody. It wasn't a person. Certain evidence suggested it."

"What evidence? I want to see it."

"You can't see anything and you can't even hint that I said anything to you. We agreed."

Eva nodded. "All right. I understand that." She worked her way around the counter again and stood by my chair, arms crossed, scowling. "Let me tell you something, John. I put up with a lot from Randy Haverhill, a hell of a lot. But child molestation? Never, I swear to you if I had ever caught Randy doing such a thing, I'd have shot him myself."

I grinned. "Careful Eva, you may have a motive."

"Do you have some sort of evidence?" Eva said, raising a hand as I started to protest. "It had better be good. I flat out refuse to believe that Randy Haverhill would ever have done anything of the sort."

It was time to head to Toby's gig. I helped Eva on with her wrap. We were quiet now. What more could we say to each other? We got into Eva's BMW, a tight car, a grand ride. I drove the downhill corkscrew, thinking about what Eva said. If Randy had been a child molester, Eva surely would have known. She would have used this as a lever in their divorce, no question, and that was why I was certain she was telling the truth. So if Randy was not a child molester, what was a bag of kiddy porn laced with portraits of his stepdaughters—portraits that Randy himself had taken—doing in his house?

SEVENTY-FIVE

Mama Hana taught classical hula at the Kamehameha School. My sister Emmy had been brought up on hula gigs and so it was natural that she should go to Kamehameha where she'd trained in the fine points of traditional dance and music. In my mind, Emmy dances in her slim satin gown and her bare feet caress a stage, a plumeria lei winds around her forehead and her long black hair fans over a mound of leis on her long, slim neck. Her hands sway, talking story while her hips play out the rhythm of the sharkskin drums and the uli uli shakers and it is forever this very time of year when I think of her, dancing hula gigs all through Honolulu during Aloha week.

How sad, how odd, that Randy should be taken now, the time of year when I was meant to be haunting the hula fests and the falsetto contests and the parades and the Downtown Mele with half a mind that I'd see my sister once again, or some semblance of her, somewhere in the crowds. And now, on Saturday night, in downtown Honolulu, the crowds poured into the streets to dine on Hawaiian soul food and hear their local bands play. I found myself thinking of the two of them, Emmalaea Liliokalani Crowningburg Spyer, my beloved soulmate and twin, and Randolph Kealoha Bishop Haverhill, now dead for one week, my notorious, my famous, my earliest friend.

I found Eva a place to sit in the Mauka Tower arcade of the Dillingham Building. She was looking into the back of the stage where Kimo and Toby were helping the band set up. Eva sipped on noni juice. I went prowling for food.

I was ravenous but couldn't make up my mind what I wanted. What would it be? Lau lau and Kalua pig? Hawaiian steak & shrimp? Huli huli chicken? Then there was poi mochi, a deep fried poi and rice pudding. I'd have to come back for some of that.

I sat down with a plateful of the lau lau just as Kimo and Toby were doing their thing, backing up the singer on their electric guitars. Eva had moved out into the street where she sat on a folding chair I'd brought for her. As the band cranked up, we moved out into the street in front of them. The group launched into some classic Doors.

"Can you believe a military band doing The Doors?" Eva said, smiling, shaking her head. "This makes me a real antique, doesn't it?"

The lead singer stepped back and let Toby and Kimo rip. The guitars chimed, whined, and screamed. The office towers around us made for spectacular acoustics. The music exploded upwards, shooting up the face of the Topa Tower building across the street. Sound crackled like musical lightning in the air over our heads.

The 25th Infantry Division's Tropic Light Band wailed away for a whole set as the crowd whooped and hollered. Finally, the musicians stomped their way to a clawing, growling finish, and Eva and I were on our feet shouting and clapping as loud as any two maniacs on the scene. We were bathed in a smoky miasma from the huli huli chicken stand. Oh, yes, it was all very fine.

I bought a plate of the chicken and sat down to enjoy it before it got cold. Eva sipped her noni drink and babbled on about what wonderful performers the boys were. Then there seemed to be some sort of a scuffle in front of us. *A real melee?* I wondered.

Toby's friend Kimo came dashing toward us, hair flying, eyes wide. "John. Come wikiwiki. There's another note."

SEVENTY-SIX

I ordered Eva to stay put and followed Kimo through the crowd. The band had set up on a platform in front of the Dillingham Building and their gear was sheltered in the arched portico that runs clear underneath the building into an open plaza behind it. Toby stood beside his opened guitar case, parked on a folding table with a jumble of cables and other instruments.

"A note," he said.

"When did you find it?"

"Just now when I came off stage."

"When was the last time you opened the case?"

"Just before the set. There was no note then."

"Are you sure?"

"Positive."

"Why positive?"

"We used floodlights while we tuned up. I would have seen it."

I dug the penlight I keep on my keychain out of my pocket. It's one of those high-tech gadgets with the intense beam and the battery lasts and it has gotten me out of trouble countless times.

I flashed on the message, took a look at it, a good look. More clumsy lettering with a few reverse letters.

The same college ruled paper. Just looking at it gave me the chicken skin. It was a garbled message from someone who couldn't communicate, as my psychologist lady friend Susan Kopono said.

"At least our mento is consistent," I said. "Did you touch it?"

Toby shook his head. "No way."

"Was anybody backstage while you were playing?"

"Just Hutch on the soundboard."

Hutch was a jug-eared shave head in the band's regulation military khakis and boots. I identified myself and asked if he had seen anybody near the gear.

"No sir, but then I was busy cranking out the volume," he said. Hutch was breaking down equipment. It was then I noticed a creepy oddity. On the table sat a pizza box.

"Did you order the eats?"

"Nope, but some guy delivered the pie. Said it was from a fan."

"What did he look like?"

"Skinny. Five eight, nine, maybe. Messy dreds, gold tipped."

"A local?"

"Haole." My skin crawled, This just had to be Elihu Markham. First he bashes my car. Now he's dropping more notes. No doubt coming unglued.

"Wait here, Kimo. Don't move. Don't let anybody handle this."

"Okay. "

"Toby, come with me."

We dashed through the arcade under the building. A hulk in a white barang accosted us as we approached a roped off area in the adjacent courtyard. A garden party was in full swing. "This is a private function, gentlemen."

"No problem," I said. "I'm looking for a pizza guy. We're short half our order."

"That way," he said, waving toward the jumble of traffic on the side street.

I realised we were in luck. Traffic was going nowhere. Toby and I carefully worked our way through the departing crowd. We found a Twice-a Slice-a van parked in a loading zone a half block up, on Queen. The hazard lights were flashing. The back doors were open. The inside of the van had been trashed. I told Toby to stay on the sidewalk and worked my way through the mob to the driver's side door. The driver was slumped over the steering wheel. Sleeping it off, maybe? But when I flashed the penlight over the side of his face, he wasn't pretty. When I tried to rouse him, he moaned. His head was sticky with blood.

"Toby, find us a cop. This guy needs help." I said to the driver, "Hang on, brah. It won't take long. The patrols are out big time. Downtown Mele. Aloha Week."

SEVENTY-SEVEN

We were in the emergency room at Queen's Hospital. The pizza guy was not yet awake. His family was with him.

I sat down with Detective Tabura in the waiting room. He had taken the original note and Toby's guitar case into evidence, but I had taken a picture of it on my digital camera and we used my photo as a model. We wrote out letters from it on the backs of my business cards and shuffled them around. I reversed them in the sequence that worked before, with the first note, the one that said "Da Itch." The first try, LHUA was gibberish. Then HLUA, Then HULA, and it was bingo.

Once hula came up, GIRL was an easy pick.

Telly snorted. "Kid stuff."

I knew where this was going and tried to head it off. "Wait a minute, Telly. You don't think... "

"You watch your rope, brah." His eyes were slits. "We find Toby over dad's body with a knife and a note. Now we find one funny note in Toby's guitar case."

I found myself nodding my head, and yes, I had to remind myself that the first note, the one I'd taken with my cell phone camera, had happened in a room Toby had been working out of the night of Randy's book signing.

The family came out. Tabura went in. I tried to stick with him but Tabura waved me off, so I struck up a conversation with Dad, a wizened and wiry haole and his wife, a tall and spare strawberry blonde with the golden colouring of certain Portuguese people, and Toby's words from the juvie centre burst into my brain. "Pocho," he'd said of the woman he had seen the day Randy was murdered.

I said I wanted to talk to his son when he felt better and Dad handed me his business card, and it was a pass Go and pick up two hundred points right off the Monopoly board.

"Mr. Markham," I said, shaking his hand and hanging on. "I am so sorry about your son." Markham senior nodded.

"As I understand it, your son Tomas has one cousin Elihu, yeah?"

"Second cousin."

"Elihu sometimes works with Tomas at Twice-a-Slice-a."

"Part time, maybe," Daddy Markham said.

"Would you happen to know if Elihu was riding with your son tonight?"

"Tomas say nothing of this to me. I will ask when he wakes up."

"Would you do that? It could be important."

"No problem."

"I'd like to talk to cousin Elihu as well." A wary expression crossed Mr. Markham's face. He turned to his wife. "You hear anything about where cousin Elihu?"

She shrugged, her face stolid. "Went back to the mainland, maybe?"

I gave them my card. "I need to talk to him. It's important."

Mrs. Markham promised me she would call Elihu's sister, who would be the most likely person to know where Elihu was.

Tabura came out.

"So?"

"Cousin Tomas not remembering anything. Not yet."

SEVENTY-EIGHT

Susan Kopono suggested we meet at Bishop Square, which is not far from her office on Fort Street. The little man with the broom was whisking plumeria petals into his dustpan as fast as the breeze shook them off the trees. Bishop Square might be upscale, but the food courts beneath the office towers are fast food palaces that the locals can afford. Susan and I went for loco moco, a sushi smorgasbord: spam musubi, kappa matsuri, shiba zuke, and plenty of buckwheat noodle, all washed down with Cokes. We found a table in the plaza near the fountain.

"What?" Susan said. She put down her chopsticks and stared at me. "A child molester? Randy? You must be joking." She combed through the hair at the top of her head with her fingers. Susan's heavy blonde hair was way more blonde than it had been just a few days ago. The dark roots had disappeared.

"A suspicious aeroplane bag was found in the Haverhill house."

"Who found it?"

"This goes no further."

"Of course not."

"Hillary was packing up. She found an aeroplane carryall full of kiddy porn."

Susan squinted. "I hate this stuff. Hate it." Her mouth twitched. "I'm a professional, a therapist and I detest it."

"Hillary tells me that pics of her own daughters were in there. She freaked."

Susan crossed her chopsticks like swords in her paper plate. "Are you telling me that Randy Haverhill molested his stepdaughters?"

"Hillary doesn't think it went that far."

"Why not?"

"The photos were portraits. She showed me."

"What about the other photos, the ones she found?"

"Twisted."

"In what way?"

"I haven't seen them myself. I'm going by what Hillary told me. The police seized everything in a search. The defence isn't privy to the evidence at this point."

"Creepy," Susan got out a cigarette case and tamped the butt on the table.

"I thought you quit."

"I did quit. Consider this a placebo," Susan said. "I'm so upset I'm going through the motions."

"I quit myself."

"Good for you, John."

"But I hate looking at those things."

She spouted some theory on addiction. Susan was big on theories.

"That makes me what, Susan?"

"Irritable?" Susan gave the cig a final puff and snuffed it out. "So. Most of the photos in the bag are twisted?"

"That's the overwhelming impression I got."

Susan nodded. Her pointy nose wrinkled along its raked sides. I found this endearing. What other woman wrinkled her nose like that?

"And yet the photos of Hillary's girls are regular portraits?"

"Nice shots, too. I saw prints made from those same photos."

"Maybe Randy took portrait photos of the two daughters in order to get them used to posing. If he were a child molester, he'd gradually work them into more erotic poses." She was rubbing her arms. "Talking about this stuff gives me the creeps."

"I thought you were a sex therapist."

"I deal with the victims, John. I tried working with offenders. I just can't find the right degree of empathy for them. I admit that."

"Is there a cure?"

"Depends. Sometimes. I worked with hardcore offenders on an experimental basis. Some are plagued with kinky thoughts that can be helped by doses of female hormones. The thoughts that plague them go away and they are able to have a normal sex life."

"But who's to say they stay on these meds?"

"Exactly." Susan stared into the harbour for a moment, then turned back to me. "With others we use intense behavioural therapy to break down their rationalisations."

"Such as?"

"The old, 'I'm just initiating this child into the world of sex'. That sort of thing. A great many sex offenders were molested themselves, so they have no normal boundaries to start off with."

I drummed my chopstick on the table. "I grew up with Randy Haverhill. I knew the whole family. I can't imagine he was ever molested—at least by anyone in his own family."

"That's just it, John. Randy's behaviour pattern doesn't fit the profile of a child molester at all. Even if he were into pictures, that doesn't mean he went any further. Most child molesters have very unsatisfactory adult relationships. They can't relate to women and aren't interested in other men. That's why they prey on children. We certainly can't say the professor was unsuccessful with women." Susan shook her head, worked her lips. "If anything, Randy was too successful with the ladies. He took advantage."

"So maybe Eva is right."

"You spoke to Eva about this?"

"On the Q.T. Randy might have been a sexual thrill seeker, just as Eva said, but never with children. Eva insists that was never a part of it."

"On the face of it, I would be inclined to agree."

"Eva also said that if Randy had ever done such a thing, she'd have killed him herself."

"Hey, I'm with Eva," Susan said and we laughed.

She glanced at her watch. "I've got to run. I don't want to be late for my two o'clock. Thanks for the lunch, John. I'm sorry I couldn't be of more help."

"So we've got a child molester who shouldn't be."

"Something's not right," Susan said. "Is Hillary sure that this, er, collection, belonged to Randy?"

"No. Hillary said she'd never seen the bag before."

"If the kiddy porn *did* belong to Randy, his fingerprints will be all over the photos, his treasured trophies."

"Tabura will have every photo at the lab for sure."

"There goes what's left of Randy's reputation." Susan bussed our plates off the table. "Oh well, I suppose it doesn't matter to him at this point." She picked up her handbag and briefcase. "One thing does matter, however. Hillary's daughters. They must be seen by a professional."

"Hillary doesn't believe things went anywhere."

"Let's hope not. But hoping isn't good enough. You tell her, John. If you aren't up to it, then have Hillary call me." Susan gave me her business card.

I looked at it. "Susan Kopono, Ph.D. Nice."

"I took six weeks off last summer and finished my dissertation."

"Good for you."

"So what about you, John? Are you going back to law school?

I shrugged.

"You seem deeply conflicted about that issue."

"Maybe you'll have to put me on the couch, Doc."

"Couches went out with Freud," Susan said.

SEVENTY-NINE

I plucked a ripe papaya off the tree in Cousin Duke's yard, poured a bowl of granola and milk and went out on the screened porch. Lola had warmed her kukui and coconut oils in the microwave and was giving me the look, patting the table. I stretched out on it face down, my head turned sideways on a small pillow.

The day I'd met Hillary for drinks at the Surfrider, I had bought an orchid from Lola—Lola McCready, whom I had met back in June while she was still a volunteer at the Pacific Rim Institute. Lola McCready had escorted me right into the middle of a murder investigation, but I didn't hold that against her. Lola was a lovely person, all the way through, and a girl of all trades to boot. Lola could dance a hula or roast a pig.

I had called Lola and ordered two items from the menu on the business card she gave me: the shirts ironed and the massage given.

Maya was coming. She would return from Maui on the weekend. Maya loved aloha shirts and so I wanted mine crisp and fresh. Since Maya is also one athletic lady, it wouldn't do for me to be gimping around with a lame back. Lola had set up her portable massage table out on the screened porch, right in front of the decrepit couch sporting one of cousin Duke's surfboards-in-progress. As Lola set to work on my back, I organised my day.

So where were we? Night before last, Telly and I had rearranged the letters of note number three: Hula Girl, while we sat in the emergency room at Queen's Medical Center, waiting to talk to Cousin Tomas Markham, the Twice-a Slice-a driver whose head was bashed the night of the Downtown Mele. I'd befriended Tomas's parents who had given me their phone number. Before Lola put me down for the count I'd dialled their number and left a message on their answering machine. They were my best hope of finding Thomas Markham's cousin Elihu, car basher and number one suspect in the Haverhill murder case.

Randy's laptop was ready. I had to arrange with Telly Tabura to meet me at No Ka Oi Computers on Nuuanu Avenue. I would need to find out what the professor was up to. If Randy was into kiddy porn, it would surely show up on his laptop.

"What is with your back?" Lola had a hint of disapproval in her voice.

"A knotty problem for you, Lola. I haven't been doing my stretches." Her hands whispered along my spine, tweaking the whiney spots.

"You are so tense." Lola trolled for knots, found and pinched on them, getting kinks out of the cord, so to speak. I went limp as a shirt put through the spin cycle and hung out to dry. Let me tell you, I was purring. After a snooze there on the table, I realised I had to get moving. I went inside to shave and dress.

By the time I was ready to leave, Lola had exchanged the massage table for an ironing board and already had several shirts from the pile hanging smartly on their hangers. The cat, Kiki, massaged her own back, rubbing it against Lola's legs.

"So Lola, tell me. What did you do at Randy's institute?" I said as I strapped on my watch, clipped my cell phone to my belt and stuffed my laundry list in my pocket.

"Sometimes I filed papers. Other times I answered the phone."

"And you quit right after the book signing?"

"Too much going on. Too scary for me."

"What did Dr. Haverhill do about it?"

"He laughed it off. No big deal to him."

"I heard he didn't bother to go to the police."

"The professor never did. Maybe it was a game to the professor," Lola said as she adjusted a shirt on the ironing board and applied the iron.

"Why do you think that?"

"It was said among the volunteers who had been there longer. The professor liked to play. Some of the volunteers did, too. Some people are players. Not me," she said. "I like a quiet life."

"Tell me about these games the professor played." Lola shrugged and concentrated on her ironing. She sprayed something on the shirt. The porch took on a starchy redolence. "I don't like to talk about people, especially the dead."

"It's the living we're helping here, Lola. Think of them. Of Toby."

She stared at me. "Such a nice boy. So shy."

"Yeah. Well, the police are trying to make a case that Toby murdered his father."

"Oh, no. I didn't know," Lola said. She set the hot iron upright. Her free hand pinned the shirt to the board. Lola's black eyes went glossy. Her eyelids fluttered. "That boy do such a thing? I can't believe it."

"Do you have any idea who would?"

"I wouldn't know. But Professor Randy had this personal trainer. I think they had a fight, maybe."

"I've heard about this trainer. His name was Eddie Cooke."

"Yeah," Lola said. "Now he works part-time at the Outrigger Club."

I added The Outrigger to my list. It was turning into a very full day.

"Thanks Lola." I gave her my cell number, paid her for the massage and a half dozen shirts, and took my car keys off the hook by the door. "Hey, wait, Lola. That day I was at the Surfrider, the day I was talking to the second Mrs. Randy?"

"Last Thursday," Lola said.

"How long were you there?"

"The hotel has me on noon to eight."

"My car was bashed before seven."

Lola's eyes went big again. "Your old Mustang?"

"Did you see anyone funny go into the hotel?"

"Not especially. Just the one I reported to security."

"Okay. Who was that?"

"One haole. I passed him in the lower lobby as I went out to the parking garage. He had this big Neiman Marcus shopping bag."

"And you reported him to security? Why?"

"He looked like one of the ones on the list."

"Of troublesome types?"

"You know the ones. Some of them pickpockets. Some of them pick up ladies and go for their money. Some of them are pimps."

"What was this guy?"

"A suspected shoplifter."

"Can you give me a description?"

"Not too tall, five seven, maybe eight. skinny. Messy dreds with gold tips, thin face, good skin, kind of golden."

"Asian?"

Lola shook her head. "No. Too big for Asian. I'd say pocho."

"Portuguese?"

"Maybe," Lola said.

"Did you see his eyes?"

Lola shook her head. "He wore sunglasses. It was dark down in the mezzanine and the sunglasses seemed wrong. Maybe that is why I noticed him."

"Mahalo, Lola. I'll buy you a drink next time I'm at the hotel." I plucked her card from my pocket. "You can add some more to your list of skills: Clues given, crimes solved."

Maybe Lola liked the quiet life but her testimony was what I needed. Lola McCready had given me the first clear description of Elihu Markham as a male, a Portuguese male, pocho, the exact pidgin word Toby had used for the colouring of the woman in the rain cape. I couldn't think of a good reason for Markham to bash my car, except maybe he was feeling some heat. Needles prickled the back of my neck. Was this woman merely Lola, girl of all trades?

"Yeah?" Lola prompted, her black eyes widening and smiling big when she realised that I was staring at her, laughing mouth luscious: Lola was Madam Pele for sure, and I'd follow her anywhere, through any labyrinth. Then Lola shook her head, lifted her heavy hair and fanned the back of her neck. Her expression changed and she was Lola again, the flower seller and masseuse who also did ironing. She picked up her canned starch and sprayed it on an aloha shirt collar. "Crimes solved? I don't think so, John. No, not me. I like the quiet life."

"Too bad Lola, you are a natural in detection."

She laughed. "I'm not *a* natural, only natural, a natural girl, that's me."

The phone rang, I swear, and I swear it never would have, except for Lola's influence. It was Mrs. Markham. She gave me the break I'd been looking for, the address of our suspect, Elihu. The guy lived 'ewa, west out of Honolulu in the coastal town of Waianae. Things might soon turn tense if not downright dicey. I went back into my bedroom and collected my SIG and donned the boxiest of the fresh aloha shirts to hide the fact that I was carrying. I went into the bedroom to put in a call to Telly Tabura.

In the time it took to do this I returned to the front room to say goodbye to Lola, but she was gone, vanished like Madam P., taking the envelope of cash I'd left for her, along with a spare key to my place. Lola was going to work me into her schedule at her own convenience; I needed her to tidy up just before Maya arrived. The only way I knew for sure that Lola had been there at all was the fact that in the hall closet hung a row of fresh shirts smelling starchy and sweet. That, and the fact that my miserable sacroiliac for once felt great.

EIGHTY

I found myself out in Waianae, a half hour west of Honolulu via the Farrington Highway. I was on Halona Street in a countrified district bordering a naval reservation. Following Elihu Markham's aunt's directions, I passed an orchid nursery, hung a left at a Quonset hut where pigs were for sale, and found a two-story stucco apartment building adjacent to a taro patch.

Elihu's cousin Tomas was still in the hospital and not talking. I had talked story to Mrs. Markham on the phone until her voice thawed. It remained unclear whether cousin Tomas had been bashed in the head by cousin Elihu, but I promised Mrs. Markham that I'd ask Elihu what he knew about that, if and when I caught up with him. This is how I found myself out in Waianae on the fringe of a fringe community.

The 'ewa side of Oahu tends to be dry since the prevailing trades come out of the northeast. The neighbourhoods looked parched, but in the distance, clouds rolled across the green palisades of the Waianae Mountains. As I went to the hallway door of a cinder block building, I heard chickens clucking in coops next door. A porker snuffled behind a hedge.

I went up the narrow stairs of a decrepit building. The halls were rank with mildew. I suppressed a sneeze. Kabuki music murmured behind a closed door. I knocked on Markham's door. A gecko scurried down the doorframe. Feeling the emptiness of the place as a hollow in my gut, I knocked again, called Markham's name. Behind me a door opened on a chain. The kabuki music was louder.

An old man answered, Japanese, wearing a stained kimono. I pressed my palms together and tucked them under my chin and bowed my head, enough to convey my respect.

"So sorry to disturb you, sir. I made an appointment with my cousin Elihu, but it seems he's not around."

"Must be asleep this time of day."

I glanced portentously at my watch. "We don't get moving, he'll miss sister Lola's baby luau." I stared at the old man. I was close enough to count the moles on his face, letting him consider the gravity of the situation. "I suppose, sir, that cousin Elihu didn't leave a spare key with you?"

"Mrs. Pada has the key, downstairs, in the back." The kabuki sounds dimmed as the door closed in my face.

Downstairs in the lower hallway, sour with mildew and decay, I found Mrs. Pada's door. I rapped on it, raising a great squawking. Footsteps came and went and came back again. The door opened a crack.

"Second floor apartment already rented," she said.

"It's not about the apartment, ma'am, it's about Cousin Elihu Markham. Sister Lola asked me to pick him up for the baby luau. His attendance is mandatory."

"I didn't know she was hapai."

"Not Elihu's sister. Lola's my sister. Lola is a Markham cousin."

"I wouldn't know about that."

"Maybe you might open up the place? Cousin Elihu works two jobs and sometimes it's hard for him to wake up. Cousin Elihu wouldn't want to miss a baby luau. That would be very unlike him."

"You Elihu's cousin?"

"In a manner of speaking," I said. "Baby luau," I repeated. "Cousin Lola's firstborn? Elihu misses it, the family will be devastated."

"I get the key." The landlady was a wizened haole with bottle red hair teased into points, and hesitant movements. I watched several bright green parrots, the eight-inch variety, sitting on swings in bamboo cages. Below them an enormous orange tabby licked its chops, tail twitching now and then, watching every birdy move.

Mrs. Pada was wise to pussy. She put the cat out when she closed and locked her door. She'd brought a parrot with her, put it on her shoulder and it squawked at me as we shuffled up the stairs and down the hall.

"Mr. Elihu?" She called, tapping on the door. The bird nipped at the side of her face with its fat beak. Silence.

"Have you seen Elihu lately?"

"Never see him except when he comes by with the rent. He works nights." Mrs. Pada held out her fingers. The parrot stepped onto them. Mrs. Pada and her bird both gave me the beady eye.

"Where does Elihu work?"

"Someplace in Waikiki."

"Sometimes he works with Cousin Tomas at Twice-a Slice-a."

The landlady shook her head. "He works nights at some bookstore in Waikiki."

I winked at the bird on her shoulder as she opened the door.

I went to the window, as if to admire the view, put my back to her, slipped my cell phone out of my breast pocket, punched the speed dialer and called myself.

I had a conversation with the mechanical voice I heard in my ear telling me to hang up and dial again: "Elihu, brah," I said. "Where you be, boy? I put my hand over the phone. "Cousin Elihu's on his way over," I said to the landlady. "He's over at the Pink Market. He'll be right back." Fortunately, I knew about The Maile Pink Market from my surfer days and the mention of it won me local status in Mrs. Pada's eyes. She took her key and left me alone in Elihu's place.

EIGHTY-ONE

Elihu Markham was our number one suspect, but he was also one tidy boy. His bed was made up with ritzy linens. He was a better housekeeper than I am. He probably ironed his own aloha shirts.

I checked the bedroom closet, found various outfits. The guy stuff was on one side, the female gear on the other. Maybe Elihu had a live-in girlfriend that I hadn't heard about. However, judging what we'd seen of him in the car bashing tape, he was a cross-dresser, māhū in Hawaiian parlance. A māhū guy was fine, perfectly acceptable by Hawaiian standards, including my own. It was the car-bashing part I had trouble with.

Speaking of the bashing of poor Em, I found what I was looking for in another closet, the one next to the front door. There was a Neiman Marcus shopping bag. I didn't dare disturb anything in it, but I got a good, hi-intensity penlight look at it. Inside were duct tape, a jimmy, a Twice-a Slice-a style rain cape and one of their floppy hats. A baseball bat stood in the corner. No blonde wig, though, and we had to have that. I re-checked the girlie side of the bedroom closet and found a blonde wig on a stand. It was hidden under a pile of ladies' hats.

I had been in the place for about fifteen minutes and was antsy to get out of there, and that was why I hadn't noticed the computer desk next to the sofa in the living room. Elihu had a clunky old laptop, but the cover was open, so I punched a key with my penlight and realized the screen was on. There was a mug of tea on the desk. I smelled it. Ginseng tea. The mug was warm. A sliding glass door opened onto a small lanai. There was a distinct possibility that cousin Elihu had heard Mrs. Pada knocking and had bailed out over the rail. Maybe he was late with the rent?

I hit the spacebar and found the blog of a woman named Madam Justine, her adventures. How she's pleasured men, women, or both. The language was as clumsy as it was verbose. Imagine the worst romance novel you ever tossed into the trash. I tried to read a paragraph and decided the grappling subjects were contortionists. I clicked the mouse and went to the home page. All of the entries were more of the same, all under one main heading: The Days and Nights of Madam Justine.

Then I noticed a link at the bottom of the page. I ran the cursor to it and clicked and that was how I found out the name of the bookstore where Markham worked: *Da Itch*. All right! We were cooking. We were also cooked if Elihu caught on, so I was careful to go back to the screen that Elihu had been looking at, and as I did so, I found several screens of the same page with different wording on them. This is how I realised that Elihu Markham was a man of many talents. He wasn't reading Madam Justine's blog, he was writing it.

I looked around, making sure I hadn't left anything out of place, closed Elihu's door, locked it, trotted down the stairs, thanked Mrs. Pada, and thanked the parrot on her shoulder. I assured Mrs. Pada I'd locked Elihu's door. I told her I'd go by the Pink Market to pick up my cousin.

I couldn't raise Detective Tabura on the phone so I called the dispatcher and told her to find him. It was urgent. I called Tabura again and punched in my callback number and drove around the neighborhood. I looked for routes, how to get back to the apartment to make a wee hours social call, should that become necessary.

While waiting to hear from Telly, I checked my list and decided nothing on it was as important as finding Da Itch bookstore. All I had was a phone number. When Telly called back I asked him to run a reverse directory check on the number. The address was a match to a very small brass plate on a tony door in a very large hotel. I drove back to Honolulu via the Farrington and found myself right back in Waikiki at the Surfrider with its Monkey Pod Bar, the same place where I'd invited Hillary Haverhill for a drink.

The parking garage where my precious Em had been bashed was just a few floors directly below the bookstore. So this was how Elihu Markham had hit on my car and managed to dodge security. He'd never left the building. He'd hidden in his place of employment. I shook the knob. It was locked up tight. I couldn't get in using the old credit card trick, either. By appointment only, the card said.

Speaking of appointments, I had to move on. I was scheduled to meet Telly Tabura at the computer place for a look at Randy's laptop.

EIGHTY-TWO

No Ka Oi Computers was in the same strip mall as Twice-a Slice-a, a few doors up from The Hungry Lion, almost directly across from the Hawaii Chinese Buddhist Society, a Chinese pastry of a place. Telly and I had agreed to meet there at 2:00 PM.

The computer store had a few private offices in the back that rented by the hour, so I booked one for the afternoon while I waited for Telly to arrive, but I was careful not to claim Randy Haverhill's laptop until Telly was on the scene.

It was close to 3:00 PM when Telly came in. A few people were checking email at the internet café at the front of the store. I handed over the claim check to the moon faced Chinese girl running the shop, paid for the repairs, and the girl showed Telly and me to our new office.

"Has Markham turned up?" I plugged in the laptop top, booted it and configured the wireless connection to the internet.

"Not yet. Got surveillance on his place in Waianae." The detective swigged on his Jamba drink. "One warrant coming to toss the place."

"Maybe Markham's at the bookstore."

"Not a problem," Tabura said. "Harry Pang with hotel security waiting for him to show up."

Fortunately, the password was on the ticket, or we'd have had a tough time of it. I typed it in, *The lt3h*, and Telly and I found ourselves in Professor Randolph Haverhill's other world.

There were scores of papers by economists and statisticians, and draft after draft of Randy's lectures. He also maintained a file devoted to public appearances. Any time Randy was invited on a talk show, he'd offer the interviewer a cheat sheet of possible questions.

"No wonder the guy appeared so smooth on TV," I said.

Telly took a pull on his Jamba juice, shook his head and grinned.

As for Haverhill's avocations, there was no child porn at all. What Randy was really into was hot lit. He had scores of emails from various ladies looking for a virtual turn-on. His list of favourite websites turned out to be links to various blogs of the Madam Justine variety. Most of them were so over the top that they were either hilarious or downright turn-offs. We searched through his files for a couple of hours and found nothing at all in the way of kiddy porn.

"This leaves us no link at all to the funny bag in Randy's hall closet," I said.

"Strange, yeah?" Telly's cell phone cranked out its Hawaii Five O ditty. "Tabura." I opened another folder, labelled *Cosmos*, expecting to find scientific papers. It was an infinity of Randy's hot writing instead.

Telly was off the phone. I was so busy scrolling through the files that Telly rapped on the desk to get my attention. "I hate to spoil your fun, but I gotta run."

"The warrant?"

"Maybe," Tabura said, bugging his eyes. His unibrow framed his yellow-tinged eyes like a hip roof wrapped around a pair of dormers. A corner of his mouth turned up. Maybe meant yes.

"I need to finish here, Telly. I've just found something else."

Tabura sliced the air with his hand. "I think this garbage turn you on."

"Leave the laptop with me?"

Telly took a pull on the juice while he thought about my request.

"There's this file, *Cosmos*." I said. "Randy was writing a novel."

"Fiction?" Tabura snorted. "No good in court."

"Let me check it out."

"Okay. We got one waste of time so far. Keep the laptop for now. You find something you bring it in."

"Agreed."

Telly had been gone about twenty minutes. I'd slogged through a dozen or so chapters of *Cosmos*, the adventures of a poor little French girl, Yvette, who had a major problem. Everything—the entire cosmos—turned her on. Yvette was too oversexed to find true love as a result. Her various lovers soon became insanely jealous or else she simply wore them out.

I have to admit that after five chapters I was worn out with Yvette. I was about to shut down and give up when the email program chirped, signalling the arrival of some new mail. It was a reminder notice of a previous invitation to a costume party at Da Itch Book Club, featuring a private reading of *The Orgasmic Cosmos*, the debut novel of the late Randolph Kealoha Bishop Haverhill. Obviously Randy had not yet been struck off the bookstore's email list.

A costume party, no less. Here was the perfect opportunity to check out Da Itch Book Club. It took me about thirty seconds to email my acceptance, using my own email address. I typed in a note explaining that I was a childhood friend of Randy's. I said that I was a hotshot scholar who had been at Oxford on a Fulbright with Randy. I'd come for the Economic Conference of Pacific Nations and now that my friend was dead, I wished to be included in the testimonial costume gig. I gave myself a few advanced academic degrees and added my cell phone number.

I got a call back within fifteen minutes. "This is Ruby Chan, proprietor of Da Itch Books. May I please speak with Dr. Spyer?" said a cultured voice, not only well modulated but seductive in its breathy intonation.

"Ms. Chan. How good of you to call. My friend Randy Haverhill spoke highly of your, ah, collection."

"I have a very select client list. I'm sorry but I do not see you on our membership roster."

"You do realise of course that Dr. Haverhill is dead."

"So tragic," Ms. Chan said in her bedroom tones. I pictured her as some seductress who wooed our green troops over to the enemy in one international conflict or another. "Randolph Haverhill was a man for all seasons, truly he was. It was my very great privilege to launch him on his literary career."

"You are Randy's publisher?"

"I published a limited edition of his wonderful novel, *The Orgasmic Cosmos*, only five-thousand copies. They were snapped up by collectors at twenty-five hundred dollars each. Now that Randy has been murdered these are going for five-thousand and up."

"Is that so?"

"Sadly for me, I very much misjudged the appetite of the market. I had no idea that Professor Randy had such a following among those of us who appreciate the very finest in erotica."

"Randy promised me an autographed copy."

"I am sorry Dr. Spyer but there's a privacy issue."

"I'm a guest at Randy's house. I stayed on after the funeral at the request of Mrs. Haverhill."

"My clients prefer discretion and pay dearly for the privilege."

"Randy meant me to be at the party. That's how I found this invitation. Randy had forwarded it to me." I paused, giving her time to reconsider. "I found the invitation just now. I have been so busy helping Mrs. Haverhill settle her affairs that I had neither the time—nor the inclination—to check my mail."

I heard a windswept sigh. "I suppose I could reconsider."

"If you need somebody to vouch for me, I'll have Randy's widow call you, Mrs. Hillary. She can verify my credentials."

I heard a sharp intake of breath. "That isn't such a good idea," Ruby Chan said."I doubt very much that Mrs. Hillary was acquainted with our group. Erotica was one of Dr. Randy's exclusive…"

"Pursuits?"

"Exactly."

"Mrs. Haverhill had no knowledge of Dr. Haverhill's interests?"

A breathy sigh filled my ear, "I'd appreciate your discretion, Doctor."

"Call me John."

"John Spyer?" she said. "I don't recall that Dr. Haverhill…. "

"John Maalaea Oluhana Crowningburg Spyer." Ordinarily I leave out the Crowningburg, an old Hawaii name sullied by one of my distant—very distant—relatives, or so Mama Hana says. One of the more recent Crowningburgs once pulled a very entertaining con job, which amused everyone but the justice system. At any rate, the fact that Ruby Chan didn't pick up on this meant that she was F.O.B., fresh off the boat.

Now that I had agreed to keep Hillary in the dark, her voice thawed. "So you have Honolulu connections?"

"Way back. Randy and I were kids together."

"At Punahou?"

"That's right. This is the first time I've returned to Honolulu since Randy and I did our Fulbrights at Oxford."

"And you wanted an autographed copy?" Chan said.

"Do you have one?"

"I do not. Unfortunately, a few clients are speculators. I'll let you know if one becomes available."

"I'll look forward to seeing you at?"

"Eight, and you must be in costume."

"Fine." I thought about going as a car basher in drag.

"And your lady?"

"I may bring a guest?"

"You must. This is a couples' occasion."

"Well, I don't…"

"If your significant other isn't with you, then you may choose a professional escort. We offer the most discreet services, catering to every taste."

"Thank you," I said. "I'd prefer to bring my own date."

"In that case, I'll need the name, please. We check invitations at the door."

"Susan," I said. "Dr. Susan Kopono. A Honolulu sex therapist who specialises in helping her clients cure their, ah, inhibitions."

EIGHTY-THREE

I sincerely thought I knew every nook and cranny of the Surfrider, but I was wrong. I found myself in an annex connected by a sky bridge to the main building. Da Itch Bookstore had a suite of rooms. The bookstore proper was set up like a reading room. Leather bound volumes were locked in glass cases. The art and the bric-a-brac were nautical, and naughty. Voluptuous ships' figureheads were the main decoration. My date, Hillary Haverhill a.k.a. Dr. Susan Kopono, was amused.

"This is a play on the reading rooms the missionaries established for the ship captains," Hillary said. "What a stitch."

"The missionary idea of what constitutes fine literature was somewhat different," I intoned, using my best professor-of-string-theory lingo. I adjusted the mortarboard on my head. The tassel kept slapping me in the face. We hadn't had time to rustle up costumes so we'd made do with what Hillary had on hand.

I wore one of Randy's academic gowns and carried my dissertation, *The Merits of the Stringless String Bikini* under my arm. Hillary in a riding habit was Madam Dressage, a dominatrix waving a serious riding crop. I could just make out her pale eyes behind a spangled mask. She had stuffed her hair into an old riding helmet sprayed with glitter.

Security on the door was so tight that we had been crowded into a hallway with several other couples, a street hooker with a vice cop, a movie director with a starlet, Michael Jackson with a child, a pregnant Lacy Peterson—a cadaver with a wonderful smile—and husband Scott in prison stripes. Bill Clinton was there with Monica Lewinsky. Catherine the Great came with her horse, and a white Romeo was accompanied by a black Juliet. The security guy doing the pat downs was a tattooed freak with a rope around his neck. He wore a blue twill shirt with patch pockets with his name, Otto, embroidered on it.

"Who is that?" Hillary whispered.

"Otto Erotica, I would guess."

The main salon was done up in fussy Victorian era furniture. Garish red flocked walls were hung with portraits of various nudes. Guests helped themselves to the eats, champagne and oysters and the like, and heavy on the sushi, all quite fine.

The guy in the horse costume made a play for Hillary, demanding that she beat him. Hillary got right into the act. She waggled the whip and made the horse prance and soon she attracted a crowd.

A hand touched my arm. "Dr. Spyer?"

I turned around.

"Ruby Chan." She extended a hand, icy as it was ivory. How good of you to come." The Big Itch proprietress had long black hair down to her okole, frameless square glasses and a glacial stare. I can't say that I recalled her face, but I felt the chicken skin rising on my arms. I knew I had seen this woman before: but where?

"My pleasure," I said. "This is quite the party."

The corners of her mouth turned up a millimetre on each side of her mouth. "We do like to have a good time." Chan said in a whispery voice. She wore a red satin gown tight as skin.

"Madam Pele, I presume?"

"None other," she said, running her tongue over her glossy lips.

"Are you going to disappear on us?"

"Possibly," she said in her breathy intonation. "If I can find the right inspiration."

"Well, Madam, that's an inspiring gown," I said. The dress was a Hawaiian holoku, built to display the hourglass curves of the feminine body. There wasn't much hour to Chan's glass, however. Ruby was very tall for a Chinese woman, and stick thin. The only hope for generosity that I could see about the woman lay with her lush lips, and those must have been surgically injected. She had perfect ivory skin, no doubt due to the careful and practical use of the umbrella to shield her from the tropical sun.

She had enormous breasts as well, impossible for an Asian woman; the breastworks on that thin frame had to have been surgically constructed. It wasn't her face but her bustline that I remembered. Ruby Chan was a piece of work all right, the woman I had noticed monopolising Randy's time at his book signing party back in June, while fifty other people cooled their heels in line.

"I like a man with brains," she purred. "Tell me about your dissertation."

"I doubt string theory would interest you."

"Not so, Dr. Spyer." Ruby stepped in close and stroked my arm. "Madam Pele loves the cosmos more than anything. "

"Madam Pele is one cosmic girl."

"You'll show Madam one big bang?"

"Not tonight, I'm afraid. Dr. Susan is flogging me as soon as she's done with the horse."

"Come by the store tomorrow," she whispered, swivelling her head around as if the other guests were hanging on her every word. "I think I've found a copy of *The Orgasmic Cosmos* for you. I can't let you have it tonight. Other guests here would be so hurt if they found out I didn't give it to them. I'm letting you have it out of respect for Dr. Haverhill. I'm sure he'd want a copy to go to his friend."

"Wonderful. What time tomorrow?"

"Any time after noon."

A muscular black dude in a white sailor suit came to claim Ruby. "This is Bruce Steadman, my assistant," Ruby said.

"Bruce. My pleasure." I took his outstretched hand. No shaka, no kamaaina; this guy was one F.O.B. whose pincer grip meant he broke bricks with his bare hands for exercise. Obviously, Bruce was the Big Itch muscle.

"Join us for group activities?" he said.

"It's up to my lady." Hillary and the horse were in a clinch until the Czarina claimed her stud and I claimed Hillary. Another couple arrived, a surfer dude and a female beach hippie.

"The surfer." Hillary hissed. "That's Eddie Cooke."

"Of course. Mr. Lobo."

"Check out the great pecs. He was Toby's personal trainer. "

"Until Randy canned him," I said, "for reasons unknown."

"Randy refused to talk about it."

"Cooke interned on *The Honolulu Gazette*. He was Eva's boy toy, although I heard he wouldn't be toyed with."

"That I wouldn't know about," Hillary said.

"Who is the girl Cooke is with?"

"I don't know her," Hillary said.

"You sure?"

"Why?"

"She was with Eddie Cooke at Randy's funeral." Eddie Cooke's date was a leggy woman in a pareau. I'd seen her outfit before—in Elihu Markham's closet.

Hillary shook her head. "I can't place her. There were too many people that day. I was too upset."

Ruby Chan minced across the room, peacock style, trailing her holoku train. Ruby hugged Eddie Cooke's squeeze.

"Elihu, you make a darling girl," she gushed. "Or should I say Madam Justine? You are the most beautiful pair in the room." I restrained an urge to high five it with Hillary; and I couldn't help but notice a force from the other dimension at work. At this instant Ruby Chan was Madam P. and Madam P. hadn't failed me. Madam P. had delivered Elihu to me.

"All right," I said to Hillary, *sotto race*. "Eddie Cooke and Elihu Markham turn up as a swinging couple at Da Itch Book Club. We've done our homework for tonight. Let's beat it before we're recognized."

"We can't just dash out. We just got here, Hillary said. So Hillary helped herself to a plate of sushi at the buffet table and I had another glass of Dom Perignon and studied the paintings. We waited until Ruby Chan and her bouncer boyfriend had joined other guests in one of the private bedrooms where an attendant stood guard at the door. We slipped out as a pair of stunning lesbian lovers came in, two beautiful blondes.

I made a mental note to call Susan Kopono tomorrow and thank her for loaning us her name. I wanted to ask her about Elihu Markham. Was beating an antique Mustang with a baseball bat some sort of turn-on?

EIGHTY-FOUR

Da Itch Bookstore was one tony establishment. I was back at the hotel annex at 12:45 PM the next afternoon. The hallway was as hushed as it was lush. There was no sign outside in the hallway that a wild party had gone on there the night before. When I rang the bell, Bruce the bouncer answered. He was wearing a white stretch gym suit that showed off his impressive physique. He wiped off the back of his sweating neck with a white towel.

"Bruce, nice to see you. That was some party last night."

"You don't know nothin' brah. You left too soon." Smirking, he rolled his eyes.

Ruby Chan came to greet me. She had on a gauzy white gown. Her hair was done up in elaborate rolls and pinned on top of her head. Her eyes were cloudy and she seemed to have the sniffles. From bingeing on coke, if I had to guess.

"I didn't see you at the reading," Ruby said. Her scant smile was a cover-up for the annoyance her whispery voice couldn't hide.

"I'm so sorry, Ruby. My date demanded attention. She threatened me with bodily harm."

Bruce laughed aloud and Ruby offered me coffee and a seat across her desk. "The reading was wonderful," Ruby said, passing me a delicate cup. The brew was delicious. It crossed my mind that the security department downstairs could use Ruby's recipe.

"I'm of course familiar with Dr. Haverhill's novel," I said. "Yvette, the French character is straight out of our Paris nights. I went prowling with him along The Rive Gauche a few times."

"When you were students together at Oxford?" Ruby Chan said.

"That's right. We did our Fulbright's together."

"What can I offer you?"

"What do you have?"

"We have a first rate collection of Victorian era literary pornography."

"I'd like to see it."

Ruby handed me a brochure.

"So where are the originals?"

"In a vault downtown." She stared at me. "I couldn't depend on hotel security. These are priceless works."

"That makes sense."

"Let me give you our virtual tour." She sat me down in a comfortable chair and turned on a TV monitor. A video came on, narrated by Ruby. The Big Itch was a subscription company. Investors had rights to view the works in a private setting. Each subscription offered readers a chance to be alone with the art. There were two types of partners, limited and general. Generals bought shares at five grand each. Limited partners invested fifty thousand each. The Limited partners were guaranteed ten percent interest paid quarterly.

"I'm a university scholar," I said. " I'd be parking a part of my stipend until I need it."

"The general partnership is best for you. You must agree to stay in the partnership for at least eighteen months. So don't put in money you'll need right away."

"I see."

"After that, you are free to sell your shares at the market price."

"And what would that be?"

"Past performance is no guarantee. But look at it this way. Our original shares were five hundred dollars.

That's a fabulous return to our original investors. Their dollars are secured by certified works of art in limited quantities. "

"Priceless."

"Indeed."

"Our Lovers' Weekends are geared to your special interests. For you and your lovely partner? Here's the memoir of Madam Valencia, a famous Victorian dominatrix."

"Valencia?" I said. "I haven't heard of her." Beyond a marmalade jar, I chose not to add. Instead I folded my hands and cocked my head in my best attentive scholar's pose.

"Madam Valencia entered a convent in her later years. Her confessions came prior to her spiritual awakening. The Valencian order sold the memoir to us for seven-hundred thousand U.S. According to a recent appraisal done just last month, the memoir is now worth three times our original investment."

Ruby fast-forwarded her video a few frames. We flashed past a few paragraphs of hot quotes from Madame's writings. She stopped the frame at an appraisal document that did, indeed, say that Madame's writings were worth a small fortune and I made a mental note of the firm, Trafford and Sons Antiquities, New York.

"Excellent," I said, looking at my watch. "I'll definitely consider this."

"Do come any time. By appointment, Of course."

"Certainly." I rose to leave. "Do you have a copy of Randy's book?"

"The Orgasmic Cosmos? I brought out the novel shortly after Dr. Haverhill became the director of the Pacific Rim Institute," Ruby said. "It was a limited edition of five-thousand copies, as I mentioned. The printing was a sellout. What few copies have come on the market have doubled in value as a result of Dr. Haverhill's untimely death," Ruby said.

I found myself staring at Ruby. Surely Randy Haverhill hadn't been rubbed to juice Ruby Chan's investment? "Impressive," I said. "Can you find a copy for me?"

"I thought so. Unfortunately another member got wind of it last night and bought it on the spot for seventy-five hundred. I couldn't turn it down."

"I understand."

"I can put you on the waiting list."

"Please do."

"We never recommend selling a first edition so soon."

"Of course not." I sat studying the brochure about Randy's book and noticed something interesting. "You also have Randy's holographic manuscript?"

"Now appraised at one-point-five million," Ruby said, "due to the wild demand for the limited edition."

"I'd love to see that."

"Out of the question," she said.

"Randy began writing when we were students. I can remember certain paragraphs." I quoted a line or two that I had read on Randy's laptop. Ruby Chan smiled her smile, but her whispery voice took on a razor edge.

"I've sent the holographic manuscript to New York. I wanted the pages treated for preservation purposes, especially now that Randy is gone. The only erotic novel by a brilliant economist? Interest in the antiquities world is enormous."

"When will it be back?"

"Not for several months," Chan said. "These preservations take time."

"Thank you, Ruby. I'll get back to you," I said.

"Please give my regards to the lovely Dr. Kopono," Ruby said.

"I'll do that. I'm on my way to see her for some horsing around."

EIGHTY-FIVE

Hillary met me at the door in a flowery muu muu, face scrubbed, eyes glassy. Kahuna shimmied against my leg. I scooped the dog up and scratched him behind his ears.

Kahuna and I followed her through the hall past the murals of Hawaiian history painted on the walls. We hung a left into the kitchen at the taro patch where King Kamehameha I laboured among his subjects, thereby dignifying common labour. Or so Mama Hana taught me.

In the kitchen Hillary poured coffee and passed a plate of malasadas. "I couldn't sleep last night, that wolfish face on my mind," she said. "This morning I remembered where I'd first seen it." She handed me a flyer, the Pacific Rim Institute Newsletter, Vol. 2, Issue 3, page 2. *Edward K. Cooke joins volunteer staff.*

"A wonderful photo," I said. "All right, Hillary, very nice work. Cooke's the lynchpin of the case: Eva's boy toy; Toby's trainer, tied into Da Itch Book Club, and a part-timer at the Canoe Club."

Hillary nodded. Kahuna sat begging, his nails clicking on the tile floor. Hillary crooned at the dog, tossing him a bit of malasada, and brushed the crumbs off her hands. "And Eddie Cooke is Elihu Markham's pal."

"Here's the next question: Would Cooke have known about the storage shed under the house?"

"It's possible," Hillary said. "Randy and Toby stashed paddling gear down there."

"So we've put Cooke on the scene here at the house. We've linked him to Elihu Markham, car basher, party animal... "

"...and Randy's murderer?" Hillary's eyes squinched shut, her mouth stretched in distaste. "I can't believe Randy had a threesome going with Cooke and Markhan."

"I'm beginning to wonder whether this is a stalking case at all," I said. "Markham works at Da Itch Book Club, which published a book that Randy wrote."

I handed Hillary the advertising brochure. She left Kuhuna begging, yapping for attention, as she stared at the write-up and dug into her eyes with her fingers, as if what she'd seen had filled them with grit. When she looked up, her face was ashen.

"The Orgasmic Cosmos? I still can't believe Randy would write something like this." She threw down the brochure. "And then to sell it to the Chan woman? Are you sure this is his?"

"I found it on his laptop, Hillary. You gave me the claim check."

Hillary closed her eyes, rubbing her temples. "Wait until Daddy finds out."

"So what's next? I called the Canoe Club yesterday, asked to speak to Cooke, but now is not the time to nose around there. Now's the time to pull back."

"Why?"

"We've found out what we need to know. We've linked Cooke and Markham to each other and to Randy. The police are staking out Markham's apartment in Waianae. Hotel security is watching Da Itch Bookstore at The Surfrider in Waikiki. Once I put Telly wise, he'll get a warrant to bring Cooke in. Muscle Cooke too early and they both scurry away."

"I see."

"So here's what we do. We need to check into the scheme at Da Itch Bookstore. Ruby Chan lists a New York appraisal firm, Trafford and Sons, in her prospectus. We need to locate Trafford in New York. They must have an internet address. Once we get that, we talk to them."

"Let me find them," Hillary said.

"Ruby claims to have Randy's holographic manuscript of *The Orgasmic Cosmos.* She says it has been appraised by this Trafford outfit. We have to confirm that."

My cell phone rang. Detective Tabura's number came up on my call screen.

"Telly, what's happening?"

"I'm at your place on Leahi. Where are you?"

"I didn't make it home last night."

"You coming home now?"

"Is there some problem, Telly?"

"Come straight here." Tabura's tone was ominous.

"My place has been tossed?"

"Maybe," Telly said, and I of course knew what 'maybe' meant.

EIGHTY-SIX

In light traffic it's maybe a half hour ride from the Haverhill mansion to Duke's hale, mauka of Kapi 'olani Park. I made it in twenty minutes and knew I was in trouble as I turned off Kapahulu and down Leahi. An ambulance screeched past, followed by a patrol car.

Telly was waiting for me on the sidewalk at the bottom of the steps. I pulled the black pickup into the drive and jumped out, left the door hanging, the seat belt minder chiming, and faced a Telly Tabura looking as irritated as I'd ever seen him.

"So who is in the ambulance?"

Tabura waggled his hand that wasn't holding the Jamba Juice. "John Spyer is one busy boy. Can't keep track of his lady friends?"

I felt a sting in my back like I'd just been shot all over again. "What are you talking about, Telly? Not Maya," I said. "Can't be. Maya's on Maui, staying with Mama Hana. I talked to her first thing this morning."

"Not Maya," Telly said. "Try Lola McCready."

"Jesus Madam. How is she?" Gentle Lola? Had I put her in harm's way? Bile rose in my throat. A flash of heat seared my innards as I fought down the urge to puke on Telly's shoes.

"Alive. We've determined that much."

"So? Are you going to tell me what happened?"

Telly stared at me.

"Where were you last night, Spyer?"

"Out at a party."

"Got some witnesses?"

"Of course." I was in serious trouble. How was I going to explain to my good friend the detective that I was passing myself off as Dr. Spyer, inventor of string theory, string bikini edition? That I'd been prancing around at a swingers' party at Da Itch Book Club with all the other consenting adults?

"I escorted Mrs. Haverhill to a function. We were out late. I crashed in her guest room."

"Uh huh." Telly's unibrow rose as he suppressed a leer. *Jesus madam, I said to myself. Telly knew all about the party. Harry Pang's security detail would have monitored the comings and goings.*

"Maybe Miss Lola didn't like this?"

I shook my head. It felt as tight as a sharkskin drum subject to one heavy pounding. "Miss Lola McCready sells flowers at The Surfrider. She does housework on the side. I hired Lola to tidy up the place and iron some shirts. My friend Maya is due back from Maui in a day or two and I wanted the place to look nice."

"What time did Lola come in?"

"I haven't a clue. I gave her a key."

Telly took a long pull on the bug juice. He stared at me. "Okay, John. We wait to hear what say Miss McCready." Tabura waved me through the wooden gate at the foot of Cousin Duke's hale. The steps were steep and Telly was breathing hard by the time we arrived on the front porch. The door was open. A beat cop was posted in front of it. Behind him I caught a glimpse of the crime scene techs at work.

Telly offered me a seat on my own porch while he went inside to supervise. He brought me a cold beer when he came back.

"Okay, Spyer. You got some theory about what happened here?"

"I'd say it was Elihu Markham and his good buddy Eddie Cooke."

"Why you say that?"

"I leaned on them last night."

Telly gave me a sidelong glance. "You messing with my investigation, Spyer? Shame on you." I read the smirk on his face. *You done good, brah*, it said.

"Hey, Telly. Haven't I earned some privileges?"

Telly took a long pull at his juice. "Privilege easy to abuse."

"Da Itch Book Club invited Randy Haverhill to a costume party. That novel on Randy's laptop? Da Itch Book Club published it. They are raking in big money on it."

"One Professor not in shape to party," Tabura said.

"The invite was emailed to Randy's laptop. This was after you left. I passed myself off as a visiting professor friend of Randy's, one of his close buddies. I took Hillary Haverhill along to help scope out the place and things worked out fine. Elihu Markham was there in drag as Eddie Cooke's date. Eddie volunteered at the Pacific Rim Institute. He moonlighted as Toby's personal trainer. I've nailed the confirms on that. There was some trouble between Eddie Cooke and Randy Haverhill as Hillary will tell you. Randy fired Eddie a few weeks before the murder. Exactly why Randy dumped Eddie, that's the question. Whatever the reason, Cooke retaliated big time. Find out what the trouble was among Randy Haverhill, Eddie Cooke and his buddy Elihu Markham, and we'll have the motive for Randy's murder."

"Story," Tabura said. "The Hawaiian juror wants the story."

"And every story has a setting," I said. "So let's look at the murder scene, the storage shed under the Dowsett house. Hillary Haverhill believes Eddie Cooke was familiar with the storage shed. It's where the Haverhill males kept their athletic gear. If that's the case, Eddie knew the Haverhills' ancient shotgun was kept there. All Eddie Cooke ever had to do was clean it up enough so that it would fire. When his buddy Elihu arrived, Professor Haverhill's own weapon would be ready to be to be used against him on a Saturday morning when the deed could be pinned upon the hapless Toby."

"All very nice," Telly said. He sipped on his Jamba juice and wiped his mouth with the back of his hand. So why they attack Miss Lola?"

"Maybe they figured out that Lola was a witness. Lola McCready works as a flower seller at the Surfrider. She volunteered at the Pacific Rim Institute with Cooke. She also reported Markham to security just before he turned into a lady and bashed my car, and here's the beauty of that, Telly. She reported Markham as a male, before he donned his māhū gear. Harry Pang at The Surfrider has Lola's report."

Tabura scribbled notes. "What time you leave this party?"

"Around 11:30. We left before the going got heavy."

"Cooke and Markham still there?"

"They disappeared into one of the bedrooms with some of the rest of the crowd."

Tabura stuck his pen in his pocket and rubbed his forehead. "So Markham and Cooke were at the Surfrider Hotel, and Miss Lola McCready works there."

"There's your connection, Telly. All you have to do is find out what time she left her job last night." I felt so spaced that the sound of my own voice seemed to belong to another dimension. "Telly, what I'm guilty of where Lola McCready is concerned, I dragged her into harm's way. I got her talking about what went on at Randy's Institute. If not for me, I doubt she'd have come forward."

"Don't be hard on yourself, Spyer." Telly flicked back several pages in his notebook. "Lola took upon herself to report Markham to hotel security. This she did before your Em was trashed."

"I'm sick about Lola."

"Join the club," Tabura grunted, "And I don't mean The Outrigger."

I took Telly's remark to be a sort of absolution. I felt better. The pounding in my head eased a bit and I could think more clearly. "By the way, Telly, I have another little gift for you."

Telly grinned, showing his missing tooth. By the light of day the whites of his eyes were sallow and his face was puffy from lack of sleep. "I like practical presents, something I can use."

"Chan," I said. "Ruby Chan."

Tabura's eyes widened and his brow rose and his mouth twitched and he didn't have to say the word.

"So you know Ruby Chan?"

"So didn't I work vice for six years?"

EIGHTY-SEVEN

"Ruby Chan may have been a hooker on your beat, Telly, but she's now an oriental glamour puss, peddling pricey erotica. She published that novel I found yesterday on Randy Haverhill's laptop. The title has been changed. Ruby published it as *The Orgasmic Cosmos*. "

"One bestseller?"

"Well, Randy's death didn't hurt sales."

Tabura toyed with his juice bottle, swirling it, turning it into a green whirlpool encased in glass. "Why kill the author? Book that bad?"

"Maybe it's extortion. I was asked whether I wanted to make an investment in this club. I expressed mild interest. Let's see what happens. Maybe I'll be coerced."

"John Spyer Professor?"

"Let's hope so, Telly. Em was bashed before the party, but I don't believe that Markham and Cooke figured out who we were."

"John Spyer Investigator?"

"Markham works in the Surfrider building. He could have seen me talking to Hillary. I happen along and start making the boys nervous."

"So they bash your Shelby Mustang as a warning."

"I'm dense, don't get the message, so they hit on Lola McCready."

"One volunteer at the Pacific Rim Institute?"

"Suppose they blame Lola for putting me onto Eddie Cooke."

"Maybe."

"So there you are Telly, my gift to you: probable cause on a platter."

"Mahalo, John. I thank you. H.P.D. thank you. Next time we grind, I buy."

"Next time we grind, Telly, I want to see you eat your flowers."

Telly flipped shut the cover of his notebook and stuck his pen in his shirt pocket. "Okay, Spyer. You're good for now. You been good to the H.P.D., so I do you one favour."

"What's that?"

"You can take a few aloha shirts with you. Not so fresh, once we toss." Tabura waved a bottle of juice in his hand. "Too bad, but Miss Lola's in no shape to press."

I nodded my head. "Thanks, Telly. A pal you are. I suppose you are kicking me out of Cousin Duke's hale?"

Tabura waved his Jamba bottle in salute. "Duke's hale one crime scene, yeah?"

EIGHTY-EIGHT

Hillary Haverhill took me in. I arrived at the Dowsett mansion with what shirts I could grab and some underwear Telly let me take out in a paper bag. Hillary gave me the spare bedroom where I'd crashed last night, just off Randy's study. She was dressed in a riding habit.

"How's tricks?" I said.

Hillary laughed. She laughed until tears squeezed out of her eyes, too heavy on the mirth by half, but her laughter had nothing to do with my skills as a standup. Hillary was laughing off stress.

"I wish I was really so funny," I said.

"It's my dressage club," Hillary said. "The president called me this morning. She asked me to do the fall fundraiser this year. Here I am, I'll never see thirty again and I'm the youngest co-chair they ever had." She picked up the riding crop she'd used as a prop at Da Itch party and shook it in my face. "Wouldn't those equine snobs die if I told them they have to attend as dominatrixes and their husbands as māhū?"

At that point the fax machine on Randy's desk bleeped to life. A piece of paper crawled into the tray. Hillary wiped her eyes, tossed the whip and handed me a warm piece of paper. "For you, Professor No Strings, Exhibit A." The cover sheet was from Trafford and Sons in New York.

"Well what do you know? There really is such a place."

"I had our accountant at Oahu Land and Cane call them."

"It helps to have clout." I looked over a copy of the appraisal of *The Cosmic Orgasm*, a holographic manuscript by Professor Randolph Haverhill. It was a fancy certificate bordered in scrolls and squiggles, signed, sealed and certified by a notary for the State of New York.

"I spoke to Mr. Trafford senior. He'd read about Randy's murder in the *Times* and was very kind," Hillary said. "He's vacationing on Maui this winter."

I perused the document. "All right, here it is, a holographic manuscript valued at *fifteen* thousand dollars."

"Wait a minute," Hillary said. "You said…"

"Yeah. The figure is way off."

I flipped through the pages of Da Itch Book Club catalogue and there it was on the back page, the same certificate from Trafford and Sons with one simple change, and it wasn't just Randy's original title. Three extra zeros had been tacked on to the end of the document.

"So there you have it. Ruby Chan kites the fifteen grand into one-point-five million."

"Inflated just a bit," Hillary said. "Randy wouldn't have missed that."

"You're sure? "

"Randy might have had his problems with the ladies and he was a very busy man, but he always balanced his cheque book. His father was an accountant, you know."

My cell phone buzzed at my belt. I checked the call screen. It was Telly.

"Detective."

"I have one gift for you, Spyer."

"Not a trip to the lockup, I hope?"

"One invitation to one questioning. Not so good as functions where Dr. No String go."

"You picked up Markham?"

"We ask him why he bashes one car and one cousin. 2:00 PM sharp."

"I accept with pleasure, Telly. "This is bound to be one fine performance."

EIGHTY-NINE

Markham got himself an attorney?" I said to Detective Sergeant Terry Wynter as we settled in an interview room behind a one-way mirror, where we talked in whispers. Technically, we weren't supposed to be talking at all. We could watch Telly Tabura question Elihu Markham in the presence of his lawyer, but they couldn't see us and it was a good thing. Elihu Markham's lawyer was such a good-looking babe that Detective Wynter was having a hard time containing himself.

Wynter handed me the lawyer's card. "Kay Foil. Some babe. And what a name for an attorney." Wynter grinned, showing spectacular white teeth in his dark face. Wynter, a leather-skinned haole, was a southern California transplant known as "Surf," as in "Wynter Surf." Now in his forties, he still maintained a board at Waikiki and had the shape to prove it. His thick eyebrows went up and his tongue ran across his lips. "Ms. Foil is a junior partner in Eddie Cooke's daddy's law firm."

"Helps to have connections."

Kay Foil, Esq. was a tall blonde with a mane of hair that shook every time she moved, who proved to be as snippy as she was stunning. As for her client, Elihu Markham, he'd have looked better in drag. He wore a rumpled tee shirt and a few days' growth of beard. His eyes were cloudy, as if he'd just emerged from bed. His messy dreds were flecked with gold tips and his golden-toned flesh went sallow in the harsh light of the interview room. It was hard to equate this unmade bed of a fellow with what I knew about his fussy housekeeping.

Telly Tabura went through the preliminaries for the benefit of the tape recorder on the table and lobbed softball questions to relax his quarry. "Where do you work, Mr. Markham."

"In a bookstore."

"What store?"

As Markham reeled off the name and address of Da Itch Bookstore, I flashed a victory sign for Wynter's benefit.

"What you do there?" Tabura said.

"I'm a curator of a book collection. I have a degree in Library Science."

Tabura slapped the table, grinning, flashing the black puka in his mouth. "Say again?"

"Library science."

"Like one library lady?" Tabura said.

"Make that one māhū library lady," I whispered.

Markham flashed Telly a look of pure disdain. "I hunt for rare volumes. I see to it that they are preserved."

"How long you work for Da Itch Books?"

"Since I got my degree two years ago."

"What about Twice-a Slice-a Pizza?"

"Just on weekends, as a favour to my cousin. I have student loans to pay off."

Tabura reached for a stack of time cards and asked Markham whether he had worked at Twice-a Slice-a on the date of that particular weekend. After half a dozen of these exchanges a very bored and irritable Kay Foil, Esq. agreed to stipulate to all the time cards in the stack.

"Two for two," I said, waving a two-fingered victory sign at the backside of the mirror.

"What?" Wynter said.

"Markham's attorney has just stipulated that Elihu Markham worked for Twice-a Slice-a on the morning that Randy Haverhill was murdered."

In the interview room, we watched Tabura, a master interviewer, at work. He glanced at his notes, looked from Markham to his attorney, and back to his notes again. "Does a degree in library science teach one haole to bash one cousin?"

Markham sat back in his chair as if he'd been slapped. "What the hell you talking about?"

"What is this?" Ms. Foil snarled. "We didn't come down here for this, Detective. Please stick to the issue we agreed upon or this interview is over."

Telly feigned an apology: "Excuse me, Ma'am. Something new just came in on Elihu here. Rather than having him back in here again, I thought I'd find out what he has to say about what happened to his cousin Tomas."

"This interview is over." Ms. Foil rose and began to pack up her briefcase.

Playing the stumblebum, Telly talked on. "As Elihu well knows, his cousin Tomas wound up in Queen's hospital on the night of Sept.16th, the Downtown Mele. Tomas regained consciousness this morning. Said Cousin Elihu here throttled him."

Markham leaped out of his chair. "That's a lie!"

"Elihu, sit down." Ms. Foil hoisted the sleeve of her grey power suit. Markham glowered from his chair. "Very well, Detective," she said. "We'll need a ten minute break while I confer with my client."

Tabura used the break time to pay us a visit. "Cousin Tomas came around?" I said.

"Maybe," Tabura said, unibrow lifting, eyes widened, expression pious.

"Or maybe yes." Wynter burst out laughing.

Through the one-way glass, the three of us watched the theatrics between lawyer and client. Markham's mouth moved furiously. His lawyer glared back. Obviously this Tomas business was all new to her. After five minutes of this they came to terms, Ms. Foil made notes while Markham stared at the clock on the wall.

Tabura tapped on the adjoining door as nine minutes and thirty seconds elapsed. Ms. Foil nodded her head. Tabura turned on the recorder. Markham's attorney said she would allow questioning on Markham's alleged assault on his cousin Tomas.

"I worked the Mele for Twice-a Slice-a. It's a big night for them," Elihu said. His sentences were jerky and his nervous timbre was magnified by the speakers. "We went out with a dozen pies. We had big orders for several of the bands. My cousin Tomas stayed with the van while I went around delivering. It was a mess. Some of the groups had been moved to different locations. It took me close to an hour to find my way through the mob. By the time I got back to the van, Tomas was gone and the police had arrived."

"We have no record of you coming forward," Tabura said. He rocked back in his chair, arms crossed.

"I asked a beat cop where my cousin was. He thought maybe Queen's so I went there. It took forever to get through the mob. The emergency room clerk wouldn't tell me a thing. I tried to call my uncle but he wasn't home."

"Did you look in the waiting room?"

"I glanced around, and didn't see anyone I knew." Telly cast a veiled glance toward the mirrored wall and I read his thoughts. Neither of us saw anything of Markham in the emergency waiting room that night.

"Where were you after that?"

"I went back to the Mele. I hooked up with some buddies and we partied until dawn." Markham turned to his lawyer. "What's their problem? My cousin Tomas, he's okay. If he thinks I hit him, that's between him and me."

"My client has a point, detective." Ms. Foil said.

"Fine," Tabura said. "We'll see what your cousin says about pressing charges."

He paused, took a swing of his Jamba juice, and looked at his notes. "All right, we got one related matter, here, could be something, could be nothing."

Markham hooted. "Nothing most likely."

"Did you deliver three pies to the 25th Infantry Tropic Light band?"

Markham started. His face went white. He mumbled some sort of response.

"What's that?" Tabura said. He tapped a pen end for end on his notepad.

"How do I know?" Markham said. "I don't recall it specifically."

"You don't remember delivering one funny note along with the pies?"

"Why would I do that?" Markham said.

"What's this about?" Ms. Foil demanded. "Elihu doesn't have to answer any questions about any... "

"I didn't put any note in any guitar case." Markham blurted.

"Okay, Tabura said, "I make one note of this. You said you never put one note in one guitar case?"

"I did not." Markham sat back in his chair, relieved.

"Gotcha!" I said behind the mirror, tossing Telly an unseen shaka sign.

Wynter's white teeth flashed. "Markham boy, you walked right into that one."

Ms. Foil rose, pinned her long hair behind her ears and proceeded to stuff her notes into her briefcase, Markham was at the door.

"Wait a minute," Tabura said.

NINETY

This time Ms. Foil wasn't taking Telly's bait. She yanked her sleek briefcase off the table. "I have to be in court." She headed for the door.

"We got just one more issue," Telly said. "I thought I might do Mr. Elihu one favour, but if not, I'll go ahead and press charges."

Ms. Foil responded with a derisive gasp.

"Felony bashing of one antique Shelby Mustang, market value, two-hundred fifty thousand dollars."

"All right," Foil groaned, parking her briefcase at her feet. "Make it fast."

From where we sat behind the one way mirror, Wynter was beside himself. "Whooo baby, hubba hubba." He stared at me.

"It's a good thing I didn't hear that disgusting sexist remark."

"Hey, and Ms. Foil didn't hear it either," Wynter said, a salacious grin on his face. "Too bad she doesn't sue me. I'd offer to settle in bed."

Adopting my best Dr. John Spyer, Professor of String Bikini Theory, I stated the philosophical question Wynter raised. "If a sexist remark goes unheard, is it still a sexist remark?"

Wynter hooted, but I poked him in the ribs. Through the window, Telly had just pushed the play button: "Were you in the Surfrider hotel in Waikiki on Thursday?" Tabura said.

"I'm there every Thursday. I work there."

Telly Tabura stared at him over his reading glasses. "Is that a yes?"

"It's a possible," Markham said.

"We have you on security tape down in the lobby."

"Where's the harm in walking around?"

"Walking around in drag."

Elihu grinned. "Hey, man. The māhū tradition."

"That's right," Tabura said. "Where were you going? Off to a māhū gathering?"

"I don't remember."

"You don't remember taking a baseball bat to a Mustang?"

"Maybe I was stoned," Markham mumbled.

"All right," Foil said. "Stop the tape." She marched her client out of the room. In a minute or two they returned.

"We have Mr. Markham on tape, bashing Mr. Spyer's car with a baseball bat."

"We'll wait until such evidence is produced," Foil said wearily.

I studied Elihu's expression. His eyes widened, but he quickly composed himself so as to appear nonchalant.

"Mr. John Spyer owns the Mustang. Spyer is a generous man. Elihu here agrees to pay damages, maybe we reduce some of the charges."

"I have to be in court in seven minutes," the lawyer said.

"No problem," Tabura said. What he meant was, court was just down the street. "Let me suggest to you, Elihu, you agree to settle with Mr. Spyer by tomorrow afternoon."

"I'll think about it," Markham said.

Tabura made a show of turning off the tape. He rose, shook Ms. Foil's hand. "Thank you for helping us clear up a few things with Mr. Markham," he said in his most formal English. Telly could speak the English king's tongue when he felt like it. He turned to Elihu Markham: "Mahalo for coming in, Mr. Markham. Please give my best to your personal trainer friend, Eddie Cooke."

"Eddie Cooke?" Foil yanked her hand out of Tabura's grasp. "What about Eddie?"

"He's the son of a partner in your law firm, yeah? Also one personal trainer for Toby Haverhill, isn't that right, Elihu?"

"How do I know?" Markham said. "Eddie's a friend of mine but I don't know all of his clients."

"What we hear, Eddie Cooke was fired by Randy Haverhill. This happened shortly before Dr. Haverhill was murdered. You wouldn't know about that?"

"Let's go, Elihu," Ms. Foil tossed her blonde mane as she picked up her briefcase. "We don't have time for idle gossip."

"Mahalo, Ms. Foil," Tabura said. "I'll see to it that any charges that might come down won't be idle ones. That way you can bill Daddy's law firm for lots of hours, yeah?"

"Hey Surf," I said to Wynter. "Congratulate Telly for me on a masterful job. Tell him I'm off to see the first Mrs. Haverhill. I have to find out what she knows about Da Itch Bookstore, and Randy Haverhill's manuscript. After all, Eva is his literary executor."

NINETY-ONE

I rang Eva's doorbell and set Hone to barking. Tutu Lia's voice answered via the household intercom. "Who is it?"

"John Spyer."

"Okay, John. I'm coming."

It took awhile for Tutu to make the long shuffle down Eva's hall. Hone was with her, wagging his tail as she flung the door open. Her face was drawn.

"How is Eva?"

Tutu shook her head. "Not so good, this tachycardia."

"I need to talk to her. I'm sorry."

"You come on in," Tutu said. "Mrs. Eva's off her feeding tube. She perks up when a handsome man comes to call."

I waited in Eva's salon. Hone put his head in my lap. I scratched him behind the ears and examined his sutured eye. It had stopped running. Eventually Eva came strutting in on backless high heels. She wore what I'd call a tea gown, though I'm no expert on such things. She'd made a valiant attempt to conceal her sickbed pallor beneath a layer of rouge and her thin hair had been fluffed up. Her eyes were bright but her hands were icy as I kissed her cheek and helped her settle into her favourite wing chair. It had a matching ottoman. Eva kicked off her shoes and curled her feet beneath her. It was a way to disguise the fact that she wasn't tall enough for her feet to reach the floor.

"How are you doing?"

"I'm a junky now. The doctors put me on morphine." Her eyes flared and her chin was high. "Dr. Kojimura is dropping by sometime this afternoon. We are on the final chapters of *The Road Less Travelled.*"

"I won't keep you from your trip."

"I'm so glad you came by, John. I haven't heard from you in what?"

"Two days," I said. "Our investigation is shifting, Eva. We're closing in on Randy's real killers. Toby will be in the clear."

"Who?"

"Eva. You know better than to ask." And I knew better than to tell Eva that her boy toy Eddie Cooke and his māhū buddy Elihu Markham had murdered Randy Haverhill. Either the news would kill her outright or it would make headlines in tomorrow's *Honolulu Gazette.*

"I've got to be hospitalised on Monday. So I want Toby out of this mess before I go."

"You sound fatalistic."

"Not at all. I've always been one of the lucky ones. I don't want Toby in danger when I'm stuck in a hospital ward, that's all."

Tutu Lia brought me a beer and Eva a noni frappé. Eva sipped her drink and grimaced. I took a swallow of the beer and set it down.

"Maybe you can help us wrap this up, Eva."

The phone rang. Tutu Lia answered it in the kitchen. She listed in on her three-pronged cane to announce the caller. "It's Mr. Deter, long distance from Austria," she said, a conspiratorial grin on her face. Tutu had become Eva's gal pal. They were like two high school teens delighted over the fact that the boy from down the street was on the phone.

"Tell him I'm feeling woozy and I'll call back," Eva said.

"I won't keep you, Eva. I have just a couple of questions. Does Da Itch mean anything to you?"

"Not unless it has to do with mosquitoes."

"It's a native term for sex."

"What a hoot. What a good one. I'll have to tell Deter."

"It's also the name of a book club in Waikiki specialising in tony pornographic literature."

Eva stared at me for a minute. She sipped at her drink. "Randy was a member?"

"You knew?"

"Of course not. I never heard of the place, but it fits, doesn't it?" Eva put her drink down. "Randy loved erotica. I showed you his letters, remember?"

"So you wouldn't mind turning the letters over to the police?"

"I'll be glad to cooperate. But I don't quite follow..."

"Da Itch Book Club published Randy's pornographic novel."

"The Collected Scatological Works of Dr. Haverhill?" Eva smirked. "Randy Kailoha Bishop Haverhill had an ego that wouldn't stop. He fancied himself as a modern day Victorian."

"You told me you are Randy's literary executor."

"I was left out of the loop on that one."

"There's another person who may know something," I said. "Eddie Cooke. I heard he was Toby's personal trainer."

Eva shook her head. "A gorgeous boy from a pedigreed family. Just my type. Eddie was a summer intern in the newsroom."

"When?"

"He started last year, between his junior and senior years."

"He was working for you in June, Eva."

"That's right," Eva said. "I got him a second internship, but six weeks into summer, the publisher started cutting the budget. I could have fought for Eddie's position, but by that time..." she waved her hand. "Eddie was no longer..."

"Of sufficient interest to you, Eva?"

"Internships are meant to foster journalistic talent," Eva said, "Eddie just wanted the job to beef up his application to law school."

"Uh huh," I said.

"Eddie needed just a little more confidence, a little mothering and a lot of... "

"Itch?" I said and we both laughed.

"Eddie had no guts, though. I did make a few moves in his direction, but he had no cojones. At some point the male has to want it."

"Randy knew him as well?"

"Oh, yes. Eddie is quite the athlete, in excellent condition, great pecs, I suggested to Randy that he hire Eddie as Toby's personal trainer. I thought a little extra conditioning would help Toby get into paddling. Eddie worked with Toby for more than a year. It fizzled, though."

"Do you know when?"

"About six weeks after I turned up at the June book signing with Eddie in tow. Randy called me about Eddie. He said he didn't want Eddie training Toby. He put it off to some issue over technique, but I saw right through that."

"How so?"

"I think somebody in the newsroom tipped Randy. When Randy heard that I thought young Cooke was quite the boy toy, he fired Eddie."

"Randy? Jealous of the likes of Eddie Cooke?"

"Of course he was. Every time I acquired an interesting new lover, Randy had a fit. In his heart of hearts he feared I'd make the boy into someone even bigger than he was." Eva picked up her juice and drew circles in the slush with her straw. "Randolph Kealoha Bishop Haverhill, famous intellect, renowned scholar, television personality and all the rest of it? He thought he could get away with anything and I'd still be his slave. Phhh," she said, pursing her lips. "But I had his number, I did. I made Randy what he was, you see. I never thought of him as some Nobel laureate in the making. I saw right through Randy. To me he was Randy the lost sophomore. Without me, Randy would have been nobody. So it killed Randy when I dumped him and applied the financial screws."

The rant was too much for Eva. She slumped in her chair, her voice raspy as she fought to keep on talking. "Eddie Cooke, this insignificant newspaper intern and personal trainer, he was a threat to the great Dr. Haverhill's ego." Eva, pale as parchment, closed her eyes. "I shouldn't have gone on so. I'm feeling a little dizzy."

"Tutu?" I shouted.

"Coming. "

"Eva's eyes flicked open. She sat up. "It's nothing. I'll be all right in a minute. I have these spells now and then. I'll be ready for Dr. Kojimura."

"I'll hit the less-travelled road." I patted Eva's clammy hand. "I'm off to call on Eddie Cooke. Before I go, I need to talk to Toby."

"Not a problem," Eva said. "In fact you can catch them together. Eddie Cooke called yesterday. He said the crew at The Outrigger is putting on a race to honour Randy. He asked Toby to help plan it. You'll find them both at the Canoe Club right now."

"Toby is at the Canoe Club with Eddie Cooke?" I kept my voice calm, trying not to alarm Eva, but this news was not good.

"Eddie was *so* sweet to me on the phone. Now that Randy is out of the picture and Eddie is off the paper, I expect his interest in me has rekindled," Eva said. Her eyes dropped to half staff. I thought she was falling asleep but then her head jerked and she sat up. "You don't have to baby me, John. I'm up today," she said, her smile feeble. I'm truly on the mend. I feel it."

Or else morphine made her feel good.

Tutu brought a cordless phone so Eva could return the call from her Austrian boyfriend, so I let myself out. As I went down the hall, I could hear Eva telling Tutu Lia that Deter would be horribly jealous if he knew how sweet Eddie Cooke had been to her on the phone. Now, how could she work that into the conversation?

NINETY-TWO

On the beach, trim men were putting away outriggers. Toby wasn't out there and I didn't see Eddie Cooke. I returned to the desk and asked where the ceremony for Randy Haverhill was being held. The desk doll didn't know a thing about it, so I asked to speak to the manager. Brandon Harpham was on duty, an old surfer buddy.

"Hey, Brandon, when did they let a surfer bum join management?"

"Once I rode the board and charmed the ladies," Brandon replied, shaking his head. "Now I'm just a desk jockey."

"That's okay, man, you can still charm the girls."

Brandon grinned. He was muscular and trim from years of workouts but his haole hide was leathery from years of lifeguard duty. "What can I do for you, John?"

"I'm looking for Toby Haverhill. His mother said I'd find him here."

"He just left."

"For where, did he say?"

"I didn't ask."

"He may be with Eddie Cooke."

"I did see Eddie here, but I think he's gone." Brandon got on the phone and made some calls. "Toby had car trouble. Eddie Cooke said he would drop him off."

"What kind of car?"

"Toby's? A green Subaru, the only one in the parking lot." I found the Subaru, hood raised. No wonder it wouldn't run. The distributor cap was missing. The driver's side door hung open. Toby's backpack slumped on the passenger seat and I felt a twinge in my back. This wasn't right. If Toby were catching a ride with Cooke, he would have taken his backpack along.

I put in a call to Eva, no doubt interrupting her call from her Austrian lover. Had she heard from Toby?

"Yes," Eva said. "There's something wrong with his car. He called AAA. He said he'd wait for the tow."

"I'm with Toby's car now. Toby's not here."

"I'll call AAA myself. He's on my contract."

Eva called me back a few minutes later. "Toby cancelled the tow."

"Toby's got a cell phone with him?'

"Yes." I dialled the number Eva gave me. As it rang I was wondering what to say. If Cooke was with him, I didn't want to push him into harming Toby. When Toby's phone didn't answer, I called Eva back. I told Eva to ask Tutu Lia to call Toby's phone and leave a message. "Have Lia say that Toby needs to call

home because you aren't well. When Toby calls, keep him talking. Describe every single ailment at length.
"I'll have Detective Tabura trace the call."

"What's wrong, John?" Eva said.

"Toby is off somewhere with Eddie Cooke. I'm hoping it's strictly a social occasion."

"I'll call Eddie myself," Eva said.

"You've got his number?"

"Of course I've got his number, Eva said. "I was once Cooke's supervisor."

"Don't let him know I'm looking for them, Eva, but find out where they are."

"You don't think Cooke had anything to do with..."

"Just do as I say, Eva. Okay?"

NINETY-THREE

By the time I got through to Detective Tabura, he already knew Toby was missing. Eva had put out the alarm to her own staff at the paper. Reporters were hounding him.

"Damn the woman," I snarled, "Suppose Cooke does something stupid?"

"He lives on Kanunu," Telly said. "I'm closing in on him as we speak."

"Meet you there," I said. Kanunu was an easy shot for Telly, down S. King, down Kalākaua and hang a right into the middle-class apartment maze in the flats mauka of the Ala Moana Mall. From Eva's place on Round Top, the trip was a pain.

By the time I found the place I'd lost half an hour and feared I'd missed the action. But as I arrived and looked up to the second floor address, the door to the apartment was open due to the fact that Telly Tabura had his foot in it.

Eddie Cooke was shaking his wolfish head, one cool dude, and his protest drifted my direction on the trade wind: "Haven't seen the kid. I left him back at his Subaru in the Canoe Club parking lot."

"Let's not play games, Eddie," I said as I arrived at the door. "Toby called Eva and said you were giving him a lift. Then Toby called AAA and cancelled. There seems to be quite a mix-up."

"Mind if we come in?" Tabura said as he bullied his way through Cooke's door.

"You have no right," Eddie squalled. "Show me a search warrant."

"One warrant on its way," Tabura said. We sit down and wait."

I said I had to take a leak and headed for the bathroom. I went through the hamper and found a bloody towel. Then I heard a ringing sound.

"I'll get it," I shouted. "But the ringing wasn't coming from the handset by the bed. I opened the closet. Stashed in the corner was a taped-together guitar case. Seeing that battered guitar case made me queasy. As a matter of fact, it made me feel worse than that. Inside the case was Toby's cell phone and Eva was on it.

"Is that you, John?"

"I'm in Eddie Cooke's apartment."

"What about Toby?"

"We're getting warm."

NINETY-FOUR

I carried Toby's cell phone into Eddie Cooke's living room, furnished throughout in dark, pyramid-shaped pieces fitted with Chinese-style brass handles, Pier One Modern, I would guess. A pile of law texts obscured the couch they rested upon. A weight bench overpowered a postage stamp of a lanai. Eddie sat at a dinette table off the kitchen drinking a Coke. Cooke raised the can in his left hand. It was shaking. His right hand was bandaged.

"Eddie hasn't seen Toby," I said, "but here's Toby's cell phone."

"Interesting," Telly said.

"Even more so, Toby's guitar case is in the closet."

"That's my guitar case, " Cooke said.

"The case trimmed in duct tape? I don't think so."

"What of it?" Cooke said.

"Belongs to my cousin Duke. I loaned it to Toby. His good guitar case was taken into evidence the night of the Downtown Mele. Had one funny note in it. Right, Telly?"

"That's my case and my guitar is in it." Cooke insisted.

"That so? What's a right-handed guy doing with a left-handed Fender?"

Telly picked Cooke up, raised his feet right off the floor. He dragged Cooke out on the lanai and shoved his head over the side.

"Brutality," Cooke shrieked.

"Hey," Tabura said. "Seen any brutality, John?"

"Not yet. Shall we show the boy some?"

"Okay. Okay. So I lied."

Tabura hauled Eddie off the rail, escorted him to a chair, pulled it out, and shoved him into it. He waved a set of handcuffs in front of Eddie's face as if he intended to hypnotise Cooke.

"What do you think you are doing?"

"Shall we arrest him, John?"

"For what?" Eddie said.

"Kidnapping? Murder? What matter? In Hawaii, hardly any difference."

"Okay, Okay." Eddie said. "I can't think. I need a smoke."

"What?" Tabura said. "One fit athlete here break training?" Tabura offered Eddie a smoke while I shamelessly sucked at the fumes.

"Okay, so Toby was here. I admit it."

"Where is he now?"

"I don't know."

Tabura's fist slammed down on the table. The Coke took flight and landed upside down on the rug, spewing the brown drink all over Cooke's pristine white jogging shoes. Cooke squirmed in his chair.

"Toby said he had to get back to his car. He left. That's all I know."

"His Subaru was broken down," I said. "He told his mother he would wait with the vehicle. AAA was backed up. They said it would be an hour or more. I invited Toby over here for a cold drink."

"I thought you didn't get along with Toby."

"Who said that? I got along great with Toby. It was Randy that didn't like me."

"Because of your relationship with Eva?"

The cigarette waggled as Cooke's mouth twisted. "Eva Haverhill? That slutty old woman? Let me tell you. Eva was never my type."

I looked around. "Wait a minute. Toby was your type, wasn't that it?"

"Ahhh, Telly said. "What we got here? One māhū?"

"That's the problem, Eddie? Randy Haverhill didn't want his son turned out?"

"His son was *already* turned out." Eddie blurted.

"Randy warned you to leave Toby alone?" Tabura said.

"Randy Haverhill was a sexual libertine, but he only went so far," Eddie said. "When it came to his own son, his attitude was very conventional. So was his mother's. Toby was afraid that neither of them would understand."

"So what was your role here? Counsellor, lover, or both?"I said.

"I was never involved with Toby. He was just a kid as far as I was concerned."

"Well that's dandy," I said. "We'll clear all this up with Toby when we find him."

Tabura got in Eddie's face. "And as for you, brah, you'd better hope we find Toby wikiwiki."

I'd thought Tabura was bluffing about the warrant. Turns out he wasn't. A crime scene unit arrived. Meanwhile Tabura got tired of Eddie and had him taken downtown for booking. Eddie bragged about his father's connections as he was stuffed into a patrol car.

Tabura laughed as the car pulled away. "I stay on the crime scene, I won't have to listen to Daddy Cooke bluster. I had judge Ohiro write the warrant. He loves Eddie's daddy this much." Tabura's fingers formed a zero. Telly looked through the O and winked.

"So maybe Eddie will stay in jail," I mused, "at least overnight."

"Mitzi Wong will have it in the paper, so even if Judge Ohiro let Eddie out, Cooke Senior will have to raise one tall bail, very tall."

Detective Tabura was upstairs supervising the search of Eddie Cooke's apartment. I went down to the parking garage and found the parking space with Eddie's apartment number on it. A white Solara convertible was parked there, the same Toyota convertible I'd seen Eddie Cooke driving the day of Randy's funeral; his buddy Markham had been wearing that blonde wig, and was turned out in the pareau wrap that showed off his legs.

The Solara was locked, but I peeked in the window, admiring the grey leather interior. The trouble was, the luxurious effect was marred by a nasty-looking dark stain on the front passenger seat.

I walked down the exit ramp to get a cell call out to Tabura. I wanted to make sure the crime techs processed the car.

I heard a screech behind me on the ramp and flattened against the retaining wall. A rusted Ford Falcon careened past and a skinny, leering face flashed by, a golden tan, a tangled mop of gold-tipped dreds.

"Jesus Madam, Telly. It's Markham. Damn near ran me down." I was shaking so badly I could barely hold the phone. I managed to get my mouth working enough to give Telly the better part of the licence plate number. An arriving patrol car attempted to cut Markham off, but he was too late. I raced down the ramp and leaped into my borrowed Chevy pickup convertible and joined the chase.

Markham hung a right on Kalākua. I caught up and stayed on his tail, still breathing hard. Road rage? I had it. I was ready to flatten that Falcon like it was roadkill, but I had to get a grip. Do that and I'd be yanked from the chase. So I leaned on Markham instead. I wanted that bastard to see one hunk of black metal looming over him every time he looked in his rearview mirror. I figured we'd be hanging a left in the next block, onto Kapi'olani where Markham could make a run for the H1 freeway. He stayed on Kalākua Avenue instead, crossed the Ala Wai Canal Bridge, where Kalākua takes on the sheen of Waikiki, with hotels and apartment towers on one side and beach parks on the other. Kalākua is one way only. What this guy was doing didn't make sense.

The police strategy soon became apparent. Patrol cars blocked every mauka exit. There was no way Markham could cut 'Ewa and make a run for it. They'd tail him all day, or until his rattletrap ran out of gas. After all, it wouldn't do to spray bullet holes in the elegant sides of the Hyatt Regency Waikiki, or disrupt the click of cash registers in the Princess Ka'iulani shops, or the tendering of coin in the International Market Place.

Markham tooled along, keeping up a brisk, but not outrageous, pace and I stayed right on his tail. Several patrol cars flanked us, herding him. Much to my surprise, Markham rolled right through the Waikiki Beach Center past the sacred Tahitian stones fenced away from the hordes of surfers and tourists.

Right in front of the H.P.D. substation he slowed down to wave a group of beach bunnies across the street while a patrol car behind us whined in protest. The beat cops didn't dare shoot out his tires. What if the Falcon went wild and flattened the pulchritude? I craned my head around. Where was backup? Usually this strip of beach crawled with patrol cars, but at the moment there were no more of them in sight. It just goes to show you: Where's a cop when you need one?

Markham rolled past the statue of Olympic medalist and surfer Duke Kahanamoku. A tourist lady draped his bronzed pecs in flower leis. She paid not a whit of attention to the siren blare. The mauka side streets crawled past: Lili'uokalani, Ohua, and Pacakalani.

I heard a roar overhead and saw rotors in my rearview mirror. Was the chopper going to land in the back of my pickup? Then it whizzed past, buzzing Markham, no doubt. *Hey brah: this is your wake-up call.*

Then we reached decision junction, the corner where Kalākua tees into Kapahulu, but Markham's mind had been made up by the cops. They had barricaded Kalākua at the entrance to Kapi'olani Park. Markham swung mauka on Kapahulu like a good boy. I could see where the police were coming from.

Kapahulu offered more room to manoeuvre through less pricey real estate. Ahead, the streets had been cleared for the takedown, but evidently Markham saw this too. He suddenly floored it and screeched off the road Diamond Head. He disappeared into the parking maze next to the Honolulu Zoo.

Overhead the chopper spun around but it was too late. Now sheltered beneath the umbrella sprawl of a monkey pod grove, Markham was gone. Patrol cars closed in on the mess. They sealed off the parking lot. They located the Falcon but it was empty. Markham was nowhere to be found. There were bloodstains in the backseat of the Falcon but Toby was missing. A pedestrian pointed toward the pedestrian entrance to the zoo and a swarm of cops dashed into the exhibits.

I pulled to the side of Kapahulu to consider, forcing myself to steady my breathing and get straight in my head. No way would the cops let me in on the search. What I had to do was a second take on Toby. Somehow, Toby Haverhill had to be tied in with Markham, Cooke and the Big Itch Bookstore, and the answer wasn't going to be found at the elephant exhibit.

Most of what I knew about the case I'd found on Randy's computer. I recalled seeing that Toby had a laptop. I had seen it in the trunk of Eva's BMW the day I took her to the hospital for her chemo treatment.

I eased up to the roadblock, waved my investigator's licence at the beat cop, told him I was working with Telly Tabura on this and he checked with someone, then waved me through. The best thing I could do was to head for Eva's place on Round Top Drive at the top of Mt. Tantalus. It would be slow going in the afternoon traffic, but so be it.

NINETY-SIX

Eva was in her bedroom, propped on a mountain of pillows, lost in a king size bed. Beside her, a bag of milky fluid was feeding out of a hospital pump. I ruffled the fuzz on the top of her head. "You look like a keiki put down for a nap, Eva."

"Dr. Kojimura wants Mrs. Eva in the hospital right now," Tutu Lia said as she straightened Eva's bedding. "She won't go. You tell her, Johnny; Miz Eva won't listen to her Tutu." Lia collected Eva's water pitcher and listed out, muttering to herself.

Ignoring us, Eva flicked from channel to channel, watching the local updates on Toby's kidnapping.

"I'll get you the best private room at Queen's. They have TV, you know."

"Toby's a *hostage*, John. I have to be here for him."

"Okay Babe, it's your party."

"Did Tutu offer you a drink?"

"No thanks, but you can offer me a laptop."

This got through. Eva stopped the channel surfing and stared at me: "What?"

"I need to have a look at Toby's laptop."

"You think Toby knows something?"

"Don't you?"

"I know he didn't kill Randy."

"He didn't. But there has to be a reason why Markham and Cooke grabbed him. We find the reason, we find Toby."

"It's worth a try," she said. "Last time I saw Toby's laptop it was in the trunk of the BMW. The keys are on my dresser."

I was halfway out the door when Eva called me back. "Wait, John. If you do find anything, I want to know what it is before you give it to the police."

"No problem."

Mindful that Telly Tabura would be irritated if not furious, I borrowed a pair of rubber gloves from Tutu Lia and set to work. I spent the better part of the next two hours looking for the password. I went through every shred of paper on Toby's desk. No password turned up. Then I attacked the mess under the bed, piles of sheet music, shoe boxes full of CDs and the skeletons of various music players and keyboards.

I came across the framed photo, the one of Toby's buddy Kimo and Kimo's sister Se Se. "Bad. Bad and sad," Toby had said. At the time I had taken it to mean that Toby was talking about Randy's murder. But what if he meant something else?

I flashed my penlight around under the bed and there, way back in the corner, was a polished wooden box, striated, milo wood. Just why such a fancy box would be so hidden made me curious. When I opened it, there were bundles of snapshots of Toby and his girlfriend, Se Se. Kimo's sister was quite the woman, mature for her age. Beside her, Toby exhibited the Haverhill stance, the proud bearing.

Underneath the snapshots was a zipper-locked sandwich bag full of dark stuff. I held it up to the light.

Ashes? Toby's piece of his dad? I couldn't stuff the ashes back in the box fast enough. Then there was a bundle of letters, arranged by date. The last few had a different address, a place in Seattle. I glanced through these. They were 'Dear Toby' messages, of the *I will always love you in my heart* variety.

I'd searched the whole room top to bottom. It was time to start from square one. I started back at the desk, rechecked the surface, looked at the bottoms of the desk drawers, and picked up the mouse pad. I was about to set the pad back in place when I glanced at the back of it, and there it was, the password: CC&ToB55.

I opened the desktop icons and scrolled down Toby's favourites list. These were mostly music-related sites. There were a few teen chat sites. Then I went into his document files and that's where I found what I wanted, a blog.

The first entry dated from three years ago:

My mother is very good to me. She is a good mother. She divorced my dad and it was a shock. I thought they got along. Now she dates this Austrian guy who was one of Dad's students. Sick. He came to pick up my mother and take her out. We were sitting out on the lanai. She caught me asking Deter if he knew my mother was twenty years older than he was.

The final entry was written the night before Randy's murder.

Hillary is being nicer. At least she speaks to me when I come into the house. The girls are real T's. They are going to the country tomorrow. Good riddance. Tomorrow Dad and I are going to play beach volleyball and watch the movie. I bet Waikiki is the only place in the U.S. where you can sit on the beach and see a free movie.

All this was enlightening, but what I wanted had to do with Eddie Cooke. I started about the time the Se Se letters ended in July. Cooke had been a summer intern on Eva's paper so I backtracked to the entries for the middle of June. June 10:

I haven't written all week because I haven't been able to lift my arms. This season, Eddie's meaner. He's killing me. I'll do fifteen pushups and then he tells me he lost count and wants five more.

We were getting warm but time was of the essence here. I scrolled through the entries again and then noticed there was an unnamed file. Toby must have started it and then forget to label it: **September 12,** the Monday he got out of juvie on bail:

They have murdered my father and the police think I did it. Ha. Ha. The joke is on me. Eddie and Ms. Elihu took care of me just like they promised.

I stared at the date of the entry in Toby's diary and realised it gave us the timeline for the whole case, not to mention a completely different take on Toby. I got on my cell to Telly Tabura. His line was busy. I called the dispatcher and asked her to raise him. It was urgent. While I waited, I went back to the diary, and cruised through it, starting with the prior year, when Hillary said the stalking had started. Eddie Cooke was in his first tour as an intern at the paper. Perhaps Eva was aware of Randy's interest in Hillary. Cooke was this athletic hunk with Canoe Club connections. She engineered a side job for her boy toy, working as Toby's personal trainer.

It soon became apparent what was going on between Toby and Eddie Cooke. Eddie Cooke became Toby's mentor, doing his best to initiate Toby into his kinky lifestyle. The morning runs through Kapi'olani Park turned into physical training and side trips down one slippery slope, and it began a year earlier, the first season:

We celebrated our fifth Saturday workout. I have to admit I am feeling good. Eddie invited me to this juice bar. We met up with this Elihu Markham guy. I'd seen him before at Twice-a Slice-a. Elihu is a librarian. I didn't realise males could be librarians. Elihu said he catalogues a private collection.

"Or a collection of privates?" Eddie said. They started laughing. I told them I didn't get the joke. They asked me if I knew what Da Itch was. It turns out to be Pidgin for sex.

The next Saturday: We went out to Waianae, surfed at Makaha. Then we went on to this awesome place, the Kaneana Cave. It used to be a sacred cave. The front part is right on the road. Elihu Markham said there's another way in that most people don't know. He knows it because the other entrance is on the ranch next door. He grew up with the son of the owners.

After lunch we went to Elihu Markham's apartment way out in the country. Elihu went to the Pink Market to get some beer. While he was gone this woman came in and danced around. She sat in my lap and wiggled her okole. Her behaviour was disgusting but it turned me on.

Eddie told her she'd better cool it and get out of here before Elihu comes back. She gave me a big kiss on the cheek. She had on some stank perfume. Elihu came back about fifteen minutes after she left. He smelled of that same nasty perfume. He had blonde hairs on his shirt. I guess the woman was his girlfriend.

Eighth Saturday.

We worked out in the afternoon. Eddie invited me to the movies. Instead we went downtown. It was a porno flick. It was creepy. Eddie thought it was funny but the place was filthy and smelled like piss and I couldn't wait to get out of there.

Ninth Saturday.

I'm pretty stupid. The woman at Elihu's was Elihu in drag. We stopped at his place in Waianae after surfing Makaha. Elihu invited me to try on this blonde wig. I tried it, but that was it. This isn't my thing and neither is Elihu. I don't know what Eddie Cooke sees in him.

I got invited to Elihu's book store. It's a room in a penthouse adjoining The Surfrider in Waikiki. In the back there are all kinds of old books in leather bindings, all in locked cases. Then they showed me a handwritten manuscript in a leather folio, and it made me sick. I recognized the handwriting: The Cosmic Orgasm by Randolph Haverhill, Ph.D. I wanted to leave but Elihu sulked. He made fun of my dad.

He said Dad put the moves on any good-looking student in his classes. He said any woman who got an A from Randolph Haverhill earned it on her back. Then they got online and Elihu was reading from the blog of some woman, Madam Justine. They were so into Madam Justine, they paid no attention when I opened my guitar case and put Dad's manuscript in it, all but the first few pages. I stuffed some sheet music in there to make it look thick.

I scanned randomly through the entries, picking up on lines that caught my eye:

I told my Dad I didn't want anything to do with Eddie Cooke. I told him Eddie and his buddy Elihu were dissing him behind his back. Dad fired Eddie Cooke as my trainer and kicked him out of the Pacific Rim Institute.

Elihu Markham showed up outside my school. He warned me not to say anything about Da Itch Bookstore. His boss is some vicious woman named Ruby. She found out Dad's manuscript is missing and Elihu is in big trouble. He wants me to give it back. If I say anything Eddie Cooke will take care of me. Eddie's father is a big attorney and nobody can touch Eddie.

Tutu Lia knocked on the door. "Come, John, wikiwiki. Eva needs you."

Eva was out of bed. pacing barefoot in front of the TV. She wiped her eyes with her fingers, aimed the controller like a wand and turned up the volume.

A reporter was standing in front of the parking lot at the zoo. "A young nun believed to be Toby Haverhill, the missing son of the recently murdered economist and a Honolulu Gazette editor, was seen getting out of a green Ford Falcon. His arm was in a blood-soaked sling. A couple in a black SUV helped him into their car. The driver asked a bystander how to get to the nearest hospital. The eyewitness followed the black SUV into traffic and took down the license number when he noticed that the SUV turned in the wrong direction."

The licence number was flashing across the TV screen.

Eva and I hugged each other. "It won't be long now," I said. She was trembling, clung to me, all in. I picked her up and put her back in bed. Her cell phone buzzed on the nightstand. She checked the call screen.

"It's Mitzi Wong, the police reporter."

Eva listened, then turned to me. She looked wrecked except for her eyes, bright now: "There's a new tip. The SUV driver is a big black guy. The passenger is a local woman, an oriental with an overdone boob job, very flashy looking."

"Ruby Chan and Bruce, her bodyguard," I said.

Tutu Lia came listing in, waving my cell phone at me. I'd left it in Toby's room. Telly's private number was on the call screen.

"Detective."

"What do you know, Spyer?"

"I've got some IDs. The couple in the SUV. The woman is Ruby Chan. The black guy is her bouncer of a boyfriend, Bruce Steadman."

"So? Where do we pick them up?" Tabura said.

"'Ewa's my guess. Waianae."

"Wonderful," Tabura said. "I like Waianae, but why does Ruby?"

"Markham's place is out there, of course. Also, as it turns out, Markham and Eddie Cooke took Toby surfing at Makaha. They also explored the Kaneana Cave."

"No place to hide, Kaneana. It's right on the Farrington highway."

"There's supposed to be more to it, a spur off a back trail. There's a ranch adjacent to the Kaneana site."

"The Kihilolo Ranch?" Tabura said. "Elmer Kibura owns it. He's descended from the Cleghorns."

"Elihu Markham apparently grew up with the son of the owner. "

"Son Bryan Kibura, one nice guy."

"You downtown, Telly?"

"I'll alert the substation in Waianae and head out there."

"I'm going with you."

"Is that so?" I was staring at the call screen. I could see Tabura's unibrow ripple across his face.

"This is a hostage deal. I've talked to Ruby Chan. I've met this guy Steadman, I can negotiate."

"As Dr. Spyer, yeah?"

"And besides..." I stared at Eva. She was hanging on every word. "I'm bringing in Toby's laptop. There's a diary on it. I can explain why Markham and Eddie kidnapped Toby."

"Meet me in twenty minutes," Telly growled.

"Toby's laptop?" Eva said as I hung up the phone. "What about it?"

I sat down on the bed and took Eva's hands in mine.

"Toby held out on us, Eva. Markham and Cooke were leaning on him. Toby knew they murdered Randy all along."

She turned her face aside, pursed her lips, shook her head, turned back, blinking away tears: "Why?"

"It had to do with Randy's novel."

"Ohmigod."

"Toby found out about it. There is a holographic copy. Toby snatched it out of Da Itch bookstore. Cooke and Markham are desperate to get it back. We have to find it. That's the bargaining chip we'll need to rescue Toby. It has to be here somewhere, Eva, and you need to find it. I've gotta run. Telly's waiting for me."

"Go," Eva said. "Take the laptop."

"I'm also taking a milo wood box. I haven't looked through everything, but I have a hunch it ties in."

"Take it, John. And please. I beg you. Don't let the cops do anything rash."

NINETY-EIGHT

Not such a bad ride, my forty-seven grand loaner, As Is/No Warranty. The Akamai Guy's black Chevy convertible pickup cruised nicely at ninety miles an hour on the Farrington Highway. We followed a patrol car with lights flashing as it ploughed 'eva in the centre lane, forcing traffic aside. I was high on genuine speed, shouting at Detective Tabura over the whine of the siren, filling him in on what I knew.

"Elihu Markham and Eddie Cooke liked Toby. They saw him as new meat to initiate into their games. Markham gave Toby a tour of his kinky bookstore and showed him Dad's hot manuscript."

"Toby didn't like this?"

"No. He snatched it right out from under them."

Telly Tabura laughed outright, exposing the puka in his teeth. "One enterprising boy. How he do that?"

"He waited until Markham and Cooke were distracted and switched it out on the spot. He stuffed all but the cover pages into his guitar case and filled the bookstore folio with sheet music. That's how Ruby Chan knew who took it."

"Ruby Chan leans on Elihu Markham to recover one manuscript?" Telly said.

"Right. The so-called stalking incidents were not stalking incidents at all. These were cover-ups of a search for the manuscript. The funny notes weren't aimed at Randy. These were notes to Toby. Warnings. Threats. "

"Ms. Chan lean on Dad?"

"I'm guessing Randy was having nothing to do with Ruby. He might have discovered that she was a con artist, had kited the appraised value of his holographic manuscript from fifteen grand to a million and a half. Randy Haverhill wouldn't go along with her game—wouldn't return the manuscript."

"This explains why Professor Randy was not eager to report the stalking."

"You got it, Detective. Meanwhile, Toby tells his old man that Cooke and Markham have been dissing him. Randy fired Cooke."

"Maybe Dad never found out it was Toby who took the manuscript."

"I don't know."

"So where is this manuscript?"

"I haven't a clue."

"At Eva's house, maybe?"

"I doubt it. I went through Toby's room top to bottom looking for the password to his laptop. If it was anywhere in Toby's room I'd have found it. Eva and her housekeeper are searching for it as we speak."

Telly swigged some Green Tree Shot, smacked his lips and set the bottle back in the drink holder between the seats.

"Better watch that stuff, Telly. I'm seeing gills where your throat used to be."

"Tough for you, Spyer, when I start diving with no tanks."

"What about Randy's laptop? Did you find any kiddy porn?"

"Nothing and no fingerprints on da photos. The aeroplane bag was planted to smear one professor. That's my guess."

"Eddie Cooke could have dumped it in Haverhill's closet while he was still on the payroll."

"So now we get to da Downtown Mele. "

"Markham stashes the Hula Girl note in Toby's guitar case as a final warning."

"Cousin Tomas gets wise."

"So Elihu raps him on the head. How *is* cousin Tomas by the way?"

"Out of the hospital. So far da cousin has stonewalled. Doesn't want to get Elihu in trouble. Now we can lean on him."

"Right. And the lovely Miss McCready?"

Telly beamed. "Miss Lola, one nice lady. She goes home today. She named both Markham and Cooke as her attackers. They thought she was having an affair with you and put you onto Cooke. She was finishing up a late shift at The Surfrider the afternoon of da bookstore bash. Cooke and Markham followed her to your place."

The patrol car slowed as we entered Waianae proper, hung a left into the drive of the H.P.D. Waianae substation. Out front it was business as usual, the low key place it was. Around back it was a different story. The place swarmed with patrol cars, fire trucks, EMT units, dogs and handlers. A gaggle of civilian guys were sorting through ropes and climbing gear. A few of them had miners' lamps on their heads.

"All right," I said. "You've located them, Telly. Where are they holding the kid? Near Markham's place, am I right?"

"I wish," Telly said.

NINETY-NINE

It was standing room only in the briefing room at the H.P.D. Waianae substation. Telly Tabura brought us up to speed, switching to proper English for the occasion. The stage lights shined off the top of his bald head. Telly looked like a talking eyebrow.

"We had a break in the case from TV news of the car chase. The foreman of the Kihilolo Ranch out past Makaha called us. From a TV report he realised that the Asian woman and the black guy seen leaving the Honolulu Zoo parking lot with Toby Haverhill were in fact his good neighbours, Ruby Chan and Bruce Steadman. Chan leased a five acre parcel from the ranch several years ago. They built themselves a retreat."

Telly flashed a photo of the retreat and I recognized it as the place I'd seen in the Da Itch video Ruby had shown me on day one. 'The foreman took a ride by there. The black SUV was parked out front, so he contacted us. We had surveillance on it within the hour, obtained a search warrant and moved in.

"The SUV had been abandoned and the residence was empty. Bloody towels, ice packs and bandages were found in the bathroom, indicating that Toby Haverhill has had some rudimentary medical attention. We believe the boy may be in poor physical condition. After determining that no other vehicle had left the ranch, we began a search on foot. We located an abandoned farm tractor and trailer in the foothills."

"At this point Mr. Alvin Slade, president of the Oahu Cavers Society, is going to describe a probable location."

Slade was wiry of build and creased of skin, a shrivelled haole in a bush hat and khakis. He chalked a rough outline of Oahu's 'ewa coast from Makaha Park and Kehuni Point where the Farrington Highway turned mauka, drew the chalk line straight north, marked in places most locals knew such as Ohikilolo Beach and Barking Sands, and he x'd in the Kaneana Cave, short a virtual mile or two from the place where the Farrington curves north and eastward again until it ends at Ka'ena Beach Park.

"Most of you have probably been to see The Kaneana Cave," he boomed. Slade had a deep voice that reverberated around the room: "It was once a sacred site, home of Kane, god of creation, birthplace of all the people of the Waianae Coast in the old belief system.

"This large sea cavern is right on the Farrington Highway. However, only the most experienced explorers realise that there is a second tunnel branching off from the back of Kaneana. The entrance to this spur is high in the hills of the Kihilolo Ranch property. It was probably an inhabited cave in ancient times."

Slade paused, cleared his throat with a shot of water and went on: "The tractor and wagon were found less than a half mile from the back entrance to the cave. It's a rugged trail from there, but doable for a person in good physical condition such as Ruby Chan's henchman, Bruce Steadman."

"What about a wounded kid?" a voice asked.

"If Toby Haverhill could walk, Steadman could have helped him along."

"The woman? Mrs. Chan?" someone shouted.

"She's one tough tita," Tabura broke in: "Flies a broom, maybe." That got a laugh.

My cell phone buzzed at my hip. I checked the call screen. It was Eva. I left the presentation and went outside to answer it.

"John, where are you?"

"We're close to the action, Eva. That's all I can tell you."

"I just got off the phone with Toby and this Ruby Chan woman. I spoke to Toby. He's terrified. He says they'll kill him if I don't find that damned manuscript."

"The Cosmic Orgasm?"

"Toby insisted it's in a milo wood box in his room. You have the box."

"It's here with me, Eva."

"Thank God. Have you found the manuscript?"

"Haven't looked; but hold on." I'd stuffed the box under the front seat of the black pickup. I kept Eva on the line while I went out into the parking lot and opened the door to the truck. It was so hot inside that it smelled as if the seats had melted. I put down the cell phone, brought out the box, checked it for a secret drawer, which it didn't have, and opened the lid. There was nothing there but the letters and the packet of ash I'd seen before. I got back to Eva.

"Toby said the manuscript is in the box?"

"I'm positive," Eva said. "It has to be there."

I shuffled through the letters looking for a clue and then picked up the only other item in the box, the plastic bag of ashes, warm to the touch. I held it up to the intense daylight. The ashes were not grey, after all, but brown and black. I opened the packet and sniffed at it, took a pinch between my fingers. A few scraps were white paper with singed edges and these stuck to my fingers.

"Okay, Eva. I get what Toby means to tell us."

"You have the manuscript?"

"In a manner of speaking."

"What do 1 tell Ruby Chan?"

"Let me consult with Telly Tabura. We'll get back to you with a plan."

ONE HUNDRED

I came to with a start. A pain shot through my jawbone, sending trails of sweat coursing down my forehead. I blinked, trying to clear the sweat from my eyes. I saw nothing at all against the blackened and dripping cavern walls, neither a shadow nor a shiv. I flung my head around, trying to shake away the pain clamping at my jaw. Fully awake by this time, I realised I'd been fighting a phantom attacker in some half-conscious state, a daze, a stupor. The real problem was bad enough. My cheek was resting on the jagged end of a rock.

I shifted my face to another location but found my nose in a puddle of dust, went into bouts of sneezing and my eyes ran. My temples throbbed. My sinuses swelled shut. I had to keep my mouth open to breathe. I tasted sulphur in the dirt as bits of grime slid down my gullet, and slaked my thirst on my own blood as it trickled down my torn cheek.

I snaked my body, trying for a more comfortable position. My hands and feet were numb—trussed behind my back. My shoulders throbbed. My lower back screamed, very much on the outs with me. The constant dripping in the cave was hell on the nerves. Then came the moaning I had heard off and on the whole night through, but I have to admit I could no longer distinguish night from day and had no clear idea how long the moaning had been going on and how long I had been out of it. So much for Plan A.

"Toby?" I said. "You awake?"

Toby was trussed up in the same fashion. Our captor Bruce Steadman was nothing if not consistent. Toby was muttering, calling for his mama and I knew we were running out of time.

Steadman heard the moaning as well. I listened to the approaching crunch of his boots on rock and managed to twist my head around to follow a beam of light. I writhed as the light bit into my face. The beam passed over me and flashed on Toby, who lay some ten feet away. His face was streaked with tear trails and his teeth were chattering.

Bruce sat the boy up and helped him take a few sips of water. "You okay, kid?" he said. "You tell us where that manuscript is. Madam Chan is having a fit."

A delirious raving was Toby's response. The boy slumped into a heap the moment Steadman let go of him.

"Mr. Steadman," I said, taking care to address him as if he were an unruly student. I was playing the part of John Spyer, Ph.D. physicist, a collector of Victorian erotica, and Bruce Steadman's best friend: "Mr. Bruce Steadman, Sir."

The light returned, washing over my face, shooting needle points of pain through the backs of my eyeballs.

"Dr. Spyer?" Steadman said. He rolled me on my back and gave me some water and I thanked him profusely. A little civility, I've found, goes a long way between victim and captor. "Toby has been moaning all night. First he is burning up. Next he is freezing. My specialty is not medicine. But I am quite certain that young Toby is suffering from hypothermia. Left untreated it can be fatal. This young man needs immediate medical attention."

"Shit man, don't I know that?" Steadman said. He was down on his haunches the better to hear me. "I tried to talk to Ruby but she ain't buying. This is all your doing. You and your double cross. Ruby is pissed."

"I beg your pardon?" I said. "What double cross could you possibly be referring to?"

"You told us you would bring the manuscript."

"On the contrary, I made myself perfectly clear. I said I could arrange to *get* the manuscript for you. I brought that milo wood box clear up here to show my good faith, together with a property receipt from the Honolulu Police Department for the manuscript in question."

Telly Tabura and I had hatched a plan all right. I was outfitted like an academic on safari. We had a team of volunteer cavers ready to roll even before Ruby Chan called Eva back. Since we couldn't produce the missing manuscript, we had to go with the next best thing, the personal guarantee of Dr. John Spyer, trusted friend and confidant of the late Dr. Randolph Haverhill. I had to convince Steadman and Chan that the manuscript existed. Toby's life—and now my own—depended on that assumption.

Hours ago—though I couldn't say how many—I'd made the climb up a goat trail accompanied by a team of experienced cavers. I'd done the last twenty-five yards alone. The cavers stayed out of sight beneath a convenient overhang just down the trail from the cave entrance, lest Steadman get nervous and start taking pot shots at us.

Trouble with Ruby Chan was, things had to go her way or not at all. When she'd opened the milo wood box and found a property receipt from the H.P.D., she flew into a rage. There was an open gash above my left eyebrow where she'd pitched the box in my face.

Steadman had jumped me, had me in a choke hold, but choke holds can be broken. I let myself go limp, he relaxed his grip enough for me to get a purchase on his forearms and I flipped him over my head. Steadman was flat on his back with the wind knocked out of him. I straddled him and was about to lay him out for the duration when Ruby Chan got hold of Steadman's rifle and jammed it into the back of my neck.

"I wouldn't make a move if I were you, professor," Chan had said in that whispery tone of hers. "Have a look around, Doctor. You'll find that this cave is rigged with explosives. I would be very careful not to make a wrong move if I were you."

Steadman went surly on me by the time he'd recovered enough to get on his feet. It's not nice to cause a security guy to puke in front of his boss. Steadman took my insults out on me by trussing me in high tensile strength twine wrapped in strapping tape for good measure, which was why I'd made no headway at all trying to loosen my bonds in twelve or so hours of trying.

"Shit man. You turned the manuscript in to the police? What good will that do us?"

"Please be reasonable, Steadman. I've already explained myself. Perhaps you weren't listening. I happened to have found myself escorting Eva Haverhill to that miserable event, the downtown folk festival. Really, one of these primitive gatherings is not to my taste. I much prefer chamber music to this yowling the popular... "

"Stow the music review Doc, or I'll blast your freaking head off."

"Very well, Steadman. Suffice it to say that at the end of the performance, young Toby became very upset when he found some illegible note left in his guitar case. Indeed, the root of this entire misunderstanding is execrable penmanship."

Steadman cocked his gun and aimed it at me, silencing my treatise on the deplorable state of education. I held my breath, let him cool off. Obviously the man had nothing to speak of in the way of an attention span.

"Dammit, professor, wind it up."

"If you will be kind enough to get the rifle out of my face, I'll continue." Steadman leaned the rifle on a boulder.

"Very well, Steadman... Please don't interrupt me again."

Steadman nodded, glaring.

"I searched Toby's room, hoping to find some way to help the young man. That's how I found the milo wood box with the manuscript in it, hidden under his bed."

"Dammit man. You should have brought it to us."

"I tried that. I put in a call to Da Itch Bookstore with the intention of returning it."

"Too bad, brah. We were out here in the country getting the place ready to bring the kid in."

"Well, all right, then. My point is that I am a university scholar, a man of honour. I had no means to safeguard such valuable property. I turned it in to Detective Tabura with instructions to contact you."

"Gee thanks," Steadman said. "One of them cops is apt to lose it right out the back door."

"I'm a very busy man. I was lecturing a graduate class on the Manoa Campus yesterday morning. Scholars have no time for tabloid news, which is mostly drivel, aimed to boost ratings by inflaming the passions of the rabble. I can assure you that I was completely oblivious to the fact that the two of you had seized young Toby. It was only after Eva Haverhill brought the matter to my attention that I felt compelled to come here in person to explain the situation. I made the effort to climb all the way up here. I cancelled a graduate seminar to do so, and here I find myself being treated very shabbily indeed."

"I'm sorry man. Hey, I don't like this place any better than you do. I can't see for the life of me why these early day Hawaiians hung out in caves. The ventilation is terrible, and there must be a million spiders in here." Steadman flashed a light around on the dripping walls. He was a big man and the low ceiling in this cave was very unpleasant for him. "Hell, I'd never of signed onto this gig, except Ruby promised me we was to stay down at The Retreat. Our place is stocked. The booze is the best. The coke is…. Never mind. The beds are fine. Only reason we're here is, the freaking TV news is so bad. Ruby turns on the TV and finds out we're all over it. Crooks they call us. Kidnappers. Don't that beat all? Ruby freaks out, insists we come on up here to this miserable hole. You think it was easy to drag that half dead kid up the side of a mountain?"

"All right, Mr. Steadman. You are a reasonable man. You can see what we have to do. We must persuade Ms. Chan to reconsider her business plan. I'll get her manuscript for her, but we must do so before both of you are charged with assault, not to mention kidnapping or, God forbid, murder."

"Hell, I spent the night trying to reason with that tita. You so smart, you talk to her."

"I'd be happy to do so. However, it is hard for me to articulate with my hands tied behind my back. If you would be so kind, my good man, I would appreciate it very much if you would cut me loose."

"Fair enough," Steadman said. "Of course you do realise you try jumping me again I blow this whole place to kingdom come. Wired it myself," Steadman said. "I worked demolition in the Army, you know."

"A point well taken, sir," I replied.

Ruby Chan came into the cave with Bruce Steadman about twenty minutes later. She wore a skin tight jogging suit which showed off the absurdity of her bosom. Her long hair swung in a ponytail that hung out the back of her baseball cap. She carried a Coleman lantern in one hand and a camp stool in the other. Rifle in hand, Bruce stood watch at the cave entrance.

"How nice of you to call, Madam Chan. Pardon my bad manners, but I'm not in a position to rise, as you can see." Bruce Steadman had cut my arms loose and I was busy working out the cramps, and wiping my bloody cheek on my sleeve. Steadman insisted my feet had to stay tied, and I thought it was best to play along with him, seeing as how he had threatened to blow the place up.

"Just put your stool down anywhere you like. I'd offer you a drink, but I'm under-stocked right now." The corners of Chan's mouth turned up ever so slightly.

"Thank you, Dr. Spyer."

"I do appreciate the lantern," I said. "The lighting is rather primitive in here."

"Please. Enough of this. Bruce tells me you know where my manuscript is."

"As I have said all along, Madam, the manuscript is in the Honolulu P.D. property room."

Ruby's big lips pulled down. "You lie. "

"I showed you the receipt, Ms. Chan."

"That manuscript is mine. I paid Randy Haverhill good money for it. Toby had no right..."

"I couldn't agree more," I said. "I turned your manuscript over to the police for safekeeping when I couldn't get in touch with you."

"I must have it back."

"It's yours for the claiming, as far as I'm concerned. After all, Madam, you do own the rights to Dr. Haverhill's book."

"I most certainly do."

"The police can't keep you from taking back your own property."

"What good's some manuscript going to do us?" Bruce whined. "We'll be arrested."

"You'll turn yourselves in," I said. You'll be questioned. You'll ask for an attorney. You'll tell the truth. You weren't holding Toby Haverhill hostage, you were just taking him out for a ride. You were trying to persuade the boy to give back what was yours before you pressed charges."

"We've got him in a cave," Bruce sputtered. "Nobody will believe that."

"Maybe Toby asked you to bring him here. He loves the Kaneana Cave. Maybe he wanted to see this second entrance. He had toured the main cave with your assistants, Elihu Markham and Eddie Cooke.

He wrote all about the expedition on his laptop, which I turned in to Detective Tabura for good measure. The detective tells me that he's an old friend of yours, Ruby. He tells me that you got out of prostitution and made it into a legitimate business. He also knows that Toby's account of stealing the manuscript is on his laptop. The evidence is on your side."

"The law is on my side," Ruby said, nodding, her frown relaxing and I knew I had her. "I walk out. I won't be questioned without my lawyer. Yes? And you will vouch for me, Doctor Spyer?"

"I'll swear in court that you told me Randy's holographic manuscript is worth a million dollars or more. Who could blame you for being a trifle upset with young Haverhill?"

"Let's go, Ruby," Bruce said. "Daylight comes, the police will storm the place. We got no other option."

"Take my cell phone, Madam," I said. Go to the cave entrance and speed dial Detective Tabura. He's in my phone index. Just leave the line open. You'll be taken into custody, but simply insist on having your lawyer present during questioning."

"Why are you doing this?"

"I am one of Doctor Haverhill's oldest friends. I have an obligation to help his son. Toby is in very bad shape. His breathing is ragged. He's lost a lot of blood. He's delirious in case you haven't noticed."

"Best we do what the professor says," Bruce said.

"I'd rather go back to The Retreat and call my lawyer. "

"Call your lawyer on my cell phone, Ms. Chan," I said. "Then call Detective Tabura. The police will have you surrounded by now. I doubt that you could move ten feet from the cave entrance without being picked off by a sniper."

"Come on, Ruby. We got no choice. We turn ourselves in before they bust us."

"Wait, my good man," I said. "It is imperative you release Toby and me. You don't want it to look as if you were mistreating us."

That's right," Bruce said.

Ruby started for the mouth of the cave.

"Wait, Madam. Let me go first. Let me talk to Detective Tabura," I said.

"I can handle Telly Tabura," she said. "We go way back."

Ruby kept right on walking. Bruce hung back to cut my feet loose. I tried to stand but couldn't make my legs work. He cut Toby loose; the boy's arms flopped but otherwise he didn't move.

"Put your hands on your head, Steadman," I said.

"In fact, it would behove you to let me walk out ahead."

Bruce ignored my warning. He seemed to panic when he realised that Ruby was out of sight. Just why Bruce was so dependent on Ruby, I can't say, but Bruce Steadman rushed out of the cave entrance flailing his arms around, calling after Ruby, and that did it. He howled, twitching, and danced around in a vitus shimmy, slammed by fifty thousand volts.

ONE HUNDRED TWO

Telly Tabura had the stun gun in his hand, wrapping up the leads. A pair of beat cops dragged Bruce to his feet, cuffed him and marched him down the trail.

"The stun gun saves injury on the job," Tabura said. "Eliminates a lotta rough stuff. Less sick time for officers. Only one thing wrong with this technology."

"Yeah? What's that?"

"Save too much scum. More defence attorneys get rich." Telly tossed the stun gun aside, grabbed me, flung his arm around my shoulder. "You tell anybody I say this, Spyer, you pau."

"It's pau," I said. We laughed, traded shakas. I was propped against the cave entrance. I tried out my legs, but my knees buckled under me. My back was pau as well. Tossing Bruce Steadman around had been extremely gratifying, but it wasn't smart. Telly flung my arm around his shoulder and with his support we started off.

"Thanks for the rescue, brah. What took you?"

"Couldn't manoeuvre in the dark. Too much risk to personnel. We been planning all night, moved out at first light. Telly barked out a message: "Get the EMS unit up here wikiwiki. The Haverhill boy be in rough shape."

My legs felt better. I stepped toward the cave, headed back to look after Toby, when I felt something shift under foot. A rock came shooting out of nowhere and landed at our feet. I heard what sounded like a clap of thunder, looked up and saw it coming, a landslide.

"Jesus Madam, Telly. Run!" I shoved Telly ahead of me, down the steep trail. We half ran, half fell down the sketchy trail that zigzagged down the mountainside, headed for the nearest shelter, the narrow ledge sheltered by an outcropping. A couple of cavers were already there. Hands reached out to us, dragged us in, and we all huddled there, backs plastered against sheer rock. I prayed the overhang would hold as I watched a torrent of rocks and boulders rain past, The air went black with dust and debris. We buried our faces in our shirts in order to breathe. Five minutes tops and that was it. A second tremor followed. More rocks rained down. Then we all scrambled back up the trail, sliding over loose rock and debris, stumbling, sweating, swearing. When we reached the cave entrance it was gone.

"Toby," I croaked. "We've got to get the kid out of there."

Telly barked orders into his radio. Bodies began to emerge, some black as zombies, some dazed, a few injured, none serious. I was amazed. Telly had managed to hide fifteen or twenty people up here. I stumbled toward the rock pile, ready to move the mountain myself, if I had to, but Alvin Slade, the captain of the cavers, made the case to Telly that his group should assess the situation before the rest of us started pitching rocks around, quite possibly causing more damage. Telly agreed and ordered the rest of us to stay back. Once Telly had the operation going, he joined me, and we stood by silently waiting for a verdict from the cavers.

I bit down a rush of hot acid searing my throat. We had just had a close encounter with the other fate, eternity, heaven, hell, Lord Jesus, Madam Pele, or whatever you choose to call it. I realised there maybe wasn't much to it, maybe pau was all there was. Pau: the end. That was it. Or was that it?

I bit down acid and sweated and paced and worried for Eva and did my best to remain calm; but inside my head I rehearsed the words, what I'd say to a small and frail woman with a racing heart. What would happen to Eva if I was forced to tell her that her baby was gone, and had joined his father in some other dimension?

"Bruce Steadman thrashing around must have set off the explosives," I said.

"Good thing we had one plan B," Tabura muttered.

"What's that?"

Before he could explain, his radio crackled to life. Telly paced off the better to make sense of the uneven smatterings of speech. I read his face for a nod or a lift of that long eyebrow that framed his hooded eyes. Telly talked some, paced some, stood waiting some, arms folded, back rigid. Then came a new flood of babble and squawk. Telly grinned big and his arm shot into the air and his thick fingers made the V sign followed by the shaka All around him the shakas flew and the cheers and clapping and shouting rang on and on, reverberating off the green peaks that surrounded us.

"Praise Jesus, praise Madam," I muttered under my breath and I stumbled toward Telly and we clinched, laughing, fighting back tears.

"How do you know, Telly? Are you certain?"

"Plan B went fine," Telly said. "A team of cavers went in this morning. Kaneana side, main entrance."

"From the Farrington highway?"

Telly nodded. "Going was slow. They just now reached the back of this cave. They found the boy. He's one scared kid, but he's okay. No way they can haul him back the way they came. We have to dig them out, but it looks good. From inside they see daylight. They have air."

"I've got to call Eva."

"She'll know already. "

"That Toby's safe? How?"

Telly grinned, flashing that black puka where his tooth used to be. "Somebody tipped off the police reporter. Mitzi Wong been harassing us all night."

"Now who do you suppose tipped off Mitzi?" I said, and we both laughed.

"What about Bruce Steadman and the cops? Did they make it out okay?"

"Da back of one patrol car never felt so good to Bruce," Telly said.

"Where's our dragon lady?"

"Headed for jail. Old home week for Ruby."

"I wonder what she'll say when she takes possession of her manuscript?"

"I will personally hand it over," Telly said, grinning big. "One bag of ashes. What do you bet Ms. Chan collects one million dollars on the insurance?"

"I'm afraid she'll have to settle for fifteen thousand."

"And what do you bet her lawyers will spend every dime of it on her defence?"

"Ruby's been charged?"

"Ruby, Steadman, Markham and Cooke, they all going down on the kidnapping of Toby Haverhill. Ruby Chan and Elihu Markham, they charged with murder-one on Randy."

"What about Eddie Cooke?"

"Eddie Cooke rolled over. Couldn't confess fast enough, his daddy being a lawyer and all. Eddie claims he did mention a shotgun in the Haverhill shed to his buddy Elihu but that was it. He had no knowledge of the deed until after it was done."

"Lying bastard. "

"Cooke says Elihu Markham told him that Ruby Chan put him up to offing the professor. Offered him money. Chan said Eva Haverhill was such a crazy tita that it would be easy to pin the crime on Eva and her son.

Telly wiped a muddy bottle of Jamba Juice on his shirt, twisted off the cap, and took a long pull off the bottle. He offered me some. I was so parched that I wiped the bottle off again and drank the stuff, washed a landslide right out of my mouth. I have to admit, that Jamba jolt tasted better to me at that exact moment than the finest Drambuie I ever sipped my whole life.

Tabura grinned. "Judge Ohira denied bail. Eddie Cooke the weasel sits in jail. Maybe forensics finds Eddie's prints on some photos in one aeroplane bag."

"Maybe so, Telly," I said, grinning. "What about Ruby Chan?"

"Jailed until sentencing on violation of probation."

ONE HUNDRED FOUR

It was quite a reunion. Eva and Tutu Lia arrived at the emergency room at Queen's Hospital, to find Hillary already at Toby's bedside.

Tutu Lia pushed Eva in a wheelchair. "I don't need this ridiculous chair but Dr. Kojimura insisted," Eva said, "It's because of the morphine. He worries that it might make me dizzy."

"I'm so sorry, Eva," Hillary said, rising. "I don't mean to intrude. I was worried that you might not feel well enough to come at all. Somebody had to be here for Toby. I'll leave if you want."

"It's all right," Eva said. "I needn't have been so bitchy toward you, but there are times you were a rotten stepmother to Toby."

"I wanted Toby to fit into my world. I was hurt when he rejected the pony."

"I put him up to it."

"You did?"

"I knocked dressage. I told Toby it was an exclusionary sport. I'm sorry Hillary. I know you meant well." Eva shifted in her wheelchair. Tutu Lia fluffed a pillow behind her back. "I need to get better and it won't happen unless I let go, give up on the power trips. Tutu Lia put me up to it, didn't you dear?"

Tutu beamed. "You getting better for it already."

"I even wrote a letter to my ex, Nelson. I shouldn't have cut and run. I should have tried to work it out with him. I led him to believe we could reconcile. Then I turned right around and eloped with Randy. It was a bad thing to do and I asked Nelson to forgive me."

"You'll get well, Eva." Hillary towered over Eva, so she pulled up a plastic chair and perched on it, the better to hear the first Mrs. Haverhill.

"Toby needs a guardian," Eva said. "Harlan Kawahara is pushing me. He insists I have a plan B in place, not that I'll ever need one. It's just a formality."

"What about Dr. Kevin?" Hillary asked.

"Kevin loves Toby, but how is he going to do his internship and look after a teen? Besides, he's bitter at me for divorcing his father. I wouldn't want his attitude rubbing off on Toby."

Hillary nodded. "I've talked to Kevin. He's got some issues you may want to sort out with him."

"Toby could go to my sister, of course. Trouble is, he loves school. For the first time, he's thriving in school, the first time in his whole life."

"I'll be there for Toby," Hillary said, "If Toby will have me. If it won't work for us, he can go to your sister."

"Toby can come to Tutu Lia's," Lia offered. "Toby loves Hone. We got room, Hone and I. We got time for one boy."

Eva patted Lia's hand. "Thank you, Tutu, and you too, Hillary. I'll have Harlan put all this in writing, just to make him feel better."

It was amazing, listening to these women. How they accomplished what needed to be done by means of half-truths. Hillary became Toby's guardian with Tutu Lia's assistance. Eva saved face. As for me, I was lying on a gurney across from them and witnessed the whole scene. I must have been more out of it than I thought. I was on muscle relaxers, half asleep when I felt a chilly hand on my arm.

Eva was on her feet, out of the wheelchair, slim in a pale purple pantsuit. The ivory Hawaiian fishhook Toby had given her hung around her neck. She wore a turban that added several inches and when she leaned over me, I could see the rouge caked on to add some colour.

"God bless you, John Spyer," she said, "And Jesus, and Madam Pele. I can't thank you enough."

"Don't mention it, Eva," I said, realising how silly I sounded. I'm not good at this sort of scene.

"Toby adores you. The boys are planning a special party for you—a new musical arrangement. Come hear them for yourself. They are quite spectacular, I do believe. You must come to dinner when you are out of Queens and back on your feet."

"A little therapy and I should be out of here tomorrow."

"I'm checking into the hospital tomorrow morning for a few tests. Dr. Kojimura doesn't like my heart rate. Now that Toby is safe, I can't put it off any longer." Eva's face turned sombre. "This is totally ridiculous, but Harlan insists that I say and do all I have to where my affairs are concerned. I've done that mostly, for Kevin and for Bart. I've apologised where I needed to, where I failed them as a mother, but Toby..." the tears started. Eva wiped her eyes. "I don't want Toby going through life blaming himself for his father's death. If anything, it was my fault. I'm the one who misjudged Eddie Cooke. I'm the one who thought that pissant was so wonderful."

"My money's on you, Eva. You'll be fine. You'll have a talk with Toby when the time is right."

"I know that, John, but hear me out. You have to know how I feel, just in case." Eva sighed, sank back in her wheelchair. Her voice was a rasp. "If it comes to...if something should happen to me."

"You'll pull through, Eva."

"Of course I will. I know that," Eva said. "But if something *does* happen to me, I want Toby to know I forgive him for not being straight with me."

"He should have been straight with all of us, but on the other hand he used his head when the thugs grabbed him. If he'd admitted he burned that manuscript? Your boy would have been pau, Eva." I chopped air with the side of my hand.

Eva flinched, as if she'd been slapped. "You are right, John. I should be proud of him."

"Telling us to look in the milo wood box? That was a stroke of genius."

"I'll tell him you said that as soon as he wakes up. Thank you John, thank you for everything. If anything should happen to me, I don't want Toby blaming himself, when all this was caused by *me...my dalliances*."

Eva turned her face away, waiting to compose herself.

When she turned back to me, the fighter Eva had returned. "I can't bring myself to tell him right now. It would scare him to death, and he's already been through too much."

I took her hand. Her grasp was weak and her fingers were clammy.

"I will talk to Toby. Of course I will, but you know these lawyers. What you have to do for me, John, if it should come to.... but never mind, you know what I mean. If the time should ever come, then you must take Toby aside and tell him what I meant by this letter. He'll listen to you." She pressed a sealed envelope addressed to Toby into my hand. "It's awful writing, I know. I can't tell if... whether I've said the right thing. My thoughts are scattered. It's the morphine they've got me on. It's wonderful for the pain, but hard on the brain and I can't really write what I want to say."

"Not to worry, Eva," I said, taking her hand. "I'll take care of it for you if it should come to that, but it won't, you being Eva and all."

She smiled. "I'm one of the lucky ones," she said, "and I've got my healing charm in place. She stroked the carved ivory fish hook around her neck. "All right then, we'll see you next week." She started to rise, but I pinned her hand to the bed.

"Don't run off, hon. Not just yet. Since you are passing out apologies, where's mine?"

ONE HUNDRED SIX

Eva's eyes widened. Her big grey eyes took colour from her suit, a faint purplish grey, reminding me of the days of the purple horizons at the beginning of last week, the omens of the winter surf.

"*Mea culpa*, John. How have I offended you?"

"Just a sin of omission."

Eva sank into a bedside chair, her face grave. "Tell me."

"No, you tell me. About Se Se."

"Oh. That." She turned her face aside. "Se Se is Kimo's sister. What about her?"

"She was also the love of Toby's young life."

"Se Se is a stunning girl, vivacious, loving. I adored her, but I thought at the time she was a little too much for Toby. Se Se saw through his awkwardness, saw what a fine boy he is, and they had their affair and there was no stopping them," Eva said. "Se Se finally realised she was too young. She took off for the mainland."

"And Toby was seriously depressed."

"Of course," Eva said, averting her eyes. When she looked at me again, her voice was trembling. "Toby is...ah, Toby is....too sensitive by half."

"Eva, come on," I snarled. "Randy finished with Se Se what he'd started with your niece. With Lani."

Eva yanked her hand away. She looked around our curtained bay, went to close it off. She came back to my bedside. "We can't really go into this. Toby's in the next bay. He might hear."

"He won't hear," I said, lowering my voice to a notch above whisper. "I'm right about Randy, am I not?"

"Oh yes," Eva said. "It happened at Hillary's country place. They all went out there on a family trip. This was the weekend after the book signing in June. Toby woke up one morning. Se Se had gone out. He found Randy and Se Se on a blanket in the yard. They had been up all night, just talking, Se Se said, but Toby couldn't handle it. He just knew. He was crushed. He broke off with Se Se over it, and it was a good thing, too. Se Se is pregnant."

"Does Toby know?"

"I don't think so," Eva said, "I never told him. Se Se is off to her big sister's in Seattle and let it be. I let Toby believe he misjudged them both, and I kept pushing the Canoe Club thing so that Toby could repair his relationship with his dad."

"You should have trusted me, Eva. Do you realise what would have happened if we hadn't solved the case? The prosecution could have blind-sided us with this...the most compelling motive there is."

Eva threw up her hands, gave me the big eye. "Why John, I can't believe you said that. *I'm* the most compelling motive there is. How many motives did you need?" Eva sank into her wheelchair. "You have to forgive me, but I'm worn out," Eva said, and these were her last words to me: "Let me find Tutu Lia. She went to meet Maya down in the lobby. Aren't you lucky? Maya will be here to rub you back."

We hugged, a hard tight hug. "I take it I am forgiven," Eva said.

I nodded. "You are forgiven, Eva, and you truly are one of the lucky ones."

Lucky in everything but her heart; it ran away from her. She was killed by the cure, died on the operating table the next morning during the exploratory surgery. The tachycardia did it, Eva's racing heart.

Every so often I wonder about our last conversation and my part in it. I have this compelling need to have everything down, every detail. I have this rage not only to have solved the case but to have wrung the whole and entire truth out of it, and after all, there are times the entire truth is simply too painful. In my darker moments, my haole ones, when I sit watching the latest wedding party from my favourite corner of the Monkey Pod Bar, I wonder whether I contributed to Eva's untimely departure.

In my lighter moments, my Hawaiian ones, after a bowl of two of 'awa at Hale Kava, I see Eva paddling off to Tahiti in hot pursuit of Randy and in those times I'm quite certain that Eva is where she wanted to be all along, off with Randy in some other realm. Eva has forgiven Randy his dalliances and they've resumed their grand romance.

I knew that another dawn had arrived when the ferns took shape at the entrance to the cave at Kaneana. We had walked into the entrance past the barriers covered with graffiti. The rough ground was too much for Tutu, who clung tightly to my arm. Maya and Hillary, dressed in jeans and boots, were stable on their feet.

Toby and his friend Kimo brought up the rear. It was Tutu Lia who had organised this trip, which is how we came to be camping the prior evening, out along the fine beach at Makaha.

There in the cave, Tutu Lia lighted her taper. We all lit our candles from hers in turn. She bade us form a circle, holding our tapers, not knowing, really, what to say.

"We begin with a moment of silence for our mother Eva," Lia said, closing her eyes.

Behind us the sea was shifting, the roar of it absorbed by the facets of the black rocks. The sound of the droplets from the walls, our breathing, our shuffling of feet, were all that I heard at first, and then came the sound of Eva's voice, startling me so that I repeated Eva's words out loud. I looked around at the others' faces as their eyes met mine, seeing the elements of this odd family, this 'ohana we had become, measured out in visible bits, cheekbones, eye whites, wisps of hair. It didn't seem that the others heard as I did, Eva's tone, low and gentle, as she advised her son and so I shared what I recalled from her letter.

"Never be too full of yourself to admit to a lapse in judgement, Toby. This has been a hard lesson for me to learn. I hope by sharing my mistakes with you, your life might be made easier."

Toby wiped his nose on his sleeve and stared at his feet, where the light from the candle flames sparked the glassy flecks in the rocks and the cave seemed to dance and spin, until full daylight washed out both sparkle and shadows. Suddenly, with no warning, Tutu Lia blew out her candle and so did we all. Tutu Lia motioned us to follow her.

We crossed the road and stood for a moment before the monument, the one that explains that the cave, the ana, is named for Kane, the god of creation in the Hawaiian pantheon. Toby sidled up to me and we huddled together, staring at the brass plaque at the base of the monument as the others went on, taking a steep, sandy trail down to the rocky black apron of lava along the beach.

"My mother talked to you?"

"Your mother left me a letter. I have it for you." I'd tucked it into the inside pocket of my windbreaker. I pulled it out, offering it to him. "Your mother never believed it would come to this, Toby. She loved you dearly and wanted nothing more than to be here for you..."

Toby yanked Eva's letter out of my hands and flung it to the winds. "He killed her, God damn him. And now I suppose she wants me to forgive him."

I dashed for the pages, impaled side by side on a bush, gathered them before they were blown to the winds, forever lost, and stowed them in my pocket. I'd pass them along to Toby another time. Ahead of us, the others tossed off their outer garments and had stripped down to their bathing suits and were seated along the rocky shelf as they eased themselves one by one into the foam.

Toby took off on a suicidal march down the middle of the Farrington Highway. I ran to catch him before he got hit by some drowsy commuter heading Diamond Head to Honolulu to work.

"You've got to watch it out here, Toby. You know these Hawaiian drivers, They are the most polite bunch in the world—except they hate pedestrians," I said, trying to lighten up the situation.

"I hate him." Tears streamed down Toby's face.

"You don't hate him," I said, dragging him out of harm's way. "You love him. That's what makes it so hard. We'll never know just what caused your mother's illness. The disease was in her family. The real truth is, Eva wanted you to buy in to what she believed about your dad and his, ah, shenanigans."

"She never told me," Toby said, his face contorted. "I found out."

"Eva harboured things. That's why you found out. That's her message to you: Let it go, Toby. Let it be." From the distance, we could hear Kimo shouting for Toby, waving his arms.

"This is what you are going to do right now, Toby, you are going to let it all go. It's the ritual that your mother learned from Tutu Lia, and this is why we are here. Your mother asked Tutu Lia to share the ritual with you and we are all out here to take the plunge with you."

ONE HUNDRED EIGHT

Toby yanked free of me and stumbled down the sandy embankment. I followed him, feeling old and slow. Toby slid along the scabby lava table, the seething mass of fire frozen in time, the swirls and potholes of hell on earth clearly visible.

A plastic coffee lid filled one of these pukas; a Heineken beer label emblazoned another. Taking care not to irritate my lame back further by stepping in the wrong place, I gimped along, stopping for a moment to consider a curious, gnome-like rock a few feet high. Here was a fat thumb of a rock stuck up through Madam Pele's pie crust, so to speak.

By the time I joined the others, I could see that the bathers had each found a private space in the water and had entered their own meditative worlds. As for me, I lay back, half afloat, staring at the Kaneana Cave, home of the creation, at least in Mama Hana's realm. Eva's voice came to me, rising on the wind:

"This, and one other thing, son. If you ever do have to let go of someone you love very much, and I hope this never happens, but then these things do... if there should come such a time, then don't do as I did."

A bigger wave crashed in and sucked back and the trades rose at my back and Eva talked on.

"I loved your father very much, adored him, I did, but then he changed, and I couldn't tolerate his infidelity. Yes, he loved me all the while, I know, but even so, his ways were not for me and yet, I couldn't let him go. I held on to those awful letters, and even worse, I showed those letters to Eddie Cooke. If only I had burned them, this never would have happened. That terrible Chan woman would never have flattered your father and cajoled him into writing that awful book."

I lay in the water staring up at the massive headland that shelters the Kaneana Cave, the womb of creation to all of mankind or at least to the branch of humanity that spread along the Waianae coast.

The bathers freed themselves of whatever burdens they had to release. They swam in, found themselves back at the rocky ledge. Kimo and Toby helped Maya and Hillary and Tutu Lia out, and all of them gathered, quietly waiting. They waited for me. They waited until I'd had my time to release certain grievances I had to admit to harbouring against Emmalaea, against my sister who was lost to me, and against Maya, too complex by half to fit comfortably into my simple life. How was it that Maya and I could love each other so? How was it then that we each demanded our own private space?

We joined in the circle again and raised our arms in unison to welcome the day. Tutu Lia murmured some words that were blown away by the wind. I stared at Toby and he nodded back and was satisfied. I could read Toby, knew from his softened expression that he had found a measure of peace.

A WORD ABOUT THE LANGUAGE

In the old Polynesian culture, "The itch" was a term for sex. "One" is often used in place of the article 'a.' I've done my best to put the meaning into the context, but in field tests with readers, I've found that some readers prefer specifics, which is why I have added a glossary and a bit about the pronunciation.

There's considerable crossover between written English and Hawaiian, since Hawaiian was a spoken language only before the missionaries arrived. The missionaries did their best to commit this melodious language to paper in the way that they heard it and they used some special punctuation marks to help convey the sounds.

There are twelve English letters in the Hawaiian alphabet: a, e, i, o, u, h, k, I, m, n, p and w, plus the okina (') represented here by a single quote mark, indicating a glottal stop. A glottal stop is a guttural sound, the "uh oh" of English. The glottal stop is so important in the Hawaiian language that the okina is considered a consonant, and the thirteenth letter of the Hawaiian alphabet.

When the okina appears at the beginning of the word, the vowel sound is accented. The yellow fin tuna so frequently appearing on Hawaiian menus, 'ahi, is **a**-hi, and not a-**hi**. Leave off an okina and you may change the meaning of the word. "Ahi" with no okina, for instance, means "fire."

Another important mark is the macron, a line over a vowel, which indicates that the vowel sound is lengthened by a beat. When you go there, as I hope you do, hop on the bus and hear the gracious way this sounds as the wonderful native speakers rush through the street names with the macrons all in place, adding a graceful pace to the language.

Consonants are pronounced as in English, except for the tricky w, which, particularly at the beginning of a words may be a soft v, Woman, wahine, is (va-hee-neh). Nobody is going to get upset if you mix up Hawaii with Havaii, since either is correct.

Hawaiian vowels are: **a** as in about; **e** as in bet; **i** is the e of bee; **o** as in obey and **u** is the oo of moon. All vowels are pronounced, Hale, house, is ha-leh, and not hale, as in the English hardy person.

There are also a group of diphthongs, conjoined vowels. are as follows: **ae** as in eye; **ai** as in ice; **ao** as in how; au as in out or Maui; **ei** as eight or lay; **eu** no English equivalent, think eh-oh, run together; **iu**, ee-oo, **oi** as in voice; **ou** as in bowl.

In cases where the same vowel is repeated, both are pronounced, producing the glottal stop. In most Hawaiian newspapers and magazines the okina between doubled vowels is written out, but in this instance, due to technical difficulties, I've left the glottal stop as understood: Nuuanu (noo-oo-ah-nu); Maalaea, (Ma-ah-lah-eh-ah).

As for accents, they fall on the macron, the okina, the next to the last syllable, or in the first and fifth syllables of very long words.

ONE BIG ITCH-----CAST OF CHARACTERS

John Spyer, Hawaiian P.I.
Lola MaCready, Honolulu girl of all trades
Maya Menecal, John's lady friend from the mainland
Emmalaea, John's twin sister
Mama Hana, John's mother
Duke Shimabuka, John's cousin
Puttnam Jorgenson, reporter, *Honolulu Gazette*
Soon Amorin, Honolulu taxi driver
Dr. Randolph Haverhill, renowned economist
Hillary Rooke Haverhill, his second wife
Cameron Rooke, Hillary's father, Honolulu mogul
Eva Haverhill, ex wife, editor *Honolulu Gazette*
Toby Haverhill, Dr. Haverhill's son by Eva
Kimo Chandra, Toby's musician friend
Se Se Chandra, Kimo's sister, Toby's girlfriend
Eddie Cooke, Gazette intern/Eva's boy toy
Deter, Austrian scholar, Eva's long-distance lover
Dr. Kevin Sneddon, Eva's son, Toby's half brother
Dr. Bart Sneddon, Eva's son, Toby's half brother
Lani, "Laniki", Eva's niece
Harlan Kawahara, Eva's lawyer
Dr. Kojimura, Eva's physician
Mitzi Wong, crime reporter, *Honolulu Gazette*
Telly Tabura, Detective, Honolulu P.D.
Tutu Lia Manalolo, Haverhill neighbour, Eva's housekeeper
Yodi Noda, proprietor, Twice-a Slice-a Pizza
H.B. "Honeyboy" Noda, Yodi's son
Elihu Markham, pizza driver/curator at Da Itch Books
Ruby Chan, owner Da Itch Book Club
Bruce Steadman, Ruby Chan's bodyguard
Satch Marshall, campus security, U. of Hawaii
Harry Pang, Surfrider Hotel security

GLOSSARY OF HAWAIIAN TERMS

Localised Directions from Honolulu
Mauka (mau-ka) inland, toward the mountains
Makai (ma-ki) seaward
'Ewa (Eh va) toward the west coast town of 'Ewa
Diamond Head toward the east

General Terms

'awa /kava (ah-va; ka-va) psychedelic drink
Barang (ba-rang) Philippine, man's dress shirt
Da, Pidgin for "the"
F.O.B. Pidgin. Fresh off the boat
Grind, Pidgin for "Eat"
Hale (ha-leh) house
Hapa (ha-pa) half
Hapai (ha-pie) pregnant
Haole (how-lee) foreigner; Caucasian
Heiau (hey-ee-ow), shrine
Hone (ho-ne) Honey
Imu (ee-moo), oven
'Iolani. (ee-oh-lan-ee). "hawk of heaven," the Hawaiian royal palace
Kamaina (ka-ma-eye-na), local, long time resident
Kahuna (ka-hoo-na) big man, expert or scholar, often but incorrectly, a witch doctor
Kahili (Ka-hee-lee) feathered fly swatter; large ornamental stand
Kanaka man
Kalākaua, (Ka-la-cow-a) "the day of battle," name of Hawaiian king (1836-1891), husband of Queen Kapi Solani
Kapi'olani (ka-pee-oh-lah-nee) "arch of heaven," rainbow, a sign of royalty, name of Hawaiian queen (1834—1899), wife of King Kalākua
Keiki (kay-kee) child
Kine, Pidgin for "kind"
Koolau (Ko-o-lau) Oahu mountain chain
Kumu hula (koo-moo) teacher of hula

Kukui (koo-koo-ee) candlenut

Lē'ahi (lay-ah—hee), "forehead of the yellow fin tuna," highest point on Diamond Head

Lilikoi (lilly-koy) fruit

Māhū (ma-hoo) a gay person of either gender

Malahini (mal-a-he-ne) foreigner

Maile (my-leh) sacred vine

Mele (meh-leh) song or chant

Mento (men-toe) Pidgin for "mental case"

Muu Muu (mo-o, mo-o) long loose dress

Nuuanu (noo-oo-an-u) cool high ground

Nupapah (nu—pay-paw) pidgin. Newspaper

Nō ka 'Oi, better than anything

Noni (no-nee) medicinal fruit related to the mulberry

Okole (oh-koh-leh) rump, fanny

'Ono (Oh-no) delicious, tasty

Ono, mackerel-type fish, also known as wahoo

One, Pidgin substitute for Eng. "a"

Pareau (pa-ray-oo) Philippine. Wrap dress

Pele, Madam (pay-lay), Hawaiian goddess of fire, lightening, volcanoes, violence and dance

Pihi wiki (pee hee wick-ee) hot keys

Plumeria (ploo-mer-i-a) flowering shrub

Pocho (po-cho) Pidgin for "Portuguese"

Puka (poo-ka) hole

Puka shells. Tiny shells with holes for stringing

Pikake (pee-kah-kee) Chinese jasmine

Ratbite. Pidgin for "bad haircut"

Shaka (sha-ka) Pidgin local handshake

Solid pidgin. Beautiful

Ti plant (tea) large leaf ornamental shrub

Tita (Tee-ta) Pidgin for "tough woman"

Tutu (too too) Pidgin for "auntie" or "wise woman"

Uli uli (oo-lee hollow gourd shaker

Wahine (va-hee-neh) woman

Wikiwiki (wick-ee wick-ee) quick

For further reference, go to the online dictionaries of Hawaiian language and place names at: wehewehe.org.

Williams crafts another riveting page-turner not to be missed. ***One Big Itch*** weaves fascinating Hawaiian culture with twists and turns spurred by obsessive love, a murder, and a John Spyer investigation.
Diana Donlon, ***Editor/ Publisher,*** WOMEN'S OUTLOOK MAGAZINE